Earning A Ring

More Than A Game

Kristina Mathews

LYRICAL PRESS
Kensington Publishing Corp.
www.kensingtonbooks.com

Lyrical Press books are published by
Kensington Publishing Corp. 119 West 40th Street New York, NY 10018

All Kensington titles, imprints, and distributed lines are available at special
quantity discounts for bulk purchases for sales promotion, premiums, fund-
raising, and educational or institutional use.

Special book excerpts or customized printings can also be created to fit
specific needs. For details, write or phone the office of the Kensington
Special Sales Manager:
Kensington Publishing Corp.
119 West 40th Street
New York, NY 10018
Attn. Special Sales Department. Phone: 1-800-221-2647.

Kensington and the K logo Reg. U.S. Pat. & TM Off.
LYRICAL PRESS Reg. U.S. Pat. & TM Off.
Lyrical Press and the L logo are trademarks of Kensington Publishing Corp.

First Electronic Edition: January 2016
eISBN-13: 978-1-60183-463-8
eISBN-10: 1-60183-463-2

First Print Edition: January 2016
ISBN-13: 978-1-60183-464-5
ISBN-10: 1-60183-464-0

Printed in the United States of America

For Rachel Parker, covering the San Francisco Goliaths is the perfect opportunity to launch her career as a serious reporter. But she didn't bargain on Bryce Baxter, the team's star shortstop, tempting her more non-professional aspirations. After tearing up the base paths with him, she finds herself with a little problem, and Bryce might be the only man who can save the game.

Bryce Baxter should be living the dream. His team just won the World Series and he just signed the multi-year contract of his career. But his field of dreams has been overtaken by a fiery redheaded reporter, who's bearing a news flash that will change both of their lives forever…

Books by Kristina Mathews

More Than A Game Series
Better Than Perfect
Worth the Trade
Making A Comeback
Earning A Ring

Published by Kensington Publishing Corporation

To my mother-in-law for not only raising a great son, but for giving me my first romance novels to read.

Acknowledgements

I couldn't do any of this without the support of my family.

Author's Foreword

I love baseball. I have loved the game since I was a kid and the only girl on my Little League team. The game has been a big part of life for me and my family. It's been a great experience to be able to write about the game I love and the (fictional) men who play it. Writing a baseball romance series has been very similar to the San Francisco Giants winning three (so far) World Series in five years. Every story is unique yet equally satisfying in getting to the happily ever after. Some things I wrote actually happened on the field and some things that happened on the field made it into my books. I didn't try to embody the Giants in my books, but Giants fans will recognize some of the traits and characteristics of my favorite players, coaches, announcers, and others who are involved in the game in one way or another. When you spend 162+ games a year watching these people they're bound to rub off.

Here's to many more great seasons of baseball and as many more books as my readers will want.

Chapter 1

Bryce Baxter sat alone in the San Francisco Goliaths' clubhouse. He didn't want to go home and watch the replays of tonight's game. There was enough of that going on in his head. He'd blown the game. How many times had he made that play since he first picked up a baseball at the age of five? A thousand? Ten thousand? Probably more. Not tonight. Tonight it was as if he'd forgotten everything he knew about the game. What should have been an easy double play ended up being the game-winning run.

The loss put his team even farther behind in their division going into the second month of the season and had reporters questioning the Goliaths' chances of repeating a World Series run. Some were even questioning the team's decision to re-sign Baxter to the big contract extension. The biggest one he'd ever inked. So naturally, he was having his worst start to the season ever. He couldn't hit. Couldn't draw a walk to save his life. And when he struck out, he did it in spectacular fashion.

Last November he'd been king of the world. San Francisco's biggest hero since Willie Mays. As World Series MVP, he'd been awarded a brand new Corvette. His face had been on the cover of magazines. He'd made the talk show rounds. Met the President. Women had lined up outside his door. And he'd had his choice of endorsement deals, including a line of men's hair care products. Now, if his game didn't improve, his agent would be lucky to get him a spot peddling adult diapers.

Reluctantly, he headed toward the parking lot.

"Hey, Bryce, you got a minute?" He recognized the voice of the woman standing beside his car. A month ago, he would have been happy to see her. Professionally, personally, a little bit of both. But not now.

"Look, Rachel, I'm not giving any more interviews tonight." He was so down, all he wanted to do was go home and crawl into bed. Alone.

"I'm not here for an interview." She would have waited in the clubhouse if she were. He knew that. Rachel Parker was a professional, the in-game reporter for Bay Area Sports Network. "Can we go somewhere? Somewhere private?"

"I'm not giving that tonight either." He waited for his body to protest, recalling the dozen or so encounters with the sexy journalist. She'd been hot. Real hot. Hot enough for him to forget his rule of one and done. They'd been hooking up *off the record* since before spring training of last season.

"Look, I really do need to talk to you." She seemed a little nervous, not her usual confident, perky, and always upbeat self who was part bubbly cheerleader, part hard-hitting reporter. She was still hot. But instead of smoking, she was…smoldering. His body stirred. Enough for him to think that maybe spending the next several hours in bed might not be such a bad idea.

But it probably wasn't a good idea either.

The last time they'd hooked up had been intense. Almost too intense. Too real. But maybe he'd just been riding the high of signing his ridiculous contract. Or maybe he'd felt the pressure of the deal and had transferred it to his personal life. Something he could control.

"You know, I think maybe we should take a step back." He raked a hand through his hair, still damp from his long shower after the game. "I'm not good for anyone right now."

Rachel gave him a weird look, almost as if her eyes slipped out of focus. Her face drained of color. She turned and stumbled toward his car, bracing herself against the front fender. Then she threw up on the hood of his Corvette.

"Are you okay?" He took a step toward her.

"No, I'm not okay." She wiped her mouth with the back of her hand. "I'm pregnant."

Shit.

Bryce unlocked his car, grabbing a bottle of water he kept for emergencies. This pretty much qualified. He handed her the water. She took a sip, swished it around, and spit. Then she took a long swallow before pouring the rest on his car.

She shook out the last few drops in a futile attempt to rinse off the hood. "Sorry about the mess."

He could say the same.

"So, you're pregnant." Bryce shoved his hands in his pockets. "I'm guessing it could be mine."

The timing was about right. But he had no way of knowing for sure. He couldn't be the only guy she'd been with. Yet, here she was.

"Yes, it's yours." She took slow, deep breaths to calm her nerves. Or maybe just her stomach. "I know we had a non-exclusive agreement, but I've been exclusive."

"Yeah. Sure." He wished he could say the same. But Bryce had tried to get Rachel Parker out of his system the only way he knew how. It hadn't worked. And now she was standing here, pregnant with his kid. Talk about things getting too real.

"So what do you want from me?" Besides the obvious. He had just signed the biggest contract of his life. It was ridiculous what they were paying him. Even after giving half to his ex-wife, a third to the government, and ten percent to charity, he still had plenty of money coming in. For the next six years, at least.

"I don't want your money, if that's what you're thinking." She shook her head, as if she was offended he'd even ask.

"Really?" He laughed. "You'd be the only one. My agent, my ex-wife, hell, even my old man all want a piece of me. It seems like the only person who doesn't want my money is me."

Shit. Why did he go and say that? It had never been about the money for him. He loved the game. Even when it didn't love him back.

"That's not why I'm here." She started to reach for him, but dropped her hand. "Look, I just wanted to let you know you're going to be a father. I don't want anything from you. I just want to give you the chance to be a part of your child's life."

"You know I'll take care of you." He rubbed the back of his neck. This wasn't the first time he'd gotten himself into this situation. He thought he'd have learned a lesson from the disaster that was his short-lived marriage. Guess not.

"I don't want your money. Really. We'll be fine." She let out a frustrated sigh. "I have a good job. For now."

"What do you mean, for now?" Rachel Parker was the one reporter the Goliaths players actually looked forward to talking to. It didn't hurt that she was gorgeous. And she knew how to stroke a guy's ego just enough to make him more than willing to talk about himself.

"People are already starting to speculate." She gave him a look that said she really shouldn't have to spell it out. "Some of my fans have noticed I've put on weight. I've seen a couple of tweets about it already."

"There's nothing wrong with your weight." He was offended for her. "If anything you're a little too thin."

"Not for television." She shook her head, as if he couldn't possibly understand. "Besides, once I start showing... I could be out of a job."

"They can't fire you for being pregnant." He couldn't understand. Not really. He hoped it was just pregnancy hormones making her overreact. Not that he would say that out loud. He wasn't that stupid.

"Not technically. But damn it, Bryce..." She leaned against his car. "I'm not supposed to fraternize with the players. Let alone get knocked up by one."

"I always thought it was frowned upon, but they'd look the other way." He stood next to her, wanting to put his arm around her, but there were so many emotions going on inside him, he was almost afraid to touch her. Because once he touched her, he wouldn't be able to stop. Look where it got them. "I mean, come on, we've been sneaking around for over a year. Surely your boss has clued in."

"No. I'd be long gone. Believe me."

"You're kidding." The serious look on her face told him she wasn't. Not at all. "If this was such a risk for you...why did you take it?"

"You really have to ask?" She gave him a hopeless smile. "You're just too damned charming to resist."

"Yeah. It's the hair." He shook his head, tossing his shoulder-length hair with all the exaggeration of a late-night infomercial model.

She laughed. A real, laugh-out-loud laugh. She'd often teased him about his long hair, both on and off camera. But it hadn't stopped her from running her fingers through his manly curls and admiring its silkiness and ability to elicit giggles when he tickled her inner thighs with just a shake of his head.

"Seriously, I never wanted to hurt you. Or get you in any kind of trouble." He reached for her hand, twining his fingers through hers. What was it about this woman that felt so good? So impossible to walk away from? "Besides, you're the one with the irresistible charm. I was doomed the minute we met."

"Yeah. I'm every man's fantasy." She gave a self-deprecating laugh. At least she didn't let go of his hand.

"You are." He turned so he could look into her eyes. They were more brown than green tonight. Almost golden. "That perfect combination of girl-next-door charm and amazing skills in the bedroom. Besides, you don't put up with my shit. You're not at all impressed by a spoiled, arrogant, immature, millionaire playboy."

"I guess I was impressed enough." She let go of his hand and put both her hands on her lower belly.

Right. The baby. The reason they were standing here in the parking lot instead of tearing each other's clothes off back at his place.

He'd known that his life would change dramatically after signing the contract. What an idiot he'd been to think it would get easier. That he wouldn't have to worry about his future. Not only had his game suffered under the weight of expectations, but now he had the added pressure of becoming a father. Again.

"Look, Rachel. Everything is going to be fine." He stood there like a fool. Yeah, he was a fool, especially where Rachel was concerned. He'd tried time and again to get her out of his system. Now he'd be tied to her for life. And what scared him the most was the fact that he wasn't as terrified of the idea as he should be. "I'm going to support you. All the way. You don't have to worry about money. But I think you should fight for your job if it means that much to you."

* * * *

"Thank you." Damn it. Why did he have to be so sweet? So supportive? Rachel had expected Bryce to at least get a little pissed off at her for telling him she was pregnant with his child. Hell, the way he talked about his ex, she was surprised he wasn't completely freaking out.

She was freaking out. Big time.

"Look, I'm sure it's illegal for them to fire you for being pregnant." He was being so rational. Especially after she'd vomited on his car.

"They can make it difficult for me, that's for sure." She didn't think they'd outright fire her. But a reassignment might be in her future. They could send her to another city, but getting players and fans to trust her would be an issue. "They could make it difficult for both of us."

She couldn't bear the thought of taking his child away from him. He already had a daughter in Pittsburgh he rarely saw.

"So you don't have to tell them who the father is." Maybe he was freaking out, too. He was just better at hiding it. "Tell them it's none of their business. If they press, you could always say you were artificially inseminated. Or that you're serving as a surrogate for a gay couple. They certainly couldn't fire you then. Talk about bad press."

"Except when I kept the baby, they'd figure out I wasn't a surrogate." She welcomed his extreme suggestion. It was more like the Bryce Baxter she knew and had spent the last fifteen months trying not to fall in love with.

"Say you changed your mind." He shrugged. As if he thought it was a simple solution. "I'm sure it happens often enough."

"Bryce, I appreciate that you're trying to help. Really. But once my pregnancy becomes public, so will our relationship, and I know you want that even less than I do."

"Why? Why do you say I want it even less?" Now he was defensive. Good. She could deal with that.

"Come on, we both know you don't need any added pressure right now."

"Ah. Yes. I suck. I knew we'd get to that." Now his pride was stung. "I suck and it must be because of personal reasons. Because of our *relationship*? Well, you know what? I sucked a few hours ago. I sucked yesterday. And the day before. It has nothing to do with you, sweetheart."

"I know that. But come on, people want to blame someone." She'd been in this business long enough. She knew the score. Winning the World Series was just the beginning. Now expectations were even higher. Pressure more intense. They'd have to do it again. Or risk being called a fluke. A one-shot wonder. "They'll blame me. For getting pregnant. For distracting you."

"They'll call you a gold digger." Bryce ran his hands through his hair again. He made a fist and she could tell he was angry. "Or worse. They'll speculate that I wasn't the only one. They'll read your friendliness, your ability to joke with all of us, as something else."

Yeah. That's exactly what she was afraid of. Her on-air persona was somewhat flirtatious. She used her feminine charms to get through the players' defenses. Make them feel like big, strong, manly studs, and they'll say just about anything. She'd never crossed the line, though.

Until Bryce.

"Why don't you let me give you a ride home?" He put his hand on the small of her back, to lead her around to the passenger seat. "I don't like the idea of you taking BART at night, anyway."

"Thanks, but I have my car." She tried not to read too much into his concern. "I can't ride the train right now. I'm fine until those doors close and the train starts to lurch forward…"

She put her hand on her stomach, wishing she hadn't brought up the queasiness. Slow breaths through the nose, closing her eyes, and willing the nausea away sometimes worked. But not always.

"I'll follow you home, then. To make sure you get in okay."

"No. I'm fine. Thanks anyway." She held her hand up, as if she could keep him at bay. He could be thoughtful as well as charming. It was the charming part that had gotten her in this mess in the first place. "I've got my first doctor's appointment in the morning. So it's best if we head our separate ways for tonight."

"Do you want me to go with you?"

"No." She answered too quickly and far too forcefully. "I mean, not this time. I think we both need a little time to adjust. And you really don't need the distraction right now."

"No. I guess not." He frowned. Her timing couldn't have been worse. "But hey, let me know what the doctor says."

"Yeah. Sure. I'll be in touch."

How many times had she promised herself that she'd forget about Bryce Baxter? That each time she saw him off-camera would be the last? It didn't matter now. They were forever linked through the child growing inside her.

* * * *

Even though she'd asked him not to, Bryce followed Rachel home. He gave her enough of a head start that she was able to make it inside before he pulled up to her modest apartment in Walnut Creek.

He'd been there a few times, when he'd been desperate for her touch. It was a nice place. Small, but nice. Perfect for a single woman. Not so great for a family.

He'd have to do something about that. But Rachel Parker was the kind of woman who wouldn't just stand aside while a man told her what to do. She wouldn't take his money, either. At least not until she absolutely had to. Legally, if he was the father, he'd owe child support after the baby was born. He was fine with that. He wouldn't want his child to have to go without, not while he could still do something about it.

Why else would he agree to pay for fencing lessons for his nine-year-old daughter? Fencing? Really? But hey, if that's where her passion took her, he wasn't going to question it. He couldn't be there to play catch with Hailey, so it didn't really matter that she'd tried every sport, dance, and activity except baseball.

Bryce waited in front of Rachel's house until she turned off the lights before he drove away, satisfied that she was safe, but worried about how this was going to play out. What if she did lose her job because of him? Or worse, transferred to another city? He already had one daughter he never saw because they lived in different states. He wasn't going to do that again.

He'd just have to make sure Rachel didn't lose her job. That she stayed in San Francisco and they'd somehow manage to be a family.

He drove back over the Bay Bridge, into the city he'd come to call home. The lights were off, but the silhouette of the ballpark was still a striking view. Some of his best memories happened in that ballpark. The rest had been with Rachel.

Shit. He didn't want to lose her. That's why he couldn't stay out of her bed. It wasn't about sex. Okay, maybe a lot of it was about sex. Great sex. Uncomplicated sex. Or so he'd thought.

It had just become real complicated. Not just with the baby. But her career, too. He didn't think she should lose her job because she had a relationship with him. But he was a ballplayer. She was a reporter. Not supposed to happen, but it did. Hell, it was almost a cliché, but most of the guys he'd known who'd hooked up with a reporter had kept it casual.

Or they'd married her.

Chapter 2

After a restless night, Bryce was awoken by the phone. Scrubbing his gritty eyes, he glanced at the caller ID, hoping it was Rachel. No such luck.

"Morning, Jillian, what do you need?" With his ex-wife, it was always something. Not that he didn't send her enough money to run a small country.

"Hailey needs braces." Jillian huffed, as if it was somehow his fault.

"She's nine. Does she even have all her permanent teeth?" He usually tried to keep his interactions with his ex-wife friendly and upbeat, but he was tired and cranky and sometimes he just couldn't fake it.

"If they do it now, she shouldn't have to go through the humiliation of wearing braces in high school." She used the same tone of voice she'd used when they were married. It was as if she thought he couldn't possibly understand the burden placed upon her by parenthood. He was, after all, a dumb jock.

"So there's still a chance she'll need them again when she's older?" He'd never had to deal with braces or acne as a teenager. It was one of the few advantages of late puberty. He'd been skinny, but athletic, so he'd had to work twice as hard as the other kids on his team. But while most of his Little League teammates had peaked at twelve, he was still in the game.

"Are you going to pay for it or what?"

"Of course. Don't I always?" He'd never deny his daughter anything. If he couldn't be around, the next best thing was to make sure she had everything she needed.

"I also need twelve hundred dollars for her summer camp." Jillian let out a sigh indicating she was insulted to even have to ask.

"Is this a fencing camp?" Fencing was an Olympic sport, right? Maybe someday his little girl would win a gold medal. After all, being a champion was in her blood.

"Oh God, she gave that up ages ago." She made it sound like it was his fault he couldn't keep up with Hailey's ever-changing interests. "No. It's a theater camp."

"Theater? Like plays?"

"Yes. Musicals."

He held his breath, waiting for a request for more money to hire a voice coach.

"Well, I'm sure she'll have a great time." He just hoped the camp wasn't during the same week he'd make his one and only trip to Pittsburgh this summer. His time with his daughter was limited enough without missing out on being able to take her for lunch before he played a night game. He knew better than to ask Jillian to let her actually come to a game. But maybe when she got a little older and could start making her own decisions about spending time with him. That was if Jillian didn't brainwash her into thinking he was scum.

Maybe he should get Hailey a cell phone. That way he could talk to her without her mother controlling… Yeah, as if Jillian wouldn't try to control Hailey's cell phone usage. If she'd let her have one in the first place. Of course, if he even suggested it, she'd shoot him down faster than she could cash a check.

"Is Hailey there? Can I say hello?" He hated having to beg for his daughter's affection. For every moment of time with her.

"She's still in school." He could practically hear Jillian roll her eyes. But when he worked up to seventeen days in a row, he often lost track of what day of the week it was.

"Well, tell her I said hello and that I miss her." As if those words could even begin to state how he felt about the little girl who had her mother's eyes, but his whole heart.

"Sure." She sighed, making it sound like a big inconvenience to relay the simple message. "So are you going to send the money?"

"I'll send it this afternoon, before I go to work." He never really cared about how much he sent, as long as it was for Hailey. "Anything else?"

"No. That's it for now." Jillian's voice was like ice. She hated him. Always had, and always would. He wondered why she'd ever even slept with him. Surely she hadn't planned on getting pregnant and making his life miserable ever since? At least he'd gotten a daughter out of the deal.

Even though he only saw her a few times a year, she was worth it. And someday, he'd be able to prove to her just how much she meant to him.

Now he had another child to take care of. He'd have to split his resources between two families. Right now, he had plenty to go around. But his recent play only served to remind him that his career would only last so long. And then he'd have to pay for Hailey's college, her wedding.

And what about the new baby?

He didn't want to be just some guy who sent money, showing up only at Christmas, kind of like Santa Claus, bringing gifts and then leaving again. He wasn't sure if Hailey even believed in him anymore.

He had to do things differently this time. He had to work out something between him and Rachel. Something more than a custody arrangement.

Maybe, just maybe, he could get it right this time.

* * * *

Rachel made it to the ballpark without any morning sickness. She took it as a sign that things would turn around. Maybe keeping the news from Bryce had made things worse, and now that he knew, she would get through the rest of her pregnancy with minimal discomfort.

Rachel's producer, Steve Montoya, pulled her aside before she headed to the field for a pregame interview with Nathan Cooper. The left-handed reliever had been traded last season, but he'd been invited back to spring training and had made a good impression so far. He'd done well in relief last night, but the damage had been done when Bryce messed up on the double-play ball.

"We're in uncharted territory here." Steve had a serious note in his voice.

Rachel's stomach lurched. Had he discovered her relationship with Bryce? Her cameraman, Carl, seemed to sense something was going on between the two of them. Oh, he never said a word, but he watched her carefully, almost as if he was waiting for her to crack under the pressure of keeping a secret of this kind. She didn't think he'd rat her out. No, Carl had always had her back. But she got the feeling he was disappointed in her. They both knew she should know better than to get involved with a player. Especially a guy with Bryce's reputation and one failed marriage behind him.

Not that she was looking to get married. She wasn't that big of a fool.

So what did she want from Bryce? Besides great sex? Really great sex.

She wanted to forget him. To be able to do her job, and not have to hold her breath every time he stepped into the batter's box. She wanted to be able to interview him after the game and not secretly hope for, yet dread, an invitation back to his place once the camera stopped rolling.

"Defending a title is different than just trying to make the playoffs," Steve was saying. "Expectations are higher. Fans are less patient."

Rachel could only nod, and hold her breath while waiting for the hammer to come down. She started mentally putting her résumé together.

"I know it's been tough these first few weeks." Steve exhaled with the frustration they were all feeling. "But I need you to focus on the positive. Stay upbeat. Your job is to keep the hope alive."

She concentrated on the word "is." She still had a job. For now.

"Positive. Upbeat." She gave him her best camera-ready smile. "Always. We're behind our guys one hundred percent."

"Good. I knew I could count on you." He clapped her on the shoulder. "It's funny. We did such a good job at making the fans feel a part of last year's victory, that now they feel like they're owed back-to-back championships."

He let out a low chuckle, shaking his head.

"But I know you'll do your part to keep it going." He gave her an encouraging nod. "Seek out the first timers, the bachelorette parties. Find soldiers on leave taking in a ballgame before they head back to their mission overseas. Focus on the ballpark experience. Make them want to be here even if the team isn't winning."

"Keep them happy until the team gets back on track. I can do that." She wasn't getting fired. Just a pep talk.

"Exactly."

"So I'll interview the guys who are performing well, like Nathan Cooper or Marco Santiago."

"Sounds like a good plan. Just stay away from Bryce Baxter." He shook his head. Oh God. He knew. He knew and he was disappointed in her. Time to update her résumé, after all.

She'd been contacted by an up-and-coming network about doing a sports talk show "for women who love sports, by women who love sports." But *Jock Talk* was nothing more than a gossip show that focused more on the players' private lives than what occurred on the field of play. What they drove, where they ate—and most importantly—who they were sleeping with got more attention than anything the athletes accomplished on the field. They would have loved the story about Johnny "The Monk" Scottsdale and his child with his college sweetheart. It would have made headlines, but not the kind she wanted her name associated with.

Could she do it if it were her only option? If it was the only way she could support herself and her unborn child? It would be a lot easier if the studio wasn't located in New Jersey.

"I only interview the players who help the team." She held her voice steady. She wasn't going to give him any reason to doubt her. "If a guy contributes on the field, the fans will want to hear from him after the game."

"Right now Baxter looks about as lost as he can get." He continued to shake his head. Almost as though he was disappointed in Baxter, too. "When he's hot, he's golden. He's got that Midas touch."

He had no idea.

"Let's hope he gets it back. We need him." He placed his hand on her shoulder, a touch of familiarity she wasn't entirely comfortable with. "And the on-screen chemistry between you two is something else. The fans love it."

Breathe in. Breathe out. The last thing she needed was to faint. Or throw up.

"It's all on him." She willed her stomach to stay calm, for five more minutes. "He's one of the players who gets it. He understands that his job isn't just between the foul lines. He knows how to play to the crowd."

And she was only making things worse. She should stop talking, before Steve realized that Bryce had also been playing her.

"Everybody loves Bryce Baxter." He wasn't telling her anything she didn't already know. "But they love him even more when the Goliaths are winning."

"We all look better when the Goliaths are winning."

Rachel watched her boss walk away, leaving her feeling like a pitcher who'd somehow gotten out of a bases-loaded jam. Her stomach was starting to settle, but she felt as though she could go lie down in the clubhouse and sleep for three days.

Still, she'd have to be very careful around Bryce. She couldn't let their relationship, or lack of one, get in the way of her job. She wondered how her boss would react when he found out the chemistry between her and Bryce had developed into biology. She'd have to explain that although they were having a baby together, they weren't a couple. And sure, she would be able to maintain a professional relationship with the player who'd knocked her up.

She couldn't think about all of this right now. Not when she had a job to do. Nathan Cooper was expecting an interview.

Carl stood with his camera ready as Rachel seated herself next to Cooper in the dugout.

"In twelve appearances, you've given up only two hits and no walks, with seven strikeouts. I guess it's safe to say your shoulder's feeling pretty good." She kept her tone upbeat, her expression friendly.

"Yeah, the shoulder feels great. The surgery was a success, and I spent the offseason building strength and flexibility." He offered a warm smile for the camera. "I'm healthy and ready to go the distance."

"Keep pitching like you have been, and you'll have a chance at going all the way." No, that didn't sound cheesy at all. But her job was to stay positive, upbeat, like the t-baller's mom who smiles and praises effort, and win or lose, takes them all out for ice cream.

"Thank you. I really hope I can contribute down the stretch. The Goliaths organization has faith in me, and I don't want to let them down ever again." Cooper nodded and headed out to the field of play to join his teammates.

She signed off, relieved that the subject of Cooper's suspension last year did not come up.

"Hard to believe that's the same guy," Carl said after the camera stopped rolling. "He used to think he was hot shit. He was hot shit. But was it because he was juiced or because he was that talented?"

"He's got talent. Always has. But you're right. He's definitely humbled." She'd been doing this job for four years. She'd dealt with some pretty big egos, and Nathan Cooper had been one of the biggest. Had he really changed? Or had he been hiding behind a cocky façade, like another ballplayer she knew only too well?

She watched the game, hoping tonight would be a reversal of the team's bad luck. Because that's all it was. Luck. Some balls were hit hard, but right at someone. Others were weakly hit but they dropped in between the defenders. Baseball was like that. Teams ran into stretches where they couldn't buy a hit with a platinum card. Or the diamonds studding their World Series rings.

That was part of the problem. Once they'd reached the mountaintop, the view from the foothills wasn't enough anymore. It was like staying in a cheap motel after living the high life at a five-star resort. Or like being with another man after having been with… She really needed to get over Bryce Baxter. Maybe she should invest in a vibrator. As if that could help her keep her head in the game.

It wasn't even May and the fans, the talk show hosts, and bloggers were all ready to jump off the Golden Gate Bridge. Who did they blame the most? Bryce Baxter. World Series Most Valuable Player. He'd been the savior. The man who'd brought them to salvation. Six months ago, he'd practically walked on water. Now he was being ripped apart on the Internet and talk radio.

And every single jab struck her straight in the heart. Bryce Baxter was a friend. A lover. The father of her child. But more than that, he was someone she'd grown to care about. Maybe even love if it wasn't such a ridiculously bad idea.

There was a reason she had a rule against getting involved with players. Besides being unprofessional, it was just asking for trouble.

At least his game had improved tonight. He drew a walk his first at bat. Later, he moved the runner from second to third on a sacrifice fly. And his defense was back on track. He'd made a spectacular dive in the fourth inning, saving what would have been two runs had it gotten through the infield.

She was able to breathe. And to continue to do her job. She interviewed fans around the ballpark. The eighty-seven-year-old fan who was celebrating her birthday as she'd done every year since the Goliaths had come to San Francisco. The bride-to-be who had converted her betrothed from a die-hard L.A. fan into seeing the light and pledging his eternal allegiance to the Goliaths for as long as they both shall live.

And she'd met a half dozen babies attending their very first Goliaths game. They wouldn't remember the day, but the certificate would be proudly displayed in the nursery or placed in their baby books. Her heart warmed at the pride that the parents of these sweet little babies held at sharing their passion with the next generation. But some of them were so tiny. She marveled at the itty-bitty Goliaths headbands, onesies, and miniature jerseys. It was all she could do not to burst into tears when she was handed a tiny infant wearing a pint-sized Bryce Baxter jersey.

He came up to bat with the bases loaded and two outs in the bottom of the seventh. The score was tied. She watched with a flutter in her stomach that had nothing to do with morning sickness. A hit or walk would score the possible winning run. She and forty thousand others silently willed Bryce to get a hit.

The first two pitches caught the outside part of the plate. Bryce took the first for a ball, then swung and missed the second. With the count 1-1, the pitcher came inside. Bryce flinched as the ball hit him square on the arm. He dropped the bat and grimaced as he hustled down to first base.

A run scored, giving the Goliaths the lead. The way things had been going lately, they'd take a run any way they could get it. The next batter,

Marco Santiago, flied out to deep right and the inning was over. The score held up, and the losing streak ended.

Rachel interviewed the closer, Diego Garcia, after the game. He was usually a good interview: confident, cocky, and always entertaining. He gave the sound bite, offered Rachel a fist bump, and retreated to the clubhouse.

She was just about to wrap it up when Bryce approached her. He flashed his million-dollar grin and she hated the fact that her heart did a little flutter. Damn that man. He was too sexy for his own good. And entirely too sexy for her own good.

"Way to take one for the team." She tried to sound objective but she worried she was transparent when it came to her feelings for this man. "How's the arm?"

"Fine. Worth it to get the win." Bryce continued to grin as if he had the whole world at his feet. "I've had a rough go of it these last few weeks. But one thing that's gotten me through these painful losses and tough wins was knowing I'd see your pretty face after the game."

Rachel felt heat flash across her skin. Her stomach rolled. She was on camera, so she simply smiled, even though she had a horrible feeling he was going to do something outrageous.

Bryce reached into his back pocket, where he usually kept his batting gloves, and pulled out a small velvet-covered box. He dropped to one dirt-covered knee.

"Rachel Parker, will you marry me?"

Her jaw dropped open. She felt the earth tilt on its axis. She happened to glance up at the scoreboard. They had broadcast Bryce's proposal, right there on the big screen for everyone to see.

"Please, Rachel. Say you'll be my wife." Bryce looked up at her with his big blue eyes. His irresistible smile. And that little something that rendered her completely powerless to deny the man anything, whether it was an invitation to his bed or a preposterous proposal. The only thing she could keep from him was her heart.

"Yes." She barely got the word out before the tears sprang forth and she dropped her microphone. The crowd cheered. Many of the forty thousand people in attendance were still on hand to witness the most exciting, the most humiliating moment of her life.

Bryce slipped the ring on her finger and kissed her, bringing her to her knees and the crowd to a collective "Awww."

Her cameraman shut off the live feed. But there were still plenty of fans nearby. She had to continue the façade. They loved Bryce, and couldn't imagine why she wouldn't be thrilled to marry the sexiest shortstop in baseball.

As soon as she caught her breath, Rachel tried to gather herself together. She unclipped her earpiece, the large diamond ring weighing heavy on her hand.

Bryce stood there at the top of the dugout steps, grinning like a kid at Christmas. What could he possibly be thinking? She didn't want to get married. And there was no way he actually wanted to get married.

She checked with her producer, making sure she was finished for the day. Hopefully she wasn't finished for her career.

"Hey, I got this." Carl assured her. "You two go celebrate. And congratulations."

"Thanks." Rachel felt heat creep across her cheeks. She'd been trained to always go along with the story. Only this time she'd become the story.

"We need to talk." She followed Bryce into the clubhouse where they were greeted by applause, whistles, and catcalls.

"I'm in trouble already." Bryce grabbed her hand and if they didn't have so many witnesses, she would have pulled it away. Instead, she had to put on her best glowing-bride-to-be smile.

They found an empty training room and she pushed the door shut, keeping her hands on the frame while she took a calming breath. She turned to face him, and saw his cat that ate the canary grin.

Calmness was overrated.

"Of all the arrogant, irresponsible— Are you totally out of your mind?"

"I thought it was romantic." Bryce's eyes twinkled with merriment.

"Romantic?" She was not going to fall for his charm. Not this time. "Maybe if you actually wanted to marry me. But Bryce, you can't be serious."

"Oh, I can be serious." He closed the distance between them. Standing so close she could almost feel his heartbeat, he leaned into her space. "I can be very serious."

He placed his finger under her chin, tilting her head so he could look into her eyes.

"Please, Rachel, won't you take a chance on me?" He rested his forehead against hers. The heat from his body radiated through her. He hadn't showered yet and he smelled of sweat, glove leather, and that scent that was uniquely his. "Take a chance on us."

"You make it sound so simple. I almost want to believe you."

"So why don't you?"

"Because I don't want you to hate me. I don't want you to resent our child." She could barely get the words out past the lump in her throat.

"Never." He shook his head. "How can you even suggest that?"

"I know how you feel about your ex-wife. I've heard you say it enough times."

"That's totally different." He backed up, folded his arms across his chest.

"No, Bryce, it's not. You only married her because she was pregnant. You wouldn't have proposed to me if I wasn't pregnant."

"Ah, hell." He fisted his hands, clenched his jaw, and exhaled. "There's one crucial difference here."

"What's that?"

"I like you." He shrugged, his lips twitching with amusement.

"You like me?" Hope bloomed in her chest. But it was overrun by disbelief.

"Well, yeah. I do." He reached for her hand, brought it to his lips, and kissed her palm. "I like you a lot."

She didn't know whether to laugh or cry. So she did both.

"Rachel, look at me." This was a side of Bryce she'd never seen. Serious. Sincere. And very dangerous where her heart was concerned. "I know it seems kind of sudden, maybe a little bit crazy. But I just know that when I'm with you, everything feels right. You're good for me. You're good for my game."

"Your game?" She knew it was too good to be true. "You want to marry me because you think it will help your game?"

"No. That's not it." He let out a frustrated sigh. "All I know is that everything I accomplished last season was so much better because you were there with me. We can be great together. Let's take a swing at it."

She knew the odds were against them. They didn't have a solid relationship, and bringing a baby into the world would be hard enough without the added pressure of the spotlight given to the reigning World Series MVP and his Emmy-award-winning fiancée.

"I can't marry you, Bryce." She wanted to believe in him, but even he couldn't pull this off. "It just would never work."

"But you already said yes." He sounded a little surprised; it was the first time she'd ever turned him down.

"I didn't want to embarrass you in front of the camera."

"So what do we do? Break up after the next home stand?" Now he sounded angry. "Should we have a fight in front of the camera? How will that protect your job?"

"I don't know." This whole thing was out of her control. "I just know that getting married isn't the answer. And now that the whole world knows about our relationship, I doubt my career is going to go anywhere. Just this afternoon, my boss warned me to stay away from you. Then you go and propose live in front of everyone."

Rachel didn't know how to stay strong, but she just knew she had to. She wasn't sure why she'd said yes. Part of it was the lights, the crowd, the romanticism of the gesture. Part of it was wanting to believe he really did want her. That he wasn't just trying to deflect the spotlight away from his game.

"What do you want me to do?" He sounded bewildered. It wasn't an emotion she ever expected from him. "Do you want me to take it back? To go on camera and say the proposal was a joke? I didn't mean it?"

"You didn't mean it," she said softly. "I know you don't want to marry me. You don't even want to date me. You just wanted to sleep with me whenever you had a good game. I was like your champagne."

He looked as if she'd just slapped him. But then he recovered and he moved in with that slow, sexy grin. "I do want to marry you."

"No. You don't." She knew in her heart that he couldn't. "But don't worry. I'll think of something. You just concentrate on your game. I'll figure out how to fix this."

"So that's it?" His smile faded.

She nodded, unable to say anything more. After taking a deep breath, she opened the door. Bryce followed her into the clubhouse. Someone handed her a glass of champagne and offered another to Bryce.

"Congratulations to the happy couple." Marco Santiago lifted his own glass.

"Congratulations!"

"Cheers!"

Rachel knew everyone was watching her, expecting her to take a sip. Her hands shook both from having everyone watching her, and from wondering if one sip would hurt the baby. But if she didn't take a drink, it would only raise further questions about their sudden, if fake engagement.

She brought the glass to her lips, the lights of the clubhouse reflecting off the ridiculously large diamond on her finger.

* * * *

Bryce could tell Rachel was stressed about drinking the champagne. She couldn't because of the baby, but not participating in a celebratory toast would raise questions neither of them was ready to answer right now.

He leaned over, and whispered into her ear. "Pretend I'm saying something so funny you can't help but spit champagne all over the place."

Like a trooper, she sputtered her drink and spilled what was left in her glass.

"We appreciate your support," Bryce told his teammates. "But we'd really like to celebrate in private."

He placed his hand on her lower back and escorted her out of the clubhouse.

"Thank you for that." She sounded genuinely grateful for his rescue.

"Hey, we're in this together." Despite the fact that she was getting cold feet. But in a way he couldn't blame her. This wasn't exactly the scenario little girls dreamed of. He certainly hoped his daughter didn't pretend to meet some guy at a bar, get knocked up, married, and divorced within a year like her mother had done. "Come to my place tonight."

She shook him off.

"Look, you said yes on camera, so publicly, we are engaged. We're going to act like we're going through with the wedding."

"I really don't think—"

"You said yes. So here's the deal." He raked his hands through his hair. "We give it to the All-Star break. If I'm still in this slump, no one will blame you for dumping me."

"Oh, sure. That will make me look great. I dump you because you don't make the All-Star team? That's really professional. Especially since I'll be showing by then." Her lower lip quivered. He couldn't handle it if she cried.

He did the only thing he could think of, covered her trembling lips with his own.

She hesitated at first, then opened up for the kiss. God, he'd missed the taste of her. Pulling her close, he savored her sweetness. He was just about to deepen the kiss when she pushed him away.

"I'm not going to sleep with you." She tried to smooth her jacket, but he could tell she was flustered. Her body and her mind were in opposition. He had a bad feeling her mind was going to win this time.

"Fine. I'll take the couch." He knew he had to be patient with her. Just like he needed to be more patient at the plate.

"I'm not going to marry you either." She was lying. Maybe just to herself.

"Look, we don't have to rush into anything." Maybe if he played it cool, she'd come around. "It's not like we have to be married before the baby comes. Being engaged will probably satisfy most people. I'm sure you'll get a few crazies who will brand you as immoral."

She snorted.

"I'm constantly being told I'm going to Hell." He shrugged. "But the ride has sure been fun."

"You're impossible." She shook her head, but at least she was smiling.

"Impossible to resist, I know." He placed his hand on the small of her back and led her to his car.

"Not entirely." Rachel held her back stiff, but at least she didn't pull away. "I'll go along with the fake engagement for now. But as soon as I figure out how to keep my job, keep the fans from feeling betrayed, and come up with a good reason to break off our engagement, I'll give you back the ring."

Part of him wanted to tell her to give it back now, but that wouldn't help either of them. They were both in the public eye, and he was well aware of the double standard that he could get away with a lot more than she could. She would need a very good reason to dump his ass even though she was pregnant with his child. His game couldn't get that bad, that she'd be justified. He'd need to do something really stupid. Like get caught with another woman. Or steroids. But he was done with the first, and wouldn't ever go with the second.

He'd just have to come up with a way to convince her to marry him.

* * * *

Bryce had been good as his word. He took the couch while Rachel spent a restless night sleeping in his bed, alone, except for his scent fueling vivid and erotic dreams. She still wanted him, but she had to be stronger than ever to resist. The sexy dreams were only mildly frustrating in that she couldn't act on them. Even more disturbing was the dream that they were getting married at home plate, with the stands full of thousands of women. Instead of rice or birdseed, the newlywed couple was pelted with panties after their nuptial kiss.

And she was no closer to figuring out how to get out of this engagement without making herself or Bryce look bad. But she couldn't have said no on camera, in front of everyone. That was her problem. She just couldn't say no to the man.

After breakfast, he took her to get her car at the ballpark. She drove home, changed, and headed back into San Francisco for the day game. Before she could get to the field, her producer pulled her aside.

"I hear congratulations are in order." Steve seemed sincere.

"Thank you." She felt a warm blush heat her cheeks. "Sorry about not staying away from Baxter. But don't worry, I won't let our relationship affect my work."

"See, that's the thing," Steve said. "The fans loved it. They love Bryce Baxter, and they really want to root for him. With his poor performance lately, they haven't had much to cheer about. Haven't had much to watch. But the ratings were through the roof on the post-game last night. The replays of the proposal got more hits than any regular season show."

"Well, it was unexpected." She felt like there were a thousand seagulls diving for garlic fries in her stomach right now.

"I'm telling you, they loved it. They want more."

"I don't think any of the other players are going to propose." Did she just say that?

"No. They want more of you and Bryce." He grinned. "In fact, I was thinking of doing a regular segment. Follow the two of you as you make your wedding plans. You know, testing cakes, interviewing caterers."

"We haven't even set a date. It would have to be some time in November." But the baby was due in mid-December. The last thing she wanted was to have Carl filming her while she tried on wedding dresses that would accommodate an enormous belly. Did they even make maternity wedding dresses?

"When you do, we'd love to go along for the ride," he said. "I mean, the viewers would love to come along for the ride. I knew there was some kind of magic between you two."

"Yeah. Magic." Not to mention the little miracle growing inside her. But did she really want to turn her life into a reality show? No. Especially when the truth was not what her producer or the fans would want to see.

"So run it by your fiancé, see if he's up for doing a regular check-in on your wedding plans."

"Sure thing. I'll let you know." She was screwed. Rachel wasn't sure what would be worse. Getting fired or getting her own reality show. Had it come down to this? Did fans want to see Bryce Baxter picking out china instead of picking off runners on a double play? Were thread counts nearly as important as pitch counts? She almost wanted to return to the days when box scores were all you needed to know about a player.

But in this era of social media, twenty-four-seven sports coverage, and all-access celebrity gossip, those days were as long gone as a ten-cent hot dog.

Rachel did her job, stopping to chat with fans around the ballpark. Many of them congratulated her on the engagement, and it seemed like they were genuinely happy for her.

The game remained scoreless into the eighth inning. As it got closer to the end of the game, Rachel started to get nervous about seeing Bryce after the final out. She hoped to interview him, because that would mean he'd contributed to the win and she'd have something to talk to him about besides the idea of planning their wedding on camera.

With a runner on third, Bryce stepped to the plate in the bottom of the inning. He fouled off five pitches before launching one into the left field bleachers. The Goliaths hung on to the two-run lead and sure enough, Rachel interviewed him after the game.

"That was quite a shot." Her heart leaped at his success. "You looked like the Bryce Baxter we all know and love."

His lips twitched in a naughty grin. She shouldn't have said "love." She was talking about the way the fans felt about him, not her, but the smoldering look in his eyes made her regret her choice of words.

"I just went out there and tried to look for a pitch to hit. I wanted to put the ball in play." He rubbed the back of his neck. "Sometimes I get lucky and I get all of it."

"We often forget how much luck plays a part in the game." She tried to keep her comments upbeat, neutral. She couldn't show her feelings for Bryce, despite what her producer said the fans wanted. "You don't work any harder on the days you win than on the days you lose. You're not any less prepared when you go hitless as when you have a three-hit night. And it's not possible for you to care less about the games now than you did last season."

"You're absolutely right. If anything, I've worked harder this season than any other." He was telling the truth. "Maybe a little too hard. Maybe I need to take a step back, adjust my focus, and my game will get back on track. I do have to say I was much more relaxed tonight than I have been for some time. Thank you for that."

A blush heated her cheeks. Now all of Northern California would think she and Bryce had spent a night of passion that led to his home run. Which would mean the next time he struggled at the plate, they would assume she was holding out on him. Why, why, why did he have to throw their so-called relationship out into the public eye? And how was she going to deal with planning a wedding on camera? A wedding she wasn't sure she'd be able to go through with.

She finished the interview with a few canned phrases, sincere congratulations, and a smile for the camera.

Once Carl turned off the live feed, Bryce leaned in to whisper in her ear. "Wait for me in the clubhouse."

She simply nodded. There was a time when she'd been granted access only for a limited time before and after games. But as a player's fiancée, she would be allowed to stay as long as Bryce was there. The line between her professional life and her personal one had become very blurry and she didn't like it.

And her producer wanted her to make it even fuzzier.

* * * *

Bryce, fresh from the shower, found Rachel waiting for him in the family area of the clubhouse. Her cameraman had left with the other reporters and she was trying to make herself comfortable, but she looked as anxious as she'd been the night she threw up on his car.

"Everything all right?" He placed a quick kiss on her cheek. He didn't trust himself to kiss her on the lips, not with a few of his teammates still milling about.

"You won the game. So that's good." She was holding something back.

"What's wrong?" He ran his hand down her arm and she shivered. But not in a good way.

"The whole engagement is spinning out of control." Her voice was a little unsteady. So unlike her.

"What do you mean?" Why couldn't she just tell him what was wrong? She'd never beaten around the bush with him before. Of course, they hadn't done a lot of talking most of the time, other than *right there*. And *oh yes, just like that*.

"So my producer has this crazy idea that the fans want to be a part of our wedding plans." She said it as though she had a bad taste in her mouth. "He wants to do a regular segment, following us around as we pick out flowers, taste-test cakes, interview caterers."

She looked away, as if she was giving the worst kind of news.

"That could be fun." He watched her cringe, and knew she didn't want to do the show. "But I get the feeling you're not up for that."

"Come on, Bryce. It's hard enough pretending like we're a happy couple." She brushed her hair off her forehead. "And in a couple of months, it's going to be pretty obvious why we're faking this engagement."

"Who said anything about faking it?" He stepped closer, almost to the point of touching. "I've never faked it. And I know you've never had to fake it."

"I can't just smile at the camera and pretend that planning a wedding is the most important thing in my life."

"Do you not want to plan the wedding in front of the camera?" He knew she'd only said yes to save face. She was scared, that was clear. But he'd hoped she'd come around. "Or do you really not want to plan the wedding at all?"

She looked stricken, as if she was battling herself over telling the truth or not hurting his feelings. Since most people didn't believe he had feelings, he was almost flattered.

"We have choices here, you know." He tried to keep his voice calm. To not let on that he was hurt by her indecision. "We can tell your boss that our engagement is none of his or anyone else's business."

"You should have thought of that before you popped the question live on camera." She almost laughed. Almost. "I can't play the privacy card now."

"We can go along with the idea. It could be fun."

"Don't you have something more important to focus on? Like baseball?"

"Look, I'm not going to leave it all up to you. I want to help."

"Yeah. Lot of good that's done me so far." She covered her mouth an instant too late to keep from letting her true feelings show. "I'm sorry. I know you really are trying to make the best of things."

"What do you want?"

She closed her eyes, as if she had something in mind, but it was hard for her to ask for it. Again, a side of her he hadn't encountered in the bedroom.

"I know what I don't want." She spoke softly, almost as though she was afraid to tell him. "I don't want to have viewers wonder why all the wedding dresses I try on have an Empire waist. I don't want to spend a fortune on champagne I can't even sip. And I don't want to be as big as a house on my wedding day."

He looked at her, took in the real despair on her face. But at least she hadn't said she didn't want to marry him at all.

"We could always elope." He reached for her hand. "We could leave tonight. Reno's just a few hours away."

"You can't be serious." She stood there, her hand trembling in his.

"I think we've already determined I can be very serious." He drew her hand to his lips and kissed her. "I want to marry you. I want to be there for you and the baby. I don't need to make it a media circus or fancy party. I just want you."

* * * *

Two hours later, they were heading east on Interstate 80. Rachel had fallen asleep before they even got to Fairfield. A good thing, really. A few days ago, Bryce had been feeling sorry for himself. He wasn't hitting. His defense was crap. They were criticizing him on the radio and TV. Yeah, he'd had problems.

Like being a selfish son-of-a-bitch who couldn't see past his giant ego. Rachel getting pregnant was just the wakeup call he'd needed.

He hoped. No, he truly believed that his plan was a good one. His very public proposal and their quickie wedding would draw fans to Rachel's side. And it wouldn't hurt if it drew some of the pressure off him and the team. The season was young. No need to panic. Yet after winning it all last year, expectations were higher than ever. They needed a distraction. Perspective. Not every bad hop or missed ball was an indication that last year had been a fluke. A once-in-a-lifetime chance at something great.

If Rachel had been a onetime thing, that would have been a tragedy. His slow start? Well, that was baseball. If he put up half the numbers he'd had last year, he'd still be in elite company. He was a major league baseball player. The best in the world. And his contract was guaranteed for six years. He'd have to do something incredibly stupid to be let go. So unless he developed a gambling problem or committed a felony, he had a job. The pressure was mostly in his own head, and the sooner he got over himself, the sooner he'd start hitting again.

He glanced over at Rachel, snoring softly in the passenger seat of his Corvette. God, she was beautiful. The car was a joke. She was the true prize.

She'd agreed to marry him, but her heart wasn't in it. She was only going along with the marriage to save her job. And maybe she believed that a baby should be brought into the world by parents who were married to each other.

He had no idea of her upbringing. Was she raised by strict, traditional parents? A single mom? Did she have siblings? Pets growing up? What was her favorite flavor of ice cream? He had no idea if she even ate ice cream. Maybe she was on one of those no-dairy, gluten-free diets. What if she was a vegetarian? No way was he going to give up eating meat. He was an athlete. He needed the protein, and he'd get it the way God intended, from a big, fat, juicy steak.

The fact that he knew very little about the woman he was about to make his wife should have concerned him. Yet it felt right.

Somehow he'd have to convince Rachel that they could do this. Oh he knew the odds were against them. But the odds against the Goliaths winning the World Series had been sixteen to one at the beginning of last September.

Chapter 3

Somewhere around midnight, the minister at the Biggest Little Wedding Chapel pronounced Bryce and Rachel husband and wife. She made a mental note to check the exact time, in case their marriage did last a full year, she should know if her anniversary would be April 30th or May 1st.

"You may kiss your bride." The minister nodded to Bryce who turned to Rachel with a look she hadn't seen on his face in some time. Pure, absolute confidence. He reached his hand behind her neck, pulling her close to him, and lowered his mouth to hers, brushing her lips lightly before diving in for a deeper kiss. If a marriage could work based on nothing more than chemistry and sexual attraction, they had nothing to worry about.

Rachel forgot where she was, reaching up to run her fingers through his hair. She loved and hated his long hair. He'd earned the nickname Midas late last season when everything about him was golden. Golden touch, golden hair. And now he had a gold band on his left ring finger.

Their sole witness, Johnny Scottsdale, cleared his throat and finally, Bryce let her go.

"Congratulations." Johnny shook her hand and offered a sincere smile. "I always had a feeling about you two."

"Thank you." Rachel had a feeling, too, but it wasn't the kind of optimism expected of a bride on her wedding night.

"Why don't you two stop by our place in the morning?" Johnny gave Bryce a sly look. "Alice and I would love to help you celebrate. We can have a reception brunch."

Rachel was a little surprised by the invitation, considering she was the one who'd figured out Alice's teenage son could have been Johnny's and not her late husband's child. But he and Bryce had formed a close friendship, and since Johnny's retirement after the World Series, Bryce had been missing his friend. The fact that Johnny had left his wife and baby girl at home to attend their midnight wedding was a testament to the bond between the two men.

"We'll definitely stop by." Bryce put his arm around her waist and grinned like a real groom. As if this were a real wedding. "Not too early, of course."

He slid his hand down her hip, making her quiver in anticipation of their wedding night. If she could keep her eyes open long enough to strip out of her wedding dress. She'd chosen a simple little sheath in a pale green that was as close to white as she could find on such short notice.

Bryce on the other hand, looked like something out of GQ. He wore a silvery-blue dress shirt, black pants, and a tie with blues and greens that almost matched her dress. His hair was slicked back off his face, falling in neat waves down to his shoulders. His two-day stubble glistened like gold against his tanned skin.

She'd never been a fan of long hair on men. But on Bryce it worked. He was six feet two inches of solid muscle. Broad shoulders, square jaw, chiseled abs. The hair toned down his raw masculinity, added to his boyish charm. And it was fun to play with in the right circumstances.

She couldn't wait to run her fingers through his hair. She hated to admit it, but he was a fantastic lover. He made love with the same kind of enthusiasm he played the game with. And while they were in bed together, he made her feel like the only woman in the world.

She wondered how long she'd be the only woman in his bed. She glanced down at her still flat tummy. Would he still want her when she looked like she was trying to smuggle a beach ball into the ballpark? She'd better enjoy him while she could.

They said goodbye to Johnny, and Bryce helped her into the front seat of his Corvette. She tried to picture him driving a minivan, and giggled.

"What's so funny?" he asked.

"Just thinking of trying to fit a baby seat in this car."

"I guess I should trade it in for something more family friendly." He didn't sound amused.

"Don't you dare." She leaned back against the seat. "You worked hard for this car. You earned it."

"It's not very practical."

"No. But it is something for you to be proud of. Don't get rid of the car."

"I guess we could get some sort of SUV to drive the kid around in."

"We don't need to worry about that just yet." Because that would just make the situation seem all too real. They weren't heading to a hotel to get it on after another one of Bryce's milestones. The night they celebrated his contract extension had been one of their crazier nights together. Crazy and intense. And that was before she realized she had conceived.

"I guess we should start thinking about finding a bigger place. Look into school districts, should we go public or private?"

"Whoa, slow down." Rachel wasn't ready to think about maternity clothes, let alone school uniforms. "Can we just get to the hotel and enjoy our wedding night? We don't have to plan for college just yet."

"It's never too early to start thinking about those things. You know I'm not going to be making this kind of money forever."

"Bryce. Stop. Please. I can't think about all of this right now." Although if she'd been smart, she would have thought about at least some of it before she'd said *I do*.

"Okay. Sorry. You're right. We should be celebrating." He turned toward her, flashing his most seductive grin. "Tonight is going to be very special."

He stuck the key into the ignition, started the engine, and then drove them to the hotel.

"Do you mind if I take a quick shower?" Bryce asked once they settled into their room. "You could join me?"

"You go ahead. I'll just slip into something more comfortable." Rachel felt shy all of a sudden. They'd torn each other's clothes off enough times over the last year or so, she shouldn't need to take a minute to wonder if he was going to find her desirable.

But everything had changed. She couldn't keep telling herself that this would be the last time. That it was just sex and it didn't matter if things didn't work out.

Because now it mattered.

* * * *

Bryce took a longer shower than he'd planned. He was nervous. It wasn't like it was the first time he'd had sex. Not even the first time with Rachel. Yet, the pressure was on. And it was a hell of a lot more pressure than just living up to his contract. He was going to have a kid. And he wanted to prove to Rachel that he could step up to the plate.

He toweled off, combed his hair, and swished some mouthwash for good measure. He wanted tonight to be special. Different from all their other hookups. This was their wedding night, so it had to be spectacular.

He splashed a little bit of cologne on, and contemplated shaving, but he knew what he could do with a few days' worth of stubble.

He ran his fingers through his hair one more time and walked into the bedroom ready to make this a night neither of them would ever forget.

Too bad Rachel was sound asleep.

She had slipped into a slinky little nightgown. Arranged the pillows behind her so she was propped up and ready for him. But the late hour had caught up with her. And maybe the whole growing a human being thing. He supposed that took up a lot of energy.

He was torn between wanting to wake her up, remind her how good they could be together, and watching her sleep. God, she was beautiful. Even with her mouth open and soft snores escaping her perfect lips. She'd worn her auburn hair up for the wedding, but had taken it down and the red and gold and copper-colored strands framed her sweet face. Her left arm was flung overhead and her right hand rested protectively on her lower abdomen. Her chest heaved with each breath.

His own chest felt like it was shrinking, his ribcage growing smaller by the minute. He couldn't breathe. Rachel was his. Officially. He had the ring on his finger and the piece of paper to prove it.

Now he just had to make sure he didn't screw it up.

* * * *

Rachel woke to sunlight streaming into an empty room. She'd fallen asleep on Bryce. On their wedding night. Instead of two or three rounds of hot, sweaty, mind-blowing sex, she hadn't even made it to a goodnight kiss.

She was just stepping out of the shower when she heard Bryce's keycard in the lock. Rachel dried off, wrapped her hair in a towel, and slipped into a robe. She stepped out of the bathroom.

He was carrying a paper cup from Starbucks and she waited for her stomach to recoil at the smell of coffee. But there was no smell.

"I started to get you a cup of coffee but then I remembered pregnant women shouldn't have too much caffeine." Bryce offered her a sweet smile along with the familiar green and white cup. "So I got hot chocolate. I also thought you might need a little something to tide you over until we get to Johnny and Alice's. I hope you like those little mini scones."

"Thank you." She took the hot cocoa and the bag of scones over to the table by the window. They had a great view of the city and the mountains surrounding it. She took a tentative sip, hoping it wasn't too hot.

"I finished my coffee downstairs. In case the smell of it bothers you." He stood as she pulled a vanilla frosted scone out of the paper sack. "Does the smell bother you?"

"Sometimes." She took a tiny bite, not trusting her stomach much these days. When the first bite seemed to pass the test, she took another. "But I miss it, too."

"If you have to give up coffee, I will, too." Bryce continued to stand there, hovering. "We're in this together."

"Stop. Please." She took a sip of hot cocoa to soothe the stinging in the back of her throat. Tears welled in her eyes. She hated being so damn emotional all of a sudden. "And please, sit down. I can't stand this overprotective thing you've got going."

"I'm not overprotective." He sat carefully on the edge of the bed. "I just want to take care of you. And the baby."

"It's too much." She shoved the cocoa and the rest of the scones away from her. "You finish your coffee downstairs so I don't have to smell it. You bring me scones and hot chocolate and stare at me while I eat. It's like you're waiting for me to fall apart."

"I'm not waiting for you to fall apart." Bryce rested his forearms on his knees. "I'm just trying to help."

"Yeah. Well, I don't need your help." Now she sounded ungrateful. "I don't need your understanding. Or you sacrificing your morning coffee for me."

"Okay." He said the word as if he thought she was overreacting. Maybe she was. But this wasn't them. They weren't a couple. They'd never even shared a meal together. Not even late night room service.

"Maybe I'm being a little…" He ran his fingers through his hair. "I guess I just don't want you to throw up in my car. It was bad enough you threw up *on* my car."

He looked up at her and grinned. That stupid, adorable, impossible-to-resist grin.

Her heart did a crazy little lurch, and she knew she was going to end up in bed with him once again. Of course she was. They were married.

She stood up, walked over to the bed, and placed both hands on his shoulders. She shoved him down and started kissing him. He tasted like coffee and vanilla and Bryce. She pressed her breasts against his chest and wove her hands into his hair.

He wrapped his arms around her waist and she could feel his erection pressing against her belly. He felt his way underneath her robe, and grabbed her ass. She wriggled, moving her hips to give him better access. This was more like it. This was what they did together better than anything.

"Do you have a condom?" She stopped kissing him long enough to ask the question she'd asked him dozens of times.

"You're pregnant," he said with a look of surprise.

"Yes. Even more reason to be careful." She didn't want to imply that she didn't trust him, but… "Unless you can tell me you haven't been with anyone since the last time we were together."

Before he could confirm or deny her suspicions, her phone on the nightstand buzzed. She knew by the ringtone she couldn't ignore it.

"Shit." Rachel rolled off him. "I've got to get that."

"Really? Now?" Bryce sounded irritated. Of course he was.

"Believe me, it's better to get it over with." Rachel scrambled off the bed and grabbed the phone.

"Hi, Mom. What a nice surprise." She sat on the edge of the bed with her back to Bryce and smoothed her robe down around her thighs. She felt the bed shake as he got up, and she tried not to cry when she heard his footsteps cross the room.

"Speaking of surprises." Her mother's tone was all too predictable. "I was watching the news last night, and before they even got to the sports highlights, there was my sweet baby girl onscreen, accepting a marriage proposal from one of the Goliaths' players. Please tell me it was a joke. Or a publicity stunt. Please tell me you're not engaged."

"I'm not engaged." She gripped the phone, digging her nails into the shockproof cover. "I'm married. Bryce and I are in Reno, and actually, we don't have a lot of time left on our honeymoon, so—"

"Married? I see." Her mother sounded like a woman who had just learned her daughter had run away and joined the circus. "I suppose informing your own mother of your intention to get married just sort of slipped your mind."

"Look, Mom, I'm sorry I didn't call you, I didn't have time. It all happened so fast. We had an off day and decided to take advantage of it while we could."

"You just up and decided to marry this guy on a whim?"

"It wasn't a whim. It was…" She rubbed the back of her neck. "We decided it would be better to make the wedding small. Stay out of the spotlight."

"I don't understand. I've never even met this man." Mom sounded more hurt than offended, now. "Never even heard you mention him. I talked to your sister. She said the only thing you ever said about him was that he drives you crazy."

"He does drive me crazy." Rachel sighed. She turned to see if Bryce was listening, but he'd left the room. "But he also makes me laugh. And I don't expect you to understand, but I do hope you'll support me. Support us."

"It would be easier to support you if I wasn't so blindsided. I didn't even know you were seeing someone." Rachel supposed it would be a shock. "I mean, you were with Carter for three years. You brought him to Megan's wedding. We were all expecting you two to be next."

"Well, Carter wasn't the man for me." She was glad Bryce wasn't in the room. She didn't want him to overhear her defending her choice to dump a man who had charmed her family so convincingly. "He cheated on me, for one. And he didn't take my career seriously."

"He cheated on you?" Mom sounded genuinely shocked. "I'm so sorry."

"He wanted me to quit my job." That still stung even more than his infidelity. "Thought I'd be content to simply be Mrs. Bigshot Attorney."

She flopped down on the bed just as Bryce came out of the bathroom. He saw that she was still on the phone and started to back away. She smiled at him, motioning for him to stay.

"Look, Mom. I'm sorry you didn't get to come to the wedding. But I've got to go. We need to head back to San Francisco. We both have to work tomorrow."

She glanced over at Bryce, and a warm feeling bloomed in her chest. Part of the reason they were here in Reno was so she could keep her job. Hopefully. But the fact that Bryce recognized how important her career was made him a hero in her heart.

* * * *

She didn't trust him. It shouldn't come as a surprise, but it still hurt. She wanted him to wear a condom. Because she knew he'd slept with other women. Not as many as he could have, but more than he should have. The question he had to ask himself was why? To prove he was hot stuff? He was Bryce Freaking Baxter. World Series Champion. MVP. The highest paid player on the Goliaths. He made even more than Marco Santiago. But Marco was set for life. He'd married the Goliaths' former owner. She'd basically traded her interest in the team for Marco. Not to mention a large sum of money.

Bryce had done everything he could not to let anyone get close to him. He knew his time at the top was only temporary. He wasn't going to be the man forever. He didn't want to set someone up for disappointment.

It had worked for him just fine until he met Rachel. He'd thought she was just using him for a story. Not a big deal. He'd been used for most of his life. From the minute his talent had become a little more than average, his dad, coaches, and yes, girls had all jumped on the Bryce Baxter bandwagon. He didn't mind. Too much.

But when he'd gone back to Rachel to plead Johnny Scottsdale's case, to ask her to keep the story to herself, she'd agreed. And he'd been totally screwed.

Chapter 4

Rachel put on her best smile-no-matter-what smile. She was a guest of Johnny Scottsdale and his wife, Alice. If she hadn't been trying to get the scoop on Johnny's relationship with Alice's thirteen-year-old son, she never would have ended up in Bryce Baxter's bed. She didn't sleep with him for a story. In fact, she'd only approached him because he was the only player who had spent any time with the reclusive Scottsdale. They'd shared an autograph table at Fan Fest and had been seen working out together.

She hadn't expected Bryce's fierce loyalty to a man he'd only known a week. Part of it was the fact that they were teammates, both new to the club. But the affection between the two men seemed genuine.

And the chemistry between her and Bryce? That was very real as well.

They'd connected that night, and when she woke up the next morning in his bed, she'd chalked it up as a one-time thing. But when he came back to her a few days later, asking her to sit on the Johnny Scottsdale story, she'd found herself once again impressed by his loyalty. And she'd found herself once again in his bed.

Now she stood on the doorstep of the last two people she'd expect to invite her into their home.

"Congratulations, you two." Johnny answered the door with a huge grin. "I wouldn't have believed it if I hadn't been there."

"Thanks for stepping up at the last minute." Bryce held out his hand in gratitude.

"Anytime, man. Anytime." Johnny pulled his friend into a fierce embrace.

Rachel stood just behind her new husband. She knew the only reason she was here was because the two men were close. A brief stab of envy rose into her heart. She could never hope to be as close to Bryce as Johnny was. They had been through a long season together. A championship season. And she knew that the rings the two of them shared would always mean more to Bryce than the one she'd placed on his finger last night.

"Alice is putting Emily down for a nap." Johnny finally acknowledged Rachel. "She'll be down in a minute. Why don't we head on back to the kitchen?"

"Thank you." Rachel felt like a stranger. Sure she'd interviewed Johnny several times. She may have even flirted with him a little bit during the first interview before she'd connected the dots between him and Alice and their son, Zach.

They followed Johnny through their large, yet welcoming home. They were on the outskirts of town, with a bit of property surrounding their house. The kitchen opened up to the back yard, where a large stone patio led to a fenced-in pool.

"We could eat outside, if you'd like," Johnny offered.

"Sure." Bryce put his hand on the small of Rachel's back, ushering her out onto the patio. "Can I help with anything?"

"No, you two just relax." Johnny grinned again. As if he was genuinely happy for them. "Coffee?"

"We already had some back at the hotel." Bryce made the excuse before she could decide whether or not she should take a cup just to be polite.

"We have juice."

"That would be nice." Rachel hoped she could stomach it. Nerves and morning sickness weren't a good combination. And today, nerves seemed to be winning.

"Coming right up." Johnny headed for the kitchen. "I should have thought to pick up some champagne. We could have made mimosas."

"That would have been great, if we weren't driving back to San Francisco today." Bryce covered for her.

"Right. You have to get back to work." Johnny's voice had the slightest hint of envy. Rachel wondered if he missed the game. He probably always would.

"Look, if you want coffee, or anything else…" Rachel didn't want Bryce to go without because of her, yet she appreciated him making it easy for her to decline.

"I already had my coffee, and I never drink and drive. Not even one drink." Bryce sat next to her, picking up her hand and reassuring her with a quick squeeze.

Johnny returned with two glasses of orange juice and a cup of coffee for himself.

"Sorry I kept you waiting." Alice joined them with a weary smile and a cloth diaper draped over one shoulder. "Emily is starting to settle into a predictable nap schedule, but she took a little longer to go down today."

Johnny stood, placing a kiss on his wife's cheek, grabbing the diaper and tucking it into his pocket.

"Thank you for having us over. I hope you didn't go to too much trouble." Rachel offered what she hoped was an appreciative smile.

"No trouble at all," Alice assured her. "Johnny did most of the work." She glanced at her husband admiringly.

"Let's eat." Johnny clapped his hands together. "Ladies first."

He ushered the two women into the kitchen and Alice grabbed a stack of plates, handing one to Rachel.

"Everything looks delicious." Rachel felt a grumbling in her stomach. She waited for the accompanying dizziness and clammy skin, but it was genuine hunger, not nausea for a change. She heaped piles of fluffy scrambled eggs, crispy bacon, and golden potatoes onto her plate. Toasted wheat bread, what looked like homemade jam, and fresh fruit rounded out the meal.

* * * *

It was good to see Rachel with an appetite. She'd eaten most of her breakfast, but Bryce could tell she wasn't entirely comfortable. Sure the conversation flowed. Rachel asked questions about the baseball camp Johnny and Alice were starting. They should be up and running by mid-June.

Bryce hoped Rachel would eventually feel comfortable around the Scottsdales. Even though they weren't teammates anymore, Johnny was one of his closest friends. He wanted to include his wife in their circle.

His wife. He was starting to feel more and more comfortable with the idea. But he was kicking himself for all the time he'd wasted trying to deny how well they fit together. If he'd put half as much energy into courting her properly as he had in trying to get over her... Well, he would have given her a proper wedding. And wedding night.

Just as they were starting to wind down their meal, Emily's cries carried over the baby monitor.

"I'll get her." Johnny placed a loving hand on his wife's shoulder. "You finish your breakfast."

"Thanks." Alice gave him a grateful smile.

Bryce really wanted to go with him. Pick his brain a little. Gain some wisdom from a guy who had this fatherhood thing down. Bryce admitted to himself that he hadn't done a good job the first time around. Fear, resentment, and a complete cluelessness had kept him from being much help when Hailey had been a baby.

He'd just been called up to the majors and wanted to enjoy his time in the big leagues. He hadn't wanted to change diapers, get up for midnight feedings, or try to put the baby down for a nap. He especially hadn't wanted to be told he was doing it wrong.

As a result, he'd failed as a father and husband. He believed he just wasn't cut out to be a family man. But being around Johnny and his family made him think that anything was possible. Made him believe that he wasn't completely helpless when it came to kids. He'd spent a lot of the offseason with them, even managed to hold the baby without freaking her out. Or himself.

Johnny returned with Emily in his arms. She was a little fussy, but as soon as she saw Bryce, her face lit up and she lunged for him.

"There's my girl." Bryce took her and she giggled as he bounced her on his knee. Maybe he could do this. "Did you miss your Uncle Bryce?"

She squealed in delight and leaned forward to plant a wet baby kiss on his face.

"Whoa, now, hate to break it to you sweetheart, but I'm a married man." He shifted her to his other knee. "But maybe if you're lucky, we'll have a boy. You can marry him when you grow up."

He glanced over at Rachel just in time to see her face drain of color. Uh-oh. Either she was going to be sick or he was going to be in trouble.

"Are you having a baby?" Alice turned to Rachel with a curious look on her face.

"Yes." Rachel glared at Bryce. He was most certainly in trouble. "Why else would we get married in the middle of the season? In the middle of the night?"

"Maybe he just finally realized the most amazing catch he's ever made was the night he met you." Johnny tried to keep the peace. "He couldn't get over you any more than I could get over Alice."

They all sat there in silence until Emily grabbed a handful of Bryce's hair and yanked with glee.

"Ouch. I think it's time you go back to your daddy." Bryce grimaced, both from the stinging in his scalp and the wound in his pride. Johnny Scottsdale had held the record for emotional shutdown. Now he thought he was Dr. Phil or Dr. Oz or whoever the hell went on TV pointing out the obvious to clueless saps.

Like Bryce. Shit. He didn't need The Monk to tell him he was crazy about Rachel Parker. Probably had been since that first night. He should have been the one to tell her.

Not that she'd believe him.

Alice stepped up and saved his ass. She asked about due dates and then the two women were suddenly the best of friends discussing trimesters and morning sickness and what to expect when.

He let out a breath when they went inside to look at pregnancy books and maternity clothes.

Chapter 5

Rachel was happy to be back to work. The past seventy-two hours had been overwhelming. Engaged, married, and moved in all in the span of three days. She'd had only about two hours alone, packing the essentials to take to Bryce's apartment. He'd taken the time to clear out a closet and half his drawers. They had to share a bed because his second bedroom housed his workout equipment.

Eventually they would have to turn that room into a nursery. Or find a bigger apartment. She wasn't ready to think about buying a house together. That seemed too permanent. Something she wasn't sure she could manage with Bryce. Sure, she'd said the words, "till death do us part," but she didn't really think it would come to that.

Kip Michaels was the first to approach Rachel in the press area before the game.

"I haven't had the chance to congratulate you on your engagement." Even though he'd been a star pitcher and was now an Emmy-award-winning broadcaster, he'd always made Rachel feel like one of the team. He'd been a mentor to her from her earliest days as an intern and she didn't think she would have made it this far without his guidance and friendship. "Have you set a date yet?"

"Actually, we got married." She felt a blush creep across her cheeks. "We went to Reno after the game Sunday and it's official."

She pasted on a smile fit for a glowing bride and held up her left hand to show her wedding ring.

"Well, in that case you deserve a hug." He pulled her into a hearty embrace. She leaned into the hug, feeling like a fraud.

He stepped back and smiled warmly. "Why didn't you tell us you were seeing Baxter? We're a family here, you know."

"We kept it quiet for various reasons." She felt only slightly less guilty for keeping her relationship with Bryce a secret from Kip as she did for keeping it from her own family. "Mostly because it wasn't supposed to turn into anything."

"But he went and stole your heart anyway?" Kip chuckled. "Well I'm happy for you, kid. I wish you all the best."

"Thank you." Rachel knew he meant it.

"Now you know my partner is going to want some of the leftover cake." He and Kurt Dwyer had been in the booth for over a decade. One-time teammates and long-term friends, they were the best broadcasting team in baseball: knowledgeable, entertaining, and always respectful of the game and the men who played it.

"We didn't have any cake." She actually felt bad for not picking some up. Kurt's sweet tooth was almost as legendary as his one and only homerun in the big leagues. "It all happened so quickly."

"You know, I think you and Bryce did it right. Young people today spend way too much time and energy focusing on the wrong things, like the cake. They forget what's really important. The marriage."

"What's this about cake?" Kurt popped his head into the booth. "If you need someone to help you test out bakeries for the big day, you know who to call."

"Thank you, but since we already got married, I don't think we'll need to test cakes."

"Married? Already?" He glanced at his partner for confirmation, and when Kip nodded, Kurt turned back to Rachel. "Well, we'll just have to order a cake. You need to have a celebration, even if it is after the fact."

"That would be lovely. I'm sure you'll come up with something delicious." She tucked a strand of hair behind her ear. "Now, if you two will excuse me, I need to get to work."

"Honeymoon's over, huh?" Kip quipped.

"Yeah, that's the price we paid for not waiting until the offseason." She tried to hold her head high, not wanting to show she was a little disappointed that not only had she not had a cake, she still hadn't consummated her marriage.

But she couldn't worry about that now. The Goliaths were playing tonight and it was her job to bring the game home to the fans. She interviewed players, fans, and distinguished guests around the ballpark. She recreated the experience of being at the ballpark for the viewers at home. But more than that, she liked to think she brought out the human element of the national pastime. She provided a glimpse into the men behind the uniform.

Her fans had often commented on how she made a group of elite, and well-paid, athletes seem like just a bunch of regular guys.

She just wondered how she was going to be accepted now that she was married to one of those guys.

* * * *

Bryce wasn't sure what to expect when he walked into the clubhouse after his quickie wedding. He'd spent the last year and a half trying to hide his relationship with Rachel, and now it was official. Legal, even.

He got some ribbing. Guys saying they thought she was too smart to end up with a guy like him. Some congratulatory pats on the back, and a few raised eyebrows. But they didn't ask too many questions. Not that he'd have much to say.

Besides, he had to get back to work.

He had a decent game. Got one hit, a walk, and he scored on Marco Santiago's game-winning home run.

Rachel rushed up to interview Marco after the game. She looked up at him as if he was the biggest hero of her life. Bryce's gut twisted as he thought of all the times she'd interviewed him after a win. Back when he'd been the one who had knocked in the winning runs. More often than not, they'd ended the off-camera portion of the interview in bed.

"Even though the team has gotten off to a slow start, you're still playing like it's the postseason." She smiled for the camera, or was it for Marco?

"Thank you, Rachel, I know I've been lucky lately." Marco flashed his too-damn-good-looking grin. "And I know it's just a matter of time before the rest of the team gets hot. We had a great run last year and every single one of us wants to do it again."

"Would you say defending the championship is harder than winning it in the first place?"

"I guess in a way, it should be easier, knowing that we're capable of going all the way." He shook his head. "But baseball is a humbling game. Success is the exception, not the rule. We shouldn't be worried about whether or not we'll repeat as World Series Champions, we should be focusing on the next game. The next series. And if we can play the way we're capable of playing, then we'll talk about it more in October."

"Thank you, Marco, it's always a pleasure talking to you." Rachel tilted her head to the side, still smiling. "I do hope we'll be talking plenty in October."

Marco nodded at the camera and took off for the clubhouse.

Bryce watched Rachel wrap up her segment and waited until the camera stopped rolling before approaching her.

"Nice interview." Bryce still had his teeth clenched. "You think Marco Santiago is hot, don't you?"

"He's on a pretty good streak." She looked at him as if she didn't know what he was talking about.

"No, you think he's *hot*. Like all the women on that Facebook fan site, 'I heart Marco Santiago' where they post about how sexy he is."

"I haven't seen that one. I do know about the site devoted entirely to your hair," Rachel said. "I've thought about commenting that, yes, it is as soft and silky as it looks, but I didn't want to brag."

"Yeah, well now you can go on there and tell them we're married. Or have you forgotten?" He knew he was out of line, but he couldn't stop. "You can't keep flirting with guys like Santiago."

"I wasn't flirting. I was working. I was asking questions about the game. Like I do every night." She glared at him. "You know what, I don't need this. I'm going to my apartment. I still have a lot of stuff to deal with and I don't need you telling me how to do my job."

With that, she stomped past him.

Bryce stood there, alone on the field. Except he wasn't alone. Her cameraman had witnessed the whole exchange. Fortunately the camera had been turned off, so there wouldn't be any footage going viral about how Bryce Baxter couldn't even score with his new bride.

"I blew it, didn't I?" he asked.

Carl just laughed and shook his head. "You've been married what? Two days? You've got a lot to learn."

"Yeah. I know." Bryce knew he was screwed. But he couldn't help it. Why did Santiago have to be the first guy she interviewed? Besides being ridiculously good-looking, he was still playing like a champion. The two men had competed down the stretch. They'd fed off each other, pushed each other, and brought out the best in each other. Their rivalry played a big part in the team's success. Marco had won the Most Valuable Player award in the National League Championship Series. Bryce had won it for the World Series. Marco then signed a lucrative five-year contract, and Bryce extended his for six.

Off the field, Marco had gotten his girl. Hunter Collins had given up her share of the Goliaths for the love of her man. But everyone knew she'd be back in the game once Marco's career ended.

Bryce had gotten his girl, too. But just like with his game, he was in danger of blowing it.

* * * *

Rachel got in her car and headed east on the Bay Bridge. She was one of the few people she knew who actually enjoyed her commute. Her job wasn't particularly stressful, but she needed the drive time to unwind. She was a professional, but she was a baseball fan first. The games were often exciting, frustrating, or a combination of both. She had to maintain an impartial façade on camera, but her heart rested with the team. When they won, she was pumped up. When they lost, she was a little down. But she couldn't show it. She had to smile and ask the hard questions after a loss. She had to keep her emotions under control.

Usually by the time she pulled into her parking spot in Walnut Creek, she was relaxed and ready for a nice warm bath, a good book, and maybe a glass of wine before bed. She had to skip the wine these days, but she could still enjoy a nice long soak.

But not tonight. Tonight she was still wound up from Bryce's fit over her interview with Marco Santiago. What the hell? She was just doing her job. The job that Bryce had insisted he wanted to save.

Did he really not trust her?

She went into her closet and started pulling out her clothes. She'd only taken about a week's worth of stuff to Bryce's apartment. She needed to sort through the clothes that would still fit her in another month. Skinny jeans were out. Yoga pants in. Then there were the few dresses in her wardrobe that she had no idea if she would wear again. Including the little black number she'd worn the night of the Golden Gate Gala. The night she and Bryce had hooked up for the first time.

She hadn't gone there looking for anything other than a feel-good story about how the Goliaths' partnership with the Harrison Foundation helped kids in the community. Damn her hunch that there was a deeper connection between Johnny Scottsdale and the Harrison kid. Bryce had been quick to point out that Johnny was an upstanding guy. His only connection was that he'd dated the director of the foundation back in college.

Bryce had approached her. Made her feel like the most glamorous woman at the party. Crazy since she was probably the only one there in a consignment store bargain and faux jewelry. And the fact that she didn't use anything she'd learned that night for a story meant she couldn't write off the expense.

When she woke up the next morning in Bryce Baxter's bed, she'd sworn it was a one-time thing. They'd both agreed that as lovely as their time together was, it was a once-in-a-lifetime experience. And it would not in any way affect their working relationship.

That resolve lasted until Bryce came begging her not to do a story on his new best friend.

A small part of her wanted to tell him, too bad. She had a story that could get her national attention. Nothing like a sex scandal to elevate her career. And news that The Monk had a love child would have given her certain notoriety. The kind that could have come with job offers.

It wasn't just Bryce's begging that had kept her from running with the story. Although he was very persuasive, she realized that if she had taken the low road, she would be no better than her ex. The one who thought being a sports reporter wasn't real journalism.

She hadn't gotten very far in her packing when the doorbell rang. She stretched, rubbing her lower back before answering the door.

"I brought you pickles and ice cream." Bryce stood on her porch. His trademark smile was damn near impossible to resist. Lord help her if their child inherited his grin. "Truce?"

"I don't like pickles. The smell alone is enough to make me want to vomit. Even when I'm not pregnant." She was still mad at him. And herself for not being able to turn him away.

"What about ice cream?" Bryce pulled a carton of Mexican chocolate from the grocery sack. "You do like ice cream, don't you?"

"How did you know my favorite flavor?" Her heart did a crazy little lurch when he produced her kryptonite.

"Carl clued me in." He shrugged. "I had to beg, but he finally told me what your weakness is."

"He's dead meat." Rachel grabbed for the ice cream and stood back to let Bryce enter. "And you are not off the hook, mister."

Bryce ran a hand through his hair. She hated how sexy he was. How drop-dead-fucking gorgeous. Even more, she hated that he knew it. And knew that she, like all women, was powerless to resist.

She made a beeline for the kitchen. Grabbed a spoon and dug into the ice cream. Just a little taste of heaven. Chocolate and cinnamon danced on her tongue. Soothing and exciting her at the same time.

Just like Bryce.

"So you think you can just come over here, offering me ice cream, and all is forgiven?" She wasn't going to let him off that easy. "I was just doing my job and you had to go get all weird on me."

"I'm sorry." Bryce ran both hands through his hair. At least he knew he'd screwed up. "I got a little carried away."

"You think?" She licked the back of the spoon. She'd better put the rest of the ice cream in the freezer. She'd eat the whole carton if she wasn't careful.

He came up to her, put his arms around her. It would be so easy to just lean into him. Accept the fact that she was completely under his spell, had been since the Golden Gate Gala.

He ran his hands down her hips, pulled her close and she was tempted to surrender. To just let him have his way with her. And she'd have her way with him.

"Seriously, Bryce." She pulled away, stuck the spoon back into the ice cream. "How could you? I mean, of all people, Marco Santiago is the last person you should worry about. He absolutely worships his wife. It's almost sickening. If it wasn't so... So genuine."

"Is that what you want? A man who worships you?"

She'd settle for a man who trusted her. A man she could trust.

* * * *

Bryce wasn't about to let Santiago beat him again. It was bad enough his batting average was a hundred points higher. His RBI totals were double. And the left fielder hadn't committed any errors this season. Now Rachel thought he was the ideal husband, too.

He grabbed the spoon, scooped up a good-sized bite, and held it up to her lips. She opened her mouth, allowing him to feed her one last bite of ice cream. As soon as she closed her eyes, enjoying the tasty treat, Bryce moved in.

He withdrew the spoon, tossing it in the direction of the sink, and covered her mouth with his. Then he wrapped his arms around her, savoring the taste of her. She tasted of chocolate and cinnamon and Rachel.

Pulling her closer, he kissed her harder, worshipping her with his mouth, his tongue. He moved his hands down her shoulders, pressed his body against hers. When she threaded her fingers through his hair, he knew she had surrendered to him.

There was no better feeling than having Rachel run her hands through his hair, except when she ran her hands across his body, wrapped her legs around him, surrounded him with her sweetness.

He broke the kiss, catching his breath. Then he moved to savor the delicate skin behind her ear. He started working on the buttons of her blouse, trailing kisses down her neck, across her collarbone, dipping his tongue between her breasts.

When he got to her slightly rounded belly, he placed a reverent kiss just below her navel.

"Is there really a baby growing inside you?" He marveled. "My baby?"

"What? You don't believe me?" She backed away from him and pulled her shirt closed. "You think I made it all up?"

"No. That's not what I meant." Bryce backed up and ran a frustrated hand through his hair.

"You think you can just come over here, bringing ice cream, and I'll just fall into bed with you?"

"What's wrong with wanting to make love to my wife?" He reached out to stroke her hair.

"It's all we know how to do." The despair in her voice made him drop his hand. "I think we made a mistake. There's no way we're going to make it. Maybe we should just admit that now, before we end up hurting each other even more."

"I refuse to fail here."

"You're just saying that because your first marriage failed."

"No. That's not it." Bryce took her hands gently in his. "I deal with failure every day. My job is nothing but failure, with the occasional success here and there."

She smiled at that assessment of the game.

"I won't fail you, Rachel. I promise." He looked into her eyes and saw the fear, hope, and maybe even something more there. "I'll make mistakes, sure. But I won't fail you. Or our baby."

She fell into his arms, and he held her, stroking her back, easing her worry. He kissed her on the top of her head.

Bryce would not fail her. No matter what. Even if it meant he had to keep his hands to himself, he would earn her trust.

Chapter 6

Rachel woke the next morning to the smell of buttered toast and the sound of a man in her kitchen. Bryce had spent the night in her bed, but they hadn't made love. They'd been married three days now and still hadn't consummated the marriage.

What was wrong with her? She'd been pushing Bryce away. As if some subconscious part of her believed that if they didn't have sex, they weren't really married and it wouldn't hurt so much when it all fell apart.

Sure. Denying Bryce her body wasn't going to protect her heart. She'd already learned that the hard way.

She got up, brushed her teeth, and threw a robe on, then went to see what her husband was up to.

Packing her kitchen. He had somehow come up with cardboard boxes and a stack of newspapers, and was pulling dishes out of her cupboards and wrapping them in newsprint.

"Good morning." He glanced up at her with a grin, and resumed his task. "Your dishes are a lot nicer than mine. They match."

"Yes. They do."

"Your glasses all match too."

"My coffee cups, too." Oh, what she wouldn't give for a big steaming cup of coffee. "Do I smell toast?"

"I'll make more." Bryce stopped what he was doing to put two slices of bread in the toaster. "What would you like on it? Butter? Jam?"

"I can make my own toast." It was easier to do it herself since she wasn't sure what she wanted. She'd start with buttered toast and if that didn't quite satisfy, she'd add jam or peanut butter. But she wouldn't know until she started eating what she could handle.

"It's no trouble, really." He flashed that irresistible grin of his. "I've been making toast about as long as I've been playing baseball. I'm practically an expert."

"I'll start with just butter." She sat down, figuring she could get up if she decided she wanted something else.

"What about something to drink? A glass of milk?"

"That sounds good, actually." She decided to give in and let him wait on her while she could. He would be leaving in two days for a long road trip. Her stomach churned just thinking about him being on the road, with temptation thrown at him.

Bryce presented her with two slices of buttered toast and a large glass of ice-cold milk.

"Thank you." She nibbled on her toast, sipped her milk, and waited for the yea or nay from her tummy. So far, so good. She grabbed a hard-boiled egg from the supply she kept on hand and managed to keep that down, too.

"You're welcome." He returned to his packing. "I'd like to take a load or two to my place today, if that works for you. I figure I can take the heavy stuff, like the dishes. Then you can pack up the small stuff you want to bring over."

"Sure." She still wasn't convinced that this move was going to be permanent.

"Have you talked to your landlord about getting out of your lease?"

"No. Not yet."

"I can do it, if you want." He offered. "I can be convincing, sometimes."

"Yes, you can." She patted her belly. "I still haven't decided what I want to do about the apartment. I've got five months left on the current lease. Maybe I should wait and see."

"Wait and see what?" He set the plate he was wrapping in the box, and pushed away from the counter. "Do you want to start looking for a house? I was thinking we could get by in my apartment for a few months after the baby comes. I'm not going to have much time to house hunt until after the season ends. Then, it might take a while to find what we really want, and once we do, it can take a couple of months for everything to be finalized."

"I'm not ready to look for a house." She wasn't ready to give up on her apartment, either, but as she looked around at the tiny space, she couldn't imagine trying to fit a baby and all the things she'd need in here. "But I'll need to figure out what to do with my furniture."

"We could rent a storage unit for whatever you don't want to bring to my place," Bryce suggested. "Do you know what you want to bring over? I'll see if Juan Javier will let me borrow his truck."

"I'm sure your manager would be thrilled with the idea of you moving heavy furniture." She smirked at the idea of Bryce and his buddies carrying her couch out to the street. "He'd kill me if you hurt your back or something."

"I guess we'll have to hire someone, then." He started wrapping more dishes. "I can handle whatever we take to my apartment, but when we get a storage locker, we can call a moving service for the big stuff."

"Fine. Sounds like a good plan." She resigned herself to the idea that she wasn't going to be able to keep her apartment, not without hurting Bryce's feelings. Besides, it really wasn't big enough for more than one person. "I'll give notice to my landlord and look for a storage unit."

"If he gives you any trouble, let me know. I can get tickets, signed bats, whatever."

"I can get tickets, too." Her job did have its perks, besides the fact that her office was the ballpark. "I don't need you to get me out of my lease. I can handle things myself."

"Of course you can. I was just trying to help." He looked a little hurt by her refusal to let him act like a big shot and bribe her landlord.

"Thank you." Rachel realized she didn't need to be so hard on him. He was trying to make this easier on her. And he didn't even realize just how difficult change was for her. Especially the kind of change that she didn't plan for, and couldn't control. "And thank you for the toast. It seems to be just what the doctor ordered."

"Why don't you go take a shower? I'll clean up in here and finish packing."

She resisted the urge to get defensive about his telling her what to do.

Rachel got out of the shower feeling pretty good. Better than she'd felt in weeks. Surprising since she still felt like her whole world was out of control. As she toweled off, she glanced down at the ring on her left hand. It was beautiful. A little larger than she would have picked, but that was Bryce. He didn't do anything small. At least since she'd known him, he gave his all in anything he tried. On the field, he worked harder than anyone else, Marco Santiago included. He sometimes failed spectacularly, but it was never from lack of effort.

Maybe he'd do the same with their marriage. She knew the odds were against them. But the odds had been against the Goliaths to win the World Series last year. They'd managed to pull it off. Bryce had been a huge factor in winning the division and the series. And oh how they'd celebrated. Longing filled her. She could step into the kitchen wearing nothing but a towel, and she was pretty sure Bryce would make love to her.

But then her mind wandered to the other women he'd celebrated with in the last year. She knew there were others. How many? She didn't know and she didn't want to know.

A tear slipped down her cheek. She wiped it away, along with the idea of seducing her husband. This marriage was about the baby. That's who she had to think about. As much as she wanted Bryce in her bed, she needed him in her child's life more.

*   *   *   *

"Seriously, Bryce, it will be a lot faster if I help you carry some of these boxes." Rachel stood with her hands on her hips while he unloaded the back of her car. "I'd hate for you to strain something and get put on the DL."

"Don't worry. I'm not going to do anything to put me out of commission." He wasn't stupid. "Although, the way I've been hitting, or rather not hitting, I'm surprised they haven't been putting banana peels in front of my locker."

"You're coming out of it." She didn't say the s-word. Slump. "You've hit the ball hard the last couple of at-bats. It's only a matter of time before they start falling in, instead of getting caught."

"Thanks." He appreciated her support. It was exactly the kind of bullshit anyone would tell a player in his position, only she said it like she believed it. "I hope you're right."

"No. The correct answer is 'Yes, dear. You're right. You're always right.'" She flashed a playful grin and it was just one of the many things he loved about her.

Whoa. No. Not love. He liked her. A lot. Respected her, sure. And he really did care about her. But love? Not something he was even capable of.

"Yes, dear. You're right. You're always right." He played along. "But you're still not carrying anything heavy."

She just rolled her eyes and grabbed a small duffel bag from the back seat. She followed him into the lobby and waited for the elevator to take them up to his penthouse apartment.

"You can get the mail. That would be helpful." He appreciated the fact that she really did want to do her share. She wasn't the kind of woman who expected to be waited on or pampered or treated like a princess, which was exactly why he wanted to wait on her, pamper her, and treat her like a queen. "The keys are in my front pocket."

She reached into his jeans' pocket and pulled out the keys. She made sure to rub up against him just enough to turn him on, but not enough for him to drop the box of dishes and take her right there in the lobby. But there was a stairwell that no one used.

"It's the little key, right?" She dangled the key ring in front of him, the way she used to dangle her sweet assets. "Am I going to find a lot of lipstick-covered fan mail?"

"No. My fan mail goes to the ballpark." Or it used to. "I mostly get junk mail and bank statements in my personal mailbox. Have you changed your mailing address yet? You can do it online, don't even have to wait in line."

At the mention of changing her address, she paled. He wondered if she was having late morning sickness or was still fighting the idea that they were in fact married.

"Look, I understand why you don't want to change your name." It stung a little, but he did understand she'd made a name for herself in her career. "But you should have all your mail delivered here. No reason for you to travel across the bridge just to pick up your mail."

"I'll get to all of that." She sighed. "When you go back on the road, I'll have a few days to take care of giving notice at my apartment, changing my address, and updating my relationship status on Facebook."

"You haven't…" He realized she was kidding about that last part. "I mean, are you sure you don't want to come on the road with me? We haven't had a honeymoon, you know."

"I really should use the time to get some things done." She gave him an apologetic smile. "I have a doctor's appointment coming up, too."

She must have seen the disappointment on his face, because she added, "Maybe when you head down to San Diego later next month. We could go to the beach or something. If I'm not the size of a whale by then."

He tried to picture her expanding waistline. Her engorged breasts. He'd never considered pregnant women sexy, but just the thought of Rachel rubbing cocoa butter on her rounded belly got him hot. Too hot, as the box started to slip from his hands. He recovered just in time, as Rachel slid the key into the mailbox lock.

"Do you want me to just toss the junk mail?" She pointed to the trash can inside the lobby door.

"No, I have a shredder upstairs."

"A shredder?"

"You'd be surprised what people will steal and try to put up on eBay." He'd had a bad experience back in Pittsburgh with a too-enthusiastic fan who'd found his apartment from digging through the trash. He'd learned to be more cautious since then. "This is a secure building, but you can never be too careful these days."

The elevator doors opened. Rachel shouldered her duffel bag, and carried the stack of mail into the car. He followed with the box of her matching dishes. Once inside the apartment, he set the box on the counter and she tossed the mail on the end of table before taking her clothes back to his bedroom. Their bedroom.

He stretched his back and picked up the mail. Sure enough, most of it was junk, but there were a couple of statements from his bank, his stockbroker, and an envelope from his doctor's office.

He tore open the envelope with shaky hands. He'd gone in to get tested after Rachel had asked him to wear a condom even though she was already pregnant. He unfolded the paper containing the lab results and scanned the page, looking for anything that came back abnormal or positive.

He was in the clear. He'd tested negative for any sexually transmitted diseases and his cholesterol levels were in the healthy range. Bryce breathed a huge sigh of relief. He'd been careful ever since his encounter with his ex-wife. But, nothing was a hundred percent guaranteed.

"So let's get the next load, and then I'll start unpacking." Rachel brushed her hair back off her forehead and sighed. "Is everything okay?"

"Oh, yeah. Great." He pushed off the counter where he'd been leaning. "Good news, actually."

He handed the lab results to Rachel.

"What's this?" She scanned the page but didn't seem to understand what she was reading.

"Well, I went ahead and got tested." He felt the shame of needing proof. "And everything's good. I'm clean as a whistle."

"Oh. Great." She looked down at the paper in her hands, but she couldn't hold it steady. "Your cholesterol levels are good. That's just great."

He'd expected her to be happy. Or at least relieved. But the tone of her voice sounded like she was on the verge of tears.

"Oh, Bryce." Not on the verge, but fully in the middle of crying. "I'm so sorry I questioned you."

"I'm sorry I gave you reason to." He couldn't help it, he pulled her into his arms and stroked her hair. It was so soft, so silky. And so damn sexy.

He lowered his mouth to hers. Kissing her cautiously, tenderly, he wanted her, wanted her more than ever. But she had to want him back.

Rachel took control of the kiss, tangling her fingers through his hair and pressing her body against his. Oh yeah, she wanted him, too.

"Bryce." She came up for air. Hopefully to suggest they take this to the next level. The bedroom. "We still have five more boxes in the car."

"Right." He took a step back. Nothing like reality to cool a man off. "I'll bring those up. You can start unpacking."

"It would be faster if I helped, make it three trips instead of five." She smoothed her auburn hair back off her face. She was one of those work first kind of people. Playtime would have to wait.

"I appreciate the offer, but I'll carry the boxes, you just worry about carrying the baby." He had to focus on that, not ripping her clothes off and saying to hell with the moving in.

"I'm pregnant. I'm not an invalid." She sounded a little pissed off. "Women in my condition have run marathons, you know."

"Not my woman." Now he was pissed off. Any other woman would have been perfectly happy to sit back and watch him do all the work. Would have used her condition as an excuse to quit her job, and take advantage of his fortune. But Rachel was different. Sometimes he appreciated that about her, and sometimes it frustrated the hell out of him.

"Your woman?" She inched closer, so they were chest to chest. She had a fire in her eyes. Maybe half of it was anger, the other half lust. "You think I'm your woman?"

"Yes. Yes, you are." He kissed her again. Not gentle this time, oh no, this kiss was pure possession. He gripped her hips and held her tight against him. "You're mine, Rachel Parker. All mine."

"Bryce." She pulled away again. "It's ten o'clock in the morning."

"Yeah. So?"

"So, we can't just…" She looked away, blushing. "In the middle of the morning."

"Why not?"

* * * *

Good question. She looked at him, all hot and sweaty, with that lustful look in his eyes. He wanted her. Bryce Baxter wanted her. He could have any woman in the world, and right now, at this moment, he wanted her.

A dozen excuses flitted through her mind. The car was full of boxes. She needed to unpack and find a way to fit her dishes in his kitchen. She was worried it wouldn't be the same now that they were husband and wife. The excitement would wear off. And then they'd still have to face the day of unpacking, changing her address, and all the other details she'd have to take care of while merging households.

"What are you afraid of?" Bryce had somehow picked up on her insecurity. "Are you afraid having sex will hurt the baby?"

"No. I don't know." She shook her head. "I mean, it didn't exactly come up at the first visit. At the time, I was just another single mom. Sex was the last thing on my mind."

"Okay. We'll wait then. If you need to check with your doctor, I get that." He wasn't happy. Especially since they both knew she was being ridiculous. She was scared, but not about hurting the baby. She knew that unless things got really wild, the baby would be perfectly safe. No, she was afraid of hurting herself. She knew that every time she'd fallen into bed with Bryce, she'd also fallen a little harder, a little deeper in love with him.

And that wasn't good for anyone.

"It's not that," she protested. "It's just that there's so much to do. Change of address, getting out of my lease, and then there's stuff like insurance. Can you put me on your plan or should I add you to mine?"

"Not to mention bank accounts." He ran his hands through his hair. "I guess we should take care of adding you to all my accounts before I take off after tomorrow's game."

"You don't have—"

"Rachel." He cut her off. "You're my wife. You need access to my money. Maybe you want to hire a decorator. Get a spa treatment."

"I don't need to hire a decorator or get a spa treatment."

"Okay, but maybe you'll need to buy some maternity clothes."

"I'm sure I'm not going to need maternity clothes in the next ten days." She sighed. This had to be the world's dumbest argument. "And even if I did, I have my own money."

"Sure, but I was planning on spending that on room service and pay-per-view movies at the hotel." He grinned, knowing damn well how adorable he was.

"Don't you get a per diem for that?" She wasn't going to be swayed by his charm. Not this time.

"Babe. Come on." He moved closer, just inches from touching her. "Don't fight it. You're my wife. What's mine is yours. We're a team, now."

"A team?" She knew she was beat. "Then why won't you let me carry any of the boxes?"

"Woman, you know I can't let you do that, don't you?"

"Not even if I promise sex later?"

He got a devilish look in his eyes. And she thought she had him.

"Oh baby, you really think you can use sex as a bargaining tool?" He just laughed. "Honey, you're the one who's going to be begging me. You'll promise me just about anything, just wait and see."

With that, he walked out the door.

* * * *

Damn, crazy woman. Bryce jogged down the stairs to the parking garage, ready to pick up more boxes. The only thing that kept him from just picking her up and carrying her over his shoulder to the bedroom was the fact that he knew she was scared.

Hell, he was just as scared, but he wasn't going to let her know that. He would be calm, cool, and patient. Just like his friend Johnny. He knew the more freaked out Rachel got, the more he had to stay in control.

It just wasn't going to be easy. Especially with the way her skin glowed and her hair seemed shinier than ever. And her breasts... Oh man, her breasts were like two lush, ripe—oh hell, he was getting himself all worked up and he couldn't do anything about it.

Bryce grabbed the heaviest box, in case Rachel snuck downstairs to help when he wasn't looking. The woman was as stubborn as they came. She didn't want his money. She didn't want his body, or she pretended not to. Her kisses told him otherwise. But when she said no, well, he had to honor that. Even if she was his damned wife.

He exhaled in frustration, as the elevator doors slid shut. This season was nothing like last year. Everything was easy, then. Everything he'd touched turned to gold. Even Rachel.

Especially Rachel.

This year he had the ridiculously lucrative contract and an incredibly beautiful wife.

Now he just had to earn them.

Chapter 7

After unloading and unpacking the boxes, Rachel spent the rest of the morning taking care of the business of combining households. She put in a change of address and wrote up a letter informing her landlord that she would be vacating her apartment before the lease was up. He wasn't happy, but when Bryce offered to pay half the rent and throw in tickets to the next home stand, he agreed.

Their next stop had been to the bank. Rachel would have been perfectly happy to keep separate accounts, but Bryce wouldn't have it. She was still surprised by how he was taking all of this. She'd blindsided him with the news of her pregnancy and he'd stepped up completely. Maybe a little too much. He'd embraced her and the idea of the baby without even flinching. She'd expected such a different reaction. She'd expected him to be angry. Or at least skeptical about the baby. He didn't talk about his ex-wife much, but from what she could tell, he'd resented being trapped in a marriage he hadn't wanted and being responsible for a child he never got to see.

She figured he'd be extra cautious about getting stuck in a situation where he could be taken advantage of. Especially after he signed the huge contract. He was making more money than he'd ever dreamed of and six weeks later, an ex-lover shows up claiming to be pregnant? Most men would run straight to their lawyer's office. Not Bryce. He married her, no questions asked. For all he knew, she might not even be pregnant. Maybe that was why he was so adamant about her not lifting anything heavy. So she couldn't fake a fall and lose the baby that had never been there in the first place.

Except she wasn't faking, not about the baby, and not about her growing feelings for Bryce. He continued to surprise her in little ways. From the ice cream, to the blood tests, and now he was entrusting her with his money. And there was a lot of it.

She tried not to think about the money. That wasn't why she'd married Bryce. In fact, it scared her a little to have access to that kind of cash. She knew it worried Bryce, too, to have that much money thrown at him. Sure, he'd earned a lot of it for his performance last year, but she knew he'd be expected to be even better this year.

So far this season, he was feeling the pressure. His average was down, as well as his on-base percentage and run totals. A lot of people believed the weight of the contract was behind it. As news of their marriage became public knowledge, she imagined she'd get more than her share of blame as well.

"Come on, Bryce." Rachel forgot she was supposed to be neutral when she watched him step up to the plate in the ninth inning. He'd gone hitless in his first three at bats. The Goliaths were down by a run with two outs and two on. "Please get a hit."

She gripped her microphone tightly, wishing the collective will of forty-thousand people could put the ball into play. The first ball came right over the outside corner of the plate before tailing off as Bryce swung and missed.

Rachel's stomach clenched.

The next pitch caught the inside part of the plate as the umpire called "Strike."

Her stomach rolled.

"Please, baby, please," Rachel muttered to herself. If her heart was pounding this hard, she could only imagine what Bryce must be feeling right now.

The next pitch was in the dirt, and thankfully, Bryce was able to lay off it.

She could feel the tension rising around her. The whole ballpark was buzzing. The Goliaths were down to their last strike and last year's hero was at the plate. Could he do it again? Or would the game end in disappointment?

Here came the pitch. Rachel closed her eyes, holding her breath. It seemed like an eternity before she heard the crack of the bat, the roar of the crowd, and the rising pitch of the announcer's voice.

"He hits it high. He hits it deep." Rachel opened her eyes when she heard the home run call. "It is *gone*! A three-run shot. Goliaths win!"

Rachel rushed down to the sidelines as Bryce was congratulated at the plate. His teammates were jumping up and down, giving back slaps and high fives, and hugging Bryce. They were like a bunch of ten-year-olds after winning their first game.

It was a beautiful thing. And Bryce was in the middle of it, smiling, cheering, and embracing his teammates. When he saw Rachel, his grin grew even wider. He took off his hat, shook his head, and let his hair dance around his shoulders. With a look of pride on his face, he sauntered over to where Rachel stood to conduct the post-game interview.

Her throat closed up and she was unable to speak. She was so happy for him. And proud, and about a half dozen other emotions she couldn't name. He'd done his job and done it well. Now she needed to do her job, but all she wanted was to throw her arms around him and celebrate in private.

He must have read her mind because he gave her a look that probably wasn't suitable for prime time. This was a family show, after all.

"That had to feel pretty good." She found her voice. "Nothing like a walk-off to win the game in front of the home crowd."

"Yeah. It did feel pretty good." PG words, but the way he said it, she felt like he was describing one of their more X-rated encounters. "It's been too long."

"Yes, it has."

Rachel knew he wasn't talking about the home run, she just hoped no one else figured it out. But the heat in his eyes was enough to melt all her reservations.

"We found out last year that you're something special." She tried to maintain her composure. She had a job to do, and it wasn't to engage in verbal foreplay.

"Last year was great." He smiled as they shared the memory of their dozen or so encounters. The audience would believe he was talking about the World Series. "But I'm here for the long haul. I know it isn't always going to be easy. But I promise I'll give it my best shot, every day."

"That's all we can ask." She could hear the slight crack in her voice.

"I'll give you everything you ask for and more." He leaned closer and whispered in her ear, "Let's go back to our place."

"Bryce." Her cheeks flamed. "We're still on camera."

"Right. Sometimes I forget I have to share you." He turned toward the small group of fans standing around, perhaps hoping for an autograph after the interview. "But the best fans in the world deserve the best, and Rachel's the best, wouldn't you agree?"

The crowd cheered.

"She's beautiful, talented, and smart, too." He turned his megawatt grin back toward her. "From here on out, I'm going to make sure you have a reason to talk to me after every game."

He ran his fingers through his hair, replaced his cap, and gave her a quick kiss on the cheek before heading back to the clubhouse.

It wasn't the first time he'd ended an interview with the suggestion they hook up at his place. It was the first time she was nervous about it. And instead of trying to hide their affair, Bryce had made sure that everyone watching at home knew how he'd be celebrating the game winning home run.

* * * *

Bryce had taken a quick shower, knowing there would be several reporters wanting to speak to him after the win. None of them as pretty as Rachel, though. He'd answered the questions about his slow start with his usual positive, I'm-just-happy-to-help-the-ball-club attitude.

"Your marriage to Rachel Parker came as a big surprise." Veteran reporter Bill Radcliff wasn't quite finished. "It almost seems like a publicity stunt, aimed at distracting the fans from your slump."

"Wow." Bryce looked him straight in the eye. "I wouldn't figure you for the kind of guy who'd take a cheap shot and say the s-word to my face." He took a deep breath, trying to channel the calmness his friend Johnny always exuded. "My marriage is real." He smiled, just thinking about Rachel. "It may have come as a surprise to you, but honestly, it was inevitable. She's been behind my success since last year. She was there every step of the way."

"You were seen with other women in the past year." Radcliff glanced at his iPad, as if he were checking dates. "As recently as spring training."

"I guess I thought about testing the free agent market." He hated the fact that his encounters with other women were public knowledge. He also hated how he'd hurt Rachel. "Turns out this is where I belong."

He hoped Radcliff would drop it, but he had a sinking feeling he wouldn't.

"It just seems odd that you'd rush off to Vegas in the middle of the biggest slump of your career."

"Reno," Bryce corrected. "We were married in Reno, and if you must know why we didn't wait until the season is over, it's because when I finally realized what was missing from my life, from my game, I wasn't going to sit back and wait. I saw the opportunity and I took it."

"So you're saying you needed to get married in order to start hitting again?" Radcliff sounded more than a little skeptical. "There's a rumor going around that Cupid is at least partially responsible for the incredible run the Goliaths made last season."

"Cupid?" Now Bryce was the one who was skeptical.

"First Johnny Scottsdale reunited with his college sweetheart." The reporter couldn't quite look him in the eye. "Then Marco Santiago and Hunter Collins got married, and now you're telling us that you and Rachel Parker were together all along as well?"

"Do you need dates and times?" Bryce asked. "Or are you satisfied knowing that we've been seeing each other off and on for over a year? Does that fit with your rally cupid angle?"

"Rally cupid, huh? I think I'm going to create a hashtag with that one." Radcliff laughed.

"I've got a hashtag for you," Bryce couldn't help but give one last comment. "#Winning, #Repeat, #Baxterbetterthanever. Take your pick."

"You really think this team has what it takes to repeat?"

"With our women behind us." Bryce winked. "You bet."

"Don't you know betting on baseball will keep you out of the Hall of Fame?" Radcliff was having fun with him now.

"Ain't nothing going to keep me out of the Hall." Bryce flashed his cockiest grin. The camera ate that shit up.

"You do realize it's the sportswriters who vote on whether or not you get in?"

"You guys love me and you know it." Bryce didn't reserve his charm for Rachel only.

"You know your wife doesn't get a vote."

"And that's a shame. She's good at her job." Bryce knew some of the beat writers looked down upon the TV reporters, especially the female ones. "In a lot of ways she works harder than you hacks. She's got to think on her feet, always present a smile even after a loss, and she doesn't have a chance to edit her report before she sends it in. It's live."

"And then she's got to go home and put up with your ego." Radcliff had just the barest hint of a smirk.

"Oh, she can take it. She may be the only one who can put up with my ego." Bryce grinned like he'd just said the funniest thing ever, but he was just covering up for the fact that his chest suddenly felt too tight. He knew he'd gotten lucky when he convinced Rachel to marry him. And he was about to get even luckier.

She was waiting for him. He wondered how much of the interview she'd overheard.

* * * *

"Do you really think I'm that good at my job?" She waited until they got to his Corvette before asking.

"Of course. Why do you think I hit so many home runs last year?" He kept his tone light. Teasing. "I wanted to be the one you talked to every night."

"You know I have to talk to the other players, too."

"Yes. And I'll try to remember you're just doing your job." He put his hand on her thigh. "I'm a pretty competitive guy, you know."

"Yeah, I know."

"So when you smile at my teammates, I'm going to feel a little possessive." He gave her knee a little squeeze. "I'll work on keeping my feelings to myself."

"Just because I'm smiling doesn't mean I'm flirting. You know there's a difference."

"I know, up here." He tapped his forehead. "But I won't always like it."

"So what are you saying? I should quit?" She wasn't going to give up on something that she'd worked so hard for.

"Absolutely not." He turned to look her in the eye. "Your job is important to you. And you're good at it. I'm just saying I'm not so good at watching you interview other guys. Part of it is because I know they all think you're hot. Part of it is because you're not interviewing me."

"They don't all think I'm hot." Please. She knew what she was and what she wasn't. She was the attractive, but not too attractive, voice of the crowd. She was pretty enough to hold the attention of the male crowd, but not so much that she alienated the female fan base. She wore comfortable, casual, yet stylish clothes. Not the evening gowns female reporters wore on some of the networks. She was accessible. Not hot.

"Sure they do." He said it like it was a fact. "And even though I know they'll all respect the fact that you're my wife, I'm still going to have my moments of jealousy."

"Thanks for the heads up." She tried to play it cool, but she felt anything but.

"I can't help it. You're gorgeous." And he sounded like he really meant it.

"Stop." She spent more than eighty-two games a year in front of the camera, yet she never felt more self-conscious than she did right now, alone with Bryce.

"I'll never stop telling you you're beautiful. And talented. And smart."

"You're just trying to soften me up, so you can have your way with me." She was in danger of falling all the way in love with him.

"Do you want me to have my way with you?" There was no mistaking the desire in his voice.

"Yes." Her heart hammered with the admission. "Yes, Bryce. I think it's time."

He grinned, then put the car in gear.

By the time they pulled out of the parking lot of the ballpark, she was more than ready to make love to her husband.

Her husband.

The man who'd broken her heart a dozen times. Except when she thought of it, she'd been the one to push him away. Other than that first time, when he'd told her that he was a one and done kind of guy. After that, she'd been the one to rush out the door, swearing it was the last time. And he'd just smiled, nodded, and come back for more.

She reached over and gave his knee a squeeze.

"Careful, woman. You know what your touch does to me."

"Yes. I do." Finally they arrived at their building. Bryce pulled into the parking garage, and maneuvered the Corvette into the narrow slot. He reached down and brought her hand to his mouth. He kissed the inside of her wrist, causing her to tremble at the promise of what was to come.

The elevator seemed to take forever. But they finally reached their floor. He held the doors open for her and took her hand as they walked to the apartment. He slid the key into the lock and opened the door. Before she could step inside, he swooped her up into his arms and carried her over the threshold.

Tears stung her eyes at the clichéd romanticism of the gesture.

"Put me down," she insisted.

"Not until we get to the bed." He toed the door closed and flipped the lock.

"Bryce, I don't want you to end up on the DL."

"Then you'd better hold on tight." He shifted her weight as she wrapped her arms around his neck. "I think we're going to have a great workout."

Gently, he lowered her to the bed. He dropped a soft kiss on her forehead before reaching for the buttons on her blouse.

Slowly, meticulously, he undressed her. It was such a change from every other time. In the past, their encounters had been frantic, hurried, and a little on the wild side. But this time, it was different. He took his time. Almost as if he wanted to discover her for the first time.

"Bryce." She was getting impatient. "Hurry, please."

"Not tonight." He placed a soft, slow kiss on her lips. "Tonight we're going to savor every moment."

She was torn between wanting to slow down and enjoy each sensation, and wanting him to hurry up and get to the good part. Because she knew how good it could be. All she'd have to do was mention how tired she was, and he'd kick into a super speed. The kind of speed he had on the base paths when he had a chance to score.

But one of the things about the game they both loved was the way that it wasn't always about being faster. Sometimes working the count, waiting on the right pitch was better than being too aggressive. There was no clock in baseball. The game would unfold on its own time.

He stared at her naked body with a raw hunger. His eyes moved over each part of her, lingering on her breasts, her belly, before traveling the length of her. Did he notice the small changes as he slowly took off his clothes?

"Please…" She trembled in anticipation. "Touch me."

"God, you're gorgeous." He lowered himself carefully to the bed. He looked at her like he'd never seen her naked before. Maybe they'd never taken the time to just look. Their previous encounters had always been so rushed.

She closed her eyes as he slowly caressed her curves. Bryce ran his hand across her skin, lowered his mouth to her breasts, savoring each one like a rich dessert. Her whole body was more sensitive, but especially her nipples. She bucked as he drew her breast into his mouth. And when he scraped his teeth across her sensitive flesh, she yelped in pleasure.

He moved his hand down her body, stopping at her abdomen. He lifted his head and smiled.

"Our baby is in there." His voice held a tinge of awe.

"Yes." She closed her eyes again, so he wouldn't see the tears that sprung up unexpectedly. "Yes he is."

"Or she?" He sounded almost giddy.

"I can't help but think it's a boy." She couldn't explain it, but she was sure they were having a son.

"Either way, our kid is going to be amazing." He placed a small, sweet kiss just below her navel.

Rachel squeezed her eyes tighter.

"Bryce. Focus." She was losing her patience. "Remember how I got pregnant in the first place? Let's do that."

He laughed.

"Yes. Let's." He positioned himself on top of her, but still he hesitated.

"You're not going to hurt me." She knew he was thinking about the baby. "But I may hurt you if you don't hurry up. I want you inside me. Now."

Bryce eased the tip of his penis into her opening. He hesitated for a moment and finally pushed his way inside. Slowly, and carefully, he began to move. Delicious friction built as his body started to take over and his thrusts became more urgent.

Rachel lifted her hips, taking him deeper. She wrapped her legs around him and bucked beneath him as her climax became closer and closer. Finally her release came crashing over her and she cried out. He pumped once. Twice. A third time and then he shuddered and groaned as he emptied himself into her.

Tears leaked out of her eyes. Her body continued to throb with the aftershocks of a quick, yet intense orgasm. Her heart felt like it would burst from her chest, and her head was spinning with the realization that Bryce was her husband. The father of their unborn child.

And he would be leaving for a seven day road trip after tomorrow's game.

Chapter 8

Bryce dressed as quickly and as quietly as possible. He wanted to let Rachel sleep since she didn't have to be to the ballpark as early as he did.

She was beautiful. Her dark red hair splayed out across his pillow, her sweet mouth quivering with a hint of a smile. Was she dreaming of him? Or their lovemaking from the night before?

He got hard just remembering how sweet and hot it had been. Different from the other times, but every bit as good. If not better.

She moaned and her eyes fluttered open. Her smile was almost enough to make him crawl back in bed. But he had work to do before the final game of the home stand.

"Good morning." He brushed a soft kiss across her lips. "I wanted to let you sleep in."

"Mmmm." She reached up and pulled him down for a longer kiss. "Thanks."

"I was just about to head into work." The morning after had never been awkward before. They'd both pretended it was no big deal. "I was going to put my bags in your car, so I could head straight to the airport after the game."

"Sure. That's fine." A pained look crossed her face, but then it was gone. "So, you're not taking your car?"

"I thought I'd jog to the park." He shrugged. He didn't want to leave his 'Vette in the player's lot. "You can drive my car while I'm gone if you want."

"Thanks, but I'll stick with my Honda." She shifted and the sheet fell away, revealing her gorgeous breasts. They were lusher than he remembered. Or maybe he was just paying attention now. Appreciating what he had.

"How many miles do you have on that thing?"

She thought for a minute. "A hundred and twenty thousand?"

"You need a new car." He didn't like leaving her with such an old vehicle. "I'd hate to think of you breaking down somewhere while I'm on the road."

"First of all, that car will probably run for another hundred and fifty thousand miles." She pulled the sheet up over her breasts with a scowl on her face. "And second of all, I've been taking care of myself for quite some time."

"Of course you have." He should just shut up now. He was going to get himself into trouble. "Sorry, I'm new at this…caring for another person thing. But that's how I roll, baby, I go all out or not at all."

She laughed, and let the sheet fall away. If it was this hard leaving her this morning, how was he going to last for a seven day road trip?

"You sure you can't come with me?" He bent down to kiss her, with at least a hope of changing her mind. "We could have a lot of fun together."

"I never traveled with the team before." She sighed. "Except for the playoffs. I have my routine, and I need to stick to it as much as I can, while I can."

"So what do you do on your days off?" Bryce sat down on the edge of the bed, not ready to leave the woman he wanted to know better.

"Nothing too exciting. I work out. Catch up on laundry, pick up my dry cleaning. Get my nails done. My hair cut." She brushed her hair off her forehead. "Do a little reading, binge watch the TV shows I miss when I'm at the game. Watch chick flicks—things like that."

"Take a spa day." He could picture her naked with someone's hands sliding across her skin. "Maybe you should do that on the day I fly home."

"Why? So I'll be all relaxed and ready for you?" She seemed to be able to read the direction his thoughts were heading.

"Damn, woman. How am I supposed to survive seven nights without you?" He'd spent the last year trying to do that, and he'd been miserable.

"You'll survive." She had a teasing grin on her face. "You'd better."

"Look, Rachel, I know I haven't been…" What was he trying to say? He hadn't been faithful to a woman he hadn't technically been dating.

"You never made promises." She tried to let him off the hook. "We didn't have a relationship."

"Rachel…" He didn't want to leave her thinking about what an ass he'd been. "Let me make a promise to you now."

He reached for her, taking her hands in his.

"I promise I will be the man you deserve." He hitched a breath. "I'll live all those vows I made the other night when I made you my wife."

"I believe you." Her voice had a small catch to it. Like she wanted to have faith in him, but she wasn't going into this blind.

"Good." He pushed himself off the bed. "I can go into work with nothing on my mind except baseball."

"I hope I'll be interviewing you after the game." She started to get up. She was working today, too.

"I'll do my best to give you something to talk about." He had to get out of there before he was tempted to push her back down on the bed and let her have her way with him.

After one last kiss, he grabbed his duffel bag and headed out the door.

* * * *

Rachel usually didn't do post-game interviews after a loss. Today's game was particularly frustrating, especially for Bryce. He'd gone hitless at the plate and committed two errors in the field. She was glad she didn't have to discuss his performance on camera.

But as she made her way into the clubhouse, she wondered how he would respond to her privately. Last night had been amazing. Almost perfect. Too bad the game today had to bring them down.

"What do you want?" Bryce snapped at her when she approached him near his locker.

You. Us. A chance

"I thought I'd say goodbye to my husband before you leave for a week-long road trip." She wasn't surprised by his attitude, a little hurt, but not surprised. She'd seen it enough around the clubhouse. Still, she didn't want him to know just how hard his leaving was on her.

"You're not going to get all clingy on me? Make me check in twelve times a day?" He was obviously pissed off. Probably because of the game. His performance. She tried not to take it personally. He wasn't acting any different than most of his teammates after a loss. They just hadn't had the chance to establish a routine. Boundaries. Was Bryce the kind of guy who needed space after a tough game? Or did he respond to distraction? Maybe he just needed to be told to snap out of it. And then there was the age old method of using sex as a diversion.

Except he had to get on the plane soon.

And he was kind of being an ass.

"Your suitcase is still in my car." She held her head high. Not going to let him see her disappointment. "You want me to go grab it for you?"

"No. I'll get it." He ran his hands through his hair. "I don't need anything else to worry about. I had enough distractions today. Couldn't keep my head in the game."

"And that's my fault?" What the hell?

"You kept me up too late." Yes. He definitely thought it was her fault. "And then I kept thinking about…well, everything."

The baby. Her. Was he second guessing the decision to get married?

"Well. You have a few days where you won't have to worry about anything except your game." She clenched her jaw to keep from crying. Angry tears were the worst. "Just do me a favor, and text me when you land. So I know you're still alive."

She turned and headed for the exit.

"Rachel, wait." He stood and moved closer, but he didn't reach for her. "Let me just grab my stuff and I'll follow you to your car."

Right. His suitcase. He pulled his phone and his wallet out of his locker and shoved them in his pockets. He walked beside her, close enough that she could smell the stuff he put in his hair after his shower. She could feel his agitation vibrating through the small space between them.

If he was going to take it out on her every time he lost, they weren't going to make it to the All-Star break.

"You really should get a new car." Bryce pulled his suitcase out of the trunk after she unlocked it. "I hate the idea of you breaking down on the bridge when I'm so far away."

"I've had this car for six years, never had a problem." She slammed the trunk shut. "Besides, I have Triple A. I can call for roadside assistance and get free maps."

"Like I want some tow truck driver picking you up on the side of the road." He flung his duffel bag over his shoulder and crossed his arms. "You could get one of those snappy SUVs. With lots of room for, you know, car seats."

"I'm not going to pull into the dealership the minute you leave town and just buy a new car." The last thing she wanted was to be seen as a gold-digger. The terms of his contract were very well-known. "It would make me look bad."

"Making my wife drive around in a 1997 Honda makes me look bad."

"It's a 2008." And she'd just paid it off last year. "It's a perfectly good car. It will last another ten years."

"Sure, it's fine." He glanced over to the bus that was waiting to take the team to the airport. "I gotta go."

"Yeah. Have a good trip." She had a slight hitch in her voice. This was hardly the goodbye she'd hoped to have.

"Thanks." He gave her a quick kiss before walking toward the bus, taking her heart with him.

It was so much simpler when they were just having sex. When she could pretend it didn't matter what he did when he was on the road. That they weren't really a couple and they didn't have a future together.

She'd known sleeping with him was going to get her into trouble. She'd known that very first night. But somehow being around him had turned her into this stupid girl who let her hormones make decisions for her. And what did it get her? A whole new set of hormones flooding her system. Making her believe she was in love with Bryce Baxter.

Chapter 9

Bryce couldn't get comfortable on the plane. The wide leather seats of the first class cabin weren't soft enough. The air seemed stuffier than normal. At least there wasn't a lot of chatter from his teammates. After a loss, most of them slipped on the noise-cancelling headphones and listened to music, watched movies, or smart guys like Marco Santiago might even read a book.

None of those distractions were going to work for Bryce, though. He was too agitated. The game was only part of the reason. For the first time since Rachel had come to him with news of her pregnancy, he had time to sit and think. Something he rarely did before he acted.

He was a married man now. About to become a father again. He'd need to start thinking about someone other than himself.

He replayed today's game in his head. That first error had been because he'd been trying too hard to look good. Thought he could hit the highlight reel with a spectacular double play, and then he could give Rachel the credit for turning him into Superman. Too bad he'd looked more like the Joker out there.

It wasn't Rachel's fault he'd been thinking of her instead of focusing on the game. Yet when she came to say goodbye, that's exactly what he'd told her. He hadn't meant it as a negative. Not really. Last night had been amazing. And he'd lain awake long after she'd fallen asleep, just thinking about what a lucky bastard he was. About how he was going to get it right this time.

Shit. He'd been a real ass. He needed to figure out a way to keep his professional worries to himself. Not take it out on Rachel when he screwed up. And what the hell was that argument about her car all about?

He got that she wouldn't want to just waltz into a dealership and whip out her brand new checkbook. She had a reputation to keep. Although she wasn't as famous as most of the players, she was well-known around San

Francisco. She had her share of fans. He'd been asked more than once about her as he was signing some guy's autograph. Mostly things like "Is she as hot up close?" or "you two ever…?" The kinds of questions he had to work really hard to keep smiling and ignore as he scrawled his name on a baseball card or program or bill of a hat.

At least now he had a comeback. "She's my wife." That ought to keep most guys from being rude. Most, but not all. Bryce hated the fact that he wasn't going to be there to protect her from jerks. Jerks who thought that just because she was on TV, she was public property. And the fact that she smiled and was friendly to them didn't mean she was interested.

He didn't have to worry about his teammates. No matter how jealous he'd been when she'd interviewed one of them, he'd always known that they respected her as a journalist. As a woman. And now they'd respect her as his wife. He trusted the guys on this plane. Every last one of them.

He trusted most of the fans, too. Goliaths fans were passionate, loyal, and enthusiastic. They'd welcomed him to San Francisco and he'd immediately felt like part of the community.

Bryce knew he should stay away from the Internet after a loss, but he was already in a pissy mood and it wasn't just the loss. He'd finally made love to his wife, and he had to leave. The frustration of not being able to hold her for the next seven nights only compounded his irritability. So checking to see what the trolls were saying about him on Twitter couldn't make him feel any worse.

There were the standard "@BryceBaxter sucks!" tweets. Sometimes even he had to agree. Like today. He'd also have to agree with "#overpaid." He scrolled down, looking to see if anyone came up with something clever or even amusing.

#Goliaths have no pride.

@BryceBaxter can't buy a hit with the diamonds in his World Series ring.

Maybe if @BryceBaxter hadn't married @RachelParker the #Goliaths would be in 1st place.

That last one was a little harsh. And totally untrue.

He looked at Rachel's Twitter feed.

Hey @RachelParker, maybe if you did your wifely duties better, Baxter would start hitting.

What the f—

Bryce punched the back of the seat.

"Hey now." Marco Santiago turned around, glaring at him from the seat in front of him. "You're not the only one who had a bad game."

"Sorry, man. Just some jerk on Twitter." Bryce hadn't meant to disturb his teammate.

"You know you shouldn't read that stuff, especially after a loss." Marco turned back around, continuing the conversation from the row in front of Bryce. "It just gets you even more frustrated."

"Yeah, well I usually think it's kind of funny." Bryce tried to laugh it off, the way he'd done so many times in his life. "But not when they bring my wife into it."

"She's strong, she can handle it." Marco had gone through similar frustrations when his relationship with Hunter first became public. But since she was the owner of the team at the time, it was even bigger news. And some of the things people had said about Hunter were pretty sexist. That she chose players based on their looks instead of talent. They'd asked him if she traded for him because of the size of his bat and they weren't talking about the ones made in Louisville. Marco had been forced to stand there and manage to avoid punching the reporter in the face.

Bryce just had to avoid responding online.

"She is strong, but she doesn't need this crap." Bryce scrolled through Rachel's timeline. She at least had plenty of fans who'd congratulated her on their marriage. A few good-natured laments about how she'd taken the hot shortstop off the market.

"No. But she's a pro," Marco reminded him. "She knows better than to get all worked up over things that don't matter."

No, they fought over stupid stuff. Like her car. He didn't understand why she wouldn't jump at the chance to upgrade. Especially since she'd need a bigger car in the next few months anyways. He couldn't imagine her trying to get a car seat in the back of her two-door car.

Maybe that was it. There were so many changes happening all at once. The pregnancy. Their marriage. Having to move into his apartment. She'd had a lot of decisions to make all at once. Having to pick out a car was probably just one more thing she didn't need to deal with right now.

He continued to scroll through her Twitter feed. He wondered how long it would be before she was getting congratulations on their impending arrival. He had a feeling her fans would be happy for her. For them.

Most of them.

Is @BryceBaxter better in bed than he's been at the plate?

None of their damn business.

@RachelParker Why did you marry #BadBoyBaxter? He sucks.

Also none of their damn business. And his suckiness would be temporary.

@RachelParker, you're too good for that loser.

Same guy. Bryce's stomach started to churn.

@RachelParker You deserve a guy who would never even look at another woman.

You're beautiful @RachelParker.

WTF. Now Bryce was getting really pissed at this guy. He clicked on the profile of SFGoliathsFan#1.

Fan of Goliaths Baseball, Rachel Parker, and Geocaching. Owner/ Operator Goliath Towing & Auto Body.

A freaking tow-truck driver. He thought of Rachel's car breaking down on the bridge late at night, as she made one last trip from her apartment. She'd have her cell phone with her and make the call for roadside assistance. Up pulls Goliath towing. It's dark. The driver gets out, in his overalls and his grease-stained Goliaths cap. He recognizes Rachel. The woman of his dreams. And once he gets her into the cab of his tow-truck...

Not going to happen. Not when he could do something about it. She needed a new car. And if she wasn't willing to go to the dealership, he would have to bring the dealership to her.

Bryce spent the rest of the flight researching cars and SUVs suitable for a growing family. He wanted something safe, reliable, and yeah, luxurious. He would make over a hundred million dollars over the life of his contract. There was no reason for his wife to drive a used Honda.

After comparing the various options, he finally settled on a Range Rover, a luxury SUV that would keep her and the baby safe. Not too flashy, but the vehicle exuded a certain amount of class.

He was able to conduct most of the transaction online. Once the money was transferred, they would even deliver the vehicle to their apartment. Rachel would only need to sign the sales agreement and the car would be hers.

And Bryce would be able to sleep at night.

* * * *

After a restless night's sleep, Rachel set out on the task of unpacking the rest of her dishes and taking over Bryce's kitchen. She had to admit, he had a great view. And the kitchen was state of the art. Too bad she'd rarely cook dinner there during the season. Most of the home games were night games. They both had to be at the ballpark several hours before the seven PM start.

Last night she'd brought home some takeout clam chowder and a large salad. She didn't even bother taking them out of the containers, so there was no need to run the energy efficient dual-drawer dishwasher.

It was a nice place, but without Bryce, she was lonely. Lonelier than she'd ever been in her own apartment. Maybe it was the fight over her stupid car. Maybe it was the fact that Bryce was on the road and she wouldn't see him for a week, wouldn't have him sleeping in the bed next to her.

It was amazing how quickly she'd grown accustomed to his presence. Even before they'd made love, she felt closer to him. Just having him next to her made her feel safe. Made her feel like everything was going to be all right. She and Bryce would manage to live together, raise their child, and have successful careers.

But then when he'd walked away from her at the ballpark, she'd started to doubt. If Bryce stayed in a slump, he'd withdraw from her. And if their personal relationship was strained, it wouldn't be long before it would show up on camera.

The camera didn't lie. Not for long.

Which is why she felt the sudden urge to pull up the video of Bryce's proposal.

She was just about to watch it a fourth time, to see if she'd really seen what she thought she saw—Bryce had really wanted to marry her. He wasn't doing it out of obligation. Or for publicity. He truly believed that they should get married. He wanted it to work.

Before she could push play, her phone rang. Work called even when the team was away. Her producer had talked her into doing a segment with the players' wives. A feel-good series asking them how they met, what they were like at home, that kind of thing.

"We have Hunter Collins-Santiago ready for her interview. Can you be at her house in an hour?" Steve asked.

"Sure. Let's do this." She was glad to have something to focus on, other than the way things were between her and Bryce. He'd called last night to let her know he'd arrived safely, but they didn't have a lot to say to each other. He was obviously still upset over the game. Or else he'd realized his usual on-the-road diversions were now a thing of the past.

She couldn't worry about Bryce. Not when she had a job to do. Rachel dressed in her best jeans that still fit, a loose yet attractive blouse, and a jacket that made her look like she still had a waistline. She did her hair and makeup and was just about to grab the keys to her Honda when the intercom buzzed.

"Mrs. Baxter, you have a delivery." Sergio, the front-desk clerk spoke with just the slightest hint of a Spanish accent.

"Go ahead and send it on up." It wasn't worth correcting the guy over her name. She figured he wouldn't be the last person to call her Mrs. Baxter.

"You're going to have to come down and sign for it." Sergio sounded almost apologetic. He'd kept her secret when she was visiting Bryce last season. He hadn't even raised an eyebrow when Bryce introduced her as his wife. "It's not something I can send upstairs."

"Oh. Okay." She didn't really have time to sign for mysterious packages, but since Bryce was out of town, it was up to her to deal with whatever it was. "I'll be right down."

After touching up her lip gloss, she headed for the elevator. She wondered what she would have to deal with before she could get on her way to her interview.

Chapter 10

Parked in front of the building was a brand new Range Rover with one of those big red bows on the hood like they had in commercials.

"Rachel Parker?" The delivery driver held a clipboard and a set of keys. "I'll just need to see your driver's license and have you sign a few forms."

She produced her ID and signed the delivery form.

"What about the loan documents?" She remembered signing form after form when she'd bought her Honda.

"There is no loan," the driver explained. "The car is paid in full."

Right. Bryce had that kind of money. He could just buy a car online the way Rachel would order a new book from Amazon, without even thinking about it.

When she looked into the interior of the car, she realized he must have thought about it quite a bit. Every detail was…well, perfect. Leather seats. Bluetooth connections. Seat warmers. Or maybe he'd just bought the most expensive, top of the line model.

She still couldn't believe he'd bought her a new car. From the road. And not just any car, but a luxury SUV. She wondered what he would have picked out for her if she wasn't expecting. Stupid. They wouldn't be married if she wasn't pregnant. He would probably be waking up in some stranger's hotel room. Instead he'd called her late last night, assuring her he was tucked into his own bed. She wanted to believe him. To believe that the car was a sign of his commitment to the marriage and not a consolation for his behavior.

Or maybe he was just trying to control her. He'd said she needed a new car. She'd said she didn't want to go out and buy a new car, so he did it for her.

"Mrs. Baxter, you can't park here." Sergio sounded a little embarrassed to have to remind her. "You'll need to move the car."

"Right." She rubbed her forehead, tying to think about what she was going to do about parking. "I've got to get going anyway. I'll try to find a spot for it when I get back."

Parking was at a premium in the city. They had two spots in the garage attached to their building, one for Bryce's Corvette and one for her old Honda. Most of the residents had only one spot, but Bryce had been able to persuade the manager into leasing him a second space. She knew even he couldn't convince them to let her have a third stall.

"I guess I'll have to figure out what to do with my Honda." It would have been simpler to trade the car in. She didn't want to deal with the hassle of selling it to a private party.

"You could always donate it to charity," Sergio suggested. "I know the Harrison Foundation accepts vehicle donations. They keep the money right here in the community. My grandson went to one of their camps and now he eats, sleeps, and breathes baseball."

"That's a good idea. I'll have to look into it." She'd first hooked up with Bryce after a Harrison Foundation fundraiser, so it would be a fitting place for her to donate her car. "In the meantime, I need to figure out where to park the darn thing."

"You could use space thirty-seven for the next seventy-two hours." He gave her a wink. "I happen to know it will be available temporarily."

"Thank you. I really appreciate it." She offered him a warm smile. "I'll get out of your way in no time."

"Take your time. It's not every day your husband surprises you with a brand new car." He looked at her as if he thought it was the most romantic gesture in the world. "He loves you very much."

"Of course." Isn't that what everyone believed? That they were in love. No one got married because of an unplanned pregnancy anymore.

"He's happier when he's with you." Sergio spoke with a fatherly affection. "I've noticed over the last year that he's a different man when he's with you. A better man."

"Thank you." She felt a sudden sting in her eyes, both at the suggestion that Bryce could ever love her and the fact that their marriage was not so much a sham as a misguided attempt at making the best of things. "I'd better get my new car off the street."

She had to get to her interview. Then she would look into the vehicle donation program with the Harrison Foundation. And she needed to call Bryce.

She missed him. And she hoped that Sergio wasn't just trying to make her feel better with what he said about Bryce being happier since she moved in. Of course she knew he seemed happy when they were together because he'd usually sought her out after the highs of the baseball season. He'd chosen to celebrate the good times in bed with her. How he'd gotten through the rough patches was his own business.

Or at least it had been. From what she'd observed, he was the kind of player who wanted to be left alone after a tough loss. Most of the guys were like that. At least in public. What they did when they got home with their families was their own business. But she would have a chance to ask their wives, when they agreed to the interviews for the new segment. Her boss wanted to call it "Diamond Divas." Not her favorite title since the word diva conjured up the image of a prima donna, and the wives she'd met so far had been pretty down to earth.

How had she gotten to this point in her career? She would be doing fluff pieces on the Goliaths Wives Club. No, still not the right title. Certainly not what she'd had in mind when she entered journalism school.

What had been her dream? Sometimes it was hard to remember the wide-eyed enthusiasm she'd had her freshman year. She'd wanted to be the voice of the Goliaths. When her girlfriends were singing along to karaoke, she would watch baseball games with the sound off, doing her best play-by-play analysis.

She worked her way up, starting as an intern in the Goliaths' minor league system. In her hometown of Fresno, she did a weekly show for her high school video broadcasting class. She developed her skills further in college. It hadn't been until she started working with the masters, Kip Michaels and Kurt Dwyer, that she'd really come into her own as a journalist.

Sure, she realized that former players were preferred in the booth. Guys who'd been there had a much better insight into the game. Plus, it was a good way to keep beloved players around for the fans. When their bodies gave out, they still had a place in baseball.

Once she realized she wasn't going to have a shot at the play-by-play, she'd started to think about going national. ESPN was still the big time, with other networks trying to compete. But as she'd learned when she almost broke the Johnny Scottsdale story, she didn't really want to put the story above all else. For her the game came first. If a story didn't affect the action on the field, maybe she didn't need to report on it.

Now that she was married to a player, she had mixed feelings about the need to dig into their personal lives. There was a fine line between being accessible and having your privacy invaded. Sure it could be fun for fans to know what restaurants the players enjoyed. Until they couldn't go there anymore because of too many fans crowding the place trying to catch a glimpse of their favorite stars.

Now she was given the task of making the fans feel like part of the families who played the game.

Sliding behind the wheel of her new Range Rover, Rachel couldn't help but feel like she was in some crazy kind of dream and she'd wake up, most likely in Bryce's bed, and realize that none of this was real. It couldn't be. Her carefully planned life hadn't spun so far out of her control.

* * * *

Bryce had about an hour before he'd have to get on the team bus for the ballpark. He missed Rachel, but at least he had a good reason to call. She should have gotten the Range Rover by now. Hopefully she'd love it. He figured he'd waited long enough to call.

"Hello? Hello?" Rachel sounded a little flustered. "Can you hear me?"

"Yeah, babe, I hear you."

"Okay, good. I wasn't sure if I'd connected it right. And I have no idea where the microphone is."

"You got the car?"

"Yes, but I'm late and don't have time to figure out all the bells and whistles." She sighed. "I have to interview Hunter Santiago for the new segment and I still don't have a better title than Diamond Divas."

"Diamond Divas?"

"Yeah, I hate the name, but I think I'll be stuck with it, since they want to air the first segment tomorrow."

"Tell me more about it." He really was interested in her work, even if he was a little disappointed she wasn't more excited about the car.

"I'm going to be interviewing all the players' wives."

"That sounds interesting."

"I guess. Look I really do need to go. I'm used to my Honda and this thing is a beast."

"So you don't like the car?" He was more than disappointed.

"No, that's not…" The sound of a horn blaring could be heard in the background. "The car's fine. I just don't need it. You shouldn't have."

"But I wanted to."

"And you always do what you want?"

"Well, yeah."

"You're impossible, you know that." She sounded a little pissed off. "I told you I didn't want to get a new car. I have nowhere to park it, and now instead of unpacking, I need to figure out what to do with my Honda."

"I was trying to make things easier on you."

"Well, nothing has been easy lately."

"Tell me about it."

"Why did you buy me a car when I told you I didn't want one?"

"You said you didn't want to go buy one. Something about waving my checkbook around. I just figured I'd order it for you. One less thing for you to have to worry about."

"No. It's not one less. It's too much. It's just all too much." Another sigh was followed by a gagging sound. "Oh damn. New car smell."

The phone disconnected. Was she really upset about the car? Or was she struck with a fresh bout of morning sickness? What was he thinking getting involved with a pregnant woman? Right. It was his fault she was pregnant in the first place. He'd been thinking about that night, going over it in his mind. It must have been the third time. He hadn't bothered with tearing open another condom. He'd just needed to be inside her, once hadn't been enough. Twice hadn't been enough. He couldn't get his fill of her then or now.

At least he'd finally figured it out. Now he just needed to figure her out. Any other woman would be ecstatic over the expensive gift. Any other woman would be more than happy to spend his money, shower herself in new clothes, and show off her newfound status as his wife. But not Rachel. Rachel was stressed about getting to an interview on time, having to figure out parking, and getting rid of her old car. Damn. He wished he wasn't on the road right now. He needed to be there for her. Especially if she was sick. He just hoped she'd been able to pull the Range Rover over before she got rid of that new car smell and replaced it with something much more pungent.

A text about fifteen minutes later assured him she was fine.

Sorry. I didn't mean to cut you off like that. Close call. The car is fine. Great actually. I never did thank you.

No problem. Glad you're A-OK. And you're welcome.

It's still too much. Gotta go, Hunter's waiting for me.

She was too much.

And he'd have to figure out a way to get her to believe in him. He wasn't going to be able to buy his way into her heart. He'd have to earn his way. He'd have to work for it every day. He'd have to prove to her that he could be the man she deserved.

Chapter 11

"Nice ride." Carl was waiting with the camera crew in front of Hunter and Marco's house.

"Bryce surprised me with it. That's why I'm late." She should be ecstatic that her husband had given her such a gift. Too bad she hated surprises. She'd had her fill of them lately.

"What's the matter, afraid he's trying too hard?" Carl asked, much closer to the truth than she'd like to admit.

"No. It's just, I've had my old Honda for so long. Since before I started working for the Goliaths. It's going to be hard to part with an old friend." Maybe part of that was true, but she didn't want to reveal the real reason the pit of her stomach was knotted, and it had little to do with the new car smell that made her pull over and nearly lose her breakfast.

Her ex, Carter, had often given her expensive gifts. A necklace, earrings, a diamond tennis bracelet. It was the last gift that came with the added bonus of a drunken confession of infidelity. The gifts were to soothe his conscience against hooking up with a waitress, a woman he'd met on a flight to New York, and the intern who was working on a big case with him.

So yeah, the TV commercials made it seem romantic to be surprised with a brand new car as a testament of love, but Rachel couldn't help but wonder if Bryce was only trying to make up for the times he'd been with other women. Like last night? No. She couldn't bear to think about that. Because deep down, she wanted this marriage to work. She wanted the kind of family she hadn't quite had growing up. She wanted her child to only know having a mommy and a daddy living in the same house, working together to create a home. She didn't want her son or daughter to ever feel like a mistake.

But she couldn't think about all that right now. She had an interview to conduct with one of her fellow wives. A woman who had been the majority owner of the team. She'd given it all up for love. It was a concept Rachel couldn't quite comprehend. She couldn't imagine giving up her career for a man. Then again, she couldn't imagine having the kind of money Hunter had. The amount she received from the sale of her team was more than all the players' salaries combined.

As if she wasn't intimidated enough by the woman who'd grown up such a daddy's girl that he'd bought her a baseball team. Rachel would have settled for a birthday card from her own father. Some acknowledgement that he even knew she existed.

Didn't matter. She was thirty years old. She'd survived this long without a father. She had Greg, and he'd been a decent stepfather. If she'd asked, he would have been more than happy to walk her down the aisle. He would have even offered a toast. But she was glad she hadn't had to ask him to foot the bill. They were still paying off her sister Megan's wedding. His daughter. The apple of his eye.

"I got dust in my eye." Rachel whipped out her compact mirror to see if she'd need to touch up her mascara before appearing on camera. Just a small smudge she could take care of with a swipe of her pinky.

"Are you ready?" Carl shouldered the heavy camera as she nodded and rang the bell.

"Sorry I'm late." Rachel apologized as Hunter opened the door. "Bryce surprised me with a new car and it took a little longer than I expected to get the paperwork taken care of, and then I had to figure out how to adjust the mirrors and such."

"No problem." Hunter opened the door and welcomed them into her home she now shared with Marco Santiago. "A new car, huh? Marco used to send me lingerie."

She laughed, as if they had been the best of friends. "He had it delivered to my office. I was mortified. Especially since the gal whipped out a tape measure to do a bra fitting right there on the spot."

"I guess that's a little more embarrassing than a brand new Range Rover with a big red bow sitting in front of the building."

"Really? A big red bow?" Hunter laughed again as she led Rachel back to the kitchen where she had pot of tea sitting on the table. "I swear, they don't know how to be subtle, do they?"

"No. Subtlety is definitely not something that gets them to the big leagues." Rachel relaxed a little at the common bond she shared with Hunter. They were both married to major league ballplayers. World Series champions. Men who had made it to the ultimate stage and thrived there.

Except for Bryce's bunt in game three of the World Series, neither of them had ever played small ball.

"You gotta love them, though." Hunter poured them each a cup of tea. "They have to show their love with actions instead of words. Even if their actions are over the top."

Hunter's face glowed with happiness. She was truly in love with her husband, and it was almost as if she expected everyone around her to be just as happy.

"I guess I need to think of it that way." Rachel still felt bad for not being as excited about the car as Bryce had clearly expected her to be. "It's just that I told him I wasn't ready to give up my old car. God, I'm so lame. You gave up your team for Marco. And here I am freaking out about losing my identity over a used Honda."

Hunter laughed and patted her on the hand.

"I can't tell you how many people have commented on that same thing. 'How could I give up my career for a man?' But you know what? I don't see it that way at all. I didn't choose being the owner of the Goliaths. I would give anything to have my father still in that position."

A quick glance out the window, followed by a small sigh, and then Hunter continued. "I was given control of the team under the worst of circumstances." She offered a brave smile. "I think I held it together okay. But it was never my lifelong goal to be the big boss. I wanted the team to do well. I wanted the Goliaths to succeed. I achieved that. I brought Marco here. And Bryce."

"Yes, you did. And both those acquisitions made a huge impact." Rachel had been so put at ease by Hunter's hospitality that she hadn't even realized that the camera had been rolling for some time.

"I got exactly what I wanted for the team." Hunter took a sip of tea with a knowing smile over the rim of the cup. "I made sure that Marco would be locked up for the future, and I strongly encouraged the re-signing of Bryce Baxter."

"Thank you." Rachel felt her cheeks warm. "It means a lot to him."

"And to you, I'm sure." Hunter smiled warmly. "I think it would be hard on you to have to worry about him ending up in another city after this season. You've made a name for yourself here in San Francisco, and I can't imagine what it would be like to have to choose between your career and following Bryce to another team."

"Yeah, that would be tough. But I guess that's the price you pay when you marry a ballplayer." Rachel tucked her hair behind her ear. "I'm sure there are plenty of players' wives who've put their careers on hold, hoping that their men could make it in the big leagues long enough that they could plan a future together."

"It's not exactly the most family-friendly lifestyle." Hunter acknowledged. "For me, it's easy to travel with the team. I have no job, no kids to demand my attention. I can follow Marco to city after city. It's almost like an extended honeymoon. Except for when they lose."

Both women laughed at the shared bond of having to deal with their cranky, frustrated men who didn't take failure too well, despite the years of experience with it.

"So I have a couple of questions that the viewers want to know. How did you and Marco meet? Did you know him personally before he came over in the trade from St. Louis?"

"I'd only seen him play a few times, but we'd never met until I picked him up from the airport." Hunter's face lit up in a love-struck glow. "If I'd known there would be something between us… No. I still would have traded for him. At the time, the team came first. I might have sent someone else to the airport. But that would have just delayed the inevitable."

"What's the most romantic thing Marco has ever done for you?"

"Won the World Series." Hunter may have been teasing. "He had help, of course, but he knew how important it was for me to make it happen last year."

"Because of your father?"

Hunter nodded, a bittersweet smile on her face.

"So what are some of the things he does that drives you crazy? Pet peeves." Rachel got the feeling Hunter didn't want to keep talking about the death of her father at the beginning of last season. This was supposed to be an upbeat piece.

"He's kind of a grump when he loses." Hunter looked grateful at the change of direction. "We both know what that's like. Our men feel that deep down they should be invincible. If they have a bad game, it's because they didn't work hard enough, or didn't focus entirely. It has nothing to do with the other team working just as hard, focusing just as much. It's funny that in a game where failure is the rule, rather than the exception, they take failure rather personally."

"Yes, indeed." Rachel couldn't agree more. "So how do you help him deal with the inevitable failures?"

"Sometimes distraction works." Hunter gave a knowing grin. "Other times when he's got that 'leave me alone, I'm mad at the world' look, I leave him alone and sooner or later he'll come up to me, maybe start by rubbing my shoulders. Then I know he's ready to connect. And he could really use a backrub."

Rachel hoped she would be able to interpret Bryce's moods so easily. Most of the time they'd spent together had been when he was riding the highs of victory. Even when they'd first met, before the season started, he'd been feeling pretty good, signing a decent free agent contract with a team he'd believed had a pretty good chance at winning it all. He'd been right about the team. They'd both been wrong about their relationship being casual.

"Okay, so I hate to ask, but I need some dirt. Does Marco help around the house? Or does he expect you to pick up after him like the clubhouse attendants?"

"Oh, he's pretty good. He likes to cook when he's home. Mostly breakfast since that's the only meal we get to share every day. At first it kind of bugged me the way he tried to take over my kitchen." Both women shared a commiserating laugh. "But then I realized I'd rather have him help than not have to spend an extra five minutes looking for the spatula because he put it in the wrong drawer."

"Sounds like the perfect guy." She cringed, knowing that comment would set Bryce off.

"He's the perfect guy for me." Hunter tucked a long strand of her deep brown hair behind her ear. "He does tend to leave his shoes lying around. And he's got really big shoes."

Her cheeks pinked.

"So besides leaving his shoes everywhere, what else drives you crazy?"

"He takes my happiness personally." Hunter's voice held a strained note. "I mean, if I'm not ecstatic every second of every day, he thinks it's his job to entertain me. Like he doesn't understand I'm trying to figure out my role in life. I was Henry Collins's daughter for so long, and then I was thrown into the role of the Goliaths' owner. He doesn't understand that I'm not quite sure what I want to be when I grow up. I mean, I went into baseball to please my father. I left baseball because I thought it would be easier on Marco and the team… But now I'm not sure."

Rachel had worried that this interview would be just another fluff piece. She hadn't expected it to get serious. But maybe she could do a better job here by asking harder questions.

"Do you regret letting the team go?"

Hunter looked off in the distance, then she shook her head.

"No. That's the really weird part. I did what I truly believed was best for the Goliaths and for Marco. The team needs him. And he needs the

Goliaths. I'm glad Marvin Dempsey took my advice and extended Bryce's contract. And I really believe that Nathan Cooper learned his lesson and will be an even stronger player for us than he ever would have been if he hadn't been suspended and traded."

"You're not finished with baseball." Rachel knew when someone was passionate about something, and Hunter was still passionate about the team. "You still have a lot to contribute."

"Maybe. But I never wanted to be in the spotlight." Hunter leaned forward. "That's for guys like Marco and Bryce. And at some point, we're going to want to start a family."

Hunter wrapped both hands around her cup and stared down into her tea.

"Best of luck with that," Rachel offered. "And thank you for this interview."

"I didn't realize the interview had started," Hunter said. "I thought we were just chatting still."

"I think that's what makes a great show. We're just a couple of friends, sharing a cup of tea and conversation about the realities of being Goliaths' wives. I hope the viewers enjoy it as much as I have."

Carl switched off the camera, signaling he'd gotten the footage he needed. There would be some editing, but for the most part, she felt pretty good about the segment. If only she could come up with a better name than "Diamond Divas."

She'd made up a list of things to talk about, but she hadn't even had to check her notes, the conversation had just flowed naturally. It seemed like the kind of piece her producer was looking for. Lightweight, upbeat, yet just personal enough to bring the fans into the inner circle.

"Would you like to stay for lunch?" Hunter asked after Carl headed for the truck.

"Sure. That would be great." Rachel was a little surprised by the invitation, but she was also kind of lonely with Bryce gone for the next week. "Let me put these files in my car."

When she opened the passenger door, the new car smell hit her hard. A fresh wave of nausea hit her and she dropped to the curb. Tucking her head between her knees, she breathed slowly, hoping it would pass.

"Rachel, are you okay?" Hunter must have seen her fall to the ground. Well, she didn't fall, but it probably looked like it from the doorway.

"Yeah. Just give me a minute." She fumbled in her purse for her stash of pita chips. With shaky hands, she opened the plastic bag and started munching on her go-to snack. Relief came after a few bites. "Maybe I should get going."

"Maybe you should come inside. Eat something." Hunter extended a hand to help her up. She had a knowing grin on her face. "Are congratulations in order?"

Rachel could only nod as she rose to her feet with the help of her new friend. "Thank you." She finally felt like she could speak without those ridiculous tears that sprang up at the most unexpected moments. She understood why diaper commercials would make her cry, but she couldn't figure out why she teared up at wireless family plan ads or the one with Jake from State Farm.

"Morning sickness, huh?" Hunter sounded curious, but maybe a little unsure how much to ask.

"Yeah. I thought it was getting better, but certain smells can set me off." And stress. Anytime she started to freak out about how her life felt so out of control, her body decided to show her what it really meant to be out of control.

"But it'll be worth it, right? When you hold your baby for the first time, you'll forget all about being sick and everything else that comes with the pregnancy."

"Yeah. I'm sure it will all be worth it." It was what she was supposed to say. She couldn't admit that she was terrified. Kids hadn't been part of her plan. It wasn't that she didn't like kids, she did. But she'd never really been one of those girls who couldn't wait to get married and have kids and a white picket fence.

"Bryce must be excited." Hunter kept the small talk going.

"I guess you could say that." Was he excited? Or was it just his way to put on a smile and act like whatever came his way was the best thing to ever happen to him? "It was kind of a surprise to both of us. But you know Bryce."

"Yeah. Midas." Hunter had been there during the postseason last year. She'd witnessed the way everything Bryce touched had been golden. Right alongside him was Marco, though. And Marco was still playing like it was that magical three weeks in October. "I have to say, Marco will be jealous."

"Marco, the guy hitting .378? Jealous of the man with a hundred point lower batting average?"

"Marco wants to start a family," Hunter informed her. "But we wanted to wait until the season began to start trying, so I wouldn't be going into labor during the playoffs."

"I can see how that would be a problem." Fortunately, Rachel's due date was in early December. That was about the only thing about this pregnancy that didn't stress her out.

"But what if it doesn't happen right away?" Hunter patted her lower abdomen. "What if I can't give him the one thing he wants more than anything?"

A year ago, both their husbands would have said they'd wanted a World Series ring more than anything. Bryce already had a daughter. Rachel really hoped she could give him a son. The one thing he didn't have yet.

"I'm sure things will work out for you." But what if they didn't? What if they went months, maybe even years without being able to conceive? It didn't seem fair that couples who were truly ready to take on the commitment of becoming parents often had trouble getting pregnant. And then there were people like her and Bryce.

* * * *

"Help me understand women." Bryce was waiting his turn for batting practice with Marco. "I mean, what do they want from us?"

"I think they want to keep us guessing." Marco chuckled. Easy for him. He had the perfect wife. She knew what she wanted and she'd gone after it. She'd gone after Marco and a lot of the guys were more than a little envious. Not that Marco had landed the former owner, but that he'd landed a woman who didn't play games. She just played to win. And they all had shiny diamond rings because of her.

"You'd think she'd be happy." Bryce still couldn't believe she wasn't more excited about the car. "I mean you spend that kind of money on a woman, and… Shit. I'm an idiot."

Marco just tapped his bat against the bottom of his shoe. He didn't want to acknowledge that fact that everyone already knew that Bryce was an idiot.

"You'd think I'd have learned my lesson with my ex-wife. It didn't matter how much I spent on her, she was never happy."

Marco tapped the other cleat.

"Rachel's not like that, though." Bryce didn't really need the other man to respond or offer advice. He just needed to get out of his own head for a few minutes. "She's almost intimidated by the money."

"It's a lot to wrap your head around." Marco wasn't telling him anything he didn't already know. "Once I signed my first big league contract, I was almost afraid to cash that first check. It was more money than my mother had made in a year. And that was working two or sometimes three jobs."

"Yeah. It can mess with a guy's head." And it could make all kinds of people show up in your life who never gave you the time of day until you were a big league ballplayer. With big league cash. And everybody wanted something from him.

Everyone except Rachel.

"I hit a grand slam my first major league at bat." Bryce wasn't bragging, just stating a fact.

"That's a great way to start your career," Marco acknowledged.

"Then I went on a six-game hitting streak before going hitless for the next seventeen at bats."

Marco shrugged. That was baseball. If you played long enough, it all evened out eventually.

"Those first few games were unreal. It was almost scary because I knew I couldn't keep that pace up forever."

"You've managed to get it back when we needed it." Marco was referring to the hot streak he'd been on during their postseason run. They'd both been on a pretty good run. Marco was still on one.

"Yeah. But as the hitting streak went on, I just knew it was going to turn around."

"It usually does."

"I don't want that to happen with Rachel," Bryce admitted. "We started off really hot, you know. And I just don't want to screw things up with her."

Marco gave an understanding nod.

"I can't fail this time."

"So don't."

"I feel like I need to do something big. Some way to prove that I'm in this for the long haul."

"You think we won the World Series because of your six home runs?"

"They helped."

"It was the little things that got us there," Marco reminded him. "Running out an infield hit. Laying off a ball in the dirt. Making the throw when the runner's bearing down on you hoping to take you out, or at least break your concentration."

"Yeah. But chicks dig the long ball."

"The good ones appreciate getting the runner over, a well-turned double play, and heads-up base running. They know that a well-pitched game with solid defense can win more games than a three-run homer."

"Yeah. But three-run homers make a big splash." Even when they didn't land in the bay.

"Marriage is a lot like baseball." Marco had taken over the philosopher's role that Johnny Scottsdale's retirement had left. "It's the little things that end up making a difference. Sure you made a big impression with the proposal. And you needed to do that. You needed the grand gesture. But even more importantly, you need to make dozens of small gestures every day."

"It would be a lot easier if I could see her every day."

"True. But you can still stay connected with her when you're on the road. Text her just to let her know you're thinking of her. Send flowers, or lingerie." Marco chuckled to himself, as if he had tried that last one out himself.

"So you're saying having a Range Rover delivered was too much?"

"You don't always need a grand slam to win the game."

"I just wish I knew what she wanted."

"Talk to her. Really listen."

"She says she doesn't want anything."

"Listen to what she doesn't say." Marco tipped his cap and then took his turn in the batting cage.

* * * *

Bryce managed to do all the little things wrong. He swung at too many pitches outside the strike zone. He didn't make the clean exchange from glove to throwing hand. And he didn't get the fly ball deep enough to score the runner from third. He didn't exactly cost them the game, but he could have. Fortunately Santiago had come through. He'd not only done the little things, but he'd hit a three-run homer to win in extra innings. Guess he was more of a "do as I say, not as I do" kind of guy.

After the game, Bryce sent Rachel a text as soon as he was back in the clubhouse. She'd texted him back while he was in the shower. Eventually they were able to catch each other and they had a short but sweet conversation over the phone before he headed straight to the hotel. He didn't feel like going out and celebrating, not when he felt as though he hadn't done anything to contribute to the win. Besides, the last thing he wanted was to be approached by any of his female fans who either weren't aware of his marriage or didn't care. It would be too easy for someone to catch that moment before he was able to make it very clear he wasn't interested in some woman putting her hand in his lap, thank you very much. One click of a cell phone camera and he'd be up all night trying to explain to Rachel that she really could trust him.

Chapter 12

It took Rachel two days to finally be ready to give up her car. The Harrison Foundation would pick it up the next day. First her apartment and now her Honda. It wouldn't be long before she gave her body up to the child growing inside her. Shouldn't she be feeling some sort of instinctive glow by now? What if the mothering instinct never came? What if she gave birth to a perfectly healthy baby and she couldn't bond with him or her? What if she resented the baby for turning her life upside down?

What if she ended up like her mother?

Her mother had wanted to go to Hollywood and become an actress, but she'd never made it out of Fresno. Well, except for that one spring break her senior year, when she'd met some guy at a party. All she had was a name that may or may not have been his real name. She'd never been able to find Rachel's father. And neither had Rachel.

At least she had that going for her. She knew the father of her child. Or at least, she thought she knew him. But Bryce continued to surprise her. She still couldn't believe that he'd bought her a Range Rover. At first she was afraid he was trying to control her, but then she remembered the conversation about him trading in his Corvette for a minivan. It just made more sense to get rid of her Honda. If they lived in the suburbs with a three-car garage, it wouldn't be an issue. As it was, Bryce had to give up a lot of tickets to get the second parking spot in the building.

Rachel had to convince herself that the car was a grand gesture on Bryce's part. He was swinging for the fences, and she had to be ready to run the bases ahead of him.

Allowing herself extra time to pull over if necessary, Rachel headed out to meet her mother and sister for lunch. She held her breath until she could get all the windows down and then she started the ignition.

As much as she dreaded this meeting, it was better than sitting around all day wondering how Bryce was preparing for the last game of the series in Atlanta. He'd had a rough start, and although he'd tried to hide it, she could hear the frustration in his voice.

Maybe it was a good thing she'd be in the middle of trying to explain to her mother that her quickie wedding was in no way meant to hurt her or get back at her for failings of her childhood. Rachel's mother sometimes went through periods of guilt over not being as close to Rachel as her sister, Megan. She'd even gone so far as to try to take Rachel on special mother-daughter outings. Unfortunately, the kinds of things her mother enjoyed doing weren't necessarily what Rachel would choose. Spending the day at the mall shopping and having their nails and makeup done weren't exactly her favorite things to do. But her mother wasn't a fan of spending the day in the library or catching a minor league double header.

As an adult, Rachel had been able to appreciate what her mother had been trying to do. And they had both realized that a nice long lunch was preferable to trying to do too much to have the kind of relationship Megan had with their mother. Rachel often wondered if she was like her father, or just reminded her mother of the mistake she'd made as an eighteen-year-old looking for a good time.

Not surprisingly, she arrived at the restaurant before the others. She ordered an iced tea, hoping there wasn't too much caffeine, but she hadn't had so much as a cup of coffee or diet soda since she found out she was pregnant. It was probably better than anything else she could order without drawing questions from her mother and sister.

She sipped slowly, so she wouldn't have to turn down the waiter's offer of a refill before her family arrived.

Finally, they showed up. Her mother made quite an entrance, all big hair and a cloud of perfume. Rachel took shallow breaths before reaching for the lemon wedge in desperation. Sucking on the sour fruit was enough to keep her from gagging on the stench.

"Sorry we're late." Lorraine Parker-Bradford brushed an air kiss across Rachel's cheek before taking the chair opposite. "But parking is a nightmare in this city."

"Yes, parking is a bit of a challenge." Rachel offered her sister the chair next to her.

"I'll bet you could just take a limo and not have to worry about it." Megan's tone held a slight note of contempt.

"No limos. I used to take BART into the city when I lived in Walnut Creek, but now it's easier to walk or take my own car." Rachel didn't want to get into it with her sister. They had never been especially close as kids. She'd been a little surprised when Megan asked her to be in her wedding. Pleased, but surprised. Through the dress fittings and shower planning, they had become almost like sisters.

"You don't still have that old Honda, do you?" Megan asked. Since her new husband was heir to Fresno's biggest Toyota dealership, she was kind of a car snob.

"No. Bryce and I decided to get something a little bigger." As if she'd had any input on the vehicle.

"It's not a Toyota is it?" Megan asked. "Because Jeff could have gotten you a good deal."

"It's a Range Rover, actually." No, that didn't sound snobby. "But if we ever decide to trade in the 'Vette, I'm sure Bryce would be happy to send some business your way."

"You have a Range Rover and a Corvette?"

"The Corvette was given to Bryce when he won the World Series MVP." A small surge of pride rose in Rachel's chest. "I'm sure he'll hang onto that car for a long time. He earned it."

"So when do we get to meet your husband?" Her mother never could stand it when the two sisters started getting into normal sibling squabbles. Distraction had always been her go-to tactic. If that didn't work, she'd send Rachel outside and Megan to her room.

"He's on the road for a few more days." Rachel had given up on trying to explain how her schedule wasn't like most people's. She didn't get weekends off during the season. Not unless the team was on the road, and that was only about two weekends a month. And they never seemed to be the weekends her family had wanted her to come for a visit. "Maybe you could come to a game, drive up the night before and we could have brunch or something."

"Where is he playing now?" her sister asked.

"They wrap up in Atlanta today." She happened to glance over to the TV in the bar. Sure enough, the Goliaths game was underway. "They're playing right now."

"Maybe we could move into the bar, and watch. I'd like to see my son-in-law in action."

Rachel flagged the waiter and they were quickly moved into the bar section of the restaurant. It wasn't until they settled so they could each see the game that the waiter recognized her.

"Rachel Parker, it's an honor to have you in my section." He offered an enthusiastic smile. "Or is it Rachel Baxter, now? Congratulations."

"Thank you." Her cheeks heated a little. She still wasn't used to so many well-wishes by her fans.

Kristina Mathews

"He's a lucky guy."

Her face felt even warmer. She knew most of her fans were Goliaths fans first. If she wasn't covering the team, they would have no reason to even follow her. Sure, on occasion, she'd have an admirer. Always an awkward feeling.

"Can I start you off with some drinks?" he asked.

"I'm fine with my tea, thanks," Rachel said.

"Oh, maybe we should order some champagne," her mother suggested.

"No. That's okay." Rachel didn't want to have to explain why she couldn't toast her own marriage.

"When do I get to celebrate my oldest daughter's marriage?"

"I'll give you all a few minutes to decide." The waiter gave a polite nod and a moment's privacy.

"We can celebrate without champagne. We didn't even have any at the wedding."

"What, are you pregnant?" Megan was joking, but it was the truth.

"Actually. Yes. I am." It wasn't exactly the way she'd planned on breaking the news to her mother, but now that she'd done it, she was relieved.

"Pregnant? Really?" Lorraine put her hand over her heart, as if it was some great shock.

"Yes, mother. I'm pregnant." It actually did get easier the more times she said it. "And that is part of the reason we hurried the wedding, instead of waiting until the offseason."

If she hadn't known better, she would have almost believed that they had been planning on tying the knot eventually, and the baby had just sped things up a bit.

"I see." Lorraine picked up a menu, glanced over it and set it back down. "So I guess I'm going to be a grandmother."

The waiter returned. "Have we decided on drinks?"

"I'll stick with water, thanks," Rachel said.

"I would like some champagne." Her mother's voice was tight, determined.

"And for you?" The waiter glanced in Megan's direction.

"Oh, what the hell. I'll toast my sister, too."

With a nod, he went off to bring them two glasses of California sparkling wine.

After the waiter left with their lunch orders, Lorraine and Megan raised their glasses.

"Congratulations, Rachel, on your marriage…" Her mother got just a little choked up. "And on your other happy news."

"Here, here." Megan lifted her glass and then took a long swallow.

Rachel simply smiled and hoped she could get through this luncheon.

After they'd finished the toast, they each glanced silently at the television. The Goliaths were trailing 2-1 in the bottom of the fifth inning. Atlanta had two runners on base with only one out. Their hottest hitter was at the plate. Rachel focused her full attention on the game. Only part of it was because she wanted to see if the Goliaths would get out of the jam. She could really empathize with the starting pitcher. Neither of them were in a position they had planned on.

The ball was hit sharply through the infield. But Bryce had been playing back at the edge of the grass, just a few steps away from the bag. He was able to dive and make the grab before it skittered into the outfield. From his knees, he flipped it to the second-baseman who fired a bullet to first base, beating the runner by a half a step. He'd made some amazing plays in his career, but this was one of the more difficult ones Rachel had ever seen.

"Wow." Megan set her half-empty glass on the table. "He's really good, isn't he?"

"Yes." A lump welled up in Rachel's throat. "He's very good."

"So I never did hear how the two of you met." Their mother was less impressed by the play.

"The first time was at Fan Fest. I interviewed him, and all the other players." She tried to recall if she'd felt anything different at that first meeting. Sure, he'd flirted with her a little, but she'd believed he was really just trying to charm the fans. "And then we ran into each other about a week later at a charity event—the Golden Gate Gala—and I guess you could say sparks flew between us."

"So, you've been dating since this Golden Gate Gala?" Her mother asked.

"Well, on and off, I guess." Rachel was relieved when their salads arrived. She had an excuse to pause and try to figure out how to explain her relationship with Bryce that had indeed started the night of the Gala.

"You guess?" Her mother raised an eyebrow as she stabbed her arugula salad.

"Neither of us were looking for a relationship when we met." She sighed. "I had only recently broken up with Carter, and Bryce…"

How did she explain that Bryce had been a free agent, in every sense of the word?

"And so it was during one of these on-again times that you managed to get pregnant?"

Rachel glanced up at the TV. "Oh look. Bryce is up to bat."

All three women turned to watch. There were two on and two outs. Bryce was behind in the count, with two strikes against him. Rachel held her breath as the pitch was released. Bryce swung his bat and made loud contact. The ball sailed towards the centerfield wall.

Oh please, please go out.

It sailed just inches over the fence. Three runs scored. And Rachel's heart swelled in her chest.

"Yes. That's the Bryce Baxter we all know and love." How many times had she said those very words on camera? Dozens?

Her ribcage shrunk even more. She felt a wave of dizziness and she abruptly stood, pushed her chair back, and made a dash for the restroom.

She pushed her way toward the larger handicapped stall. Gripping the handrail, she hovered over the toilet, waiting for the nausea to overtake her. Slowing her breathing and closing her eyes, she realized it wasn't morning sickness that had her head spinning, it was the realization that she hadn't done as good of a job at hiding her feelings for Bryce as she'd thought.

A few more slow, steady breaths helped to calm her nerves. She grabbed the paper cover and spread it over the seat, deciding to make use of the facilities while she was there. She was just washing up when her sister arrived.

"Are you okay?" Megan had a look of genuine concern on her face.

"Yes. Thanks. False alarm." She wet a paper towel and patted the back of her neck. "The morning sickness tends to creep up on me suddenly."

"Is it…horrible?"

"It was when I threw up on Bryce's Corvette."

After what seemed like forever, they both broke out into shared laughter.

"You threw up on his car?"

"Yes." Rachel had never been so mortified in her life.

"That is horrible."

"It was. But somehow he forgave me."

"He married you."

"Yes. He did." Rachel was still amazed at how it had happened.

"And you're going to have a baby?"

Rachel just nodded, her emotions too raw to speak.

"I'm a little jealous," Megan admitted.

Still, at a loss for words, Rachel just stood there.

"I want a baby *so* much." Megan blinked as if she was trying to keep tears at bay. "But we decided we were going to wait two years."

"Your anniversary is only a couple of months away."

"Yeah. I know. But…" Megan wrapped her arms around herself. "Jeff seems to be putting it off. He says the business is crazy right now, he doesn't know how he'll keep up. I'm starting to think maybe he doesn't want to have a baby at all."

Rachel didn't know what to say. They'd never been close. Megan was six years younger. By the time Megan was old enough to play with, Rachel had outgrown playing with dolls and Candyland. She'd been more of a tomboy, preferring to play sports or climb trees.

"It's just not fair," Megan whined. "You get to have everything. You're rich. You've got a hot baseball player for a husband. You live in San Francisco. And you get to have a baby."

"Bryce makes a lot of money right now, but it won't last." She'd seen enough former players who ended up nearly broke just a few years after their bodies gave out. "And living in the city is exciting, but there are tradeoffs. Look at your house. It's beautiful and brand new and you have a garage and a big backyard. Bryce's apartment is nice and has great views, but only a tiny balcony."

And just like that, Rachel could picture what she wanted. A house. With a yard. And good schools. And while the Range Rover wasn't a minivan, it was a family car. A modern day version of the station wagon. She could picture a garage full of sports equipment, baby seats and a booster chair in the backseat. And if she tried real hard, she could picture Bryce sitting next to her. If she tried hard enough she could picture the family she'd always wanted.

"Well, what good is a backyard if there's no one to play in it?" Megan pushed her way past Rachel and out of the bathroom, tossing her blond hair over her shoulder. Rachel followed, wishing she could be a better sister and offer some sort of comfort, but jealousy was hard to just brush off. She should know. She'd been jealous of her baby sister her whole life.

They walked back to the table just in time to watch the Goliaths record the final out. Bryce's homerun had sealed the win. With a headset on, he was being interviewed by Kip and Kurt from the booth.

"That shot reminded me of the one you hit in game one of the World Series last year," Kip said. "It must feel pretty good to get your swing back."

Kristina Mathews

"It feels pretty good to help the team win." Last fall, he would have taken the compliment and run with it. He would have said something about how it was just the beginning and he would keep hitting the home runs.

"You helped the team with that spectacular double-play," Kurt added.

"Just doing my job. The best I can." Bryce started to run his hands through his hair, but he seemed to remember he was wearing a headset. He'd knock it off if he wasn't careful.

Bryce continued with the interview, a little more subdued than usual.

"So that's my son-in-law?" Her mother watched the interview with added interest. "The father of my grandchild?"

"Yes. That's him."

"What's with the hair?"

Rachel laughed. "It's his signature look, I guess. I've gotten used to it."

"It's kind of hot," her sister added.

Rachel shot her a look. "Hey, that's my husband."

"Oh, come on. He is hot. Even mom thinks so."

"He is a nice-looking young man." Their mother's cheeks pinked. "Even with the hair."

Her mother and sister seemed to be having a good time. Maybe it was the champagne, or maybe it was the bond the two of them had with each other. But they seemed to be in on something Rachel didn't share. But then again, Rachel had always been the outsider, standing on the sidelines of her own family. Mom, Megan, and Megan's dad were a unit. Rachel was the bastard child, complete with red hair.

Chapter 13

"Hey, you coming out with us tonight?" Diego Garcia, the Goliaths closer, asked Bryce as they were getting off the bus at the hotel in Philadelphia. "Oh man, I forget, you're an old married man now. No more fun times on the road."

"I'm married. That doesn't mean I'm dead." Bryce was feeling pretty good after the game and the happy flight from Atlanta. "I can still grab a beer now and then."

"Yeah, but no more blondes, huh?"

"Who needs blondes when I have a gorgeous redhead at home?" Bryce made up his mind to join the party. Sure, he wouldn't be going home with anyone, but that didn't mean he had to hole up in his hotel room.

"I still don't know how you landed Rachel Parker." Diego shook his head in admiration. "She's too good for you."

"Yeah. I know."

"I thought she was pretty smart, too."

Bryce took the good-natured ribbing from his teammate. That's what guys did. They razzed each other. And Bryce often wondered himself how he'd managed to get Rachel to hook up with him in the first place. She wasn't like the women he usually went out with. She was smart, talented, and not at all impressed by his job. Sure, she was impressed by his play, when he played well, but she wasn't impressed that he was an athlete. She spent enough time in the clubhouse to know they were just as full of shit as anyone else.

Bryce looked down at the gold band on his left hand. He still couldn't believe it sometimes. Kind of like he couldn't believe he had that other ring, the one with his name and the team name and all those diamonds.

He met Diego and a few other guys at the hotel bar. He was looking forward to kicking back with his teammates, having a couple of beers, and not having to think. About his contract, his wife, or the kid who would be here in a few months.

"There he is," Diego shouted when Bryce entered the bar. "Did you have to get permission from the little woman to come out tonight?"

"Nah. She trusts me." Did she? Maybe more than she did a few months ago. He'd talked to her right after the game. She had gone to lunch with her mother and sister. Her voice had that false optimism she'd have during a seven-game losing streak. He wondered what the history was there. Everyone had issues from their childhood. Why would Rachel be any different?

Bryce took an empty chair next to the relief pitcher. They had chosen a table off to the side, with a clear view of the room. The other guys were obviously keeping their options open.

The cocktail waitress gave Bryce an appreciative smile as she took his order for a beer.

"Here you go." She lingered just a little longer than necessary after delivering his drink. Her eyes took in all of him. "Is there anything else I can get you? Anything at all?"

"I think I'm good here, thanks. But I'll let you know if I think of something." He returned the smile along with a big tip. Bryce believed in taking care of his waitresses. He knew they worked long, hard hours, on their feet, for little money. A lot of their customers were rude, cheap, and demanding. If she did her job well, he always rewarded her with a generous tip. If she was friendly and accommodating, he'd offer a little of his trademark charm. Even if she was clueless or incompetent, he still treated her with dignity. He'd ask for her to fix her mistakes and when she did, he'd tip her adequately and send her off with a smile.

"Damn, I thought she was going to crawl into your lap," Diego teased. "Maybe you need to wear a sign around your neck that says, 'Sorry ladies, I'm taken.'"

"I don't need a sign."

"Yeah, you're right. Some chicks would just take that as a challenge. You have a hard enough time fending off the ladies."

"That's why I hang out with guys like you." Bryce took a long drink. "You scare them all away."

"Hey now!" Diego gave him a quick jab in the arm. "I don't scare them all away. Some of them feel sorry for me."

Just as Diego said it, a group of three women entered the bar. They had that look. The tallest one, a brunette, locked in on their table. A slow smile spread over her face as she made eye contact with Bryce. He knew the signs. They were willing to play the game. A game he'd played too many times. A game with unwritten rules, and all the players knew how things worked.

She sauntered over; her long legs looked as if she'd been dipped in denim. Her silky silver halter clung in all the right places. Her long hair had been carefully arranged to look like she'd just rolled out of bed. Long, dangly earrings competed with the shiny gloss on her lips to draw a man's attention.

Behind her, a blonde and another brunette—this one with light brown hair—were less flashy, but still decked out to show off what they had.

"Excuse me, gentlemen," the tall brunette addressed them all, but she didn't take her eyes off Bryce. "Is that the wine list?"

She leaned over, revealing a hint of black lace, as she reached for the wine list that sat on the table in front of Bryce.

"Help yourself." Bryce leaned back in his chair, hoping she'd get the hint he wasn't interested.

"So, are you boys in town for work?" She did a quick glance around the table. "Or for play?"

"Both." Diego, on the other hand, did seem interested. "Considering we play for a living, you could definitely say both."

"Oh, and what do you play?" The woman gave Bryce one last smoldering look before turning her attention to Diego.

"We play to win." Diego said, scooting his chair back to make room for the ladies to join them. "Have a seat, we'll tell you all about it."

"Sounds fabulous." She took the chair between Bryce and Diego. "I'm Angelina. These are my friends, Tori and Elyse."

"Diego Garcia." The pitcher introduced himself first. "These are my teammates, Bryce Baxter, Gavin Owens, and the rookie here is Ryan Fletcher."

"What team do you play for?" Angelina asked as her friends took the two chairs on the end.

"We're World Champion San Francisco Goliaths." Diego flashed his World Series ring. He was one of the few players who wore it in public. "Except for the rookie, here. He's the only one of us here without a ring."

"*Yet.* I'm the only one here without a ring yet. There's still time to go for back-to-back championships." Ryan leaned in, flashing the kind of cocky, yet green smile that reminded Bryce a little of his younger self.

"So what position do you play?" Tori, or maybe it was Elyse, leaned in.

"I'm an infielder." Ryan didn't add backup. "Diego here is our closer."

At her blank stare, he explained that the closer was the relief pitcher who came in for the last three outs to close out the game. He didn't go into the details of what constituted a save,

"So you're a pitcher." Tori was the blonde. At least, he thought that was her name. "And that's really a World Series ring?"

She scooted closer to Diego, who obliged by holding out his ring.

"Oh my God, that is a ridiculous amount of diamonds."

"Damn straight. But every single one of them was earned." Diego started to puff up, knowing he had a good chance of getting laid tonight. "Most of them by our friend Bryce. The MVP. We wouldn't have gotten there without him."

"I just got the trophy." For the first time in his life, Bryce didn't care for the attention to swing in his direction. He didn't need to impress anyone, especially not any of these girls. And they were girls. None of them could be older than twenty-three. He was pretty sure they were all over eighteen, since they were out on a school night. "But there were twenty-five guys who got us there."

"Wait, I thought there were only nine guys on a team." Elyse finally joined the conversation.

"There are nine starting players," Gavin explained. "But there are twenty-five on the roster. Usually five starting pitchers, six or seven relievers and the rest are bench players. Backups for when the regulars need a rest or if someone gets hurt."

"Are you a starter or a backup?" Elyse moved in, giving the impression she was interested no matter what he said.

"I was a backup last year," Gavin told her. "But I've been getting a lot of starts at second base this season."

"Second base, huh?" She puffed up so that her second base was prominent. "You like second base?"

"Oh yeah. I love second base." He dropped his gaze to her breasts. Two down. That left the rookie for Angelina.

"So what position do you play, Bryce Baxter?" She practically purred.

"I'm a shortstop."

"And do you wear your ring?"

"Just my wedding ring." He flashed the simple gold band. No diamonds. No sparkle. Just a commitment.

Her eyes narrowed as she glanced at his left hand. As if his marriage was a personal affront.

"So where is your wife tonight?" She asked in a way that was part challenge, part contempt.

"She's home in San Francisco." He really didn't want to get into it with her. Especially since she didn't seem to give a shit that he was a married man.

"So why doesn't she come support you when you're on the road?"

"She doesn't need to follow me around all the time." Bryce was getting irritated at having to defend his wife. His marriage. "She supports me in a lot of ways. Sometimes staying home and taking care of the little things is even bigger than being there when I get off the field."

"Somehow I get the feeling you don't have any *little* needs." Someone should put this girl out of her misery. If that was supposed to be a come on, or compliment, it was like one of Diego's infamous scuds. A pitch that bounced so far out of the strike zone it might as well be a misguided missile.

Bryce drained his glass, but before he could make his excuses, the waitress had come around again.

"The next round is on me." He smiled at the waitress, waiting until she'd taken everyone's orders before handing over his card. As soon as he'd signed the charge slip, he excused himself from the party.

Angelina gave him a pouty look before sliding over to take on the rookie. He hoped Ryan was up for a challenge. She was going to be a piece of work. Not sure if she'd be worth the piece of ass.

He nodded to his teammates, said goodbye to the ladies, and made his way to the elevator.

He had stepped inside, punched his floor number into the panel, when a harried looking man with a baby strapped to his chest, a toddler in a stroller, and diaper bag slung over his shoulder called out to hold the elevator.

"Thanks man. I appreciate it."

"Looks like you've got your hands full."

"You have no idea." The guy patted the baby, who was starting to fuss. "This Mr. Mom thing is a lot harder than it looks. Especially when my wife gets bumped from her flight. She'll be spending a quiet night in Denver, alone, while I've got to figure out how to get them down after they both slept during the whole flight."

Bryce just gave a sympathetic nod, hoping the kids would settle down soon. He was starting to get a headache.

"I quit my job when my wife took the promotion." The guy bounced slightly, trying to calm the baby. "She'd have to travel more, she said, but the money would be worth it."

Bryce tried to smile in sympathy. But the subject of money was never something he discussed with anyone other than his agent.

"Sometimes I wonder, you know. She gets home after the kids are in bed. She's out the door before they wake up. And sex? Forget about it."

How did you politely tell a stranger that he was oversharing?

"This was supposed to be a mini-vacation for us. Before she heads to London for three weeks. But now, we'll be lucky if we get a whole weekend."

The baby's fussing turned into full-blown crying. The toddler joined in, and Bryce was more than relieved when the trio got off three floors later.

He sank against the back of the elevator. Was that what his life was going to be like? Would Rachel keep working even when his contract was up? When his body gave out? Would he be hobbling around, trying to lift a squirming toddler with a shoulder that had turned a few too many double plays?

He wasn't ready for diapers, midnight feedings, and trying to juggle work schedules that happened to be the same. They'd have to hire a nanny, since there weren't many day care centers open from three to midnight.

The elevator stopped on his floor. He stepped into the hallway, trying to remember which direction his room was in. After a while, the hotels all started to look alike. Two nights at one hotel, three at the next.

The elevator next to him opened and a couple tore themselves apart. The woman smoothed her hair while the man reached into his pocket for his room key.

"This is my floor." The guy sounded a little like he was afraid she'd come to her senses before they got to the room.

She followed, still fussing over her dress, as if she needed to make herself presentable before they tore each other's clothes off once they got behind closed doors.

Would he bump into them again in the morning? Or just her, as she slunk out of the room in the early morning hours, still wearing the same dress from the night before?

That wasn't the life he wanted either. Those women back at the bar were like the plastic key cards issued by the hotel. Interchangeable. Disposable. Used for the night and then tossed aside or left behind after checking out of the room.

No, he didn't want that life anymore. He'd grown tired of it maybe even before he'd met Rachel. But old habits die hard. It had been easier to keep doing what he'd always been doing. It was familiar. Safe. He'd known what the next morning would bring. An empty bed. A slight headache. And no messy emotions.

Then he'd met Rachel. She'd left his bed, but she'd stuck around in his head. Maybe even his heart. It was messy. And in a few months it would get even messier. A kid.

He didn't want all that. He just wanted to play baseball. Win a championship. Get a long-term contract so he could play out his career and have something to be proud of. And he'd done it, made his dreams come true.

Baseball had saved him more than once in his life. He had a feeling it could save him again. If he just focused on his game, then everything else would fall into place.

It had to.

Chapter 14

The representative from the Harrison Foundation was right on time. Rachel signed the donation paperwork and then watched as a big burly guy loaded her faithful Honda onto the flatbed of his tow truck. How ridiculous was it for her to mourn the loss of a seven-year-old car? It was just a mode of transportation. It wasn't as if she'd lost her virginity or conceived her child in the backseat or anything. It was just a car.

Time to get over it. Seriously. She had a great new vehicle, and as the new car smell faded, she was getting used to it. Actually, she really liked driving the Range Rover. She was bigger than a lot of cars, so she felt somewhat more protected.

"Are you sure you have everything out of the car that you need?" The tow truck driver wiped his palms on the front of his coveralls, almost as if he was nervous. "I could check one more time before I haul it off."

"No. I went through it." Twice. "But thank you, Dave."

She glanced at the name stitched on the left side of his uniform. There was something almost familiar about the guy. Since she'd never had to call a towing service, she figured she may have met him at a game or something.

"It's my pleasure. Believe me." His ears turned red, as did the skin above his dark brown beard. "I'm actually a big fan."

He kicked at a small piece of gravel in the street. "A really *big* fan."

"Thank you." She wasn't sure if he was referring to his size or the size of his admiration. Either way, she got that little shiver up her spine that made her just a little bit wary. He was a big dude, easily six-four, at least two-hundred fifty pounds. His hair was cut short, almost military style. He had a thick beard and his hands were like two catchers' mitts.

"No, thank you." The guy looked down at his feet in an "aw-shucks" kind of way. "I'm just glad I got to meet you in person. And I'm happy for you. Really."

He lumbered over to the cab of his tow truck and gave a shy wave as he closed the door.

Rachel swallowed a lump in her throat as she watched him drive away with a piece of her past.

Time to get moving. She had a whole host of errands to run. She wasn't quite ready for maternity clothes, but her jeans were getting a little snug. She figured she could go up a size if she chose the styles with a little bit of Lycra in them. She'd pick out a few blouses that would hide her expanding waistline. Hopefully that would get her through the next month or two until she was ready to inform her boss about her condition.

Then she needed to go grocery shopping. She was almost out of her favorite conditioner, and she wanted to pick up a small gift for Bryce. Just because. Nothing she'd find could match a new car, but she wanted to show how much she appreciated everything he'd done. She just didn't really know him well enough to know what he'd like. Other than the obvious, and she'd given him that enough times over the last year and a half. She'd give him that, too, because, well, it was a gift that gave right back.

How was it that going a week without being in his bed was so much harder now? She'd gone months at a time before. But a small part of her knew she was hopelessly hooked on him. She should have gone on the road with him. He'd called her late last night—well, it was late in Philly, almost midnight. He'd gone out with his teammates to celebrate the win. He'd sounded tired, despite having had a great game. Their conversation had been short; it was obvious he was just checking in before turning in.

Rachel made it to Macy's and headed to her favorite section of designer jeans. She grabbed the next size up, and then after hesitating a moment, the size after that. After browsing for a few loose blouses, she had enough to take to the fitting room. Once inside she marveled at the subtle changes in her body. Her breasts were fuller, much to Bryce's delight. Her belly was more rounded, but she didn't exactly look pregnant. Yet.

The first pair of jeans was too tight and she couldn't even get them buttoned. Bummer. She knew size shouldn't matter, but she'd long been conditioned to see the smaller number as better, which was ridiculous since every brand had a different version of what size actually fit.

Next size up fit around her expanding waistline, but they were too loose in the hips and butt. She looked like she was wearing a saggy diaper. Definitely not going to work. But she couldn't just walk over to the maternity section and start trying on clothes. It would be just her luck that she'd be recognized and then have to worry about it hitting the Internet.

The last thing she'd need would be to have her boss find out she was pregnant on Twitter.

She selected three blouses that would hide her baby bump. At least she hoped they would. After handing the jeans back to the dressing room attendant with a shrug, she went in search of a nightgown that would make Bryce realize just how much she appreciated him. And wanted him.

The lingerie section was one of her least favorites. On one end, you had the body shapers. Hard-core Lycra meant to squeeze women into a size and shape that was unnatural. Some women raved at the miracle they offered. But for Rachel, the only miracle was that she had been able to get out of the darn device that one time she'd tried one on.

At the other end of the spectrum were the racy, see-through, ooh-la-la numbers. Bras that offered no support but did come with feathers or rhinestones. And they came with matching G-strings. Because those were comfortable.

Somewhere in the middle was where she was more comfortable. Sexy, but not overly sleazy. After some browsing, Rachel found a black satin chemise, it hugged her breasts and flowed over her belly, hitting mid-thigh. It made her feel pretty. And special. She just hoped Bryce would find it enticing. Especially if she skipped the matching thong altogether.

By the time she checked out, she was starving. A good thing they had restaurants in the basement level of the department store. She could get some clam chowder from Boudin's, pick up a chopped salad from Mixed Greens, or she could even stop by the Burger Bar, except she had a hard time stomaching red meat. She'd always appreciated a nice juicy steak now and again, just not since the pregnancy test came back positive. She couldn't even watch those commercials with the dripping cheeseburgers.

She settled on a salad and a small round of sourdough to keep with her in the car. She had a feeling it wouldn't make it home.

The next stop was to the grocery store to stock up on healthy, easy to stomach foods. Plenty of fresh fruits and vegetables, lean meats, mostly chicken and fish. She thought about picking up another loaf of bread, but she figured she could hit the sourdough store if she ran out. It wasn't like she had a lot to do with Bryce and the team still on the road.

She busied herself putting away groceries, weeding through old and expired condiments, and making a list of things she thought Bryce might want her to replace. Staples such as ketchup and mustard, hot sauce and soy sauce. She figured a bachelor living alone and on the road half the year might not use up even the smallest bottles of condiments.

Sudden longing filled her. She missed him. Not just physically, but she'd gotten used to the goofy way he was trying so hard to make this work. Sure, he'd made mistakes. They both had. But he was trying to make the best of the situation and for that she was truly grateful.

After starting a load of laundry, she hand washed the new nightgown and hung it up to dry in the shower. Sunday night couldn't come fast enough for her. She just hoped Bryce would still want her when he returned. She hoped he'd be turned on by the black satin, and not appalled by the fact that none of her jeans fit her anymore.

Glancing over at his dresser, she wondered if she would fit into his jeans. Not that she could wear them to work, but to get through the weekend. She pulled on a pair of faded Levi's. They were a little loose, but infinitely more comfortable than leaving the top button undone and the zipper pulled down. While she was at it, she grabbed one of his long sleeved t-shirts and pulled it on. Why not? She wasn't going anywhere the rest of the day. If she couldn't have Bryce, she'd have the next best thing.

Sitting on the plush leather sofa, wearing Bryce's clothes, she watched him on TV. He was having a great game. He looked much more like the Bryce of last season when nothing could stop him on or off the field. Rachel was happy for him, even as she was ordering her first three pairs of maternity jeans online.

This was really happening. She was really sitting in Bryce's apartment, in his clothes, carrying his child. They were married. She twirled the ring on her left hand, marveling at the size and the weight of it. Not just the ring, but all of it.

She desperately wanted to believe that it was all going to be okay. They would somehow manage to make a life together. To have a family.

As she watched Bryce round the bases on his second home run of the night, she wiped the tears from her face and hoped that it was a sign of good things to come.

Chapter 15

Bryce continued to have a good series and the Goliaths ended up sweeping in Philly. He finally felt as though he was getting back on track. It helped that he didn't have any distractions while on the road. He woke up, had breakfast, and reported to the ballpark for his workouts before game time. He finally had his head back in the game where it belonged.

Sure, he checked in with Rachel every night, but their conversations had been short. Everything was fine on her end; she was feeling better, and getting used to the new car. She was just taking it easy while she could. Who knew when she'd have to cover an extra inning game that went deep into the night?

So yeah, he was feeling pretty good as he packed up his locker in the visitors' clubhouse. The bus to the airport would load shortly, and it would be a happy flight.

"Mr. Baxter?" A stern voice interrupted his solitude.

He turned to find a uniformed police officer standing a few feet away, an iPad in hand.

"Yes, can I help you?" He had no idea what Philadelphia's finest would want with him.

"I hope so. I have some questions about an incident that occurred at the Ritz-Carlton Thursday night." The officer said.

"We checked in Thursday after flying in from Atlanta." Bryce had no reason to hide anything.

"And were you in the bar between the hours of ten PM and midnight?"

"I stopped to have a drink with a few teammates, but I'm sure I left well before midnight."

"And what about your teammates? What time did they leave?"

"After me, I guess. I really don't know. I had a couple of beers and then turned in for the night."

"Do you recall a young lady named Angela Hartman?"

"There were a couple of ladies who showed up. I think one of them was named Angelina or something like that. I wasn't really interested. See, I'm a married man." Bryce held up his wedding ring, as if to prove it.

"Ms. Hartman says she arrived with two friends, and they met up with some ballplayers from San Francisco."

"Yeah, I guess that was her, then." He remembered how predatory she'd seemed. She'd been after something, And he'd learned the hard way that girls like her could be looking for a good time or looking for a sugar daddy. Another reason to be grateful he had Rachel. He could put that kind of nonsense behind him.

"Do you know which of your teammates she hooked up with?"

"Nope. Sorry." He didn't like where this was going. "Like I said, I turned in early. All I wanted was to relax with my friends, have a beer or two. But then these gals showed up, dressed to kill, and I was out of there. The whole scene got old for me a while ago."

"Ms. Hartman was sexually assaulted by one of your teammates."

"What? No. I'm sure it's a misunderstanding." He had to weigh his words carefully. "I mean, she was definitely looking for some action."

"And how do you know that?"

Oh shit. He was in a real tough spot. First of all, he'd been there. Angelina had been on the prowl. From her tight clothing, her overdone makeup, and the way she practically crawled into his lap trying to reach the wine list. But he couldn't say that. He'd sound like a misogynistic jerk. But he also knew his teammates. Sure, they had been looking for a good time, but he didn't think any of them would take it too far. Would they?

"Look, I've been around awhile. And I've met my share of groupies, cleat chasers, whatever you want to call them. I know when a woman is looking to score with a ballplayer. And these women were most certainly looking to score. Angelina, or Angela, whatever her name is, she tried to come on to me, but when I turned her down, twice, she turned her attention to the rookie."

Shit. He shouldn't have said that.

"Does this rookie have a name?"

"What does any of this have to do with me?"

"Ms. Hartman could only identify you out of the four players in the bar. She did clarify that you were not one of the men who assaulted her, but you were the only one she knew by name."

"What do you mean 'one of the men'?" There was no way the guys had pulled any kind of crap like that.

"She said that there was a lot of alcohol involved and she didn't remember how she got to the room, only that she woke up naked and violated."

"I'm sorry, I can't help you with that." Bryce ran a hand through his hair. "I was there for maybe one round of drinks after the girls showed up."

"Can you tell us the names of the other players who were there that night?"

"Doesn't the bartender have the charge slips?"

"Just yours. The rest of the guys paid cash."

"Of course they did." Bryce was getting annoyed with this whole conversation.

"Look, Mr. Baxter, this is a serious matter. I know guys like you are used to getting away with things, but not in my city."

"I'm not trying to get away with anything. I'm just trying to get on a bus and get home to my wife."

"And I'm trying to do my job."

"I really don't know what happened after I left. It looked like everyone was having a good time. I don't know if anyone hooked up with anyone. It really is none of my business."

"You Goliaths players are known as a tight-knit group. A band of brothers. You'd do anything for each other."

"On the field, absolutely."

"So why are covering for your brothers in this case?"

"Oh, is there a case? Should I get a lawyer?"

"You don't need a lawyer."

"Good. Because I'd much rather get home to my wife."

"So you said. A few times. Sounds like someone's trying a little too hard to play the dutiful husband card."

Bryce shoved his hands deep into his pockets.

"You married?"

The police officer nodded.

"How long has it been since you've seen your wife?"

"This morning."

"I haven't seen my wife in over a week. So yeah, I'm anxious to see her. But first I have to get on that bus. Then a plane will take me to San Francisco, home to my wife."

The clubhouse door opened, Ryan Fletcher came in. "Hey, Bryce, you're holding up the bus."

He looked at Bryce, then looked at the police officer. His face drained of color. The officer picked up on it and turned his questioning toward Ryan.

"Were you in the hotel bar Thursday night?"

Ryan simply nodded.

"And did you meet a woman named Angela Hartman?"

"She said her name was Angelina." Ryan's voice had a nervous edge to it. "But nothing happened, I swear. She fell asleep. I tried to wake her up before I left for the ballpark but she was out cold. I made sure she was breathing and left a trash can by the bed, in case she got sick."

"Well, Ms. Hartman has reported a sexual assault."

"No sir. We made out a little in the elevator." Ryan's face was red now. "And the bar. But that's it. We went back to my room, but like I said, she fell asleep before we could, you know, do anything."

"I'm going to let Javier know we might need a few more minutes." Bryce had heard enough. He believed Ryan. He'd been there, that chick was all over him. But to pass out and then go on to accuse the poor kid of rape was low.

Bryce kind of felt as if he had something to do with this whole nightmare. He'd passed her off on Ryan. He was just a kid. He still hadn't figured out how to turn down an attractive woman who seemed to want nothing more than to stroke a guy's ego, among other things.

Hell, Bryce had only recently figured that one out.

Finally, about a half hour later, Ryan boarded the bus. He looked weary and dejected and a little scared.

Bryce waved him back to the seat next to him.

"Everything okay?" he asked when Ryan slumped into the seat.

"It's all fucked up." Ryan leaned his head back and closed his eyes.

"Do you need a lawyer?" Bryce kept his voice low, so the others couldn't hear. Hopefully. Most of them had their headphones on, so there was a good chance they wouldn't be overheard even in a normal speaking voice. "I'd be willing to help you find someone if you do."

"I don't know man. The whole thing is just crazy. I mean, you were there."

"I was at the bar. I know how the night started." Bryce looked the other man in the eye. "But how did it end?"

"Just like I told the cop. Nothing happened." Ryan held his gaze. "At least not once we got to the room. I went to the bathroom to get a condom and when I came back, she was passed out naked on the bed. I pulled the blanket over her and slept in the chair. I've still got the kink in my neck to prove it."

"If only that was enough," Bryce said. "You sure nothing happened?"

"Nothing happened to her." Ryan looked around before adding, "She went down on me in the elevator. One minute we're kissing, and the next, she's on her knees."

"You do know there are security camera in those elevators."

"Shit."

"No. That could be a good thing. If it comes down to it, the tape could prove that she went willingly to your room with the intention to engage in sexual activity."

"Man, I didn't want all this. I was just looking for a good time, you know?"

He knew all too well.

"I mean, I wanted to blow off some steam. I'm sure a lot of people think I've got nothing to worry about. I get paid to watch baseball. I don't even have to play and I still make more money than most people."

"Yeah." Bryce could understand the frustration of the kid. He finally made a major league roster—a dream come true—only to sit on the bench, watching.

"Do you think that's what this is about? She wants me to buy her off? I ain't got that much money." Ryan leaned back in the seat, frustrated. "Maybe that's why she went after you first."

"Could be." Bryce leaned forward as the bus took the off-ramp to the airport. "Or maybe she was just someone who was also looking for a good time and got carried away. She had too much to drink and when she couldn't remember what happened, assumed the worst."

"Even if that's the case, I've still disgraced the team. The fans." The rookie sounded discouraged. "I've disgraced my family, my hometown."

"Hey, don't worry. Once we get on a hot streak, no one will care."

"Easy for you to say. You've got it all. A ring. A big fat contract." Ryan sighed, his envy showing. "A beautiful wife. You're lucky you don't have to deal with this kind of shit anymore."

"Yeah." Yet he'd spent twenty minutes talking to a Philly cop that afternoon. And somehow he was going to have to explain it to Rachel. Hopefully he'd get to her before the news did.

Chapter 16

An hour before the Goliaths' flight was due to land in San Francisco, the reports started coming in that Bryce Baxter and several other players had been questioned by Philadelphia police regarding a sexual assault that occurred at the team's hotel. *Allegedly* occurred. No charges had been filed, but speculation was flying all over the Internet.

Rachel searched for the official reports, but they were entirely too vague. The only fact she could find was that a woman contacted the police after waking up naked in a player's hotel room. Bryce was the only player named, although it didn't come right out and say it was his hotel room. Other Goliaths players were also questioned before being released to catch their flight home.

With few facts to go on, the Internet exploded with allegations. There were plenty of angry outbursts claiming over-privileged jocks once again getting away with breaking the law and abusing women. Cynicism about special treatment was balanced by those questioning the woman's motives. More than once, Bryce's contract was brought up along with speculation that the woman was hoping for a big payout.

Many were publically calling for the Goliaths to release Bryce from his contract. Others wondered whatever happened to the concept of innocent until proven guilty.

Rachel didn't know what to believe. In her heart, she knew Bryce wasn't the kind of man to force someone into having sex against her will. But if there was alcohol involved, consent was a tricky thing.

She needed to hear the true story from Bryce. Have him look her in the eye and tell her what happened in that hotel room in Philly. Then she would... The problem was, she wasn't sure what she was going to do. The obvious choice was to move out. But where would she go? Her apartment had been leased already.

By the time she got to the airport, Rachel's stomach was a mess. Only she couldn't blame it on the baby. Not this time. This time it was all on Bryce. And the worst part of it was that she was just starting to believe that they could be happy. That they could make this work.

What a fool. She only got to report on others' successes.

Bryce was the first one out of baggage claim. Damn the man. He looked good. A little ragged, but good. He saw her and dropped his bags, rushing to her side.

"I missed you." He pulled her into his arms and her stupid body responded as it always did. With longing. Desire. Need.

Rachel wrestled free from his embrace. She couldn't give in to the man. Not anymore.

"Rachel, what's wrong?" He looked alarmed. "Is the baby okay?"

He spoke those last words in a panicked whisper as his hand slid protectively over her belly.

"The baby's fine." Would she have to come right out and say it? Tears pricked her eyes but she fought them back.

"How could you?" Her voiced cracked as her throat tightened; it felt as if she'd swallowed seawater.

Understanding dawned on his face.

"Oh, baby, I didn't do anything." He reached for her hand. "I swear."

She wanted to believe him. But if the police were involved, something had to have happened.

"So what did you hear?" He gave her hand a squeeze. Was he trying to reassure her or was he trying to keep her from pulling away?

"You were questioned by the police, involving a...a sexual assault." She had a hard time even saying the words, at least in connection with her husband.

"As a witness." He pulled her closer. Still holding her right hand, he tilted her chin with his left hand. "They questioned me as a witness, only I didn't see anything. I had gone to bed. Alone."

"So what happened?" Hope sprung in her heart.

"As far as I can tell, nothing. I mean, yeah these girls showed up in the bar looking for a good time." He let go of her hand and dragged his own through his hair. "I was there having a couple beers with the guys. But I wasn't interested in hanging out with those girls, so I paid for everyone's drinks and left. I guess one of the women hooked up with one of the guys and went up to his room, but she passed out before anything could happen."

"Are you sure?" Rachel hoped that was the case. Even though she now knew it wasn't Bryce, she still didn't want any of the other Goliaths to have committed a sexual assault.

"Like I said, I wasn't there, but I think he's telling the truth." He let out a ragged breath. "I've been in his shoes, before. Not long after my divorce. I took this girl up to my room, but she'd had too much to drink and nothing happened. Only instead of accusing me of sexual assault, she tried to name me in a paternity suit a year later."

"Wait, if nothing happened, how could she claim paternity?"

"I took the test, knowing it would come up negative. I don't know, maybe she thought she had a chance. Even my first contract was worth more than your average guy would make."

Rachel's heart sank. She'd known about his ex-wife. But were there others? Women who hadn't come forward? How many half siblings would her child have?

"Maybe this gal's just looking to cash in. She went after me first, but then she had to settle for one of the guys least likely to keep her in the lap of luxury."

"Who did she pick?" Now her curiosity was getting the better of her.

"Ah, there's my reporter. Always wanting the scoop." Bryce smiled and tucked a strand of her hair behind her ear.

"So who was it?"

He shook his head. "Look, I don't really know everything that happened after I left the bar. And I'm sure you wouldn't want to run with a story based on speculation and rumors."

"The Internet is full of speculation and rumors." She shook her head, frustrated, yet somewhat pleased he wouldn't sell out a teammate. Especially if what he'd said was true. "Most of them about you."

"Rachel. Look at me." He reached up to cup her face in both of his big, strong, yet incredibly gentle hands. "I would never do anything like that. Even when I was single and...playing the field. But now that we're married... Oh, Rachel, I could never hurt you like that. I swear."

The sincere look in his eyes had her wanting so desperately to believe him. Sure, she believed he wouldn't ever take advantage of a woman who wasn't one hundred percent willing. The problem was that there were still many women who were more than willing to hook up with a guy like him.

"So you met this woman, the one making the accusations? And she tried to hook up with you?"

He flinched. "Yeah, she came after me, but I blew her off."

"So what was she like?"

"Look. I know you're not supposed to think that a woman dressed in tight jeans and a low-cut blouse is necessarily looking for sex." He let out an exasperated sigh. "It shouldn't matter what she's wearing, 'no means no' and all that. But when she's shaking her ass and rubbing her tits in a guy's face..."

He clenched his fists, frustration clearly getting the best of him.

"I mean, when a guy has to say 'no thanks, I'm married' three times before she removes her damn hand from his thigh."

"She had her hand on your thigh?" Rachel's possessive instincts rose. "She shook her tits in your face?"

"I tried to be civil, but when she didn't take no for an answer, I left." He raked his hands through his hair. "I should have taken the kid with me."

At this point, she didn't need to ask who he was talking about. There were two or three rookies who could have been at that bar with him. Didn't matter, at least not if charges weren't filed.

"I can't help but think that she went after him to get back at me." His statement would have sounded conceited if not for the utter despair in his voice. "I don't know... It was like she walked into that bar with an agenda. And when she didn't get what she was after, she went all psycho bitch the next day. Or maybe it was the day after. We were at the bar on Thursday night. The cops didn't show up in the locker room until Sunday afternoon."

"Well, hopefully, the truth will prevail."

"Even if it does, the damage is done." He smoothed her hair back off her face. "I'm sorry you had to spend even one second doubting me. And I'm sure you'll have to defend me, defend us, to a few people who will believe the worst even without the facts."

"Hey, I knew what I was getting into. I know you're a public figure. People will say things about you, most of which isn't true." She tried to keep a positive front. "They say stuff about me, too. It comes with the territory."

"Yeah, but it's one thing to have to put up with fans complaining about my on-field performance, or lack thereof. It's another to be accused of a sexual assault. Especially when it's her word against ours. Some have even said it was a group thing. That we were all involved. The fact that no charges were filed doesn't mean some people won't believe the worst."

"True." Her heart ached for Bryce, and the as yet unnamed player who had taken the woman to his room. It ached even more for true victims. The ones who had to defend their choices in clothing, refreshments, and whether or not they were looking for it when they walked into a bar or party or even a date.

"But you believe me?" He reached for her, tenderly, but with a hint of doubt. "As long as you believe in me, that's all that matters."

"Yes. I believe in you." And she did. He may have been a bad boy, but he was a good man. She knew that, deep down.

* * * *

It killed Bryce to see the doubt in Rachel's eyes. Even though she'd accepted his version of the story, he hated that she'd even wondered if any of it was true. Hated even more that she'd thought he was involved.

He now realized that everything he did—and even things he didn't do—would affect Rachel. And their baby.

He'd spent the last several years not caring what people thought about him, off the field. He prided himself in his performance on the diamond. He was paid to be good. Very good. An All-Star. His fans expected his best when he slipped on his glove.

Just like they'd come to expect his worst off the field. He'd somehow fallen into the stereotypical *player* role. The bad boy who could charm the ladies out of their panties with little more than a smile. And a multi-million dollar salary.

It had been a part he played. And it had served him well. No one expected anything more of him. No one got too close.

Not even his wife.

"Let's go home." He placed a gentle kiss on her forehead.

"I'll drive." She gave him a weak smile. While he was chilling out on the flight from Philadelphia, she'd been inundated with accusations about her husband. The most harmful kind. The kind that would have jeopardized their marriage, his career, and freedom, had they been true.

How could he make this up to her? Buying her things wasn't enough. Sure, he was happy to do it. Would buy her more if she'd let him. He smiled as he got in the new Range Rover he'd picked out for her. It was a sweet ride.

"So how's the car?" he asked as she slid behind the wheel. "Do you like driving it?"

"It took me a little while to get used to being so high off the ground, but I actually do like it." She turned to him, her smile this time a little more genuine. "Thank you. I know you were just trying to take care of me and the baby. I guess I'll have to get used to it."

"The car?"

"No. Being taken care of." She let out a soft chuckle. "I've worked hard for everything I have. My car was no exception."

"Yeah, I guess that's why Marco Santiago still drives that old Mustang." He knew a thing or two about working to get somewhere. "That'll change when Hunter gets pregnant, though. You'll see."

Rachel let out a sign, and turned the key to start the ignition. "So you're saying it's a guy thing?"

"Oh, yeah." Bring on a debate. "Totally a protective instinct. You're carrying my baby. You get to nurture, grow, and protect our baby inside your...body."

"What? Does the word uterus make you uncomfortable?" She was fully engaged now. "What about vagina? Does vagina make you uncomfortable?"

"Oh, hell no. I've found quite a bit of comfort in your vagina." She had no idea how much.

"Is that so?"

"Yeah, babe. And I had a rough couple of weeks. I could use some comfort."

"You are such a guy." She laughed as she merged onto the freeway, heading toward the apartment they now shared. Home.

"You seem to like my guy parts."

"Yeah, except those guy parts got me knocked up."

"And now I need to protect you. And the little peanut inside you." He leaned back against the plush leather seat. How the hell was he going to pull this off? He not only needed to keep her safe with half a dozen air bags, antilock brakes, and stability control, but it was also up to him to protect her from his reputation, his past and future mistakes. And the media. Only she was the media. Or part of it.

"You sound like such a caveman."

"Yeah. Well, you've got protective instincts, too." He glanced over at her and smiled. "Every time we talk about the baby, you move one hand over your uterus. Although, if you had really good instincts, you would have run as far and as fast from me as possible."

"How can you say that?" She placed both hands on the wheel and stared straight ahead. "If anyone should have run, it would be you. I mean, you weren't expecting this. All of this."

She waved her arm around the interior of the vehicle before resting briefly on her stomach.

"No. I certainly wasn't. There's nothing quite as frightening as being told you're going to be a father." He stared out the passenger window. He hadn't wanted to tell her how scared he was. But he couldn't protect her by keeping it to himself, either.

"What are you afraid of?" Unspoken worries carried in her tone of voice.

"What if it's a boy?" He turned toward her. "What if he's just like me? I was quite a handful when I was younger."

"I hate to break it to you, but you're still quite a handful." She smiled as she stared into his lap. "Oh, yeah, you're quite the handful."

Now, he couldn't think about anything other than getting her home. Into his bed.

"You can handle me." He grew hard just thinking about how well she handled him. "You're the only woman who can handle me."

"I better be." She accelerated, moving into the HOV lane, driving them closer to their bed.

The traffic wasn't too bad, but it still felt like forever before they pulled into the parking garage of their building. He gathered up his luggage and followed Rachel to the elevator. He dropped his bags, and glancing up at the security camera, settled for taking her hand instead of taking her right there in the elevator.

When the finally made it inside their apartment, he tossed his luggage aside and pulled her against him. "I've missed you."

"I missed you too." She barely got the words out before he covered her mouth with his.

He drank her in as if she was a long, cool drink of water on a hot day. He needed her. And the way she pressed against him, running her fingers through his hair and taking him in, she needed him too.

"Let's go to bed," he whispered.

"Have you had dinner?" Rachel tossed her head back as he nibbled on her ear.

"No. Dinner can wait." He flicked his tongue on that delicate spot on her neck. Her skin was the only thing he wanted to taste. "I can't. I want you now. I need you. *Now*."

"Mmm." She moaned as he continued to taste her neck.

"Is that a yes?"

"Yes. Let's go to bed." She tugged his hand and led him to their bedroom.

Chapter 17

The next morning Rachel stepped into the shower, with Bryce not far behind her. He ran his hands over her belly, her suddenly rounded belly. She'd swear not two days ago, she couldn't tell she was pregnant, at least not from the waist down. Sure, her boobs had gotten bigger and she'd already gained five pounds, but she didn't look pregnant. Until now.

"I guess I should think about making the announcement, soon." She leaned back against Bryce's hard, damp chest.

"You want to make an announcement that you want to have sex? A simple yes is fine." Encouraged, Bryce dipped his hands lower.

"Twice last night wasn't enough?" She couldn't help but laugh at his eagerness. Besides, she might as well enjoy it while she still could.

"Nope. I've got seven nights to make up for." He started kissing her neck, flipping her damp hair out of his way. "So I need five more times before we're even."

"Are you really that insatiable?"

"Yes." His hand slipped between her thighs. "And you are, too."

She moaned as he found just the right spot. Seconds later, her legs went weak as he brought her to climax with just his fingers. She turned around and pushed him down on the marble bench seat at the back of the shower. A bottle of body wash clattered to the floor as she straddled him. He groaned as she slid down on top of him. Gripping her hips, he thrust upward. Slowly building like the steam of the shower, he moved deep inside her. After another earth-shattering climax, Rachel collapsed against him.

"Now what was I saying?" She stood so she could get back to washing her hair and getting ready for work. "Oh, right. I'm thinking we might need to make the announcement about the baby soon."

The minute she mentioned the baby, Bryce's hands moved from her hips to her abdomen. Then he placed a gentle kiss just below her navel.

"Yeah, I guess we should." He grinned. "Do you want to go big? Make a huge announcement? Or make it simple, like a quick tweet about a player to be named later?"

"Well, I need to tell my boss first."

"Yeah. And probably our families."

"I kind of already told my mom and my sister. Well, they guessed."

"I guess I should let my dad know." He got a worried look on his face. "And I'd like to tell Hailey myself before it becomes public."

His daughter. Rachel nodded and then turned to grab the shampoo.

Bryce got out of the shower a little bit before her. He was already in the kitchen making breakfast by the time she found a pair of jeans that fit. The maternity jeans she'd ordered were too big, and most of her old clothes were too small. She could wear a skirt, but the nights at the ballpark could be a little too chilly, even in May.

"She's already at school." Bryce sounded disappointed he hadn't been able to speak to his daughter. "I asked Jillian to have Hailey call when she gets home, but she made up some excuse about having some club after school. The woman has no trouble dialing my number whenever she needs something, but I want to have a five-minute conversation with my daughter and she acts like it would be a major disruption."

"I'm sorry you have such a hard time with your ex." What else could she say? At some point, she would have to deal with the woman herself.

"I know part of it's my own damn fault." He stirred the eggs. "But it's been almost ten years. I guess she'll never really forgive me, but it'd be nice to think at some point she can move past the joke that was our marriage."

"What is it that she can never forgive you for?"

He turned off the stove, scooped the eggs onto two plates, and stared at the wall.

"I never gave our marriage a chance. I wasn't there for her or for Hailey." He turned around and crossed his arms over his chest. "I always got the feeling all she really wanted was my money, so that's all I gave her. I knew we weren't in love or anything."

Rachel just swallowed the hard lump in her throat. Was their marriage much different? She knew Bryce didn't love her. And even though she didn't want his money, that was all he was able to give. That and great sex.

"She's just so *angry*." Bryce sounded as if he felt like it was his fault. "I mean she was angry when she told me she was pregnant. Angry when I proposed. And when Hailey was born... I just couldn't make her happy."

"Maybe your job wasn't to make her happy. Maybe your job was to just be there." The words came out so softly, Rachel wasn't sure she'd said them out loud.

"I swear. I'll be there for you." He was at her side, holding her. Holding on as if his life depended on it. "I want to do everything I can to make you happy."

"You can't make me happy." He flinched at her words. "What I mean is, you can only try to be happy with me."

"I am happy with you." He relaxed a bit, but still held her. "Really. Happier than I ever thought I could be."

A tear slid down her cheek. It was a happy tear. Sort of. Her heart ached for what he had to go through with his ex. But the thought that she made him happy warmed her heart.

"Let's eat." Bryce broke away and clapped his hands together. "We worked up quite an appetite, huh?"

In other words, he was done talking.

* * * *

Bryce ate quickly and got a jump on the cleanup. He loaded the dishwasher and wiped down the counters while Rachel did her hair and makeup. She would be going to work today. And she'd most likely tell her boss she was pregnant.

He wasn't sure if he was ready for everything that came with the announcement. But ready or not the baby was coming.

Could he get it right this time? Or would it all go to hell again? Rachel had just admitted he didn't make her happy. He'd made her come, but he hadn't made her happy.

Maybe he wasn't capable of making a woman happy.

Screw that. How many times had he been told he couldn't do something, only to prove them all wrong? He'd been too immature, too fidgety, too out of control to make it as a student. Too small, too wild, too inconsistent to be a good ballplayer. But he'd settled down. Learned how to sit still long enough to get through class so he could make it to the ballpark where he worked longer, harder, and with more determination than the rest of his teammates.

He'd made it through school. So he didn't go to college, but when he was drafted out of high school, he didn't see a need. And he'd worked his tail off to make it through the minors into the major league. He'd played his heart out in Pittsburgh. Made a few All-Star teams and earned his shot at free agency. And he'd been able to sign with the Goliaths at exactly the right time. When they'd been on the unstoppable path to the World Series Championship.

He'd been a big part of that winning team.

Rachel had, too. She'd been there through the highest of the highs. And his lows seemed to come about when she hadn't been around.

So what would it take to make her happy? What was important to her?

Her job. She took her job seriously. And she would soon have to inform her boss that she was expecting. That couldn't be easy, especially in such a public job. But then again, it might be seen as a good thing. The fans loved her. She was a friendly link to the players. They would be happy for her.

Maybe he could find a way to make her job easier. Would she want him to give his version of what had happened—or not happened—in Philly? He could offer the name of the police officer who'd interviewed him. He hesitated at offering up Ryan Fletcher's version of the story. The kid deserved to have some privacy in the matter. But if she asked, he supposed he had to give her the information. Or at least offer to have Ryan talk to her and give his side of things.

He found her in the bathroom, finishing up on her hair and makeup. Her hair was perfect. Almost the color of the crushed brick infield, only shinier. He laughed to himself, realizing no woman would want her hair compared to dirt. But he loved that dirt. It was home to him. Rachel was home, too.

Watching her put on lipstick, he wondered why she even wore makeup. Oh, he knew it was for television, but she really didn't need it. She was beautiful without it. She had great skin, especially when her cheeks were flushed with arousal or satisfaction. Her hazel eyes changed color sometimes depending on what she was wearing. And her mouth. Good lord, how he loved her mouth.

He came up behind her and wrapped his arms around her waist. He wanted to kiss her but was afraid he'd get in trouble for messing up her lipstick. Besides, if he took her to bed for the fourth time in the last twenty-four hours he might not make it to the ballpark.

When she closed her eyes and leaned against him, a soft moan escaping her lips, he considered giving it a go. But he needed to find ways to make her happy with their clothes on.

"So, I thought you might want the contact info for the cop who talked to me in Philly." He pulled a card out of his wallet. "In case you need to do a story on it or something."

Rachel gave the card a cursory glance before tossing it on the bathroom counter. "Thanks. I hope I won't need it."

"Me, too. But I thought if I can do anything to help..." He hated the whole situation. Especially the media's tendency to run with a story before they even had a story. Well, some members of the media. They weren't all bad. Rachel would never sell him, or any of the Goliaths players, out without getting the facts first.

She picked up the card and tucked it in her back pocket.

"It's not exactly the kind of story I would be assigned." She gave him a small smile. "I'm more of the feel-good girl." Her cheeks turned a deep pink at her statement. "You know what I mean."

Bryce answered with a quick kiss on that delicate spot behind her ear. "You feel pretty good to me."

She moved away from his touch, busying herself with cleaning up her makeup and beauty supplies. "I tend to report on the fluff."

"I like your fluff." He moved toward her, unable to keep his hands off her.

She swatted his hand away.

"Bryce." She tried to sound offended, but couldn't quite pull it off. "Please, I have to get ready for work. And it's not always easy to pretend like everything is sunshine and rainbows."

"Well, then maybe you should make the big announcement. I mean, what's more sunshiny and rainbowish than a baby on the way?"

"Rainbowish?"

He shrugged. "You want good news? I can't think of anything better."

"What about your daughter?" Her voiced softened, as if she understood how hard it was for him to be so damned far away and at the mercy of his ex-wife's whims.

"I'll try to call before we leave for the ballpark, but if I wait until Jillian is ready to let me break the news, the baby will be able to drive out there and do it for me."

Rachel's face twisted into a frown. Was she worried that Jillian would cause trouble? Or did she think he was being childish and bitter?

"Will she be able to spend time with us when she's out of school?"

"I usually just go there, during the offseason. But yeah, I'd like to have her come spend some time in San Francisco." He wondered, not for the first time, if maybe he should have pushed harder for more time with his daughter. He'd mistakenly believed that if he gave his ex-wife everything she'd wanted, she would be more accommodating when he asked for time with Hailey. "I just don't know what I'd do with her while I'm working. I can't exactly have her in the clubhouse."

"How old is she?"

"Nine. She's a great kid. Smart. Funny." Bryce felt his chest constrict just thinking of his little girl, and how fast she'd grown. "She's pretty independent, too. You'd like her."

"I'm sure I will." Rachel's smile was encouraging. He could picture her offering a similar smile to Hailey. Welcoming her to the family. "Maybe she could hang out with me. She could go around the ballpark with me when I do my fan interviews. And I'm sure Kip and Kurt would help keep an eye on her, too. The broadcast booth would be better for a young girl than a clubhouse full of half-naked men."

"Kip and Kurt don't want kids running around while they're doing the post-game wrap up."

"Are you kidding? They love kids. Kip's a grandpa now, and Kurt's counting the days until his kids get married and start having babies."

"That's cool. But still, they don't want to babysit." It was hard enough to be a dad in this business, let alone a single dad. Although, he wasn't single anymore. But his wife had her own career. And they'd have to deal with that in a few short months, not just for a week or so, but for the entire season.

"We're like family." She must have been thinking along the same lines because her brows furrowed into a worried look. Her hand moved instinctively over the baby.

"I guess we'll need to get a nanny."

"How long do you think your daughter will stay with us?" Now she sounded a little hesitant. "Do you think your ex will give her up for the whole summer?"

"She won't even have her call me." Bryce had the sinking feeling that an extended visit of any kind was nothing more than wishful thinking. "I mean when the baby comes, we'll need to hire a nanny. Unless you want to conduct player interviews with an infant strapped to you. But if anyone could pull it off, you could."

"I guess we need to start making plans." Both hands now rested on her lower abdomen. "I need to tell my boss. But the good news is that when the baby comes, it'll be the offseason. So I'll have a couple of months before I have to figure everything out."

"Yeah. The timing is good in that respect." Bryce wrapped his arms around her. "Neither of us will miss any games in December."

"Nope, you should be finished by the end of October."

"A few weeks ago, I was feeling like I'd be out of the race by September." If not sooner. "But I think we've got our groove back."

He just hoped the media attention surrounding the police inquiry wouldn't be a distraction for the team.

Chapter 18

Rachel texted her producer to let him know she wanted to speak with him privately. She knew he'd probably think it was about the sexual assault rumors. In some ways, that would be an easier topic of conversation than informing her boss that she was expecting. Steve was in the studio, waiting for her. He was working on one of the computers when she arrived. Whatever it was, he didn't seem too happy about it.

"Someone sent me a link to a YouTube video." Steve didn't even look up when Rachel entered the room. "I think you should take a look. It's from the hotel security camera in Philly where that woman was allegedly assaulted."

"Sure." She wasn't in a position to question her boss.

He pulled up the feed, but paused before clicking the play button. "I'm going to grab some coffee, would you like a cup?"

"No thanks. I'm good." Here was an opportunity to casually mention the reason she couldn't have coffee, but she chickened out. She wondered what he'd seen on the video that would make him so eager to leave the room.

As soon as the door closed behind him, Rachel played the video.

It was obviously inside an elevator. The doors opened and a young man entered with a woman draped against him, she had one arm sprawled across his chest and her head leaning on his shoulder.

It wasn't Bryce. This man had shorter hair. Light brown or dark blond, it was hard to tell in the poor lighting of the elevator. The woman was a brunette, with long, glossy hair, expensive designer clothes, and very high heels. The woman was obviously very drunk, as she was having a hard time keeping her balance.

All of a sudden, the woman dropped to her knees. The look of concern on the man's face quickly turned to surprise as she undid his zipper. Her head blocked most of the view, but the man's face was very clear. His

Kristina Mathews

eyes fluttered shut in pleasure as the woman continued to go down on him. At one point, he reached out against the wall of the elevator, as if he was grasping for something to hold on to.

Rachel was trying to figure out which Goliath player he was. One of the rookies, Brian? No, it was Ryan. Ryan Fletcher. He was a backup infielder, just called up this season. She'd had one quick interview with the kid in spring training. He'd seemed kind of shy. Apparently he wasn't that shy. At least not after a few drinks.

The camera was still zoomed on his face when his features contorted into that intense look a man got when he was having an orgasm. Poor kid. This was not something he'd likely want to hit ESPN. A ballplayer wanted his first national TV exposure to be for making a great play on the field, not making out in a hotel elevator. Well, it was a little more than just making out.

At least the video showed that the woman was in no way forced to go up to his room. If anything, it made it look as if she had been the aggressor. Of course, things might have changed once they got to the room. But from the looks of this, it was clearly consensual.

Rachel breathed a sigh of relief. She wondered how this whole mess was going to play out and how it would affect her job. Would she be expected to interview Fletcher? Talk about an uncomfortable spot to put both of them in.

Steve returned with a cup of coffee and a questioning look on his face.

"So? It was hard to tell, but that wasn't Bryce in the video?" He looked away briefly. "Was it?"

"No. Not Bryce." She was pleased to see his relief. He'd been worried about her. About her relationship with Bryce. "It was, oh, how do I put this delicately? Some woman, I'm assuming it's the one who filed the complaint, she's um. She's… Well, it looks like she's giving Ryan Fletcher a blow job in an elevator."

"Ryan Fletcher?"

"I think that's who it was. The kid does kind of look like a younger, more clean-cut version of Bryce." Or maybe it was the orgasm face that caused the resemblance. She was very familiar with the look on Bryce's face when he came. But maybe all men made the same face.

"Interesting." Was he referring to the video or the idea of Ryan and Bryce looking somewhat alike? "Well, I guess that clears up the question of consent."

"Maybe. We may never know what happened after the video ended." Rachel didn't like to think of anyone being accused of a crime they didn't commit, especially not one of the Goliaths players. But the woman must have had some reason to go to the police. "Besides, she looked like she was pretty drunk. And alcohol makes the question of consent rather tricky."

"She could have been too drunk to say yes or no."

"So where does that leave me? Do we wait and see if anything comes of it? Do you want me to interview the kid?"

"Let's go with the wait and see approach. Hopefully we'll have something better to talk about, like a good start to the home stand."

"Let's hope so." Rachel was starting to relax. "Although... Where did you get the video?"

"It was emailed, anonymously."

"I'll bet we weren't the only ones to receive it."

"Probably not."

"Which is why we should be prepared to address it with Fletcher."

"I knew I could count on you." Steve smiled, almost as if he was proud of her.

"There was something else I wanted to talk to you about." Rachel's knees started to quiver. She slid into a nearby chair. "I-I have some news."

This was so much harder than telling Bryce.

"I'm pregnant." She tried to sound calm; this would in no way affect her career. "I'm not due until December, so you don't have to worry about me missing any games or anything. And I won't have to take maternity leave, so that's convenient."

"Congratulations." His smile seemed genuine enough. "That's great. Just great. I'm happy for you. And Bryce, too."

"Thank you." That wasn't so bad. "We're excited. A little nervous, but mostly excited."

"Let's go with the excitement." Steve broke into a wide grin. "The fans have loved the segments on the players' wives. Let's give them more. We can follow your pregnancy, maybe even take the camera along when you and Bryce go shopping for a crib. Oh, maybe we could do a virtual baby shower, only instead of sending gifts, viewers could send in their best tips for dealing with a newborn."

"A virtual baby shower? What have you got in that coffee?" She usually liked how her boss tended to think outside the box. Sure, the regular broadcast consisted of baseball-related segments. Pregame interviews conducted during batting practice. The occasional in-the-moment spotlight after a milestone was reached such as hitting a grand slam on a rookie's first at bat, retiring a record number of consecutive batters over several games, or breaking some obscure batting record held since the turn of the *last* century.

She'd also done webcasts to show a more personal side of the Goliaths family. Interviews at players' favorite restaurants. A tour of Alcatraz with Johnny 'The Monk' Scottsdale. She'd even kneaded sourdough with Marco Santiago down at Fisherman's Wharf as a way of showing the players enjoying some of San Francisco's popular attractions. And one of her favorite segments was filming Nathan Cooper at Golden Gate Park, playing his guitar and singing a love song for his fiancée Annabelle Jones.

But shopping for baby furniture with a camera crew in tow? That was taking the whole "We Are Goliaths, We Are Family" slogan too far.

"I'm sure no one wants to see Bryce and me pick out a changing table or argue over cloth versus disposable diapers."

"You'd be surprised." Steve grinned as if he knew something she didn't.

"Look, I'm all for making our announcement public." Hopefully Bryce would be able to break the news to his daughter first. "But I don't want it to overshadow the progress he's made on the field."

Steve just nodded, as if he were considering her words.

"I know we pride ourselves on bringing the game home to the fans." She knew what her job really was. "But we have to keep the focus on the game. As much as we enjoy teasing Bryce about his hair, it's his performance on the field that makes anyone even care about what kind of shampoo he uses and whether or not he's about to become a father."

"But they do care." Steve placed a gentle hand on her shoulder. "They want to be a part of your lives."

"A glimpse. They only want to see a glimpse into our lives." Rachel didn't want to turn her marriage and her pregnancy into a reality show. "They don't need to know what brand of breast pump I ultimately end up with."

Did she just say 'breast pump?' To her boss? Why the hell not? On a day where she'd watched a young player get a blow job in an elevator, there wasn't much more to be embarrassed about.

At his raised eyebrows, she backpedalled. "Look. I'm all for bringing the fans up to speed with the baby. It's not like I'll be able to hide it from them in a few months, if not weeks, anyway. But I don't want to make too big of a deal about it. Really. I'll post baby pictures, but no ultrasounds. And there is absolutely no way I'm having a camera, any kind of camera, in the delivery room."

"That's fair. But if this Philadelphia problem gets any bigger, we might need you to ramp up the excitement over the baby."

"Bryce needs to tell his daughter first." Rachel stood her ground. "She doesn't need to find out she's going to be a big sister from a webcast."

"Bryce has a daughter?"

"Yes. From his first marriage. She's nine and lives in Pittsburgh. I haven't met her yet."

She looked forward to meeting the little girl. Her mother? Not so much.

* * * *

Bryce entered the clubhouse to the sounds of Aerosmith blasting above male laughter and ribbing. Poor Ryan Fletcher was getting the full locker-room experience. But instead of making stuff up to impress the other guys, he'd had to endure repeated playbacks of the surveillance video that had caught him in the act.

At least it would help his case. No one would see the chick from the bar as an innocent victim. If anything, it looked like Ryan was the one taken advantage of. Other than the final moments, it didn't look like he'd been too comfortable getting a little love in an elevator.

He looked even more uncomfortable by the loud music, reminding him of the experience, and the teasing by his teammates.

When he saw Bryce walk over to his spot a few lockers down, Ryan looked up at him with eyes that begged for a rescue.

"Hey." Bryce gave a friendly nod, acknowledging the kid's pain.

"I suppose everyone knows what happened, huh?" Ryan looked defeated. "No keeping it with the Philadelphia police department."

"The story broke before we even landed. Rachel had seen dozens of rumors while waiting to pick me up from the airport. Many of them insinuated that her husband was involved."

"Oh man, I'm sorry." Ryan's face got even redder at the mention of Rachel. "The last thing I wanted was to cause trouble for anyone. So, does she know the whole story?"

"She knows the parts that were mine to tell." Bryce came over and sat down next to him. "She knows my part in the whole thing. That I was questioned as a potential witness, and that I believed you when you said nothing happened when you got to the room."

"Nothing happened. I swear." Poor kid looked like he was going to be sick. "Did she believe you?"

"Yeah. She did." Bryce wondered why Ryan was so concerned with what Rachel believed. "The early reports were pretty vague. Only linking my name and 'sexual assault.' But she knows I'd never... And she has faith in this team. She was relieved to hear that it was a misunderstanding, brought about by too much alcohol, and that none of her players are—you know—rapists."

"Oh, hell," Ryan said. "I can't believe I got myself into this mess. And I dragged you, your wife, and the whole damned team into it."

"Look, we've all been there. Just trying to have a good time."

"Yeah, but have you had the police involved?"

Lawyers, yes. Police, no.

"Hey, one of the things you'll learn in the big leagues is how to be more selective." How could he explain this so a kid, a pretty raw one at that, would understand? "It's like when you step up to the plate the first few times. Every pitch looks so fat and juicy, you just can't help but swing away. But with experience, you start to figure out which ones you can hit, and which ones to lay off."

Ryan nodded, an expression of understanding spreading across his young features.

"Same thing with women." Man, when did Bryce get to be the wise old veteran? "At first, they all look spectacular. Hotter than anything you ever even dreamed of in the minors. But you've got to be careful. You've got to learn how to sit on a pitch, or in this case, a come-on, and only take the ones you can do something with."

"I just hope I get another chance." Ryan sank into the folding chair in front of his locker. "With hitting, I mean. I'm done with women. Especially the kind of women who would go up to a hotel room with a guy they just met." A pained look passed over Ryan's face. "I guess I shouldn't judge. I mean, I did invite her up to my room."

"True."

"It's just that I didn't feel right about leaving her there in the bar, all by herself." He leaned over, his forearms resting on twitching knees. "Her friends had already abandoned her for, you know, the other guys who were there. And I couldn't just put her in a cab. Who knows what would have happened to her."

"So you invited her up to your room?"

"Yeah. And she was pretty enthusiastic. As you, and everyone else, could see." He exhaled and raked his hands through his hair. "But once we got to the room, I had second thoughts. And by the time I could work my nerve up to tell her I'd changed my mind, she was passed out on the bed. Naked."

"Only it's your word against hers."

"Yeah. And that video makes my insistence that nothing happened seem like a lie."

"It also makes it clear she was a willing participant."

"But she was in no shape to participate, you know…" Ryan searched for the right words. "She wasn't exactly making good decisions."

Couldn't argue there. "Look. I know some people will think the worst. Of you. Of her. Of professional athletes. Hell, some people will think the worst of our whole culture. You've just got to live with what you actually did, and your intentions."

"That's the thing. I wanted to. I had every intention of following through." He lowered his voice, and leaned closer so only Bryce could hear the rest of what he had to say. "Until the elevator. She came on a little too strong. And I couldn't help but think that something wasn't quite right with the situation."

"You think she set you up?" Bryce's blood began to boil. "You think she had this planned before she even walked into the bar?"

"No. No. That's not what I mean." Ryan looked around, as if he was checking to see if their teammates would be too busy getting ready for the game to listen in on their conversation. "It just seemed too easy, you know? I haven't always had the best luck with girls. Then all of a sudden, I've got this really hot chick who can't even wait until we're in my room to…get busy."

The way the kid blushed, Bryce would think he was sixteen and recalling his first make out session in the backseat of his parents' minivan.

"Maybe I just wanted my first time to be… I don't know. Special."

Whoa. Did the kid just say his first time?

"Yeah, I know. How can a guy make it to the majors and still be a…" Another glance about the clubhouse. "Technically, I'm still a virgin."

When Bryce recovered from the shock, he patted the rookie on the back.

"Look. What we need, more than anything, is to get the focus back where it belongs. On the game." Bryce had learned a long time ago that the only thing he could control in this life was his approach to the game. When the rest of his life started getting to be too much, all he had to do was step into the batting cage. A few dozen swings and all was right with the world again.

At least that had been his go-to stress relief. Until he met Rachel. She was better than any workout at clearing his head. And not just when they were in bed. Just being in the same room with her seemed to center him somehow. He could be having the worst day, and just seeing her pretty smile would make him forget all about whatever was troubling him.

After talking to the police in Philadelphia, the only thing he could think about was coming home to Rachel. Taking her hand, looking into her eyes, and letting the whole world just fall away. Only she'd been affected by the accusations, and he'd been the one to comfort and protect. He'd had to assure her that they were stronger than any false accusations and rumors. They were a team, the two of them, and no one—not the media, the public, or a messed-up groupie who didn't know the name of a guy she'd gone down on in an elevator, so she'd used the only name she knew, his—no one would come between them.

Bryce grabbed his glove to go out and take infield practice. He was about seven steps from his locker when he heard his phone buzz from inside his locker. He took two more steps before realizing it could be Hailey.

The phone stopped buzzing just as he reached it. Damn. Jillian's number was at the top of the missed calls list. Bryce hit redial only to have his call go straight to voice mail.

"Hey, sorry I missed your call. I was on my way out to the field. Call me right back."

He paced in front of his locker, staring helplessly at his phone, hoping she'd call back before he got fined for being late for warmups.

The alert for a voicemail popped up. They must have been leaving messages at the same time.

"I thought you wanted to talk to Hailey. Guess it couldn't have been that important." Jillian sounded put out. But then again, he couldn't recall a conversation with her that hadn't been an inconvenience on her part.

He waited about ten seconds before dialing her number. Again, it went straight to voice mail. After the third try, he gave up. Bryce tossed the phone into his locker and headed out to the field, more frustrated than he'd been in a long time.

Nothing like fielding a few grounders to get his head back on straight. By the time his turn for batting practice came up, Bryce had put his annoyance with his ex-wife behind him. He was able to set an example for the rookie by leaving his personal problems back in the clubhouse and only bringing his A game onto the field.

Fletcher must have taken some of his words to heart, because he was raking the shit out of the ball in BP. Bryce was proud of the kid. He'd taken a messed up situation and channeled it into his game. He just hoped he'd get a chance to showcase that fire in a game soon.

By the bottom of the seventh inning, the rookie got his chance. The Goliaths were up by two runs heading into the top of the inning, but the opposing team managed to tie the game before the Goliaths were able to record the final out.

A leadoff walk, sacrifice bunt, and an infield hit put Goliaths runners at the corners with the pitcher's spot coming up. Javier had seen Fletcher's impressive performance in batting practice and took a chance. After two quick strikes, he called for time and stepped out of the box. Fletcher glanced over at Bryce, who made a motion for the kid to take a deep breath. Bryce hoped he'd remember their conversation about laying off the hot and fast ones.

The rookie stepped back into the batter's box. He looked a little more relaxed. And confident. The next pitch was a little high. Just like the first two he'd chased out of the strike zone. A ball in the dirt and the count was tied at two balls and two strikes.

Come on kid. You got this.

Bryce closed his eyes but he could hear the contact. He looked up just in time to see the ball sail over the left field wall. A three-run homer put the game back in the Goliaths' favor. The dugout cleared to congratulate the rookie as he crossed home plate.

Bryce gave his teammate a hearty pat on the back. "What did I tell you about being a little more selective?"

"I guess you know what's up." Fletcher grinned, the excitement of his first big league homer showing on his face.

The Goliaths ended up winning the game and Rachel was on hand to interview the rookie. A small sliver of jealousy was overshadowed by pride in his young teammate.

Chapter 19

"Congratulations, Ryan, on your first major league homerun." Rachel didn't have to fake a smile. "I have a feeling it won't be your last."

"Thank you." The rookie infielder had the right combination of humility and pride. "I'm just glad I could come through at a time when my team needed it."

"A team can always use a three-run homer." Rachel laughed, so grateful to be talking about the on-field action and not the video she'd seen earlier that day. "But it's especially exciting in the late innings of a tie ballgame."

"I tried not to put too much pressure on myself. Tried not to think of the situation." He seemed to grow more confident as the interview went on. "I got some advice recently, about being patient. Sometimes when a guy comes up, he wants to make a big impression right away. Prove to himself and the team that being here isn't a mistake."

"Sounds like good advice."

"Yeah, well, when the World Series MVP talks, a smart man listens."

"Bryce does know his baseball." Rachel felt her cheeks warm just a little. Maybe someday she wouldn't feel like her relationship with Bryce was somewhat scandalous.

"I'm just honored to be able to work with him. Have him as a teammate."

A sudden flood of emotion filled her. Pride was only part of it.

"I hope I'll be able to learn from him for years to come."

"Just as long as you don't try to take his spot." Rachel could tease now, as Bryce's game was turning around. He'd had a great road trip. The pressure of the contract seemed to be lifting. She liked to think she was helping get his mind off the incredible salary he was pulling in and focus on the game, their marriage, and their growing family.

"I'm more of a third baseman," Ryan admitted. "But I can fill in at any of the infield spots if needed."

"I look forward to seeing more of you on the field." Rachel gave a polite nod to signal the interview was coming to an end, but before she could send it back up to the broadcast booth, Bryce appeared with a shaving cream pie which he shoved in Ryan's face.

Ah, the age-old prank welcoming the young player into the exclusive club of major league home run hitters. Nothing like a face full of Barbasol to make a guy feel successful.

Marco Santiago came up and gave him a pat on the back with one hand and offered a towel with the other. Ryan wiped his face, removing most of the white foam, but not the grin that made him look even younger than his twenty-four years.

With a final congratulations, Rachel smiled and signed off from the interview. Carl switched the camera off and started packing his equipment away. Another night at the ballpark had come to an end. The players would return to the clubhouse to shower and then make themselves available for the beat writers and national networks. She would wait until Bryce was released before they could go home.

Rachel relaxed her shoulders and let out a tired sigh. It had been a long couple of days, and they were barely two months into the season. She hoped she could make it through the next four or five months without becoming too exhausted. Especially as her pregnancy advanced, she wondered how she could maintain her energy level without the aid of caffeine.

She stifled a yawn before noticing that Ryan Fletcher was still standing in front of the dugout. He didn't seem to be in any hurry to hit the shower and wash off the evidence of his acceptance on the team.

"Um, excuse me Ms. Parker... Or is it Mrs. Baxter?"

"You can call me Rachel." The kid had a genuineness and she couldn't help but like him.

"Okay, Rachel." His cheeks turned a deep red. "I...uh... I wanted to thank you. You know, for not mentioning what happened in Philadelphia. I'm sure you've seen the video."

"I was shown the video." She felt bad for him. She also couldn't help but wonder if a similar video existed somewhere of her and Bryce. There was that one stairwell in the hotel in Dallas after the Goliaths had won the World Series... "But I think most of our viewers are much more interested in your first major league home run than anything else."

"I'd like to think so, but..." He shifted uncomfortably, his large frame all arms and legs, reminding her of a puppy who hadn't quite grown into his feet. "Anyway, I'm glad you didn't ask any of those kinds of questions. Especially since… Well, I wouldn't want you to think I was the kind of guy who'd, you know, take advantage of a woman like that."

"I'd hope not." She wanted to believe the best about their Goliaths family. "Besides, it looked like she was more than a willing partner."

"See that's the thing." He rubbed the back of his neck. "By the time I realized she was so drunk, I didn't know what to do about it. So, I kind of hung out in the bathroom, hoping she'd just fall asleep. Only she took off all her clothes first and flopped down on the bed. I covered her as best I could, and I swear, I did not have sex with that woman."

"I believe you." And she did. "I hope others will, too. If you're innocent, then you shouldn't have to deal with this anymore."

"But we both know this won't be the end of it." Ryan toed the dirt in front of the dugout. "Some people will always believe the worst. They'll always question me."

"Then maybe you should come up with a statement. Honest, concise, and heartfelt. Just like you told me. I think if you hold your head high, go about your business—the business of baseball—with dignity and respect, you'll be fine."

"I appreciate your faith in me." He looked up at her with a glimmer of hope in his eyes. "Especially since…Well, you're one of my favorite reporters. And you're married to my teammate."

The darkening of his cheeks only made him seem more genuine. Or maybe he was just incredibly charming. Again, she noticed the resemblance between him and Bryce. They could almost be brothers. A protective instinct rose in her.

"Look, here's what you should say, when the question comes up." She wanted to help him. As long as his story was true. "Although the video shows what looks like an act of foreplay, there was no further sexual contact. The reason the young woman doesn't remember what happened once we got to the room is that nothing happened."

"I think I can say that."

"If they keep pressing, you'll want to mention something about her not being able to give consent due to her level of intoxication."

"I don't want to make her look bad."

"The girl didn't even remember your name," Rachel reminded him. "She went to the police and dragged my husband's name through the mud."

"I'm so sorry about that." He looked almost pained. "I'm just glad you and Bryce are solid. You have faith in him, and won't let this come between you two."

If he only knew how close she'd been to believing the worst.

"You're kind of an inspiration." He flashed a shy grin. "You and Bryce. I just hope that someday I'll meet a woman like you. Someone who will be strong enough to withstand the rumors. Someone who would make it impossible to even consider doing anything rumor worthy."

Ah, to be so young and idealistic.

"Well, you probably won't meet a woman like that in a bar."

"Or an elevator." Ryan Fletcher replaced his cap and retreated to the clubhouse.

Rachel couldn't wait to get home. It had been a long day. A long couple of days. She just hoped this whole incident would blow over, but she couldn't help but think Ryan's homerun would only add fuel to the media fire. If he remained firmly planted on the bench, the story would fade a lot quicker. But an up-and-coming star might sell more copies or ad-clicks or airtime. And throw in a sex-tape, even if it was taken from a hotel security camera, it would create even more buzz.

At least she didn't have to worry about Bryce being a part of it. Sure his name had been mentioned in the initial report, and she knew some people would never keep reading beyond the headline until they uncovered actual facts, but that was their problem, not hers.

Her problem was that she had initially jumped on the bandwagon of doubt. She'd believed the worst before Bryce had a chance to even give his side of the story. She'd let his reputation speak louder than his actions since they'd married. She'd let her own insecurities override what she'd come to know about the man he'd shown himself to be.

Bryce emerged from the clubhouse, his hair glistening from his shower, and whatever sponsored product he used to make his hair so soft and shiny. A good wife would know these things. But when he smiled at her, she forgot her own name, let alone what brand of shampoo either one of them used.

"You weren't too hard on my boy tonight were you?" Bryce put his arm around her waist.

"Did you adopt him?" she teased. "Because that's one of those joint decisions we should make together."

"Like purchasing a new vehicle?"

"I like the car, okay. I didn't mean to freak out about it." She was starting to relax a bit and enjoy Bryce's playful side. She had come to realize that the more he joked about something, the more it meant to him.

"I don't know, maybe I should have gotten you a minivan."

"No. Definitely not. Unless you do plan on adopting a few rookies."

"We'd need a bigger place." Bryce grinned. He was in his element. "Although from what I've heard, Fletcher is a pro at sleeping in chairs."

When Rachel gave him a puzzled look, he explained. "From what he told me, when he found that girl passed out on his bed, he slept in the chair. It's a miracle he was able to even lift the bat, let alone crush one over the fence."

"Can we not discuss the incident in the hotel anymore?" She was sick of the subject. Now that she knew it didn't affect her husband or her family, she would rather talk about anything else. Including minivans, school districts, and even white picket fences.

"What incident?" Bryce pulled her even closer. "Let's go home, babe."

Home. She was finally starting to believe that they could make a home together. A shelter from the outside world. A place where they could each be who they were, not who they pretended to be for the camera.

* * * *

It was too early in the season to feel this tired. Bryce leaned back into the plush leather seat of Rachel's new Range Rover. She'd insisted on driving, and he was wiped out enough to let her. Besides, it felt like a truce of sorts, her accepting the car. Accepting the idea of being married to him.

Maybe he was the one who was coming around. It hadn't been that long ago that he'd vowed to never get married again. To never have more kids. And here he was in a rushed marriage with a baby on the way. His career was at its peak and the idea of settling down was actually starting to appeal to him.

Especially after the fiasco in Philly.

He felt bad for Fletcher. The guy had been in the big leagues for a little over a month, and people weren't going to remember his first home run. They'd remember that stupid elevator video. The guy could hit 780 home runs and people would still talk about the elevator. At least that would be the first thing to pop up in a Google search.

And the kid had never even gotten laid.

Bryce must have chuckled out loud because Rachel turned to him and asked, "What's so funny?"

"Nothing, actually." He looked over at his wife. His *wife*. She'd pulled her hair back into a loose ponytail and her earrings dangled from her earlobes. She was beautiful. And she was his. He'd do well to make sure she stayed his. "I was just thinking about stuff."

"Did you ever get to talk to your daughter?"

"No. I kept getting Jillian's voice mail." He exhaled in frustration. The woman had no problem getting a hold of him if she needed something. "I'll try again tomorrow."

"I told my boss about the baby." Rachel turned her attention back to the road. "I told him we wanted to keep it quiet until your daughter knows. But he wants us to really embrace the pregnancy. Get the fans involved."

"He wants what?" He must be more tired than he'd thought. "Get the fans involved in what exactly?"

"You know, just get them excited for us. Put updates on my social media pages. Invite them to share tips, maybe bring a camera along to Babies"R"Us. Nothing too invasive."

"Cameras?"

"I told him I'd have to run it by you. If you're uncomfortable with the idea, we can scale it back."

"I'm comfortable with whatever you're comfortable with." This was her thing, the media. Television. He'd be perfectly happy to just play ball. But he knew it didn't work that way. If it weren't for the television contracts, he wouldn't be pulling in the kind of change he was making. If the fans didn't feel a part of the game, they wouldn't plunk down their hard-earned money on tickets, T-shirts and jerseys, and even game-used batting helmets.

"I'm not sure how much I'm comfortable with," Rachel admitted as she pulled into the parking garage. "I mean, I get that the promotional theme this year is 'We are Goliaths. We are Family.' But that doesn't mean I want to invite them all to my baby shower, virtual or otherwise."

"What's a virtual baby shower?"

"I don't know. Something my producer came up with. I think he overestimates the fans' interest in all this." She shut off the engine and looked a Bryce. "I'm not having a camera in the delivery room. Or anyone other than you and the doctor and the nurses. No contests to name the baby. It's a child, not a promo opportunity."

"I don't know. Maybe they would do a prenatal care awareness night."

"You can't be serious?"

"I was joking, but actually, it's not a bad idea. Maybe pair with the local hospitals and clinics. I'm sure there is a need in the community for low-cost prenatal care."

"I think most of the promotions are already set, but I'll mention it." She gave him a watery smile as she reached for her seatbelt. "We're really doing this? We're really going to have a baby. Together."

"Absolutely together." Bryce reached for her hand and gave her a reassuring squeeze. "Rachel, I—"

He almost said "I love you," but he was afraid she wasn't ready to hear it. Funny. He'd always thought he'd be the one to bolt at the thought of falling in love.

"You're doing it again." Rachel shook her head. "You're laughing at some private joke. You want to let me in on it?"

"Someday." Bryce leaned over and gave her a quick kiss on the cheek. "It's kind of hard to explain."

Besides, he didn't want to say it for the first time sitting in the parking garage. No. He'd have to make it extra special. Their wedding had been rushed, and kind of a blur. He'd thought the proposal was romantic, and so did the forty thousand fans who'd witnessed it, but Rachel had been more embarrassed than impressed. He'd have to do a much better job of this.

Chapter 20

The home stand went all too quickly. They'd played nine games in ten days. Won six of them. It was starting to look like the Goliaths had shaken off their World Series hangover and were getting back to championship form. Bryce had been playing a lot better and he credited Rachel for most of it.

Rachel. Sometimes he'd sit in the dugout and take a deep breath, realizing just how lucky he was to have her. How lucky he was, period.

It was late in the game on the final night before they would take off on another road trip, this time to Washington D.C. and then Pittsburgh. He looked out at the packed ballpark. The night sky was crystal clear, without so much as a trace of fog. A few seagulls were swirling around, not yet ready to make their assault on the stands in their search for leftover popcorn and garlic fries.

Bryce leaned back against the wall of the dugout, stretching his legs in front of him. In the sanctuary of the dugout, he realized he wasn't a screw-up. He'd managed to actually make something of himself. And he brought a lot of joy to people around him. His teammates had come to rely on his defense at shortstop, and he had become more consistent with his hitting, enough that he'd been named National League Player of the Week.

He wondered what his mother thought of him now. Did she still think he was out of control? Too hard to handle? Did she ever watch his games? Was she ever sorry she'd left?

At least Rachel had stuck around. She'd even come to trust him. They had settled into a comfortable routine. It was a lot more comfortable than he'd ever envisioned. He always thought he'd feel trapped by marriage. He certainly had the first time around. And while both marriages had started under similar circumstances, they could not be more different.

He enjoyed spending time with Rachel. Instead of itching to get out of the city, he was dreading this road trip. The only thing that made it bearable was knowing he would see his daughter. It had taken three days before Jillian had her call at a time when he'd been able to talk. She didn't sound terribly excited about the idea of having a little brother or sister, but she probably figured she'd never see him or her. Never get to play with her sibling.

That was something he would have to work on. Maybe he could convince Rachel to travel with him. At least until the child started school. But maybe by then, he'd be ready to retire. No. He couldn't imagine life without baseball.

And it was getting harder and harder to imagine life without Rachel.

He still hadn't told her he loved her. He'd come close several times. When they were in bed together, basking in the afterglow of the most amazing sex they'd ever had. He would run his hand over the increasingly roundness of her belly. But something held him back. He tried to convince himself it was that she wasn't ready. The truth was he wasn't ready to find out whether or not she returned his feelings. In case she didn't.

It was time to get back to work. Bryce grabbed his batting helmet and his favorite bat, and stepped into the on-deck circle to take his warm up swings and time the pitcher. He seemed to have lost a little bit of velocity. Bryce planned to take advantage if he could.

The second baseman, Gavin Owens, bunted to put the leadoff man in scoring position. The Goliaths clung to a one-run lead and Bryce knew that if he couldn't get the runner home, Santiago was behind him. They'd had a team meeting a few days ago. Javier had realized that a lot of them were pressing, trying too hard. The pressure of defending the title weighing on all of them. Then he'd proceeded to look each man in the eye and remind them of some small way in which they'd contributed to that title. When every returning player had been recognized, Javier made a point of staring Bryce down and stating that no one man was responsible for the trophy that now stood in a place of honor in the club level of the ballpark. No one man had earned the rings they all had sitting in a safe deposit box or the top dresser drawer. It took twenty-five of them to pull it off. And all twenty-five of those guys had done their part. Not all at once, but that was the beauty of the game. The beauty of this team. They could and did pick each other up.

Bryce relaxed as he stepped into the batter's box. He would do his best, just like his teammates behind him. The first pitch was a little high, and

Bryce took ball one. Just as he'd thought, it was a little slower that the last at bat, when he'd grounded out to third.

Digging in, he prepared for the next pitch. A fastball, right in his wheelhouse, and Bryce crushed it just down the left field line. A two-run lead energized the ballpark, the atmosphere of last October had returned.

Life was good. Life was definitely good.

Marco Santiago doubled and then the game broke wide open.

Rachel was ready at the top of the dugout steps after the game, her trusty cameraman, Carl, ready for the post-game interview. She could have picked any one of a half dozen guys, but she eyed Bryce with that special gleam in her eyes. The gleam that meant she was going to do her job with joy and verve and a kind of energy that made the win seem all that sweeter.

"You really set the spark that got the team rolling in the late innings." Rachel sounded almost giddy. And why not? The team was back on track. They were back on track. And Bryce couldn't help but think the two were related. "What do you attribute to the quick turn around? Just a few weeks ago, it looked like you guys were wiped out. Like the extended season had taken its toll on all of you."

"I think we just had to take a step back and realize what we have here." Bryce ran his left hand through his hair, the weight of his gold band sending a little shiver across his scalp. "We've accomplished something a lot of guys wait a lifetime for and never achieve."

"It is important to take the time to enjoy the moment."

"Yes. But once the next season starts, the moment is over." He longed to reach for her. But the camera was rolling, and some things were private. "It's time to work towards the next great moment."

"Tonight it looked like you really believe there will be more great moments."

"Absolutely."

Rachel tucked a strand of her gorgeous red hair behind her ear. Her cheeks darkened to a fresh pink. They'd had their share of moments together, just the two of them. And he really believed they would have a lifetime of moments ahead of them.

"The best of times aren't behind us." He did reach for her hand now. "I think we can look forward to many more unforgettable experiences."

"You do have a lot of great baseball left in you." She tried to pull her hand away, but Bryce refused to let go.

"I think we've got plenty of game left." He wanted to say it. More than anything, he wanted to tell her how he felt about her. About them and the family they were creating. But in front of the camera wasn't the place to confess his feelings for the first time. He'd proposed publically because he knew she wouldn't say no, not in front of everyone.

And if he professed his undying love for her on camera, she would say it in return. But would she mean it? That wasn't something he wanted to wonder about. When she said it, he wanted it to be one thousand percent true.

* * * *

Rachel's heart was pounding. Sure, she was excited after the win and she was happy for Bryce. His game was back on track and she had a feeling it would stay that way for the rest of the season. But she also felt like there was something else going on. He was going to say something. Something big. And in front of everyone.

"We have a lot to look forward to, not just on the field." Bryce had a twinkle in his eye. He was up to something. He stepped closer, put his arm around her, and faced the camera. "We have some exciting news. We're expanding the Goliaths' family with a player to be named later."

He leaned over and gave her a kiss on the cheek, his right hand moving to caress her baby bump.

The cheer from the crowd was almost overwhelming. Even more than when he'd proposed. That had been a complete surprise. She'd spent the last ten days trying to figure out how to break the news to her fans, and Bryce had just run with it. It was spontaneous and genuine—just like Bryce.

Her heart swelled. Oh how she loved this man. And she knew she needed to tell him. But she couldn't just whisper it in his ear as he drifted off to sleep. With Bryce, there was only one way to do things. All out.

Other than the time she threw up on his Corvette, she hadn't done any grand gestures. She would have to come up with something spectacular. Something to show him just how much he meant to her.

After he'd showered and changed into his street clothes, Rachel handed Bryce the keys.

"You trust me?" He grinned, knowing how hard it had been for her to give up control, or at least control of her vehicle. He'd humored her and let her drive, saying he didn't like to drive in the city.

"Yeah." Funny how he made light of the issue. Trust was never easy for her. It would be easy to blame her cheating ex, but that was only part of it. And even though Bryce's image had been that of a carefree playboy, it wasn't entirely about him either.

Rachel had never really trusted her place in the world. She'd never really fit in with her family. They'd tried to make her feel included, but she was just…different. Her mother, half sister, and stepfather were a unit. A team. And she was there on the sidelines, like the fan who stood at the edge of the stands hoping for the slightest acknowledgement.

Bryce held the passenger side door open for her and helped her step up into the SUV. She sank back into the luxurious leather seats. Had she really freaked out about getting such a generous gift? Yes. She had.

She had seven days to figure out how to make it all up to him. He would go to Washington D.C. and then Pittsburgh. Then he'd be home for eight days before leaving for the next ten.

"Are you sure you can't come with me?" he asked as he pulled into the parking garage.

"I have a doctor's appointment on Wednesday." It was just easier to schedule for days she wasn't working. And he didn't need to come to all of the prenatal appointments. "Plus, now that we've made the announcement, I'm sure I'll have plenty to keep myself busy with responding to tweets, e-mails, and Facebook posts congratulating us."

"You know you can hire someone to manage your social media."

"Yeah, but then it's not genuine." She had a love-hate relationship with the time-consuming aspect of social media. But sometimes, something a fan took the time to post made it all worthwhile. "People can tell when you're faking it."

"Honey, you don't ever have to fake anything." Bryce reached over and ran his hand along her thigh, sending shivers up her spine. "I'll make sure of it."

She laughed because she knew he was talking about sex. And yes, with him, she'd never had to fake it. But outside of the bedroom, she felt like she faked everything. Her marriage, her job—hell her whole life had been one big fake smile.

She followed Bryce to their bedroom, where she pretended that she was okay with the fact that Bryce had only married her because of the baby. Because of her job. And maybe even a little bit to help his job. He had been playing better since the wedding, and he often gave her credit when asked about the quick turnaround by other reporters.

And the fans ate up his new image. As much as they'd loved the bad boy bachelor, they swooned even more over his "Sorry, ladies, I'm a married man, now" act. He'd become the golden boy once again.

And in the morning she would smile and wave as he boarded the bus for the airport. She'd pretend she belonged with the other wives as they gave goodbye kisses and best wishes. She'd pretend she couldn't hear their whispered "I love you's," while wondering what it would be like to hear those words herself someday. Or to say them.

Chapter 21

After settling into his hotel, Bryce took a cab over to his ex-wife's house. He was looking forward to seeing his daughter. His ex-wife had been, well, not exactly pleasant, but she'd been less hostile than usual, so he hoped that meant she wasn't going to cause too much trouble.

He paid the driver and walked up to the oversized house. What did two people need with 4,500 square feet of living space? When he'd lived there, he could go hours, if not days, without crossing paths with Jillian. He'd had his bedroom, bathroom, and man cave. Jillian had the rest of the house.

He rang the bell three times before remembering he still had a key. Maybe they were out by the pool. It was a warm evening, so why not?

"Hello," he called as he stepped into the foyer. "Jillian? Hailey? I let myself in when you didn't answer."

Nothing. He headed toward the backyard, but there was no one out there. He went back into the kitchen, but there was nothing but an empty bottle of wine on the counter. It was early, but maybe she'd been nursing it for a week.

He called out again, but got no response. He searched the downstairs and found it empty. With growing trepidation, he headed up the stairs.

Hailey's room was empty. Not even a school bag tossed on the floor. Either the maid had come that afternoon or no one had been in there in a few days. Odd, since Hailey still had a few weeks left of school before getting out for the summer. And her theater camp. He'd have to get the exact dates from Jillian. He was determined to have Hailey come and spend some time with him in San Francisco over the summer. They had two ten-game home stands that would give them plenty of time to spend together. And he'd definitely want her over the Christmas holidays. Maybe take her up to Tahoe and enjoy the snow.

Bryce was about to give up on them being home when he heard a loud noise coming from Jillian's bedroom. A crash, like a lamp being knocked over or something.

Cautiously, he pushed the door open. "Are you all right?"

"Go to hell." Jillian stood next to the bed, watching half a bottle of red wine soak into the carpet. The lamp and a broken wineglass had been knocked over as well. A mound of used tissues was piled up on the floor about two feet away from the empty wastebasket.

"Jillian, what's wrong?" He was used to walking on eggshells around her, but tonight she seemed extra fragile. "Where's Hailey?"

"Hailey?" She looked up at him, her features twisted in a painful grimace. "She's...at a friend's. They have a school project they're working on and it was just...easier...for them to do it there."

For a minute there, he'd been sure something was wrong with Hailey. Breathing a sigh of relief, he now focused on Jillian. There was definitely something wrong with Jillian. It wasn't like her to go through a bottle and a half of wine all by herself on a weekday afternoon. But then again, how would he know? He hadn't seen her since the end of January.

"I guess you forgot I was coming tonight?"

"No. I didn't forget. I can never forget." Her voice sounded hollow as she reached for the remains of the wine.

"Let me help you with that." Bryce was quicker and he upended the bottle with maybe a quarter of it left inside. "Where do you keep your towels? We should clean this up before it stains."

He knew it was too late. He'd have to add new carpet to the ever-increasing list of things Jillian needed.

"Leave it. I don't care." She grabbed the bottle out of his hand and started to take a drink.

"Maybe you should take it easy on the wine." He took the bottle back from her.

"Fuck you." She reached for the wine, but he held it out of her reach.

"You talk like that in front of our daughter?"

Jillian just laughed. A bitter sound that told him she was itching for a fight. At least Hailey wasn't around to witness it.

"How much have you had to drink today, Jillian?" He knew it would piss her off, but he wasn't leaving until he understood the situation around here. Was this a one-time only thing, brought about by his return and his recent announcement? Or was this something Hailey lived with every day?

"Why do you care?" She made another weak attempt at grabbing the bottle from him, but he had the advantage of height and sobriety over her. "You never gave a shit about me."

"I care, Jillian. You were my wife." Although neither of them had taken their marriage very seriously. "You're the mother of my child and I need to know you're both okay."

"We're fine." She fell back against the bed. "You don't need to worry about us."

"Well, I do. I know I haven't always been around." He sat down on the bed, a few feet away from where his ex-wife lay. "But I want to work on that. I want to spend more time with Hailey. When she's out of school, I'd like to have her come to San Francisco. Get to know Rachel."

And yeah, get to know him a little better.

"No." Jillian sat up, but couldn't stay upright. "You can't have her."

"She's my daughter, too." Maybe he was an idiot for even trying to have this conversation with Jillian now. But he knew it would take more than one request. "I know I've let you raise her your way, according to your rules. And she's a great kid. But she's growing up. She needs her father more as she gets older."

"Too bad you're not her father." Jillian's bitterness took on a whole new level.

"What did you say?" He must have heard her wrong.

She lifted herself off the bed, sitting up so she could look him in the eye.

"I said, too bad you're not her father." She jumped up and ran for the bathroom.

He could hear her throwing up. If what she said was true, he felt like he could be right there next to her. Not Hailey's father? Had she fucking lied to him? Trapped him for eighteen long months in hell? Taken him for a small fortune?

He waited until he heard the toilet flush before making a slow walk toward the bathroom.

Jillian came out, wiping her mouth with a plush white towel. Her hair was damp from where she must have washed her face, but her eyes were hard.

"I know it's gotta be hard on you to see me married...and with a baby on the way." He knew she'd never loved him, but that didn't mean she'd be happy about sharing him—or his money. "And if you were looking for the one thing you could say that would hurt me the most, well...you hit that one right on the screws."

"I'm not just saying it to hurt you." She tossed the towel toward the hamper and missed. "Hailey isn't your child. You weren't the only man I was with that month and… Well, the timing was wrong."

"The timing was wrong? So you knew she wasn't mine and you married me anyway?" He was reeling. Not just from the shock, but the fact that he could have been that stupid.

"I never thought you'd marry me."

"So what? You were hoping I'd offer you money, make the whole problem go away?"

"Something like that."

He stood there, feeling like he'd just been drilled by a ninety-eight mile an hour fastball, right in the chest.

"Does Hailey know?"

Jillian's eyes welled up with tears and she shook her head. "No. She has no idea."

His anger was understandable, but he also felt huge sense of loss. Even though he hadn't always been around to show it, he loved Hailey. He was proud of her and he couldn't imagine not being a part of her life.

Jillian stumbled toward the bed, and she'd probably pass out soon.

Bryce took the bottle of wine to the bathroom and poured the contents down the drain. He noticed a bottle of prescription drugs on the counter. A popular anti-anxiety medication that probably shouldn't be mixed with alcohol.

He had to get out of there. Before he said something to Jillian they'd both regret.

Jillian was passed out on the bed. Still in her designer jeans, but he wasn't about to undress her. He folded the bedspread over her and left the room.

He paused at Hailey's door. He could be furious with Jillian; he could lawyer up and restructure the divorce settlement or maybe even have their marriage annulled, and then he could cut her off financially. But anything he did to Jillian would only hurt Hailey. And DNA or not, she was his responsibility. Especially if her mother was as messed up as he now feared.

Bryce stepped inside the room of a nine-year-old girl who needed his protection. He flipped on the light, to get a better look at the environment where his little girl spent so much of her time.

The room had been professionally decorated. The delicate pink walls bore a hand-painted mural of fairy princesses. But the bulletin board over her desk had magazine cutouts of some boy band. He had no idea who the little prepubescent punks were, but what the hell were they doing pinned up on his baby girl's wall? He looked at the wall next to her bed. There was a whole collage of pictures. He stepped closer to examine what pop culture idol was the last thing she looked at before she fell asleep.

It was him. Most of the pictures were from the World Series, but there were some throughout the season. She didn't hate him, after all. Maybe she even looked up to him.

He had to get out of there. There were too many emotions swirling through his mind. And he had a game tomorrow. He couldn't show up at the ballpark this wound up.

He called for a cab and had the driver drop him off at one of the bars he used to frequent when he needed to get away from the pressures of living with Jillian. It wasn't a trendy spot, more of a locals' place. A place where a guy could get a drink and sip in peace. Or he could meet up with friends or new acquaintances. It wasn't a meat market, but it wasn't a monastery either.

Anyway, it wasn't too far from his hotel, but it was far enough that he wouldn't likely run into any of his teammates.

He just wanted a beer. Something to take the edge off. He didn't want to get plastered and end up with his head in the toilet like Jillian.

He downed the first IPA faster than usual. Normally he liked to savor the hoppy brew. But he barely noticed the complex aroma, just let the liquid slide down his throat. He ordered another and tried to take his time, but the fury inside him made him down the bottle like it was a light beer.

After ordering his third beer, he texted Jillian informing her that he'd be at the house at ten A.M. to pick up Hailey. She'd better be ready or there would be hell to pay. He would be taking his daughter to the game and if Jillian had a problem with that, she just might find her funds cut off.

Yeah, he knew it was a low blow, but it was the only thing that his ex-wife understood.

And he really did want to see his daughter. He didn't give a damn if she wasn't really his, except for the way Jillian had fucked him over. And as much as he wanted to get back at his ex, he couldn't do anything to hurt Hailey, who was innocent in the whole thing. And he still wanted to spoil her and protect her and take care of her.

By the fourth beer, Bryce realized he needed backup. Needed someone to talk to while his feelings were still raw. Before they festered and became toxic.

He dialed his teammate. "Yo, Marco! You still awake?"

"Yeah. What's up, Bryce?" Marco sounded concerned, but cool. He was a good dude. He'd sort of taken over the leadership role that Johnny had vacated. "Everything all right?"

"No, man. Everything is not all right." Fuck. He didn't need to drag his left-fielder into his mess. "But, hell, I'm sorry to bother you."

"No. It's all right." Bryce could practically picture his teammate run his fingers through his dark hair. "Where are you?"

Bryce told him, and was relieved when Marco said he'd come. He needed a friend in the worst way. And except for Johnny Scottsdale, Marco had been the one guy he'd been closest too in all his years of professional baseball.

Marco entered the bar, looking a little intimidating. Bryce ordered two more beers even though he knew he should have stopped by now. He didn't know if he was going to talk about what went down tonight, but he needed to have something to do with his hands either way.

With a quick nod, Marco made himself comfortable on the barstool next to Bryce. He took a long pull on his beer and waited for Bryce to talk, or not. It seemed he was cool either way.

"This is good stuff." Marco finally broke the ice after he'd downed about a third of his beer. "Really good."

"Yeah. It's a local brew. Can't get it in California. At least not yet."

"It's a mighty fine brew, but I don't think you called me down here just to try it."

"No." But Bryce didn't even know how to begin telling him what was really going on.

"I thought you were going to spend the evening with your daughter."

"Yeah. Me, too." Too many emotions were swirling through him. Anger. Fear. Resentment. Trepidation. "But my ex had other plans."

"So what are you going to do?"

"I'm going to pick up my daughter tomorrow. Bring her to the ballpark."

"She'll like that." Marco took another sip from his bottle. "I bet you can't wait to show her off."

"If she even shows up." Bryce couldn't hide the bitterness in his voice. "My ex... Oh, she's a real piece of work."

Marco just grunted. Yeah. He got it.

"She lied to me. Deceived me. Flat out screwed me over in the worst way."

"Sorry to hear that."

"I gotta get out of here." Bryce drained his beer. He'd lost count as to how many he'd had. Four? Five? Didn't matter. He couldn't drink enough to forget about the shit Jillian had pulled. He couldn't even drink enough to catch up to her. She'd been pretty messed up. Was this a regular thing, or just because he was in town, newly married and ready to have another child?

Or maybe Rachel's baby was his only child.

Bryce stood up and tossed a few bills on the bar. Marco offered up his own tip and they turned toward the exit. Before they could reach the door, two attractive female fans approached, squealing in recognition.

"Oh my God, you're Bryce Baxter," the blonde screeched.

"And Marco Santiago." The brunette seemed to sigh his teammate's name.

The years of professionalism prompted them both to smile and acknowledge their fans.

"Can we get a picture?" the blonde requested.

Bryce couldn't give a fuck, so he shrugged. Marco was a little more polite, offering his trademark smile.

The girls surrounded them, holding their smartphones at arm's reach, ready for the selfies.

Just before clicking the camera phone, the blonde placed a kiss on Bryce's cheek. They squealed again, stumbling away with "Oh my God" and "Can you believe it?"

Bryce was sick of the whole scene. If he never stepped into another bar in his life, he'd be more than happy. He'd met Jillian in a bar. Look where that had gotten him.

Chapter 22

A slight hangover clouded Bryce's head the next morning. Or maybe it was just lack of sleep and the situation with Jillian that had his stomach turning and his head pounding. He'd texted her saying he'd be there by ten. But since he couldn't sleep, he was ready to head over to her place by a quarter to nine. He'd downed a full bottle of water and two cups of coffee before the cab pulled up to take him to get his daughter.

This time, he paid the driver to wait for him. He rang the bell, but wasn't too surprised when she didn't answer. He unlocked the door, and once again, his instincts told him that something wasn't right. He headed straight to Jillian's room and pushed open the door.

She was passed out on the floor, face down in a pile of vomit. An empty glass of wine was knocked over and the pills he'd seen in the bathroom were scattered across the floor.

Oh fuck.

Bryce rushed to her side, checking her wrist for a pulse. It was weak and erratic, but there.

She was still alive. But he wasn't sure for how long.

He lunged for the phone next to her bed, dialing 911 and praying he wasn't too late.

As soon as the paramedics arrived, he was sent out of the room. He staggered downstairs, and remembered the cab that was still waiting in the driveway. Bryce grabbed his wallet and paid the cabbie for his time, but dismissed him since he didn't think he'd be going anywhere until he knew if Jillian was going to make it.

This was all his fault. He shouldn't have been so hard on her. This had to be a difficult time for her, with everything in his life going so well—his career, his marriage, his impending fatherhood. Maybe she was worried that he would cut her off financially. She had to know that he was bound by the terms of her divorce to keep paying her a very generous alimony and child support. Maybe she was worried that his new wife would nix all the extras he had been more than willing to shell out whenever she'd asked.

Now he wondered how much of that money had gone to Hailey. And how much of it had ended up in her wineglass.

But if she wanted to make sure his financial contributions remained, why would she tell him Hailey wasn't his? Surely she knew how simple a paternity test was these days. If Hailey wasn't his, he wouldn't be responsible for child support and all the extras he paid for because he wanted to keep Hailey happy.

Or maybe she knew he was a sucker. Despite his bad boy image, deep down, he was a good guy. He was a pushover when it came to denying that little girl anything.

A minivan pulled into the driveway, the tires screeching when the driver pulled up short of the ambulance. With the engine still running, a woman in stylish cropped jeans, a sparkly top, and oversized sunglasses jumped out of the van.

"What did you do to her?" Her perfectly manicured claws were aimed at his throat.

"I found her on the floor of the bedroom..." Before he could add in a pool of vomit, Hailey had exited the vehicle.

"Your mom had a bad reaction to some medication." He directed his words to his daughter. "She's going to be okay. The paramedics are going to make sure of that."

He hoped he was telling the truth.

Momzilla seemed to deflate slightly at his words. She took off her sunglasses and eyed him carefully before turning to Hailey.

"Hailey, honey, why don't you run up to your room and grab some clothes for a few more nights."

"I don't think that's a good idea." Bryce noticed Hailey glance from one adult to another, unsure of who to listen to. "I don't want to get in the way of the paramedics. Maybe we should go out back by the pool."

He hoped his voice sounded calm and reassuring. The last thing he needed was for Hailey to realize that he was scared to death.

"Yeah, that's a great idea. I'm Darlene, by the way." The woman offered a shaky hand and Bryce shook it.

"Bryce Baxter." He let go of the woman's hand. "I'm Hailey's father."

He waited for a look that said she knew otherwise, but when she gave him a shaky smile and said, "Nice to meet you," he got the feeling she didn't have any knowledge to the contrary.

Kristina Mathews

"Hailey, why don't you grab your bag and you and McKenzie can go sit by the pool." She gave a smile that was even faker than her tits.

As soon as the girls were situated in the backyard, Darlene pulled Bryce into the kitchen. "So what is really going on here? Jillian called me this morning all freaked out, crying and saying you were threatening her. That you were going to show up at ten to try to take Hailey from her."

"If you were so worried, why did you bring Hailey here?"

"I…" She cast a nervous glance out the window toward the girls. "Jillian has been… Oh, how do I put this?"

"Unstable?"

"I've been worried about her." She stood against the counter, her arms crossed firmly over her chest. "The last few weeks especially."

"Since I got married?"

Before they could continue the conversation, the paramedics brought Jillian downstairs on the stretcher.

"Is she going to be okay?" Bryce asked, wishing he were a praying man.

"It looks like we got to her in time," one of the paramedics said. "Ten more minutes and…"

"What hospital are you taking her to?" Darlene asked.

The paramedic gave the name of the hospital where Hailey had been born. Guilt slammed into him even harder than he ever imagined.

"Do you want me to take Hailey home with me?" Darlene asked.

"No. She needs to be with family right now." Bryce felt like he was somehow outside his body. "I'll take care of her. I promise."

"Can I give you a ride to the hospital?"

"Yeah. Thanks."

"I can take you and Hailey. We'll follow the ambulance."

"Yeah. That would be great." Bryce scrubbed his hands over his face. "I just need to clean up in her room.

"Why don't you grab the girls, we'll go to the hospital, and I'll come back and clean up for you. It's the least I could do."

"You don't have to—"

"I know." She reached out and touched Bryce's arm. "But Hailey is practically family. She's at our house almost every weekend. She's like another daughter to us. I want to help in any way I can."

"Thanks. I appreciate this." He started toward the backyard to fetch Hailey and her friend, but there was one more thing he needed to know.

"Do you think Jillian did this on purpose? I mean, we had a fight last night. We both said some things…"

"I have to believe it was an accident." Darlene reached for his hand. "For Hailey's sake."

"Yeah. Me, too." Bryce didn't want to think about what it meant if she'd taken the entire bottle of pills he'd found on the bathroom counter and washed it down with a lot of wine because of him. "Either way, she's going to need help when she gets out of the hospital."

He didn't want to add *if* she got out of the hospital.

* * * *

Rachel hadn't heard from Bryce in over twenty-four hours. He usually called or at least texted her before he went to bed while on the road. Not last night. And not a word from him this morning, unless you counted the Instagram pictures posted by some bimbo in the bar who had her tongue in his ear, while her friend ran her hand up Marco Santiago's bicep.

What the hell? He was supposed to be spending his free time in Pittsburgh with his daughter. Instead he was out carousing with another married player. The quality of the photograph wasn't great, but it looked like Bryce had been a little drunk. He had a wild look in his eyes, and his hair was messed up as if someone had been running their fingers through it.

How could he do this to her?

Especially now, when they'd made such a big deal about the baby. The fans had been so supportive. It was overwhelming how positive they'd been. How excited for her and Bryce.

And now they would be crushed. Almost as much as she was.

It hurt. More than she had ever imagined.

Just think, she'd been this close to telling him she loved him. Would it have made a difference? Or maybe he knew, and this was his way of showing her that he did not return the feeling.

Obviously, if he loved her, he wouldn't be getting cozy with some stranger in a bar. If he loved her, he would call her. If he cared about her at all, he'd at least make up a lie about how the picture wasn't what it looked like. He'd offer an explanation. Even if it was bullshit, it would be better than acting like she didn't matter at all.

Rachel started packing.

She'd known all along that Bryce Baxter would break her heart.

* * * *

The hospital was stuffy, with that nauseating smell of disinfectant and sickness. Maybe bringing Hailey here had been a mistake. All this sitting around and not knowing what was happening was driving him crazy. What must she be going through? Her mother was in the emergency room and she was sitting in the waiting room next to a guy with a nail sticking out of his thumb, a crying toddler tugging on his ears and drooling on his mother, and a woman who looked like she hadn't had a meal or sleep in days, complaining loudly about the service in this place and who the hell had taken her cigarettes.

"Maybe I should take the girls home," Darlene offered.

"If we don't hear anything in the next half hour, that might be a good idea." He hated to leave Hailey, even for a minute. The longer this dragged on, the more he was determined to be there for her. He could be the only family—no he couldn't think like that. He had to stay strong, for his daughter.

Even if she wasn't his flesh and blood, she was still his daughter.

He wondered if Jillian had shared the information she'd dropped on him last night? Did Darlene know he might not be Hailey's father? Did Jillian's parents know? Or was she just making it up, saying the one thing that would hurt him the most?

The doctor came out and asked to speak with Bryce privately, a look of concern on her face.

He was glad Darlene had come, he'd hate to leave Hailey alone, and it looked like the doctor had something to say that wasn't appropriate for a nine-year-old's ears.

Bryce followed the doctor into the room where Jillian lay resting, with tubes coming out of her, and machines beeping softly behind her.

"Is she going to make it?" It was the only question that mattered.

"She's lucky you found her in time."

Relief washed over Bryce like a monsoon.

"I have to ask a few questions before we admit her for the night."

Bryce just nodded, his brain still having a hard time processing the whole situation.

"Are you Mrs. Baxter's husband?"

"Ex-husband. We've been divorced for about eight years."

"I see." The doctor clasped her hands together, almost in a praying motion, but not quite. "And you still have a relationship with her?"

"We have a daughter. She's nine."

The doctor gave a sympathetic half-smile. Did she know Hailey wasn't his? Was he the only one who didn't have a fucking clue?

"Does Ms. Baxter have a history of depression? Anxiety?"

"We had an argument last night." Bryce ran his fingers through his hair. "I recently got remarried, and my wife is expecting. I suppose the news is a little hard on Jillian."

He felt like the world's biggest asshole.

"The amount of drugs and alcohol in her system suggest this might not have been an accidental overdose."

"You think she was trying to—" Bryce couldn't breathe. He couldn't think about what the doctor was suggesting.

"I'm recommending a psychiatric hold." The doctor had a calm, professional, and sympathetic tone to her voice. "We'll keep her under observation for seventy-two hours, until we can make sure she isn't a danger to herself."

"What if it was intentional?" Bryce had to prepare for the worst. "Is there some sort of treatment we can get for her? Even if it wasn't a suicide attempt, I think she might have an addiction problem."

Either way, she was in a world of trouble. And he'd just been sucked into it.

"I can recommend a few treatment facilities that take most insurance."

"Cost is not an issue." Bryce exhaled. "I only want the best. I want her to get better. For our daughter's sake."

The doctor gave him an impatient smile. "I'll have a nurse bring you some brochures."

He returned to the waiting room.

"Is Mommy going to be okay?" Hailey's concern was understandable. It still broke his heart.

"Yeah. She's going to have to stay in the hospital for a couple of days, though."

"Hailey is more than welcome to stay with us," Darlene offered, and while he appreciated it, there was no way he was letting the girl out of his sight.

"Thanks, but I'll be here."

"Don't you have a game tonight?"

It took him a few seconds for the words to sink in. Right. Baseball. Not something he could even remotely think about right now.

"I'll call in, tell them there's a family thing. They'll understand."

Hailey inched toward him, her fear palpable.

Bryce knelt down, pulling his daughter into a hug.

"It's going to be okay, Princess. I promise." He just patted her long, dark hair, hoping he could fix this. What was the point of making millions if he couldn't somehow make this right?

Chapter 23

Rachel turned on the Goliaths game. She still hadn't heard from Bryce, and was surprised to see he wasn't in the lineup. Ryan Fletcher would be taking his place at shortstop. The broadcasters only said a family emergency had come up and he was not at the ballpark.

So Kip and Kurt knew more about her husband's absence than she did? That made her feel about as significant as the sunflower seed shells spit on the floor of the dugout.

She knew the fastest way to find information was to check her Twitter feed; she followed several other journalists who worked with the team and would have access to inside information. But there would be no way to filter all the speculation and false reports about why he wasn't with the team.

The morning sickness she'd thought was behind her had returned with a vengeance. Rachel curled up on the couch with a bag of pita chips and water infused with lemon and ginger at her side. She watched the game through blurry eyes, hoping to hear more details about Bryce, but the game went on without him.

Fletcher played solid defense, and had moderate success at the plate. He reached base twice, on a single and an error, and scored one run in the win. Bryce's absence didn't hurt the team on the road, but the home team was miserable.

Most of the clothes that still fit her were packed in two suitcases. She had them in the bedroom, ready to throw in her toothbrush as soon as he returned home. She wasn't going to take the coward's way out and leave before he returned. No. She would have to look him in the eye to know that it was truly over.

And he would know just how much he'd hurt her.

* * * *

His manager was more understanding than Bryce could have imagined. He'd had to tell the whole story, including the need to get Jillian checked into rehab and get Hailey checked out of school two full weeks before the end of the school year.

He hoped he could bring Hailey on the team's charter Monday afternoon, but had a feeling they would be flying commercial, probably getting in late at night. Too late to have Rachel pick them up from the airport.

Rachel. He'd tried calling her, but was relieved when she didn't pick up. He knew just hearing her voice would wreck him, and he had to stay strong. So he'd left a text telling her they needed to talk when he got home. Maybe he should have left a message, explaining all that had happened, but he didn't even know where to start. He needed to see her, to hold her, while he confessed his biggest failure.

How could he have not known how bad Jillian had gotten? How could he have thought that all his money could have kept her demons at bay? He should have known that his moving to the other side of the country would devastate her. She hadn't loved him, but she'd counted on him. Needed him to check up on her and Hailey from time to time.

Cheating on Jillian had been one thing, but nothing compared to the guilt he now felt over leaving them to further his career on the other side of the country. He'd found the ultimate success. He'd even found a woman he'd wanted to share it with. But now the weight of his ring—of both his rings—felt more like a burden than anything. His happiness had come at too great of a price.

Hailey had fallen asleep on the way home from the hospital. He'd put her to bed and poured himself a glass of wine from Jillian's extensive collection. Guilt gave the wine a bitter aftertaste, and he ended up pouring the rest of the bottle down the drain.

"Daddy?" Hailey stood at the far end of the kitchen. Her dark hair and dark blue eyes stood in stark relief to the paleness of her skin. "I can't sleep."

"Come here, Princess." He held his arms wide open and she rushed toward him. Her little body felt so fragile, and he was almost afraid he'd hurt her if he squeezed too tight. But he hugged her anyway. With the fierceness of the love he felt for this little girl.

"It's my fault Mommy's in the hospital." Hailey's voice was wise beyond her years. "I shouldn't have left her by herself. She gets lonely. And it's more fun at McKenzie's house 'cause she has sisters and a dog and a cat and she has to do chores before we can watch a movie and sometimes I help, too."

"That's great sweetheart, I'm glad you help out when you're at your friend's house."

"It's like being a part of the family." She stepped out of his embrace. "A big, *happy* family."

Her emphasis on the word happy nearly broke his heart.

"Mommy's sad a lot." Hailey looked down at the floor, as if it was somehow her fault. "And now she's in the hospital."

"Oh sweetie. It's not your fault. It's not anyone's fault." At least for now, he was sticking to his original story. That Jillian's overdose was an accident. "She had a reaction to some medicine she was taking. Like an allergy."

"She took the medicine because she was sad." Hailey held onto him as if she was afraid he'd go away, too. "Why was she sad?"

"I don't know." He had an idea, and it was because of him, but he didn't want to share that with Hailey. Didn't want her to have to take sides between her mother and him. "It's even possible she doesn't know why she was sad."

"I thought it was because I was excited about being a big sister." She started to tremble in his arms. "Maybe if I wasn't happy…"

"Oh sweetheart." He stroked her dark hair, so much like her mother's, but softer. Shinier. "Don't ever think that your happiness will make someone else feel bad. It doesn't work that way."

"When you won the World Series, you were happy, right?"

"Yes. I was. We all were."

"But what about the other team?" She took a step back, looking up at him with such innocence it killed him. "Didn't they feel sad?"

"Yes. I suppose they did." He had to keep a grin from escaping his lips. She was a good kid. Kind. Empathetic. Innocent. "But in baseball, you're prepared to lose. You hope you win, but you know there's a really good chance you'll lose. That's one of the things that makes the winning so great, is knowing how hard it is."

He didn't know if she could understand, or even how it would help her grasp what her mother was going through. He had a feeling Jillian was like the fans who, when their teams didn't make the playoffs, they cheered against their rivals rather than picking another team to root for. And sometimes seeing their rivals win was worse than their team losing.

For years, as long as he wasn't happily involved with anyone else, Jillian had been content with their divorce. If they couldn't be happy together, at least he wasn't happy with anyone else.

Until Rachel.

And his happiness had destroyed Jillian's.

"Is Mommy going to go away for a while?"

"She's going to get the help she needs."

"Can I go with her?"

"You're going to come to San Francisco with me." He hoped he was doing the right thing. Jillian's friend had offered to keep her until the end of the school year, but he knew in his heart she needed family more than she needed to attend the field trips, parties, and end of the year celebrations that would take up the last ten days of third grade. "It's going to be great. You'll see."

He was tempted to offer to buy her a pony, but there weren't any stables in his apartment building. If only he could buy a time machine, go back in time and be there for her all along. Maybe if he'd insisted on spending more time with her these past nine years, his request to have her over the summer wouldn't have sent Jillian over the edge.

There were a lot of things he would have done differently.

"What about earthquakes?" She sounded genuinely worried.

He picked her up and she wrapped her arms around his neck. "You have nothing to worry about. The big ones are pretty rare. And I live in a new building that is built to withstand any major shaking."

Hailey nodded, but he wasn't sure if she was convinced.

"Come on, Princess, let's get you back to bed."

"Will you stay with me?" Her voice sounded so small and fragile.

"Of course." If he had to sleep on the floor of her room, he'd do it. Anything to make her feel safe.

He tucked her into bed and found a chapter book to read to her. She grabbed his hand, clinging to him as if her world depended on it.

Finally, after two and a half chapters, he felt her grip loosen. Her eyes closed, and soft snores escaped her innocent lips. She was asleep. But Bryce couldn't tear himself away from her side.

* * * *

After an uncomfortable night's sleep on the floor of Hailey's room, Bryce woke around dawn to prepare for the task ahead of him. He had to pack a few essentials for Jillian's month-long stay at a very exclusive and expensive substance abuse clinic. With the amount of money he would be paying, they had better keep their promise of absolute confidentiality.

Fortunately, the woman had a large selection of designer sweat suits. Or maybe they were yoga pants. Whatever. They would be comfortable while she was doing whatever she would be doing. He couldn't imagine. He just hoped it would help. He truly wanted her to be able to get past the bitterness that had festered between them for so long.

He wanted her to be able to move on with her life, so he could get on with his.

It was way too early to call Rachel. But damn. He missed her. If only she had been with him, this would have been so much easier to deal with.

Or would it? Would Jillian have gone even farther over the edge if he'd brought his new wife into her messed up world? Or worse. Would she have tried to take Rachel down with her?

No. He couldn't think like that. Couldn't let his mind wander into the kind of scenario that would end up on one of those true crime shows.

Bryce would just have to figure out a way to protect all of the women in his life.

Rachel could take care of herself. She was one of the strongest women he knew. And that was one of the things he loved about her.

Jillian would be in the capable hands of the well-paid doctors and therapists at the rehab facility he'd arranged for her.

It was Hailey he had to turn his attention to now. She was the one who needed him most. A little girl caught in the middle of a huge mess. If Jillian had been telling the truth—in other words, if she'd lied to him—and she was in fact the daughter of some nameless stranger, then… No. He couldn't even let his brain go there. Hailey was his. And he would fight for her. No matter what.

After packing Jillian's suitcases, he made his way downstairs. Hailey would need breakfast. And a distraction to keep her mind off the situation with her mother. Her impending cross-country move. And the fact that she would be missing the last two weeks of school.

There was only one thing that could make the rest of the world go away.

Baseball.

He would take her to the game with him. Let her become a part of his world. He'd buy her some peanuts and Cracker Jack. Maybe an ice cream sundae in one of those little helmets. Sully would look after her in the clubhouse since she was too young to be in the dugout as a bat girl. At least she'd be at the ballpark. With people he trusted. He just wished Rachel had come on the trip with him. Not that he would have wanted her to have to deal with the shit Jillian had pulled.

Still. He missed her. And he hadn't been able to connect with her. When he couldn't reach his wife by phone, Bryce sent another text.

Taking Hailey to the game tonight. Hope she has a good time.

There was so much more he wanted to say, but some things could only be said in person.

* * * *

Well, wasn't that sweet?

Bryce had texted saying he was taking his daughter to the game tonight. As if he didn't have a care in the world. He hadn't missed a game for some mysterious family emergency. He hadn't been at a bar two nights ago with some bimbo.

Did he really think so little of her? Apparently marriage hadn't really changed their relationship. It was no different from that whole first year, where he'd chased her with all the intensity of a team just a few games behind their division rival in the last few weeks of the season. But once he'd made the score, he was like the teams who thought they could just walk into the playoffs, toss their jock on the field and end up with a ring.

There was a reason most teams didn't repeat as World Series Champions. Complacency played a big part in it. That and the attitude that whatever they touched would always be golden. Was Bryce thinking he could do no wrong? That she'd just forgive him because he was an MVP? Did he think he could just toss money her way and she'd forgive anything? Some women could look the other way if it meant financial security. She wasn't one of them.

But sadly, she realized that money could buy her a new place to live. She didn't have to stay with Bryce. And she didn't have to go crawling back to her mother in Fresno. Not that she would do that even if she didn't have the financial resources to stay in the Bay Area. She still had a job to do. And now, keeping it was more important than ever.

Even though it was a Sunday afternoon, she was able to make an appointment with a real estate agent. The young woman seemed more than enthusiastic to show her two-bedroom apartments in and around the city. And that was before Rachel told her who she was, and who her husband was.

Rachel was early, so she stood in the lobby of the real estate office, looking at flyers for everything from studio apartments to a ten-million-dollar Victorian mansion. Her stomach rolled just thinking about the taxes on such a property.

Why had she given up her apartment? It was a nice place. And eventually, maybe she could have put in for one of the larger units.

But no. She'd been charmed by Bryce. He'd somehow managed to sweep her off her feet and into his beautiful downtown apartment. He still had his workout equipment in the second bedroom. He wasn't any more ready to welcome a child into this world than she was. He was perfectly happy playing weekend dad and taking his kid to the ballpark. No doubt the poor thing would end up in the company of Sully, the clubhouse manager. Mike Sullivan was a great guy, had been with the team since they came over from New York, but he wasn't exactly any little girl's favorite companion.

"Hi, I'm Catherine Beck," a young, blonde, and very polished woman extended a confident hand. "Oh, you're Rachel Parker. I'm a huge fan."

"Thank you." It still surprised her when people recognized her outside of the ballpark.

"Really." Catherine sounded almost giddy. "I was only a casual fan, watching mostly because my dad or brothers had the game on. But then you came along and made the game more interesting. You bring out the human side of the game."

"I try."

"And it's so much more fun rooting for the guys because you make us feel like we know them." The other woman was gushing now. "I mean, how can you not love Marco Santiago? A guy who still drives a '65 Mustang because he wanted to buy his mother a house instead of a fancy car for himself."

She started to fan herself.

"And Bryce Baxter." Catherine sighed. Rachel had heard that sigh before. She'd even uttered it herself. "Okay, you have to tell me. Is his hair… Oh, how rude of me. He's your husband. Is it weird knowing that thousands of women are madly in love with your husband?"

"A little, I guess." Rachel tried to keep a brave face. "Most of the time I try not to think about it."

"Oh, I almost died when he proposed." Catherine put her hand over her heart, as if it was the most romantic thing in the world. "And, I'll admit. I cried a little. But I'm happy for you. Truly. And now you're having a baby."

The woman's eyes glistened. She reached out and took Rachel's hands and squeezed. "Oh, we have to find the perfect house for your family."

"That would be great." Rachel swallowed the lump that had formed in her throat. She didn't have the heart to tell this sweet lady that she really wanted to look at apartments for just her and the baby.

"Come on back to my office, and we'll pull up the listings." She turned on her sensible, yet stylish heels. "I'm sure schools will be a consideration. Are you looking to buy within the city? Or are neighboring communities acceptable? But then you'd have to factor in commute time, and with a baby... You are planning on keeping your job after the baby comes?"

The questions came flying faster than Rachel had a chance to respond.

Her hand moved protectively over her abdomen. The baby. She had to keep her focus on the baby. It was the only thing that had kept her from falling apart these last twenty-four hours. Or was it thirty-six? She couldn't keep track of time since she'd seen that horrible Instagram picture of Bryce and the bimbo. Anger boiled up inside her, but she pushed it aside for the sake of her child.

She would move forward. Make a home for herself and her child. She had a feeling it was a boy, so the idea of finding a house with a yard had a certain appeal. That ruled out a lot of places in the city, but she could commute. She'd done it before.

Chapter 24

Hailey had fallen asleep in the clubhouse. She'd watched the first couple of innings but since she hadn't grown up watching the game, she'd quickly become bored. But Sully had done a good job with her. He had several grandchildren and had practically raised Hunter Collins from the time she was seven.

Bryce got her to school just minutes before the bell, and after she went off to class for the last time, he went to the office to disenroll her. Or was it unenroll?

"I'll be with you in just a minute." The school secretary was busy giving out tardy slips and fielding phone calls. "If you're here to volunteer you can sign in and as soon as I check your ID, we can issue a visitor's pass."

He gave her a polite smile and stood off to the side with his hands in his pockets. He'd only been to the auditorium of Hailey's school, on the rare occasions when her school performances hadn't conflicted with his baseball games. God, he'd missed so much.

Finally the schoolchildren cleared out, the phone stopped ringing, and the secretary could give Bryce her attention.

"How may I help you?" She seemed friendlier than she had a few minutes ago. Maybe not friendlier, just less harried.

"I'm Bryce Baxter, Hailey Baxter's father."

The woman kept her helpful smile on her face, with a questioning look in her eyes.

"I'm going to need to check Hailey out of school."

She glanced at the clock, probably noting that the school day had just started.

"See, her mother is ill…" Bryce let out a breath. "And I'm going to be taking care of Hailey until she's better."

The woman didn't need to know that he'd decided to seek custody of Hailey, hoping that her mother's current state would keep the issue of paternity from coming up.

"I see."

"I live in San Francisco now. And we're flying out this afternoon." Why did he feel like she was about ready to push a secret button, the one that would send the police rushing to thwart an attempted kidnapping?

She gave a polite smile and then started typing something into her computer. Nodding her head, she seemed to find the information she was looking for.

"You're the baseball player. Thank you so much for your generous donations. You have no idea what a difference it makes for these kids to have proper PE equipment." Her tone was suddenly as helpful and friendly as could be.

"I'm glad I could help." He still hated the fact that he hadn't been here to help show those kids how to use that equipment. Especially Hailey. He thought back to his own school days. The fundraisers that had come home and not been returned. But his dad at least had helped out. He'd done the heavy lifting for school carnivals and field days and all the things Hailey would miss out on.

"Do you have the name and address of the school she'll be attending?" Madame secretary brought him back from that little trip down memory lane. "We'll want to get her file out to them as soon as possible."

"It's my understanding that there are only two weeks left of school. I'm not sure if it will be the best thing to enroll her in a new school for just a few days."

"Yes, that could be disruptive, but she is required by law to attend school."

"Is there a way to get work sent with her? I can work with her. We could email the assignments." He'd never felt so powerless. No, he had. When he'd walked in on Jillian's limp body.

"A lot of the learning activities these last few weeks are more hands-on. I'm not sure how she could make them up."

"Surely there must be something you can do to help us." He flashed the smile that used to charm most people. Especially women. But he probably looked like hell. He hadn't slept very well in days, and worry wasn't exactly good for his skin or hair. He wasn't even sure if he'd washed it this morning, he'd been so preoccupied with trying to tie up loose ends so he could get Hailey home with him.

"Usually we give teachers a few days' notice to come up with an independent study packet."

"I don't have a few days." He ran his fingers through his hair. It wasn't too greasy, so maybe he'd remembered the shampoo after all. "I have a few hours. I'll be back to pick up Hailey after school. And what time, exactly, does the bell ring?"

"Two fifty-seven." She answered the easy part first. "I'll see what we can pull together, Mr. Baxter."

"Thank you. I appreciate it." He felt the load lighten just a little. The first hurdle of his day had been cleared. "I'll be back at two fifty-seven."

"Oh, you should get here by at least two forty. If not earlier. The parking lot fills up."

He nodded, and gave her his full-watt Bryce Baxter grin. "Thanks, again."

He started to tip his cap but realized he wasn't wearing one.

The walk to the parking lot, back to Jillian's BMW, was longer than he remembered. The hardest part of his day was still ahead of him. The hardest part of his life.

He would be checking his ex-wife into a residential substance abuse treatment facility.

For years, he'd approached the game of baseball with the attitude that he'd face failure more often than not. He'd embraced the idea of failing again and again, of getting back into the box with the attitude that the failures only made his successes that much sweeter. And sure, his triumphs were only about a third of his attempts, but he'd never felt like he'd been a *failure*.

Until now.

Now he felt like the world's biggest loser.

With that feeling, he entered the hospital, ready to take the next step. His shoulders felt as heavy as if he'd been swinging a thirty-two-pound bat instead of a thirty-two-ounce one.

It was a bit of a blur, signing Jillian out of the hospital, loading her into her car, and driving her to what looked like a five-star resort, but in reality was only a step above a prison.

She didn't say much as they went through the motions of checking her in. It was as if she'd lost all the fight that she'd so frequently taken out on him. He'd rather have her venom than this zoned-out complacency.

He wondered if she'd been drugged. It would explain her defeated demeanor. Maybe they'd noted it in her paperwork. The hospital had assured him that her file would be transferred over. Confidentially, of course. Hopefully, if they had given her something to make the transition easier, they would alert the rehab facility so that they didn't give her an additional dose, or mix medications. Shit. Why hadn't he paid closer attention? Asked questions?

He'd just wanted to get this over with.

He was handed a stack of forms; he took the pen from the receptionist and started to sign his autograph. Shaking his head, he remembered they needed his signature, which was very different from what he wrote on baseballs, photos, and more than once, on some woman's chest.

After scrawling his legal signature on a stack of papers, he watched Jillian do the same. With a pang of regret, he remembered signing for the house she would leave abandoned for a month. Sure the cleaning lady would come, the gardener would make his rounds, and Darlene had promised to pick up the mail and check on the house every couple of days.

Once the formalities were taken care of, Bryce waited for Jillian to say something. To ask after Hailey. To accuse him of ruining her life. Anything other than this awful silence.

"So. You take care." Yeah. That was what she needed to hear. "Don't worry about Hailey. I'll make sure she's got everything she needs. And Rachel will help."

"Rachel. Your wife." Jillian's voice was so soft. So defeated. "Do you love her?"

"Yes." No use lying to her, even if the truth hurt. Maybe if they'd been honest with each other years ago… No. He couldn't let regret take over.

"And you're going to have a baby together?"

He nodded.

She looked away, obviously hurt by the news. "I'm so sorry."

Bryce didn't know exactly what she was apologizing for. And now was not the time to get into it. "Me too."

"You don't have to…" She struggled to find her voice. "Hailey's not your responsibility."

"Don't say that." He tried to keep control over his own voice. He couldn't show anger. Not now. "The minute I signed that marriage certificate, she became my responsibility. The second I looked into her eyes, I became her father. Nothing else matters."

"Bryce. Thank you."

He looked at the woman who'd basically been a stranger for the last ten years. She'd been a one-night stand, then a desperate woman who'd come to him, crying and freaked out about a baby she'd led him to believe was his. Then she'd become his wife, at least in name. She'd never been happy. Not as long as he'd known her.

He just hoped that while she was here, she'd be able to figure out why.

* * * *

"I'm sorry none of these homes are quite what you're looking for." Catherine Beck pulled her Mercedes into the real estate office parking lot. "But don't worry, we'll keep looking."

She'd been such a sweetheart, working her tail off to find the perfect house for Rachel Parker and Bryce Baxter.

There were so many great places, in and out of the city. But none of them felt like home.

They returned to the office where Catherine pulled up listing after listing, shaking her head at her inability to find the perfect house for her client.

Finally, she pushed back from the desk. She looked around, as if to make sure no one was listening.

"There is a house—it's not on the market yet, so technically I can't show it to you—I think it's exactly what you're looking for."

She grabbed a pen and a notepad from the top drawer of her neat desk. She jotted down an address and handed the slip of paper to Rachel. "I hope to have it listed in a few weeks. But it will go fast. Real fast."

She stood up, poked her head out into the corridor, and satisfied that she wasn't being overheard, sat back down.

"Drive by, take a look, and if you can wait, I'll make sure you're one of the first to see it when it finally does come on the market."

Rachel wanted to ask why this woman was being so accommodating, but it didn't really matter if it was because she was a good agent, a huge Goliaths fan, or if it was because she would potentially make a killing on the commission.

The minute she turned up the street, Rachel knew Catherine was right. It was exactly the house Rachel had dreamed of. A wide stone path welcomed family and friends. A large tree begged to be climbed.

Surrounded by native vegetation, the house looked like it was placed into the environment, instead of carefully selected landscaping added after the fact. The only plants that seemed to have been added by the homeowners were camellias. But even those looked like they'd been there forever, planted a generation ago to add colorful winter blooms in an otherwise dreary season.

Even from the street, she could tell the view was incredible.

She could make out a fence extending to the backyard. Not a white picket one, it looked more like the kind that would fully enclose a pool.

No. She couldn't sit here any longer, parked across the street from her dream home. Not when that dream wouldn't include having Bryce to share it with.

She turned around, but not before noticing the remnants of a rope swing in the tree. It looked like it had been awhile since any children had swung from its branches.

And her child wouldn't be the one to resurrect the old swing. He (or she) wouldn't learn how to swim in the pool. And Bryce's Corvette would not be parked in the garage.

Chapter 25

"Come on, sweetheart, just pick a few of your favorite things that you'll need in San Francisco for a few weeks." Bryce had thrown most of Hailey's wardrobe into Jillian's matched luggage set. Four suitcases held more than a month's worth of clothes. But Bryce didn't know what her favorites were, what clothes she'd outgrown, and what she'd actually need for her extended stay with him. Sure, he could buy her anything he'd left behind, but he wanted her to have mostly her own things with her.

The problem was, she had a lot of things. Toys. Dolls. Stuffed animals. Books. An iPod. Her bedroom looked like an upscale toy store. He supposed it would be hard to choose just a few items to take with her. To pack up and leave everything she knew behind. To go live with a man she saw only a few times a year and the rest of the time it had been just her and her mom.

She must be worried about her mom. He certainly was.

Hailey grabbed her iPod and earbuds. She shoved a book that she'd been reading into her backpack and then she looked around the room. It was almost as if she were taking inventory. Trying to determine what was most important to her.

Finally, she approached her bed and rifled through a huge stack of pillows. She grabbed one and hugged it to her chest.

It took Bryce a minute before he realized it had been made out of one his jerseys.

"Okay, we can go now." She picked up her backpack and slung it over one shoulder. She smiled at him and his heart stopped. She'd left behind her American Girl dolls, her video games, and her stuffed animals. But she'd brought a pillow made out of her dad's jersey.

They hadn't been able to leave early enough to fly out with the team. He texted Rachel to tell her he'd be taking a later flight and he'd get a shuttle from the airport since it wouldn't arrive until late that night. There was so much he needed to talk to her about. More than anything, he just wanted to hold her. She had become his center and he needed her now more than ever. It had been the longest weekend of his life. But as much as he wished Rachel had been with him, she didn't need to be put through all this shit.

The flight was uneventful and Hailey had fallen asleep on the ride from the airport. He left the luggage in the lobby and carried her up to the apartment. He would lay her on the bed while he made up the couch. He'd have to order furniture for her bedroom. And move out his exercise equipment. It was time to start looking for a bigger place. A house. With a yard, and maybe a pool. He wondered if Rachel was ready to take that next step.

Funny, he was supposed to be the bachelor playboy afraid of commitment, yet she'd been the one freaking out about things moving too fast.

He just hoped Hailey would love Rachel as much as he did. Because there was no way he could do this without her. Especially if he was going to have to fight Jillian for custody.

He turned the key in the lock, pushed open the door, and carefully carried his daughter into the apartment. He hoped Rachel was still up. He wanted to make love to her, but it would probably have to wait until Hailey had her own room.

He just needed to see her. To hold her. To know that everything was going to be all right.

* * * *

Rachel heard his key in the lock. Heard the door open. She tried to prepare herself to face the man who had broken her heart for the last time.

He carried a sleeping child in his arms. The look of weariness in his eyes made Rachel wonder how he could stand himself, let alone carry his daughter.

"I'm just going to set her on the bed while I make up the couch for tonight." He sounded like he could collapse on the bed himself.

"I can take the couch." Rachel offered, her resolve to have it out with him before she loaded her suitcases into her Range Rover melted as he laid the girl gently on the mattress.

"You don't have to make it up for her." He didn't seem to understand her offer to sleep on the couch herself. "I'll just run downstairs and grab her suitcases and…"

His eyes rested on Rachel's suitcases that stood by the door of the bedroom they had shared.

Kristina Mathews

Bryce stumbled backward as if he'd been slapped.

"Rachel, what's going on?" His features twisted in a look of shock and fear.

"I..." She was such an idiot. She had a whole speech prepared. About how she wasn't going to live a lie. That their marriage had been a mistake from the beginning and it was time they both acknowledged that fact.

She glanced over at Bryce's sleeping daughter and something tugged at her heart.

"Let's go in the other room." She didn't want to wake the girl.

Bryce nodded and motioned for her to go first.

"What happened in Pittsburgh?" Rachel walked into the kitchen and poured herself a glass of water. "You missed a game and no one knew why. And you didn't call. Then there was that picture."

"What picture?"

"Of you and that girl."

"There was a picture of me and my daughter?" Bryce sounded confused. Angry.

"No. The girl from the bar." Now Rachel was confused. And she needed to hang on to that anger she'd felt. She couldn't give in to his act of innocence. "The blonde. The one with her tongue in your ear."

"I don't know what you're talking about. Look, it's been a really shitty couple of days." Bryce ran his hands through his hair. "I had a fight with Jillian over Hailey and—"

"Oh my God, Bryce, you didn't kidnap her did you?"

"No." He smiled. It was that same charming, self-deprecating grin that had melted her heart the first time she'd met him. "I didn't kidnap my daughter. Jillian is in rehab. She... I keep telling myself it was an accident, but...she almost died."

"Oh, Bryce. I'm so sorry." Rachel felt herself going toward him, but she stopped at the last minute. "Why didn't you tell me?"

"Oh, baby, I didn't want to worry you." He closed the space between them and tried to put his arms around her.

"But you did." She stepped back. "You had me thinking the worst. You missed a game. And the last I saw or heard from you was an Instagram picture of some girl licking your ear. I thought you had spent the night with her. That you were unable to make the game because you were shacked up with some bimbo."

"No, Rachel. I would never do that to you."

"How the hell was I supposed to know that?"

"You could have trusted me."

"Like you trusted me with what was happening with your family?"

"Rachel, please…" He started toward her, his arms out.

"I was going to go to a hotel."

"I need you." He let his hands fall to his sides. "And Hailey needs both of us."

"That's not fair."

"No, it isn't. But it's the truth." He ran both hands through his hair. "Look. I know I fucked up. It's all I've ever done. But please. Don't walk out on me now."

Before she could respond, the doorbell rang.

Bryce went to answer it.

"Mr. Baxter, I brought your luggage up from the lobby. You seemed to have your hands full." The front-desk clerk stood in the hallway with Bryce's duffel bag and a matched set of luggage.

"Thanks, Sergio." Bryce stepped aside as Sergio brought in the first two suitcases. Then he stepped out into the hall to bring in the rest himself. "I appreciate it."

Bryce reached for his wallet.

"No. No. Mr. Baxter, you put that away." Sergio smiled warmly. "You know I don't accept tips. I was happy to do it."

"Just let me know when you can catch a game, and I'll make sure the tickets are waiting for you."

"Will do, Mr. Baxter." Sergio nodded, and turned his attention to Rachel with a polite smile. "You two have a nice night."

"Thank you." The words sounded forced from her lips. "Goodnight."

Bryce shut the door and fell back against the heavy wood. "Should I call him back? Have him carry your luggage down?"

"No." Her head was spinning. She didn't know what to think anymore. She'd packed her bags believing Bryce had been sidelined because of girl. She was right, in a way. But the girl was his daughter. An innocent child who was caught up in adult problems. Rachel didn't want to add to the drama. "I'll stay. On the couch. You and your daughter can have the bed for tonight. We'll figure out the next step tomorrow."

"Rachel, I'm sorry to involve you in this mess." His shoulders slumped as he pushed off from his position against the door.

"That's the problem, Bryce." How could she make him understand how much his silence hurt her? "You don't want me in your life, except when everything is going great. When you're winning, you can't wait to share the glory. But when you get into a slump, you shut down. And when something really hard comes along, you disappear altogether. You don't want a partner. You want a cheerleader."

He hung his head, and without another word, trudged off to the bedroom.

Rachel wrapped a throw blanket around her and curled up on the couch. She fell asleep quickly, but was plagued by distressing dreams. They were in her old Honda and Bryce was trying to back into a parking space, but they were on a hill and he backed up too far and they started sliding down, down, a mountainside, with nothing to stop them. Brakes didn't work, and there were no trees or other barriers to slow their progress. Would they burst into flames? Or would they walk away unscathed? Would the car eventually roll, causing her or Bryce to be crushed in the wreckage? And what about the children? How could she possibly protect them? She woke with a start, unwilling to find out what would happen when the car made its inevitable stop.

Her heart racing, she got up and went to get a drink of water. She downed it in one long gulp and set the glass carefully on the counter. The dream pretty much summed up how she'd felt since the moment she'd peed on a stick. Her life was suddenly out of her control. And even with Bryce at her side, she didn't know how they could possibly avert disaster.

* * * *

Bryce heard Rachel get up in the middle of the night. He had been lying on the floor, trying to sleep, but he couldn't get comfortable. It wasn't the hardwood that was making him toss and turn. It was the monumental way he'd messed up with Rachel.

All he'd wanted to do was protect her from the shit storm that had taken over his life when he landed in Pittsburgh. Instead, he'd only made things worse. By not calling and talking to her, he'd led her to believe the worst. She didn't trust him. And he couldn't blame her.

Oh how he wanted to go to her. To make up some bullshit about how everything was going to work out. How he'd make it up to her. But she'd see right through him. He couldn't fake confidence until he figured things out. Not with this.

He wondered if he would be able to sort this situation out. If Hailey wasn't his daughter, Jillian could make it damned hard to get even partial custody of her. And after what he saw Friday night, he wanted to fight for permanent custody. But if the judge ordered a DNA test and it came up negative...

No. He couldn't go there. He had to think about what was best for Hailey. Everything else was irrelevant.

Except for Rachel. And the child she carried. His child. He was sure of it. Rachel wouldn't have come to him if it wasn't. She had too much integrity.

God, he was a fool. He'd found a good woman. Or she had found him. Either way, he had failed her.

He knew she'd stay, for Hailey's sake. She'd help him take care of her until he could make permanent arrangements. Hire a nanny. Enroll her in summer camp. Finally be the dad he'd always wanted to be, but had been afraid of stepping on Jillian's toes.

And he knew, if he asked, she'd stand by him if he was able to sue for custody. She'd keep up the appearance of their marriage if it meant an innocent child would be safe.

He just had to convince her that keeping Hailey was the right thing to do.

First, he had to convince himself.

Chapter 26

Rachel felt like someone was watching her. She opened her eyes, and sure enough, the little girl stood over her, a pillow made out of a shirt of some sort clutched in her hands. On closer inspection, she realized it was one of Bryce's jerseys, the name "Baxter" sewn on the back. A smile escaped her lips before she could remember that Bryce had let her down.

"Good morning." Rachel sat up slowly, hoping her stomach would cooperate. "You must be Hailey."

The little girl nodded and offered an uncertain smile. "Are you my dad's wife?"

"Yes. I'm Rachel." She held out her hand. "It's nice to finally meet you."

The girl gave a tentative handshake. "You, too."

"I'll bet you're hungry."

"A little." Hailey shrugged.

"Give me a few minutes to get cleaned up and I'll make us some breakfast." Rachel slowly rose from the couch; her back was a little stiff and her bladder was full. Why had she drunk so much water in the middle of the night?

"You're really going to have a baby?" The child's voiced was laced with curiosity and awe.

"Yes, I am." She couldn't help but rest her hand on her expanding waistline. "And I'm sure you're going to be terrific big sister."

The girl just nodded, and gaped at her as if she'd never seen a pregnant woman. If she was astonished now, just wait a few more months when Rachel would be unable to see her own feet. Rachel made her way to the bathroom, trying not to wake Bryce. She almost stepped on him, since he was lying on the floor, sound asleep.

A little something tugged at her heart. He'd sacrificed his comfort for his daughter. Although there was plenty of room in the king-sized bed, he let the little girl have it all to herself.

Maybe she wet the bed. But the spot where she'd tossed the covers aside looked clean and dry, if a little rumpled. The other side of the bed, where Bryce usually slept, was undisturbed. It wasn't as if he'd crawled into bed with her and given up when the little girl had become too restless.

She wondered if he'd have felt more comfortable sharing a bed if he'd spent more time with his daughter all along. From what he'd told her, they barely spent three or four weeks together throughout the year. And those visits had been with his ex-wife nearby.

Damn it. She was doing it again. Letting her heart take over, when she really needed to rely on her head. Now was not the time to soften, just because he'd slept on the floor didn't mean she should forgive him.

But what, exactly, did she need to forgive him for? Putting his daughter's needs above everything else? Including baseball?

As long as she'd know him, he'd never missed a game. He'd had the playboy reputation for much of his career, but he'd never missed a game. He'd never been unable to work because of it.

Rachel splashed cold water on her face. She needed to wake up. Just because he had a good reason to hide away from the public didn't give him an excuse to hide from her. How could they move forward together if they didn't lean on each other in times of trouble? Their wedding had been somewhat of a blur, but she clearly remembered the part about for better or *worse*. The fact that he'd shut her out at the first sign of trouble didn't bode well for their future together.

After rinsing her toothbrush and straightening the hand towels, Rachel made her way to the kitchen. A little girl needed her breakfast. She needed her father, and in some small way, needed her stepmother, too.

"So, do you like pancakes?" Rachel put on her least wicked stepmom smile and motioned for Hailey to join her in the kitchen.

The little girl just nodded.

"Would you like to help?"

She shrugged and clutched her pillow tighter.

"I'm not the best cook in the world." Rachel hoped to sound encouraging. She got the feeling the child was frightened. Whether it was of cooking or the whole ordeal, she didn't know. "But I'm pretty sure I'm the messiest cook in San Francisco."

A tiny smile escaped Hailey's lips.

"So if you don't mind a little flour in your hair, and syrup on the counters, you're welcome to join me." Rachel reached for the apron and held it out to Hailey. "You might want to leave your pillow in the living room, though. It looks like it's pretty special."

"My mom made it for me." The girl hugged it even tighter. "When Daddy moved to San Francisco, she ordered one of his jerseys, and made me a pillow so I wouldn't miss him so much."

"That's sweet." A big lump formed in Rachel's throat. She couldn't imagine anything easing the pain that Bryce's absence from her life would bring.

Hailey walked slowly to the couch, and carefully set her pillow on the leather cushions.

"I've never made pancakes before." Hailey's eyes were wide with trepidation and eagerness.

"Well, it's time you learn how." Rachel grabbed the cookbook from the shelf. "I find it's helpful to follow a recipe until you get the hang of things. Then you can get adventurous and add things like chocolate chips."

"Chocolate chips?"

"You've never had chocolate chip pancakes?"

Hailey shook her head.

"Then you haven't lived." Rachel hoped she hadn't eaten them all. She kept a bag on hand for cravings. She checked the pantry. Whew. Half full. And then she spied a couple of bananas that were getting a little too ripe. "You know what's even better than chocolate chip pancakes?"

"No?"

"Banana chocolate chip pancakes." A memory slammed into Rachel of her stepfather trying to help in the kitchen when her mother had been on bedrest with her sister. At first, Rachel had wanted nothing to do with the strange concoction. First of all, the pancakes were too big, almost the size of the plate. Her mother had always made silver dollar pancakes, barely bigger than bite-sized. And the ones Greg made had stuff in them. Mushed up bananas, and chocolate chips that were supposed to be for cookies, not breakfast.

"Okay, I guess." Hailey still sounded unsure.

"Try them. You might like them."

"Like green eggs and ham?"

"I guess so." It had been a while since Rachel had read the Dr. Seuss classic. But if the pancakes were a bust, she could always break out the food coloring and at least make the eggs green.

"Do you like bacon?" Rachel asked, a sudden craving hitting like a tsunami. "Because I feel like also making some bacon."

"Okay."

Soon they were working together like an all-star team. A few miscommunications along the way, but for the most part, they were doing their best and having fun. The bacon was getting crisp in the oven, all the dry ingredients were measured and blended together. The bananas were mashed and ready to be added after the eggs and buttermilk were mixed in. Last, but not least, came the chocolate chips, carefully folded into the batter.

"Now, let's make sure the griddle is nice and hot." Rachel placed a small dot of batter on the surface of the pan. When it quickly browned and bubbled, she flicked it over, pleased with the perfect color. "Looks like it's ready."

She helped the little girl stand on a chair, and guided her in pouring half-cup scoops of batter onto the hot griddle. A few drips would make those crispy little micro pancakes that her stepfather always used to swipe through the butter dish before popping them into his mouth.

"Something smells good." Bryce stumbled into the kitchen, his hair matted and his clothes rumpled from sleeping on the floor. "Almost good enough to eat."

"We're making pancakes." Hailey's face lit up at the sight of him. "With banana and chocolate chips."

"Wow. What a treat." He started for the coffee pot, but stopped short.

"It's okay. If you want coffee, go ahead." Rachel could use some herself, but she'd forego it for the sake of her child. Bryce looked like he needed it. And she didn't want him having to go down the street to order it like he usually did. "I can handle it."

"Are you sure?"

"Yes." To prove it, she pulled the coffee out of the cupboard, opened the package, and inhaled. The aroma was comforting more than anything.

Bryce took over making the coffee, while Rachel finished the pancakes. Soon they all sat down at the small kitchen table to have their breakfast.

With a sigh, Bryce sipped his coffee. He looked exhausted. As if he hadn't slept in days. Well, neither had she. Having her husband communicate only via short texts while the Internet exploded with rumors did that to a person.

He twisted his neck, an audible crack sounding a little bit like corn popping.

"The first thing we need to do is order some bedroom furniture for Hailey's room." Bryce dug into his pancakes. He washed the first few bites down with more coffee. "And we'll have to get the exercise equipment moved out."

"We could use my bedroom furniture." Rachel realized she wouldn't need it as long as Hailey was living here. With Bryce's schedule, there was no way he could take care of a nine-year-old on his own. "And make room in the storage shed at the same time."

"That would be fine." Bryce looked a little surprised by her suggestion. "But I was thinking Hailey might like to pick out something for herself."

"That's okay." Hailey shrugged. "I don't need anything fancy. I'm only going to be her for a month, right?"

A look of concern passed over Bryce's features, but he quickly changed his expression to a carefree grin. The one she'd learned was a mask. One he used to shut out the world. Including her.

"Why don't we call the movers and have them take out the treadmill, weight bench, and stuff we don't need." Bryce sounded entirely too cheerful. "We'll take them to the storage place and if Hailey likes the furniture set we've got stored there, great. If not, we'll go shopping."

"That sounds like a great plan." Rachel tried to sound positive, but it still bothered her that he was putting on a show. Maybe it was for Hailey's benefit, not because he didn't want to open up to her.

And he never would. Especially not with Hailey in the house.

So for the next thirty days, they would live together, under one roof, pretending to be a family.

* * * *

When Hailey found Rachel's bedroom furniture acceptable, Bryce had the movers load it in the truck and deliver it to the apartment. Getting it set up didn't leave much time to shop for bedding and accessories. But there would be no time after tonight's game.

"So let's go downtown and buy you some new sheets and a bedspread." Bryce tried to sound more excited than stressed.

"Okay." Hailey agreed, but didn't seem too enthusiastic.

The three of them piled in Rachel's Range Rover. Rachel let him drive. She'd suggested Target and Hailey agreed. A far cry from the exclusive children's boutique he'd been dragged to when picking out Hailey's nursery. But that trip had taken hours, looking at all the perfectly coordinating bedrooms organized by theme. Then arguing over whether to do fairies, princesses, or fairy princesses. He didn't remember what they'd (Jillian) decided, since she'd gone and changed the bedroom several times before Hailey even started school.

"Okay, here we are. Pick out anything you want." They stood in the bedding section, where he was bombarded with an assortment of choices. He supposed she was too old for the Disney princesses and Hello Kitty sheets. And he didn't want to think about her sleeping with this year's version of N'Sync on her comforter. He shuddered at the image of a boy band on a little girl's bed.

Hailey shrugged, as if nothing really appealed to her. She walked past the little girl comforter sets, and reached for a plain set of white sheets.

"I want you pick out something that will make you feel comfortable in your room." He knew what it was like to stay in an unfamiliar room. He'd lived with host families when he first started in the minor leagues. He'd slept in recently vacated teen rooms, antique furnished guest rooms, and he'd shared a room or two with fax machines or sewing machines, sleeping on a futon in basements. "It will be your space for as long as you're here."

"You're just buying me lots of stuff and then you're going to go away." Hailey's voice was so soft, he almost didn't hear her.

"Hey." He knelt down in front of her. "Is that what you think? That I'm just going to go away?"

She nodded.

"I know I've been gone a lot. Even when I lived in Pittsburgh, I spent a lot of time on the road." His heart sank. He'd still spend a lot of time traveling over the next month. "I'll be here for a little more than a week. And then maybe you can come with me on my next road trip. We'll go to San Diego and Los Angeles. Would you like that?"

"I guess." She didn't sound too excited about the idea.

He had to remember the girl had been through a lot in the last few days. Maybe he should have let her stay in Pittsburgh with her friend. At least she would have familiar surroundings. And she wouldn't have to travel to the ballpark with him and fall asleep in the clubhouse. He really hadn't thought this through.

And he'd made a huge mistake in not discussing his decision with Rachel.

"Well, good. That's settled." He stood up and clapped his hands together. "Now, you still need sheets for your bed. And blankets and a comforter."

"Okay." She walked slowly up and down the bedding aisle, her hands behind her back, as she inspected the choices.

"Do you think it's a good idea taking her to San Diego?" he whispered to Rachel.

"Yeah. I think we'll have a good time."

"We?" He didn't want to get his hopes up too high, but it sounded like she was willing to join them.

"Yeah, I think you need me to come with you."

"I do need you, Rachel." And not just because of Hailey. But he didn't know how to tell her.

"You should have talked to me."

"Yeah. I know." Bryce swallowed the big lump in his throat. He knew he'd screwed up.

"We'll get through this." She patted him on the shoulder and turned her attention to Hailey. "Oh, that's perfect."

Hailey had selected a multicolored quilt, with a bold, almost tribal pattern. The pinks were vibrant, not prissy. She chose mismatched sheets in bright pink and green with bright blue pillowcases. He wondered if she'd get much sleep. But at least her room would be cheerful.

"That looks great." Bryce added, "What else do you need?"

Hailey shrugged again.

He and Rachel exchanged a look that said neither of them knew what a nine-year-old girl needed either.

When she was younger, he'd constantly been scolded for using the wrong toothpaste, the wrong laundry soap. Did she still need special soaps, shampoos, and detergents, or could she use what he and Rachel used?

They ended up getting shampoo, conditioner, toothpaste, and strawberry-scented body wash. It wasn't everything she'd need to make her feel at home, but it was a start.

Chapter 27

They had barely put the sheets on Hailey's bed before they had to report to the ballpark. Rachel had agreed to look after the girl, show her what she did to get ready for the game, and introduce her to the television crew. She couldn't imagine what the poor child must be going through. She'd had to leave her home, her mother, and her friends to fly across the country and stay with the father she barely knew and his new wife.

Rachel's heart ached for the little girl. She had often felt like a stranger in her own family. And she knew that it would take time for her to trust her new stepparent.

Time. That was something neither Rachel nor Bryce would have enough of. The baseball schedule was grueling enough to a single person. But throw in a family—children with bedtimes around the seventh inning stretch—and it would be darned near impossible to have a normal family life.

Something that would be more than just a temporary problem next season. No. She couldn't think about next year. They just had to get through this month. Keep Bryce's daughter safe and as happy as a child of an addict could be.

Rationally, Rachel knew that Bryce's ex-wife hadn't overdosed on booze and prescription drugs because of her marriage and impending motherhood, but she wondered if Hailey would blame her. A nine-year-old would be looking for a reason. Someone to blame. A way to make sense of it all.

"So, Hailey, are you okay following me around tonight?" Rachel kept her voice as cheerful as possible. "I can show you an insider's view of the ballpark."

"Okay." Hailey shrugged.

"I'm sure you'd rather be with your dad, but all those smelly guys?" Rachel made a face and fanned her hand in front of her nose, eliciting a little giggle from Hailey.

"My mom never let me watch baseball." She bit her lower lip, as if it was something to be ashamed of. "But when I went to McKenzie's house, I got to watch my dad play sometimes."

Rachel wanted to sweep the poor girl into her arms.

"My mom wasn't a big sports fan, either," Rachel admitted. "But my stepdad is. He's one of the reasons I got interested in watching and playing sports."

"You play sports?"

"Not anymore, but I played softball as a kid, and in high school." Rachel hoped to encourage her. Playing sports had been a huge confidence builder for her. Maybe it could do the same for Hailey.

"My mom seemed to think sports were a waste of time. That I should be interested in dance or music or stuff like that." Hailey brushed a lock of hair off her forehead. "She even signed me up for a theater camp. Like I want to get on stage in front of people and make a fool of myself."

"Maybe she just wants you to have many experiences. The only way to find out what your passions are is to try new things."

"Yeah, I guess." The girl sounded disappointed. "It's just the experiences were always what she wanted, not what I was interested in."

"So what are you interested in?"

"I like to draw and write stories." Hailey's eyes lit up as she talked about her hobby.

"I wish I'd known. We could have brought a notebook." Rachel was pleased that the girl felt comfortable enough to share her passion with her. "Oh, I'll bet my friends Kip and Kurt would know where you could get some paper and pens."

"Who are Kip and Kurt?"

"They're the broadcast team. They talk about the games on TV. Kurt does the play by play and Kip is the color commentator."

"Huh?"

"I forgot. You don't watch a lot of baseball, do you?"

Hailey shook her head and looked down at the ground as though she was ashamed.

"Well, we'll fix that, won't we?" Rachel gave what she hoped was an encouraging smile.

"Okay." Hailey looked up at her with big blue eyes. They weren't the same blue as Bryce's eyes. She must take after her mother. A flood of emotions filled her. Jealousy was one of them. This little girl was the product of a one-night stand between Bryce and some woman he'd met in a bar. Rachel wasn't sure if the fact that he'd married the woman made things better or worse. She supposed it was better for Hailey, even if things didn't work out between her parents. At least the little girl wasn't a bastard. Even if she didn't know what a bastard was.

Rachel knew. She'd known the feeling even before she'd heard the word. Before she'd seen the blank spot on her birth certificate where her father's name should have been. It meant feeling inferior. There was something about her that was lacking. Roots. A history. A daddy.

Hailey had a daddy. And he was damn good one, despite what he thought about not having been around. He still held his little girl's heart in his two steady hands.

"Let's go on up to the booth. You'll get a great view of the ballpark, and maybe even learn a few things about the game."

"Okay." Hailey was a sweet, agreeable girl. Rachel was in danger of becoming attached. No. It was already too late. Just like her father, the girl had charmed her way into Rachel's heart the moment they'd met.

Hailey slipped her hand into Rachel's as they made their way up to the club level where the broadcast booth was located. Yep. She was a goner. It was going to be really hard to say goodbye to the child at the end of the month.

And Bryce? She didn't know what she was going to do about Bryce.

The man had broken her heart more times than she could count. The other women were one thing, back when they weren't even dating and he didn't even owe her anything. But this…this was a major life crisis and he'd completely shut her out. Didn't even bother to tell her what was happening. He'd acted like nothing had happened. That it was no big deal he'd missed a game to take care of a family emergency. Hell, she'd thought she was family.

Her hand moved on its own over her abdomen. The child growing inside her reminded her of what it meant to be a parent. It meant that sometimes you'd do whatever it took to protect that child. Even if that meant shutting out the rest of the world during a crisis.

She just wished that Bryce had trusted her enough to include her in his crisis. Oh, he was leaning on her now, but she couldn't be sure if he needed her, or if Hailey needed her.

She knocked on the broadcast booth door, and pushed it open, entering with her most show-worthy smile.

"Kip, Kurt, there's someone I'd like you to meet." Rachel ushered Hailey into the room. "This is Hailey Baxter, Bryce's daughter."

"Well, hello there, Miss Hailey." Kip stood and offered his hand. The former pitcher was almost as much of a charmer as Bryce. "It's very nice to meet you."

"Nice to meet you too." The girl's hand was swallowed up by Kip's two-handed handshake.

"Welcome to San Francisco." Kurt exuded a more subtle charm. He was the laid-back, rational half of the dynamic duo. His low-key persona balanced Kip's over-the-top enthusiasm. "I hope you'll enjoy your stay here."

"Thank you." Hailey blushed and tucked a dark strand of hair behind her ear.

"So Hailey is an artist," Rachel said with pride. "And a writer. I was wondering if you guys knew where we could find some paper and maybe some pens or pencils."

Kurt jumped up with a smile. "I'm sure we could borrow some paper from the printer."

He walked over to the back wall where the office machines stood. He opened up the copier/printer/fax machine and pulled out a handful of white copy paper.

"I think we can round up some pens from over here." Kip opened a drawer and grabbed a handful of writing implements.

"Thanks guys." Rachel didn't know what she'd do without her partners. "Do you think she could come back up here and work on her drawings if she gets tired later?"

"Absolutely." Kip grinned.

"We'd love to have her," Kurt agreed.

"Thanks, guys." Rachel breathed a sigh of relief. She knew that Hailey would be in good hands if the game dragged on, and she was needed to report on happenings around the ballpark.

"Have you ever been inside a real broadcaster's booth?" Kip invited Hailey to step up to the microphone where he would be giving his insight into the game once it started.

"No. I went to a game with my dad in Pittsburgh, but I stayed mostly in the locker room."

Kip proceeded to show Hailey the view from the announcers' booth. He pointed out how they could see the whole field from up here, and the view of the city, and he told her about the seagulls who would show up just before the game ended even though there wasn't a set time in baseball.

Rachel leaned against the wall, and Kurt must have picked up on her worry.

"Everything okay with the home team?" he asked in a low voice.

"Yeah. Hailey will be staying with us for about a month." She tried to sound cheerful.

"That's great." Kurt was ever the optimist.

"Yeah. It is. I just hope she doesn't get too bored coming to the ballpark every night."

"How can you get bored at the ballpark?" Kurt teased.

"Maybe not necessarily bored, but I worry that some of the nights will be kind of late for a girl her age."

"How old is she?"

"Nine."

"A great age." Kurt smiled. "I remember when my girls were that age. Now my youngest is in college. Time flies."

"Yeah." Rachel couldn't even think that far ahead. She was still anxiously awaiting the birth of her child. She didn't want to even think about college.

"She's home for the summer, though. Maybe for the last time." Kurt gave a proud, yet resigned sigh. "You know, Kaitlyn might be able to help you out here."

"What do you mean?"

"She's studying to be a teacher. Loves kids." Kurt's face lit up like it did during a late inning rally. "She might be available to fill in as a part-time nanny."

"You know, that might be a really good idea." Rachel had been wondering how she'd find someone on short notice. "Do you really think she'd be interested in giving up her evenings?"

"Yeah. She's got a boyfriend, but he's back in Indiana for the summer. She's bored, but she doesn't want to go out and feel like she's betraying him. Besides, she doesn't turn twenty-one until late August."

"It wouldn't hurt to see if she's interested." Rachel was surprised by how the weight had lifted from her shoulders. "It would actually be a huge help."

"I'll text her and let you know."

"That would be great, thanks."

"And if Hailey gets bored out there, or tired, you're welcome to bring her back to the booth, here," Kip added. "My granddaughter is about her age. She's taken a few naps up here when my son has taken her mother out for a nice dinner and the old man's idea of babysitting is to bring her to the park."

"I appreciate it." Rachel breathed a sigh of relief. They really were a family here. It wasn't just a marketing ploy.

"So, what did you think of my mentors? You think you could hang out with them for a bit while I go around the ballpark doing interviews?" She crouched down just enough to look the little girl in the eye.

"What's a mentor?" Hailey asked. "I know what dementors are. They're those creepy floaty things in Harry Potter."

"Sorry, I haven't seen Harry Potter." Rachel wondered what other kid's pop culture she would need to take a crash course in. "But a mentor is someone who teaches and leads by example. Like Obi Wan Kenobi."

"Who?"

"From Star Wars."

"Oh. Was he the green guy? Or the old guy in the robe?"

"The old guy. The one who taught Luke the ways of the Force."

"I like the robots. And the princess with the weird hair. She's cool."

"Yeah. Princess Leia is pretty cool."

"So how are those guys your mentors?" Hailey was a bright, curious child.

"Well, they've been in the broadcasting business a long time. They taught me a lot about being a reporter and a lot about the game. They both were players, like your dad."

"Do you like being a reporter?"

"I do. I meet a lot of interesting people, and it's my job to watch baseball."

"Why do you like baseball?"

It was a good question. Not necessarily an easy question, but a good one.

"Well, for one thing, it's an interesting game. Anything can happen, and often does. It isn't always the game's biggest stars who make the biggest impact."

"Is my daddy a star?"

"Oh yeah." Rachel's heart thumped and bumped with pride in her husband and sadness that his daughter didn't know how great he was. "He's one of the best. He was named the Most Valuable Player in the World Series last season."

"Cool." The little girl's face shone with pride.

"Yeah, it was very cool. I wish you could have come to the games." Rachel wondered why she hadn't been there. She couldn't imagine the girl's mother being so bitter as to keep her child from witnessing her father's greatest professional accomplishment. But then again, it seemed that Bryce's ex wasn't exactly in a good place.

The urge to pull Hailey into her arms and just hold tight came over Rachel. Instead, she offered a warm smile.

"My mom doesn't really like sports." Hailey sounded so resigned to the fact. "And I don't think she really likes my dad all that much."

This time Rachel couldn't resist putting her arm around the little girl's shoulder.

"Divorce can be tough for some people." Not that she had any experience in the matter. "Sometimes moms and dads try to make it work, but they just can't. But that doesn't mean they don't both love you."

"I know." Hailey shrugged, as if it was just something she dealt with, like being picked last for the team or dropping the ice cream off her ice cream cone.

"So would you like to follow me around the ballpark and learn about the game?"

"Okay."

"They're about to start batting practice." Rachel ushered Hailey down to the lower level, so they could get a close up view of the field. "Your dad lights it up during BP."

At the puzzled look on Hailey's face, Rachel felt the need to explain. "Baseball is full of colorful language. We use a lot of metaphors."

"We learned about figurative language in school. You know, similes and metaphors and idioms. We had to do an art project illustrating idioms. Some kids did ones like ants in your pants or open a can of worms."

"So what idiom did you illustrate?"

"The one I turned in was about flying colors." Her cheeks stained pink. "But I actually did a whole notebook of them."

"I'd like to see it sometime." Rachel motioned for Hailey to sit in one of the seats down in front. The ones she knew wouldn't fill with the season ticket holders until closer to game time. Frank and Gladys took the ferry to the games. They stopped for a drink at the bar where they'd met almost fifty years ago, and then arrived at the ballpark in time to sing along to the National Anthem.

"Okay." Hailey sat down and looked around the ballpark with wide eyes and wonder.

The batting cage was rolled out, and the screen was set up to protect the pitcher from balls hit hard up the middle. The pitchers came out first, so they could have plenty of time to warm up after batting practice.

"There's Nathan Cooper and Diego Garcia. They're relief pitchers." Rachel explained. "They'll come out of the bullpen late in the game. Cooper will face mostly lefties, and Garcia is the closer. That means he'll come into the game in the ninth inning if there's a lead of three or fewer runs and try to close out the game. It's called a save if he keeps the other team from tying or going ahead."

Hailey nodded, taking in the information.

"And that's Mark Carson." Rachel pointed to the big guy who looked a little like a lumberjack with the bat tossed casually over his shoulder. "He's our Ace. That means he's the best starting pitcher on the team. He's not a bad hitter, either. He's been known to knock one out of the park on occasion."

"That means he hits home runs?" Hailey inquired.

"Yes. But see, most pitchers aren't very good hitters. The starters only play every five games." Rachel hoped she was explaining it without sounding like she was dumbing it down. "And the relievers almost never get an at bat. They usually only pitch an inning or less, so they don't get a turn to hit. I think the last time Cooper stepped into the batter's box was in 2013."

"So why do they get to practice hitting first?"

"Just to keep sharp, I guess." Rachel sat back, as if she was merely an observer. "Like I said earlier, you never know what can happen. A game can go extra innings and the manager might not want to burn all his pitchers so he might give them a turn at the plate. Especially if it's a bunt situation."

"What's a bunt situation? I thought that was a kind of cake. You know, with the hole in the middle."

"That's a Bundt cake. No, a bunt is where the batter squares up and hits the ball really softly, so that the infielders will have to come up to field it, and most of the time, their only chance is to get the batter out at first base."

"Why would they make an out on purpose?"

"It's called a sacrifice. The runner who was at first moves over to second, and is more likely to score on a ground ball to the outfield."

"A sacrifice." Hailey filed the information away.

"It's not as exciting as a home run, but sometimes a sacrifice makes all the difference in the game."

And sometimes a sacrifice could make all the difference in life.

Bryce had sacrificed everything to bring Hailey here. To keep her safe. He'd put his job in jeopardy, even his marriage.

The question was, would it be enough?

Chapter 28

Bryce had never let himself get distracted by ladies in the stands. At least not in the regular season. Spring training had been a different animal. Flirting before the games was part of the ritual, part of the game. Or it had been.

Now, as he waited his turn for batting practice his attention was drawn to two special ladies. Rachel had brought Hailey down to the prime seats at field level. As the in-game reporter, she had access regular fans didn't have. He glanced over to see Rachel cheerfully explaining the game to his daughter. Yes. She was his daughter. Even if she wasn't his flesh and blood.

At least the two of them seemed to be getting along. He'd made a big assumption in thinking that Rachel would help him with looking after Hailey. Especially since he'd given her absolutely no warning. And yet she'd stepped up to the plate. She was doing a better job at making Hailey feel at home than he had.

He would be forever grateful for her help. But he had to wonder if she was only sticking around for Hailey's sake. He'd seen the packed bags. Knew exactly what they'd meant. She was done with him. With his thoughtlessness. His past had finally caught up to him. She couldn't trust him. When he'd been out of reach, she'd believed the worst.

And he had no way of making it up to her. He couldn't buy his way out of this. Couldn't charm his way, either. He'd already married her, so he couldn't just drop down on one knee and propose.

The only thing he could do would be to be there for both of them. To be steady and strong. And he'd have to fight for them. Even though he didn't deserve either of them.

But he loved them. He loved Hailey more than he'd ever thought possible. Hearing that she might not be his had been devastating. But it didn't make him love her any less.

His love for Rachel was different, but just as fierce. Only he hadn't told her. He'd been too afraid of spooking her. Funny, considering he was the one who was supposed to be the *player*. He was supposed to be the one afraid of commitment. But he'd come to realize that Rachel had been just as scared to give her whole heart as he'd been.

Somehow this crisis with Jillian had made him realize that hiding how he really felt wasn't doing anyone any good. Sure, there had never been any love between him and his ex-wife. But maybe if he'd told her how much he'd admired the job she'd done raising Hailey, or if he'd stepped up and taken some of the burden off her… Well, he couldn't undo the past. But he could do better in the future.

And he'd start by focusing on the present. He stepped into the batter's box and missed the first two pitches. He fouled off a third. It took him a little longer than usual to find his stroke. But once he found it, he was dialed in. The ball sailed over the fences and he was able to hit to all fields. True, it was only batting practice and having a good BP didn't always translate into success in a game, but it added to his confidence and sometimes that did carry over.

Tonight felt like one of those nights.

When he came up in the first inning with the first two runners on, he hit a screaming double down the left field line to give the Goliaths a quick two-run lead. Santiago knocked him in with a double to the gap in right center and the rally was on.

Bryce ended the night going three for four, with a double, single, and a home run to cap off the six to two win. It felt good to get back on track. The whole team was back to where they'd been last October, playing as a smooth-running machine. The starting pitching was solid, the bullpen held the lead, and the hitters were making a contribution up and down the lineup.

Last year, he'd been just as lucky off the field when things were going well. Maybe he could get that back on track, too.

Rachel approached him with her microphone in hand, her cameraman in tow.

"That's the Bryce Baxter we all know and love." She started the interview with her signature line. "You looked like the same team that was tearing it up last fall."

"Thanks." He tried not to think about whether or not she meant the love part.

"We could tell right off the bat that you would have a great night."

"I felt it, too." He often got a sixth sense kind of thing going when he had a particularly good game. There was a buzzing feeling when he stepped onto the field. Of course, maybe he always had that feeling, he just ignored it when he had a bad game.

"You've gained some of the ground you lost in the early part of the season. L.A. has dropped a few games but San Diego is starting to pick up some momentum."

"And we face both of those teams in the next couple of weeks. In their house." He tried not to look ahead. "But we've got to take care of business at home first."

"Yes. We do."

He looked around, wondering where his daughter was. He hadn't seen her since the game started, but then he didn't look into the crowd once the first pitch was thrown. It was just a big blur of color and noise and support.

"Where's Hailey?" he asked, forgetting he was on camera still.

"She's up in the booth with Kip and Kurt. They're showing your daughter a behind-the-scenes look at broadcasting from the most beautiful ballpark in the world."

Smooth. She'd answered his question in a way that wouldn't confuse the viewers.

"Maybe you can start a junior broadcasters program."

"I'll run it by the studio." Her smile was genuine, not just for TV. He liked the way she lit up when she was doing her job. It was obvious she enjoyed her work. "Until then, I'll just say congratulations on another great game."

"Thank you." He tipped his hat to her and to the fans and trotted into the clubhouse to shower.

When he reached his locker, he found a text from Rachel. Hailey had fallen asleep upstairs in the broadcast booth and she didn't want to wake her until he was ready.

I'm ready now.

Okay. Will meet you at the car.

I can come up.

It's easier for us to come down.

Bryce beat them to the parking lot. He was just about to start the engine when he saw Rachel leading a swaying Hailey. She looked about as steady as he had after he first learned of Jillian's betrayal.

"Let's get you home and into bed." Bryce realized how tired he was now that the adrenaline from the win had worn off.

"Okay, Daddy." Hailey leaned against him and he wrapped his arm around her.

Rachel undid the locks and went around to the driver's side while he got Hailey into the backseat and buckled into her seatbelt.

"Do you want me to drive?" he asked, but it didn't really matter to him.

"I'm okay." Rachel slid behind the wheel.

"You know, I can't thank you enough for all you've done for Hailey." He climbed into the passenger's seat.

"She's a great kid," Rachel acknowledged. "We had a good time tonight. Didn't we?"

She glanced back in the rearview mirror and smiled.

"Uh-huh," came a sleepy voice from the backseat.

"I'm going to call Kaitlyn Dwyer tomorrow. She's home from college and might be available to look after Hailey at night so she doesn't have to sleep in the corner of the booth." Leave it to Rachel to start looking for a nanny, even if it was only for the summer.

He'd have to find someone permanently if he was able to get custody of Hailey.

"Thanks. I appreciate it." He leaned back into the leather seat. It really was a nice car. Or SUV or crossover, whatever they were calling this kind of vehicle these days. "Have you met her before?"

"Oh yeah. She's a great girl. She's going to school to be a teacher, so she loves kids. She'll be terrific." Rachel had it all figured out. She was going to be one hell of a mother. "If she's available."

"That will be a big help."

"The nights can get pretty late at the ballpark." They were down to making small talk. Like an old married couple. Or estranged lovers.

They rode the rest of the way in quiet. Hailey had fallen asleep on the short drive and he carried her into the elevator and up to the apartment. He tucked her in bed still wearing her skinny jeans and long sleeved t-shirt.

"Don't you think you should get her undressed?" Rachel stood in the doorway.

How did he explain why he didn't feel comfortable undressing the child? He had to be very careful if he was going to pursue custody.

"I don't want to wake her." He stepped away from the bed and ran his hand through his hair.

"We should at least get her jeans off." Rachel approached. She seemed to have no qualms about stepping right in. She gently peeled off Hailey's pants. Hailey grumbled and then rolled over, reaching for her jersey pillow.

Bryce couldn't breathe. Both of his girls had taken hold of his heart.

He followed Rachel out into the hall.

"So shall I take the couch tonight?" The packed suitcases still weighed heavily on his mind.

"What? Why?"

"I get the feeling the only reason you're still here is because of Hailey." He felt raw. Exposed.

Rachel shook her head, pasted on a smile, and marched into their bedroom.

Not sure if he should follow, in case she was heading straight for the packed bags, he took a deep breath before going after her.

"I was hurt." Rachel sat on the edge of the bed. Her smile had faded and a weary expression had taken its place. "I didn't know what was going on and I didn't want to stick around to have you throw an affair in my face."

"I didn't have an affair." He could see now how it could look like he had.

"I know that now." She lifted her shoulders in a half-shrug. "But at the time I couldn't imagine any other reason why you wouldn't talk to me."

"I'm sorry I didn't think to keep you in the loop. I was too scared, I guess."

"Scared of what? That I wouldn't understand? That I'd be jealous of your ex-wife?"

"No." Well, maybe. But that was only part of it. "I was scared that Jillian wouldn't make it. And it was all my fault. I was afraid dragging you into it would only make things worse."

Without another word, Rachel rose, and headed for the bathroom.

He fell to the bed. The bed he would share with Rachel. At least for now. He had no illusions of them spending the night in each other's arms. First of all, Hailey was just down the hall. But he also knew Rachel didn't trust him.

He only had himself to blame.

* * * *

Rachel brushed her teeth and put on her pajamas. Hopefully, she wasn't being a fool by sleeping in the same bed with Bryce. Her heart was a jumbled mess. She loved him, but he had hurt her. And it wasn't just because she'd thought he was with another woman. That would have almost been easier. Then she would be justified in feeling betrayed.

No. He'd simply been dealing with an accidental (or not) overdose by his ex-wife. He'd gone from being the fun-time dad who spent more money than time on his daughter to being the full-time caregiver to the precious little girl.

Maybe she was being unreasonable, but the fact that he didn't trust her enough with the information was what hurt the most. It was as if Hailey and his ex were his first family. His real family. And Rachel wasn't even an afterthought.

Only now he needed her. He couldn't take care of his little girl on his own. Even if the rules hadn't changed and Hailey could serve as bat girl—after a near collision with the three-year-old bat boy during the 2002 World Series, they now had to be fourteen—life at the ballpark night after night would be tough on a young girl.

It wasn't much easier having her tag along as Rachel did her in-game interviews and highlights around the ballpark. But at least she wasn't stuck inside the clubhouse, watching the game on the monitors. Hailey had been able to see her father's double and home run. She'd watched him turn two double plays, and she'd been swept up in the excitement of the game.

The girl had also been given tutelage from two of the best TV broadcasters in all of baseball. At least in Rachel's opinion. As well as the opinion of Goliaths fans who'd been dismayed to find the World Series had been called by national broadcasters and not their hometown guys.

Hailey had asked a lot of questions and listened to their answers. She was a great kid. But a month of being dragged to work with her father and stepmother would try the patience of the most saintly child. Eventually she'd want to go home to her mother, her friends, and everything that was familiar.

Right now was a honeymoon phase. She was eager to please her dad, but that would change when he told her no for the first time. Or when she wouldn't eat her dinner or pick up her clothes or when she wanted to watch a show that he didn't think was appropriate for someone her age.

And it would be even harder when Rachel had to be the one to step in and correct the child. Not only wasn't she the girl's mother, but at some point, just the fact that Rachel was here and her mother wasn't would become an issue. And who knew how she'd deal with her worry and fear and uncertainty.

She wasn't sure she was up for all of this.

But she also knew she couldn't just walk away either. From Hailey or Bryce.

Chapter 29

The rest of the home stand had gone smoothly. Kaitlyn Dwyer had been more than happy to stay with Hailey at night. They paid her a modest sum, just enough to keep her from sponging off her father but not so much that she'd abandon her dream of becoming a teacher for a more lucrative career as nanny to the stars.

Now they were in San Diego for the first leg of a road trip. Hailey had been excited to fly on the chartered jet with the team. She'd received the royal treatment as the daughter of the reigning World Series MVP. It probably helped that Bryce had been named player of the week for his offensive production over the last several games.

Although, the more he thought about it, he realized that she would have been welcomed by the Goliaths family no matter what his stats were. They were indeed a family. Many players' wives and kids were along for this trip. Who wouldn't want to spend a few days in San Diego in mid-June? Perfect weather, sandy beaches, and a friendly, yet competitive rivalry from their opponents and their fans.

Hunter Collins-Santiago had made the trip. She told stories about growing up in the Goliaths' clubhouse and made Hailey feel like a part of the family.

Annabelle Jones had joined her fiancé Nathan Cooper and brought her twins. Sophie and Olivia were a few years younger than Hailey, but the girls had become fast friends on the flight down.

They had barely dropped their suitcases in the hotel room when Hailey asked if she could go swimming with the twins. Rachel volunteered to go down to the pool to help supervise. That would give him time to chill for a little while before he had to head to the ballpark for tonight's game.

Bryce stretched out on the bed while Hailey raced into the adjoining room to change into her swimsuit. When she came back out in a tiny little string bikini, he sat up.

"What are you wearing?" His eyes must be playing tricks on him. No way was that skimpy thing designed for a little girl.

"My bathing suit." Hailey had a look of innocence on her face.

"I don't think so." Bryce shook his head. "You're not going out in public in that. Don't you have something more…um, appropriate for a girl your age? Where did you even get such a thing?"

"Mommy bought it for me." Tears welled up in her eyes. "We had a girls' day with shopping and pedicures and…" Her bottom lip started to quiver. She wrapped her arms around herself as if she suddenly realized how exposed she was. "She was happy then." Hailey said quietly before returning to her room and slamming the door.

Shit. Bryce rubbed his hands over his face.

"Maybe I can help her find a tank top or something to wear over it," Rachel offered. "Then maybe we can look for a more modest suit."

"No." He didn't mean to take his frustration out on Rachel. "I mean, I don't know if it would help. What the hell was Jillian thinking? The damn thing looks like it came from Victoria's Secret. Do they have a little girls' section?"

"I don't know."

"Do you think I'm being unreasonable?" He ran his hand through his hair. "I mean, she's a little girl. She shouldn't dress like a twenty-two-year-old."

"I'm afraid it's only going to get worse," Rachel informed him. "As she gets older and wants to look more grown up. But right now the important thing is that she's upset and thinking about her mother."

"Yeah. I know. I just don't know what to do about it."

"Try talking to her. Not at her, but to her."

"Talk to her? Not exactly my strong suit." Bryce knew he was more of an action kind of guy. But when his actions had been limited to buying love, he hadn't exactly hit it out of the park. Time for a new game plan.

He crossed to the second room of the suite and knocked on Hailey's door. "Can I come in?"

A muffled, "whatever," came from the other side.

Pushing the door open, he stepped inside.

"Hey." Yeah, there was an invitation to some real communication.

Hailey sat on the bed. She'd slipped a t-shirt on and had tucked her knees under the fabric. Her eyes were red and swollen from crying.

"I'm sorry. I guess I overreacted." Approaching her carefully, he hesitated before sitting down next to her. "Do you mind?"

She simply shrugged.

He started to say the swimsuit was fine, but that wasn't really the issue.

"You miss your mom, don't you?"

Hailey nodded.

"You probably went shopping together a lot."

"Uh-huh."

"And I just drag you around to baseball games. Probably not as much fun for a girl your age as getting new clothes and pedicures."

She shrugged again.

"Maybe tomorrow we can go down to the beach."

"What about my bathing suit?"

"The girls here in California wear board shorts over their bathing suits. It's kind of surfer style." Bryce thought maybe if he made it sound cool to cover up, she'd be more willing. "We can pick up some really cool ones at a surf shop. They have several right there on the beach. Would you like that?"

"I guess."

"So that's settled then. We'll get you some surfer shorts first thing in the morning, and we'll spend a few hours at the beach before I have to go to work." He stood, feeling a little better, but once again, he was offering money to solve the problem.

"Dad?" Her voice sounded incredibly small and fragile.

"What is it, sweetheart?" He returned to the side of the bed.

"Is Mommy going to be okay?"

"Of course she is. She just needs…" What did he know what his ex-wife needed? Time? Space? Months, if not years of therapy? "She just needs us to think positive, and know that she's doing her best to get better."

"What if she doesn't get better?"

"She will."

"But what if she doesn't?" Hailey was truly scared; he could hear it in her voice.

"I'll be here for you. No matter what. You got that?" He scooted closer and scooped her up in his arms. "I'm going to be here for you from now on."

"Promise?"

"I promise." He wondered if now was the time to bring up his plans. "Now do you want to come to the game tonight or hang out here with Rachel?"

"She's pretty." Hailey had breathless admiration in her voice. "And nice."

"Yes, she is."

"And she's going to have a baby."

"She is."

"Is it a boy or a girl?"

"We don't know yet." Bryce smiled; he would be happy with either. "The only thing I know is that you'll be a terrific big sister."

"Will I get to see the baby much after it's born?"

"I hope so." Maybe he should get her input on his plans. After all, she was the one who would be affected by the judge's decision. "So, I was wondering, what would you think about living with me, more permanently?"

"In San Francisco?"

"Yes. That's where I live and work."

"And where Rachel works, too. I'd have to go to a new school." She didn't sound too excited about the prospect. "And leave all my friends behind."

"Well, you'd make new friends." The look on her face showed that wasn't her favorite idea. "And we'd be able to visit Pittsburgh in the winter."

"I think I'd rather have winter in California." She gave a small smile. Maybe she was warming to the idea.

"Well, then we'll bring your friends out here."

"What about my mom?"

"Well, we'll have to see." He had a feeling that one month at a treatment facility wasn't going to solve all her problems. And if he took Hailey away from her, she could relapse. But as much as her health was important, Hailey's safety and well-being was even more important. "One thing I know is that I'm going to try a lot harder at working with your mother and together, we'll do what's best for you."

Hailey leaned toward him and threw her arms around him. "I love you, Daddy."

"I love you, too, sweetheart. I love you too."

Rachel knocked softly on the door. "Sorry to interrupt, but Annabelle just texted me. Her girls are waiting down by the pool."

"Did you still want to go swimming?" Bryce turned his attention back to his daughter.

"What about my bathing suit?"

"You could wear something over it. A t-shirt or shorts."

"Really?" She almost rolled her eyes.

"Look, Hailey. You're my little girl. You're always going to be my little girl. Even when you're married and have kids of your own." The thought hit him hard, knowing those things would come sooner than he'd ever be ready for. "You're already growing up too fast for me."

She just shook her head, bounded off the bed, and dove into her suitcase. She slipped a tiny pair of shorts on over her teeny-weeny bikini bottom. "Is this better?"

Barely. But he held his tongue. Maybe she'd just grown so fast that the shorts had become too small for her. They couldn't be designed as short-shorts for a nine-year-old girl. Could they?

"Okay, so let's head down to the pool." Bryce followed Hailey into the adjoining room.

"Do you want me to take her?" Rachel offered.

"We can all go." He was determined to spend as much time with Hailey, and Rachel, as possible when he wasn't on the field.

"Okay. Let me just grab my Kindle." Rachel had softened over the last few days. She'd been great with Hailey. But then, he wasn't surprised. She was going to make a great mother. He wanted to tell her that, but they hadn't had much time alone. By the time they got home from the ballpark, they'd both been exhausted. And he didn't dare push things by trying to make love. He knew he was on borrowed time. She'd been all set to leave him from the moment they'd said "I do." He'd pushed her into this marriage before she'd been ready. Maybe she would never be ready and that was why she was prepared to bolt at the first opportunity.

Yet, she hadn't quite made it out the door. She kept finding reasons to stay. Their baby. Her job. And now Hailey.

He needed to give her a reason to stay. For him. With him. Forever.

* * * *

The three of them met Annabelle and the twins at the hotel pool. Rachel was surprised by Bryce's reaction to Hailey's swimsuit. Yeah, it was a little skimpy, but she was just a little girl. She didn't have anything to reveal. Still, it touched something inside Rachel to see him so fiercely protective. He'd put his foot down, but he'd also talked to his daughter and whatever he'd said must have worked, because they had both come out of the room smiling.

Hailey was wearing shorts over her suit and she jumped into the pool with them on. Didn't seem to slow her down one bit.

"Do you know of a mall around here?" Bryce asked. "I need to take Hailey shopping."

"There's an open-air mall not far from here," Annabelle suggested as she pulled out her phone. "I'll send Rachel the address."

"Thanks." Bryce smiled at the supermodel. Rachel knew she had no business feeling jealous. Just because Bryce smiled at a beautiful woman didn't mean he was interested. Besides, Annabelle was engaged to Nathan Cooper. They were planning a wedding for some time around Christmas. "I need to take Hailey shopping for some new clothes."

"You know, you don't have to buy her affection." Rachel was only half-teasing.

"True, but I do have to buy her new clothes. I think she's outgrowing everything she owns. Look how short those shorts are. They must be from last summer."

Annabelle laughed so hard she almost fell out of her chaise.

"What's so funny?" Bryce asked.

"You obviously haven't been shopping for little girls' clothes lately." Annabelle gave Rachel a look that said she thought he was pretty clueless. "Good luck finding anything longer. Unless you shop in the school uniform section, but she won't want to wear those."

Bryce looked stunned. And not very amused.

"Let me make a few recommendations." Annabelle removed her oversized sunglasses. "Leggings, skirts, and capri pants are your friends."

"Oh brother." Bryce leaned against the back of his chaise. "When do we find out if we're having a boy or a girl?"

"Not until the middle of July." Rachel smiled, knowing he was hoping for a boy, if only for the wardrobe.

"July huh?" He turned toward her with warmth and pride in his eyes. "I guess we'll just have to wait and see."

"Yeah." Rachel's throat suddenly felt dry and tight. She turned her attention to the pool, where Hailey was playing big sister to the younger girls. She was leading Sophie and Olivia in a game of Marco Polo, only they'd changed it to Marco Santiago.

Rachel watched Bryce watch his daughter with pride and love on his face. He couldn't take his eyes off the little girl.

All those times he'd told her he'd been an inadequate father and a horrible husband—he could not have been more wrong.

Chapter 30

After a successful road trip, Bryce was glad to be back home. He'd had a good time with Rachel and Hailey and he was pretty sure his girls had had a good time, too. They'd spent the early part of their days on the beach in San Diego, their nights at the ballpark.

In Los Angeles, they did touristy things, seeing the Hollywood stars on the Walk of Fame, driving through Beverly Hills and pointing out which mansions they'd want to live in. He'd taken them to Rodeo Drive, but Rachel had balked at actually doing more than window shopping. He'd practically had to drag her into the upscale maternity boutique where she'd headed straight for the sale racks. At least she'd found a few blouses she could wear on the air now that she was no longer worried about covering up her pregnancy. Now she could really flaunt it.

Hailey had been happy with the clothes he'd bought her in San Diego. The only thing she wanted was a T-shirt with the Beverly Hills sign logo printed on the front.

The team had done well, coming home with only one loss, an extra-inning heartbreaker to open the L.A. series. But they'd beaten their rivals five to nothing on the last game of the road trip so spirits were high on the flight home.

The only thing missing had been making love to Rachel. Hailey's presence had only been a part of it. He was scared. Afraid she'd reject him. And a part of him was afraid she wouldn't. That she'd slip into his arms and they'd find themselves living a dream. A dream he'd never planned on.

Maybe he could have it all. He was at the top of his game, and he had a beautiful wife to share his success with. Hailey and Rachel got along great. Hell, he was even thinking about getting a dog, although he knew better than to even consider such a thing without discussing it with Rachel.

There were other things he wanted to discuss with Rachel. Such as how he could make her scream without making any noise. Yeah. The apartment was too small. But maybe it would be a fun challenge, to see how hot he could get his wife without waking up his daughter in the next room.

Rachel had let him drive home after they'd landed. Progress. He just hoped she wasn't too tired once they got home. After pulling into the garage and unloading the suitcases, Bryce checked the mailbox before heading toward the elevator.

There was a larger stack than usual, but he'd wait until they got upstairs before tossing the junk mail. Some of it might be for Rachel, too. And he supposed Hailey could get a postcard from a friend, if any of them were traveling and wanted to let her know they were thinking of her.

Hailey went straight to bed, but made sure to give him a goodnight hug and kiss before falling asleep, her arms wrapped tight around her favorite pillow.

"Why don't you take a nice warm bath while I go through the mail?" Bryce wished he could offer her a glass of wine, but that would have to wait until after she stopped nursing. "Relax a bit."

"Mmmm. That sounds nice." She rubbed her lower back. "Maybe after I unpack."

She headed toward the bedroom, but not before giving him an encouraging glance. Desire shone in her eyes, just like he'd remembered.

Bryce reached for the mail. Junk. Junk. And more junk. He made a pile of envelopes and flyers headed for the shredder. In the middle of the stack was a letter. From Jillian.

He slid the flap open, trepidation filling him as he unfolded the single sheet of paper.

Dear Bryce,

This isn't an easy letter for me to write, but as part of my treatment, I need to clear up a few things. And try to make amends, although I wouldn't blame you if you never forgive me for tricking you into marrying me.

I realize how much I hurt you when I told you Hailey is not your daughter. But I was in a pretty dark place and lashed out, wanting someone else to feel as bad as I did. But instead of making me feel better, I only added to my guilt and shame.

Guilt at letting you marry me knowing I carried a child who wasn't yours. And shame at the way she was conceived. But I'll never be able to move forward if I don't confront the past. And since you are Hailey's father in her heart, if not in her genes, you need to know how it happened.

About ten days after we spent the night together, I went back to the bar where we'd met. My girlfriend was supposed to meet me, but she never showed. Instead I started talking to some guys who were in town for a few days. They were ballplayers, just called up from the minors and enjoying their first road trip as major leaguers. There were three of them, although one of them really seemed to like me. He bought me drinks and tried to impress me. Then he invited me to a party with several of his teammates. He even promised to introduce me to their All-Star shortstop who was hosting the party.

Like a fool, I went. The guy was pretty good-looking and I knew you wouldn't be calling me. Although you'd been sweet and generous and eager to please, I knew you weren't looking for a girl like me—at least not for more than one night.

The party was crowded and loud and this guy kept shoving drinks at me. We kissed a little, and I figured we'd end up going back to his room at some point. But after a while I realized I'd had a little too much to drink. I asked my new "friend" to call me a cab. But instead of fulfilling my request, he got angry.

"You came here to party," he said. "So we're going to party." He grabbed my arm and led me toward the bathroom. His two friends followed.

I told him I didn't feel so well. My head was starting to spin and my feet felt a little unsteady.

"I'll make you feel good. I'll make you feel so fucking good." He pressed me against the door and kissed me hard. Possessive. But it wasn't sexy. It was scary. But he had me pinned beneath his weight. And then he shoved me into the bathroom. I tried to get away, but his friends had followed us into the bathroom. One blocked the door and the other held me down while he yanked my jeans off.

Bryce couldn't read any more. He let out a growl of rage and pushed away from the table.

Rachel came running from the bedroom.

"Is everything okay?" Concern laced her voice.

"No. I can't even…" He didn't want to take his anger and feeling of helplessness out on her. "I have to get out of here."

"What's wrong?"

"Jillian…" He pointed toward the letter. "I have to get out of here."

His jaw locked tight. His fists clenched with a fury he'd never felt before. He understood the desire to murder someone, only the person— or persons—wasn't around. He didn't have a name, and it was probably for the best. Sure, he could go through the record books to see which players had been called up around the same time he had made it to the big leagues. Found the names of three or four guys who would have been in Pittsburgh that September. But having a name or a face wouldn't do him any good right now.

The only thing that he could do was to get outside, hit the streets, and run. Just like when he was a kid and his dad would tell him to take a lap. He would run around the block, or the track, or if the weather was terrible, around the living room, and eventually he would calm down.

The way he felt right now, he could run to Pittsburgh and back and it wouldn't do any good.

By the time he hit the bottom of the stairs, his rage ebbed, just enough for him to realize he hadn't brought his phone. He stopped by the front desk to let Sergio know he was going for a run, if anyone wanted to know.

Oh, he knew he probably should go back and tell Rachel what was going on, but he didn't trust himself at the moment.

He'd never felt like a bigger failure in all his life.

* * * *

Rachel wanted to go after Bryce, but she couldn't leave Hailey alone in the apartment. Something horrible had happened, but she didn't know what.

An overwhelming sense of dread came over her. She glanced at the letter, sitting open on the table next to Bryce's cell phone. She didn't want to get in the middle of things between him and his ex-wife, but there was an innocent child stuck in the middle. A child Rachel had grown to love.

Oh God.

What if… What if it was a suicide letter? Bryce would need her. And so would Hailey.

With shaking hands, Rachel picked up the letter.

She got as far as the part describing the rape before her stomach lurched. She made a mad dash for the bathroom and hurled what was left of her dinner into the toilet.

Her heart broke for the woman who had been Bryce's first wife. Who was Hailey's mother.

After rinsing her mouth, she went back to finish reading the letter. She'd come this far, she needed to know the whole story. She skipped to the part where Jillian described the events of that night.

I know you're wondering why I didn't go to the police. But I think you already know the answer to that question. No one would believe me. I went to the hotel room of a famous professional athlete. I'd been seen at a bar well-known as a place to hook up with jocks. I'd been seen leaving that same bar with you less than two weeks before. Not to mention the clothes I wore that night could be considered slutty.

Rachel felt sorry for the woman, and angry at the way the world worked.

I tried to put the whole incident out of my mind. A two-day hangover went a long way toward convincing myself that it had just been a nightmare, brought on by too much alcohol and possibly drugs slipped into my drink. But just when I'd convinced myself that it hadn't really happened, I missed my period. Two more weeks of denial, a desperate plea with God, and finally a shoplifted pregnancy test convinced me that the nightmare was real.

Then I saw you on TV. You stepped up to the plate like you were meant for greatness. There was something about you that I couldn't quite put my finger on, but I suddenly felt a sense of peace. Like you would somehow save the day.

There was a small part of me that hoped you would simply offer to pay for an abortion. But deep down, I knew you would step up and you did. I never expected you to propose, but I couldn't say no. Not when you offered hope, not only for me, but for my child.

I know you think I did it for your money. Even though you didn't have a lot when we were first married, it was clear that you would be the star you've become. But that wasn't the reason I went along with the wedding. I knew you'd be a great dad. And you were. From the moment Hailey was born, you were all in. And it scared me. I was afraid you'd love her more than you could ever love me, even though I knew deep down you'd never love me. So I pushed you away. I made you feel like you weren't needed for anything more than your bank account.

For that I am truly sorry.

I wish I could have done so many things differently. But since I can't change the past, I can only hope that you haven't changed your mind about being Hailey's dad, even though you are not her biological father. She's such a sweet and loving child, and she absolutely worships you. My therapist says I should someday tell her the truth about her conception, but I disagree. If she only knows you as her father, she'll be better off.

Rachel folded up the letter. So many emotions poured through her. Hailey wasn't Bryce's biological daughter. He knew she wasn't his, and he'd still brought her home when she needed him.

But he'd had no idea the facts behind Hailey's birth. He'd found his ex-wife in crisis and he'd done the only thing he could do—protected his daughter.

Now he'd been told the ugly truth. And he'd run, literally, out the door.

After what felt like hours, but had been only thirty minutes, Bryce returned. He was sweaty and flushed, looking like a man who'd just been through hell and survived.

"Oh Bryce, I'm so sorry." She couldn't help herself; she pulled him into her arms. "I read the letter. I was worried about you."

He held on as if she were an anchor in a storm.

"Are you okay?" She leaned against his chest, feeling his heart rate steady with each breath. "I can only imagine what you must be feeling right now."

"I was going to tell you." He relaxed against her. "I just needed to clear my head a little first."

"Of course." This wasn't the time to get pouty about him shutting her out. Or to worry about how she measured up to his first wife. Her insecurities were so trivial in comparison that she felt foolish for even feeling an ounce of doubt. "Just tell me what you need."

"I don't know right now." He pulled away. The anguish in his eyes was devastating.

"It wasn't your money she was after." Somehow reading the letter made Rachel feel like she knew the woman a little better. "It was your heart she wanted."

"She didn't love me. And she knew I didn't love her." He sounded like a man so full of regret that her heart ached for him. Even more than when she'd first read the letter.

"No. But she knew you'd love Hailey." Her hands instinctively moved over her own womb. "She knew you'd be a good father."

"But I wasn't. I wasn't there for the first nine years of Hailey's life." He raked his hands through his hair.

"You're here for her now. When she needs you the most."

Bryce sank against the sofa.

"If I'd only known. I could have…" He heaved a great sigh.

"Would it have saved your marriage?" Rachel's heart lodged in her throat.

"No." He sounded weary. "But, I could have been kinder. Maybe more understanding."

Bryce leaned forward and rested his forearms on his thighs. "I don't know what to do."

"I guess just try to be as supportive as possible." Rachel couldn't believe she was encouraging her husband to be there for his ex-wife.

"No. I mean, I don't know what to do about Hailey. I was going to file for permanent custody." He lifted his head; the anguish in his eyes was heartbreaking. "I can't take the chance that Jillian will relapse, but if I take Hailey away from her I can almost guarantee that she will."

Chapter 31

For the next two days, Rachel stood by while Bryce struggled with the knowledge that Hailey had been conceived during a rape. And ten years later, his ex-wife was still traumatized by it. The reports of Bryce being involved in a sexual assault, even though false, must have brought back horrible memories for her.

If only he would talk to her. But he kept his feelings well-guarded. What else was new? Besides his complete and utter devotion to his daughter. He'd taken on a whole new role as an all-star father. And this time, instead of spoiling her with things, he was giving her what she needed most. Time. Attention.

Rachel was torn herself. On the one hand, she was proud of how Bryce had stepped up as a father. She was encouraged for his future relationship with their child. But she wished he had more time for her.

Patience. He had to get through this crisis with his first family. The child came first. And if he was serious about pursuing custody, the devotion he showed her would go a long way.

He hadn't asked Rachel to stand by him, but he'd been noticeably relieved when she'd asked him to put her suitcases away for her.

She wasn't going anywhere and they still had a few months before the baby came. Would the baby's big sister be living with them? They would definitely need a bigger place.

The house she'd looked at when she thought Bryce had been partying in Pittsburgh came into her mind. She wondered if it had come on the market yet. Even if it hadn't, she needed to step up the house hunting. Bryce was too busy with Hailey to do the preliminary research. And if she could find the perfect house for them, it would show him that she was ready to commit to this family.

Rachel texted her real estate agent explaining that some family things had come up, but she was ready to view properties in earnest.

* * * *

"Are you sure you don't want to come with us to the Exploratorium?" Bryce had to admit he was disappointed. They were starting to feel like a family. Him, Hailey, and Rachel. Soon there would be a baby, and more than anything, he wanted for them to come together as a team.

"I would love to, but I'm not feeling great. I think I need to save my energy for work tonight." Rachel gave him an apologetic smile.

"I thought you were past the morning sickness."

"I thought so, too. Now I'm just tired." She rubbed her lower back, and if Hailey hadn't been standing right next to them, he would have offered to give Rachel a massage. A full body massage. But he supposed the last thing she needed right now was to get naked.

God, he missed sex. He missed the taste of Rachel's skin. The feel of her hands on him. And those little noises she made when she climaxed. Well, the noises weren't always little, which was one of the main reasons he hadn't made an effort to seduce her. The apartment was too small.

Rachel probably wasn't feeling up to rounding the bases with him anyway. If she was too tired to spend the morning exploring the science museum, she probably wouldn't have the energy for a marathon lovemaking session.

"Well, get some rest." He kissed her on the cheek and it was enough to get his blood pumping. Not good when he couldn't do anything about it.

"I will." She had that pregnancy glow thing he'd heard about. "You two have fun."

Rachel ruffled Hailey's hair, bringing a big grin from his daughter.

"I hope you feel better." Hailey smoothed her hair down, but she was still smiling.

"Thanks. You keep your dad out of trouble, okay?"

Hailey giggled and grabbed his hand as they headed out the door. "Do you think she's really tired, or do you think maybe she's tired of me?"

"Oh honey, I know Rachel adores you." Bryce pulled his little girl into a reassuring hug. "It's hard work making a baby."

That didn't quite come out right.

"I mean, it's hard work growing a baby inside her body." Bryce took Hailey's hand and led her to the elevator. "Think about it, the baby is growing a heart, lungs, a brain. And arms and legs and a cute little nose."

He tweaked her nose, eliciting a smile and a slight eye roll.

"Was my mom tired a lot when she was pregnant with me?"

"Yeah. She was pretty sick the first few months, too." Not to mention she'd survived a rape. She may have had some PTSD, as well. So many things about his marriage now made sense. Jillian hadn't hated him; she'd been hurting. Hurting in a way he hadn't been equipped to handle.

"Why do babies make their moms sick?"

"I don't know." He wished he had a better answer. "I guess that's just the way it works."

"Sometimes babies even make their moms sad. Like really sad."

Had Jillian made Hailey feel responsible for her problems? Anger flared, but he was able to keep it under control.

"Honey, it's not your fault your mom is sick."

She shrugged, as if she didn't quite believe him.

"Hailey, look at me." He turned her around to face him and placed his hands squarely on her shoulders. "Your mother loves you very much. And so do I."

Tears filled her eyes and she nodded before wrapping her arms around him in a death grip.

"Hailey, I love you and I'm going to make sure everything will be all right."

Somehow he would have to make good on his promise.

* * * *

"I'm so glad you contacted me." Catherine Beck greeted Rachel when she arrived at her office. "That house you were interested in just came on the market this morning. You'll be the first to see it."

"Great." Rachel was nervous. What if Bryce didn't love it as much as she did? And how did she negotiate price? The whole world knew what Bryce's current salary was, but they wouldn't think about how it wouldn't last forever. "I look forward to seeing the inside."

"The kitchen was recently remodeled in the main house." Catherine's enthusiasm was contagious. She chattered on about the home's features as they drove to the house. "But the pool house could use some updating. Everything is functional, but it's a little 1990s with the whitewashed oak cabinets and ivy wallpaper borders."

"There's a pool house? With a full kitchen?"

"Yes. It also has two bedrooms and one bathroom."

An idea formed in her mind. But it was crazy. Just not done.

"So let's take a look at the main house, shall we?" Catherine retrieved the key from the lock box and opened the door.

From the moment she stepped inside, Rachel knew she was home. The view was incredible from the large open living space. An open floorplan flowed from the kitchen into the dining room and out onto the deck. It was a park-like setting, the built-in pool had the feel of a mountain spring with rock outcroppings built around the edges and forming a small waterslide.

Beyond the pool was a pool house. The main structure was built in 1963, reminiscent of a Frank Lloyd Wright style. The pool house appeared to be a more recent addition. It was on the other side of the full acre property, tucked into the trees so that it almost felt like a completely separate home.

What if?

Bryce needed to be in Hailey's life. Sending her back to Pittsburgh would devastate him. But since she wasn't his biological child, getting full custody would be difficult, especially if Jillian chose to fight him.

Jillian would be getting out of rehab in a few weeks. Maybe she would need a change of scenery. Maybe she would be willing to come to California. She would need a place to stay. A place close to her daughter, but not exactly under the same roof as her ex-husband.

It would be a temporary solution until the courts or Bryce and his ex could sort things out.

"Let's take a look at the master bedroom, shall we?" Catherine pulled Rachel out of her head. "It's got a good-sized closet for a home of this age."

Rachel followed down the hall, but she'd already been sold on the property. The view, the landscaping, and the pool house were enough to make her fall in love. But it was the overall feel of the home. It was open, spacious, yet very private. A place where she and Bryce could get away from it all and cozy up with their family. So the fact that she was picturing an extra member of the family—a woman she'd never even met—wasn't weird at all.

Chapter 32

Bryce was one of the last ones in the clubhouse after a tough loss. Hopefully it wouldn't stretch into a June swoon. There was a lot of season left to play, he knew that, but tonight he felt like he usually felt in August. Dog tired. Sore. And there was still a month until the All-Star break. He'd like to blame his fatigue on the extended postseason.

That wasn't the problem. For the first time, he'd let his personal life interfere with his career. Hell, he'd missed a game, and he'd had to work a lot harder at staying focused since then. He managed most nights. Muscle memory, training, and the fact that he'd been playing baseball longer than he'd done anything else in his life except eat had kept him from losing all his focus.

But keeping his head in the game was getting harder and harder with each passing day. He'd been in contact with his lawyer, and he knew he had a better shot at hitting over .400 for the season than he did of gaining full custody of Hailey without a fight.

And if Jillian chose to fight him, it could get real ugly. Especially considering that up until recently, his only parental contributions had been financial.

He was worried about what a lengthy court battle would do to Hailey. She was just starting to open up to him about how worried she was about her mom. She was like him in some ways, even if not genetically. She didn't like to talk about her problems. She preferred to act like everything was just fine and as long as she kept a smile on her face and a bounce in her step, no one would know she was hurting. Her sweet and docile behavior worried him more than if she'd been a brat. If she'd complained about having to leave school two weeks before the end of the year and miss out on all the fun activities. If she'd whined about having to leave her home and her things behind. If she'd shown any of that preteen angst, he'd feel a lot better. He'd feel like he was a real dad.

A *real* dad. What did that even mean? Was it about genetics? A legal definition? According to his lawyer, removing his name from the birth certificate would require more than just his ex-wife's assertion that someone else might be the father. Might.

There was still the possibility that Jillian was trying to hurt him, that her pain was too great to withstand his happiness.

But the letter. It seemed genuine. So full of anguish. He believed she'd been raped—his teeth ground together at the thought—but maybe after ten years, she could be confused about the timing.

The timing of this crisis couldn't be any worse.

He was married. For now. He woke up some nights drenched in sweat, the image of Rachel's packed bags and the look of betrayal in her eyes haunting his dreams.

What would a court battle do to her? How could he protect her and their baby from Jillian's pain and the shitstorm that came with it?

Rachel wasn't in the clubhouse. After a loss, she usually didn't do a post-game interview. It was late, so Kaitlyn would have taken Hailey back to the apartment so she could go to bed at a reasonable hour. Maybe Rachel had gone home with them.

Or maybe she'd been waiting for him in the parking lot.

He made his way out to the nearly empty players' lot. Her Range Rover stood under one of the bright lights and Bryce had a flashback to that day back in April. When she'd puked all over his Corvette. He'd thought he had problems then. Oh, the contract was intimidating. He wasn't hitting. One-night stands hadn't satisfied him.

He'd been a World Series champion and a world class idiot.

"Hey, Bryce." Rachel stepped forward and took his breath away.

"Rachel." Somehow she was standing there before him. A lesser woman would have run a long time ago. The rumors, allegations, and pictures circulating the Internet would have been enough to send her packing. Throw in a crazy ex-wife—in all fairness she was suffering from post-traumatic stress disorder—and it was a wonder that she hadn't thrown those packed bags out the window and followed right behind.

"Rough night, huh?" Her voice was like a healing balm. His muscles felt looser, his head clearer.

"It's part of the game." He shrugged, even though he knew she could see right through him. She understood him better than anyone, and he'd taken her for granted so many times. "But it's looking up."

She smiled, her cheeks turning pink as he approached her.

"There's something I want to show you." Her eyes shone with nervous excitement.

"Did you have the ultrasound? Do you know if we're having a boy or a girl?" Had he been so focused on Hailey that he'd missed an important milestone?

"We still have a few more weeks before we can find out." She reached for his hand. "There's something else I want to show you."

Bryce breathed a huge sigh of relief. He wouldn't worry about whether or not he'd be on the road when she did get the ultrasound.

"Come on. Let's take a ride." Rachel dangled her keys. "I'll drive."

Bryce climbed into the passenger seat with a sense of anticipation. Where was she taking him, and why was she almost giddy at the prospect?

He was just tired enough to sit back and enjoy the ride across the Bay Bridge, into the city of Orinda. She pulled off the freeway and onto a side street that led up into a quiet neighborhood. Only a few miles from the BART station, yet it felt like they were in the woods. To accentuate that feeling, a deer darted across the road and Rachel slowed, allowing the doe and her fawn to cross safely.

She turned into a driveway in front of a "For Sale" sign.

"I know we haven't really discussed what we wanted in a house." Rachel turned toward him, a nervous smile on her beautiful face. "But something about this place feels like home to me."

"You picked out a house?" Was this the same woman who had been afraid to even think about school districts, minivans, and college savings plans? "I thought you were allergic to white picket fences."

"The fence is black, and made of steel. It's required around swimming pools." She was trying to sound defensive, but there was an underlying note of excitement in her voice. "It has great views, a hot tub..."

She winked at him and his mind filled with all kinds of things they could do in a hot tub together.

"Come on, let's look inside." Her enthusiasm had convinced him already. He could care less about the square footage, the architectural details, or location, location, location. If this was the house Rachel wanted, he'd be more than happy to put his autograph on the mortgage paperwork.

"Did you find an agent willing to show us the house this late at night?"

"She gave me a key." Rachel held out a shiny brass key. "Guess celebrity comes with some perks."

"Lead the way, darling."

Rachel opened the front door and flipped on the lights. He tried to notice the details. A fireplace in the living room, the kitchen with a stove, refrigerator, and sink. The view was pretty sweet standing on the deck. Damn, Rachel had a fine ass. Oh, and there were trees and hills and stuff in the distance.

"The pool and hot tub take up a lot of the back yard, but there's a great big tree in the front that will be great for climbing."

"I think tree climbing is one of the activities my contract forbids, along with skydiving, and base jumping."

"I was thinking of the kids." She gave his shoulder a friendly shove.

"Kids. Yeah, I guess some kids like climbing trees."

"I suppose Hailey will be more interested in swimming." She started down the steps to the pool below. "And then there's the pool house."

Rachel pointed to a structure on the far corner of the property. It was bigger than the childhood home he'd shared with his dad the first few years after his mother left.

"Is that your way of telling me I'm still in the doghouse?" He let out a nervous laugh.

"Actually…" She grasped his hand. "Maybe it's a crazy idea, but I'm willing to give it a shot."

Had he missed something? What was a crazy idea?

"I was thinking that maybe Hailey's mom could stay there." She pointed to the pool house or guest house or mansion in some parts of the world. "You know, until she gets back on her feet."

"Wait. What?" Bryce tried to remember if maybe he'd been hit on the head earlier that night. "You want my ex-wife to live in our pool house?"

"Well, yeah. I guess it does seem weird." Rachel let go of his hand, and clasped her hands together. "I just thought that it was a way for you to have your cake and eat it too. Or in this case, Hailey could have her father and her mother, too."

Powerful emotions whipped around inside him like the flags in center field on a windy night.

"But what about you? And our baby?"

"Well, we'll have the master bedroom. And after Hailey picks out her room, we can start decorating the nursery for the baby."

"And you're okay with my ex-wife living in the pool house?"

"Well, temporarily, yes." Rachel's confidence seemed to waiver. "I just thought that it would be a way to keep Hailey from having to travel back and forth from here to Pittsburgh. I mean, that would be nearly impossible when she goes back to school. And I know you don't want to let her go back. I just thought this would be an easy solution."

Her lower lip started to quiver. He had to reassure her somehow.

"I think it's a brilliant and very generous idea. " He reached for her, taking both of her hands in his. "I-I just can't believe that you would be willing to make such a sacrifice."

"If it keeps our family together, it's not really a sacrifice."

"Even if it means having Jillian so close by?"

"I know she's in a rough place right now," Rachel said. "But maybe if she doesn't have to fight you over Hailey, we can all heal."

"Wow." Not only was this woman beautiful and sexy and witty, but she was also very wise. "Not many women would offer their home to their husband's ex-wife and stepdaughter."

"I'm not most women. I thought you knew that by now." Rachel stepped toward the pool. In the moonlight, she looked more beautiful than ever. And for a moment, he thought, *why not?* Why couldn't they make it work? Why couldn't they find a happily-ever-after with his ex-wife in the backyard? As long as Hailey was safe and Rachel was happy, he was game for anything.

"No, you are not like most women." Bryce put his arms around her. "And that's why I love you."

"You love me?"

"Yeah. I know I've been an idiot for not telling you." He slid his hands up under her loose-fitting blouse. Her skin felt so soft. So warm. He pressed his lips against her neck. "I love you. I thought I could just buy my way into your heart, but I failed."

"No, Bryce, you haven't failed." She melted into his arms. "You found your way into my heart. You've been there all along."

"So I don't need to buy this house for you?" He dropped tiny kisses along her neck and collarbone.

"I was hoping you'd want this house for us." Her head fell back, soft murmurs of pleasure escaping her lips. "For all of us."

"I don't know. I think we need to check out the pool first." He tore his shirt off and started working on hers. He started at the top button, working his way down, his lips following his fingers as he made his way to her breasts. Sliding her blouse off her shoulders, he reached behind and unfastened her bra.

A sense of urgency followed as they reached for the buttons on each other's pants. The next thing he knew, they were both naked. He pulled his bride into the pool.

The combination of the water and the moonlight made her skin sparkle. Her full breasts seemed to float in the pool. He grabbed her, caressing her curves that were becoming curvier by the day. His child grew inside her. He had no doubt that this baby was the fruit of his loins.

Bryce chuckled softly. Like DNA was what it took to make a family.

"You know, if we consecrate the pool, we'll have to buy the place."

"I think you mean 'desecrate.'" Rachel splashed water at him.

"No. I mean consecrate. As in make sacred." He pressed his body against hers. "Rachel, your love has blessed me more than I could ever dream of."

"I do love you, Bryce Baxter."

"Good. Now let's get this pool dirty. Maybe we can knock a few hundred grand off the asking price if we clog up the filter."

"You're so bad."

"I used to be." He ran his hands through her damp hair. "Then I met you."

"No Bryce, you've always been a good man. You just were afraid to admit it." Rachel swam away, enticing him to chase after her.

"But you love the bad boy side of me, admit it." He swam toward her.

"I love all of you." She let him catch her. Let him kiss her. She let him sink himself inside her. "Even your hair."

Epilogue

Bryce Baxter sat in his old clubhouse in Pittsburgh for his third All-Star game appearance. The first two times, he'd been worried about living up to the hype. Now, as he returned to the city that had given him his first break, the place where he'd come close, but hadn't quite lived up to the promise, he was able to appreciate the honor. He'd left Pittsburgh feeling like he'd done his best, but he'd still failed the team, the city, and most of all, his family.

As an older, wiser veteran, he now understood that he wasn't that special. Baseball, like marriage, was a team game. It wasn't up to just one person to ensure success.

He'd learned about teamwork as a member of the San Francisco Goliaths. It wasn't about ego, or talent, or luck. Sure, those things played a part in a team's overall performance. The first was often to the detriment of the team. Talent and luck could contribute to success, but the most important thing was sticking together, through thick and thin. Through hot stretches and losing streaks. In front of packed home crowds or empty, yet hostile road venues.

Marriage wasn't all that different. Sure, it was easy when things were going well. When they couldn't keep their hands off each other, or when Rachel would take his breath away with just a smile.

But there were tough times, too. And sometimes going through the hard times made the good times that much sweeter. Getting through those hard times made them that much closer.

Rachel had been there when Jillian got out of the residential treatment center. She'd stood by when he'd requested to have Hailey live with him full time. And she'd shared his relief when Jillian agreed that giving him temporary custody was the best thing for the child.

They'd revisit the arrangement in six months. If Jillian felt like she'd recovered enough to be a part of Hailey's life, she would move to California. As much as she'd appreciated the offer to live in the pool house, she insisted on finding her own place nearby.

The only thing left to settle was what color to paint the nursery. Hailey had picked out her room and decided to paint it in neon pink, green, and yellow. Bryce just hoped she'd be able to sleep in such a colorful room.

Rachel had stayed behind for a doctor's appointment. He hated missing the sonogram, but he'd been selected to take part in the home run derby and other All-Star festivities. Rachel had been asked to cover the All-Star game, but she'd had to decline doing a three-day behind-the-scenes extravaganza. She'd agreed to cover the game itself, but before and after were reserved for family time.

The clubhouse doors opened. It was too early for the press, but his favorite reporter approached his locker. She had a smile on her face, as if she had a secret of some sort.

"Hey." She tried to play it cool, but he knew exactly the kind of news she was here to share. "You look relaxed and ready to play."

"I'm always ready to play." He removed his hat and ran his hands through his hair. He'd considered cutting it, but it was a part of his image. A part he didn't mind keeping. The arrogant playboy image had morphed into something different. A fun-loving, yet responsible husband and father had replaced the guy who'd once been rated a home run on a groupie's blog of players she'd scored with.

"I'm proud of you." Rachel approached him and put her hands on his shoulders. "You worked hard to get here. You deserve the honor."

Her words lifted him up more than any award or trophy ever could.

"I never used to believe it." He grabbed her by the waist and pulled her onto his lap. "I often thought I was only in the big leagues by mistake."

Rachel didn't say anything, just put her arms around his neck and leaned against him.

"I always thought it was only a matter of time before everyone saw through me. Before they realized I was a failure."

"You're not a failure." She snuggled closer. "You're not here by a fluke, or a mistake. You've earned your spot on the Goliaths. You've earned your spot on this All-Star team."

"I finally believe that." He brushed her auburn hair off her neck and placed tiny kisses in the exposed spot. "But the important question is have I earned a spot in your heart?"

"You know you have." She rolled her head back, giving him better access. "I love you, Bryce."

"I love you, too." If he wasn't careful, he was going to give the media and his teammates a real show when the clubhouse opened in the next twenty minutes or so.

"So don't you want to know my news?" Rachel pulled away slightly.

"You have news?" He already knew it was good. Whatever the results were, he was game. If it was a girl, he would welcome another daughter into his life. And if it was a boy… Well, he had visions of having a catch with his son.

"I had the sonogram." She beamed, pride radiating off her like the bright lights of the stadium.

"And?"

"We're having a boy."

"A boy?" His throat felt smaller than normal, his heart so much larger.

"I hope he grows up to be just like his father." Rachel's voice was tinged with emotion. The kind of emotion a guy like him could never put into words, even if he shared that feeling.

Bryce was at a loss for words. In the past year, he'd had several milestones. He'd won the World Series, been named MVP, and been rewarded with a huge contract.

He'd learned how to be a father, even if Hailey wasn't his own flesh and blood.

He'd married the only woman he'd ever loved and now they would be having a son.

It was more than he'd ever dreamed of. Definitely more than he deserved. But he would spend the rest of his life earning the blessings he'd been given.

Meet the Author

Kristina Mathews doesn't remember a time when she didn't have a book in her hand. Or in her head. Kristina lives in Northern California with her husband of twenty years, two sons and a black lab. She is a veteran road tripper, amateur renovator and sports fanatic. She hopes to one day travel all 3,073 miles of Highway 50 from Sacramento, CA, to Ocean City, MD, replace her carpet with hardwood floors and serve as a "Ball Dudette" for the San Francisco Giants. Visit her on the web at kristinamathews.com.

Keep reading to see where the series began, with an excerpt from:

BETTER THAN PERFECT

Life beyond the game...

Johnny "The Monk" Scottsdale has won it all on the baseball diamond. He's even pitched a perfect game. Known for his legendary control both on and off the field, his pristine public image makes him the ideal person to work with young players in a preseason minicamp. Except the camp is run by the one woman he can't forget...the woman who made him a "monk."

Alice Harrison once traded her dreams so that Johnny Scottsdale could make it to the Majors—and then her dreams fell apart. Now here comes Johnny back into her life, just when she's ready to finally go after her dreams. This time she's not letting up. Even if she has to reveal what she kept secret for too long from her son and Johnny. She can't be sure how things will turn out, but she's not leaving until she swings for the fences...

A Lyrical book on sale now.

Learn more about Kristina at
http://www.kensingtonbooks.com/author.aspx/30540

Chapter 1

"Pitchers and catchers report to spring training in thirteen days, twenty-one hours and seventeen minutes," Hall of Fame broadcaster Kip Michaels announced, and the crowd went wild. "Kicking off today's Fan Fest, I'd like to introduce one of our newest players. Two-time Cy Young Award winner, perennial All-Star, and the last man to pitch a perfect game. Give a warm San Francisco welcome to Johnny 'The Monk' Scottsdale."

Thirty thousand people were expected at the ballpark today. A great crowd—for a baseball game. But instead of working the count, Johnny would be working the crowd. Answering questions. Signing autographs. Putting himself out there in a way he wasn't entirely comfortable with. He was as nervous as the day he'd made his professional debut fourteen years ago. Butterflies? Try every seagull on the West Coast taking roost in his stomach.

Focus. Breathe. Let it go.

"Thank you. I'm thrilled to be here." He'd much rather face the 1927 Yankees than sit in front of a camera and a microphone talking about his game instead of playing it. "I hope I can help the team bring home a World Series Championship."

He tried to relax his shoulders. Tried to hide his nerves. The Goliaths could be his last team. His last shot at a ring. His final chance to prove himself and leave a legacy that went beyond the diamond.

After fielding a few questions about what he could bring to the team, and deflecting some praise about his success so far, Johnny was released to another part of the park to sign autographs. Little Leaguers approached with wide eyes and big league dreams. Tiny tots with painted faces squirmed with excitement about getting cotton candy while their parents shoved them forward to collect an autograph. A shy boy with a broken arm asked him to sign his cast. The look on his face was more than worth the discomfort of being in the spotlight for something other than his on-field performance.

Johnny had signed the big contract. The team paid him a lot of money to pitch every five games. They also paid him to interact with the fans, to be an ambassador for the game he'd loved for so long. The game that had saved him from a completely different kind of life.

He shared a table with another new player, shortstop Bryce Baxter. They were set up near the home bullpen along the third base line. Several other stations were set up around the park, giving fans a chance to get up close and personal with the players. Some tried to get a little too personal.

"So you're the hot new pitcher." A busty brunette leaned over the autograph table, wearing what appeared to be a toddler-sized tank top. The team logo sparkled in rhinestones and she was obviously well aware of the attention she drew. "I'd be more than happy to show you around."

"No thanks. I'm pretty familiar with the city." He held his pen ready, although she didn't seem to have anything to autograph. Nothing he was willing to sign, anyway.

"I could take you places you've never been." She leaned over even more.

Johnny kept his head down, trying to avoid gazing at what she had to offer. He reached for a stock photo, scrawled his signature across the bottom, and slid the picture forward, hoping she'd take the hint and leave.

"You forgot your number." She pouted.

"Sorry. I don't give that out." Johnny wished he could retreat to the locker room. Get away from her and the crowd that seemed to be growing. He never understood why people would wait in line to make small talk and take his picture. He gripped the black marker, needing something to do with his hands. If he only had a baseball, he could roll it around in his palm. Feel the smoothness of the leather, the rough contrast of the raised stitches. Find comfort in the weight and the symmetry of the one thing he could always control.

His teammate inserted himself into the conversation. "Do you know who this is? The one and only Johnny 'The Monk' Scottsdale."

"The Monk?" She drew her gaze over Bryce, then glanced at Johnny before settling on Bryce once more.

"He's a god." He flashed a grin indicating he was more than willing to play her game. "Me? I'm a mere mortal." Bryce leaned toward her, clearly enjoying the interaction.

"You're new, too." She scooted over to his side of the table, dismissing Johnny's rejection as strike one. She must think she had a better chance of scoring with Bryce.

"I am. I think I left my heart somewhere in the city. Could you help me find it?" He slid one of his photos across the table to her.

"I can help you find whatever you're looking for." She took the pen from him and wrote something on the inside of his forearm. Her number, most likely.

Bryce grinned as if he enjoyed having a stranger tattoo him with a permanent marker.

"Bring your friend, too. If he's up for a challenge."

"I'll see what I can do, sweetheart." Bryce tipped his cap and winked at the woman.

Johnny exhaled, realizing he'd been holding his breath during the entire conversation.

"Thanks man, I owe you one." Johnny shook his head, as relieved as if Bryce had just snagged a line drive with two outs and the bases loaded.

"So it really isn't an act." Baxter eyed him carefully. "You really do walk the walk."

"What walk?"

"The celibacy thing. It's for real." A lot of guys thought he was full of it. That it was just for show. A way to get attention, and women. But once they realized he was genuine, most of the other players accepted him. Some even respected him. "You really don't mess around."

"No. I don't. I'm not perfect, but I try to stay out of trouble." Johnny removed his cap and ran his fingers through his hair. Since they were both new to the team, their booth wasn't as crowded as some of the others. They had a chance to catch their breath. He was able to finally sit back and enjoy the perfect weather. It was one of those glorious Northern California days when the sun came out to tease, dropping hints of spring and the fever that came with it.

"You looked like you were a little uncomfortable there." Bryce, on the other hand, seemed to relish the attention.

"I know it's part of the job, but it's not the part I'm good at."

"You let your game speak for itself. That's cool." Bryce reclined in his chair, looking as relaxed as if he was sitting in his own back yard. "Some of us have to use our charm to make up for lack of talent."

Johnny laughed. Baxter had plenty of talent. And more than enough charm to go around.

"She was pretty fine, though." Bryce continued to check her out as she walked away, collecting ballplayer's numbers like kids collected baseball cards. "Exactly what I need to get me in shape for spring training."

"Is that so?" Johnny managed to avoid the whole groupie scene. His entire career had been about control, both on and off the field. The Monk kept his cool. The Monk never got rattled. And The Monk maintained a spotless reputation. He had to, considering where he'd come from.

"There he is. Come on, Mom." A kid, about twelve or thirteen, rushed up to the booth, practically dragging his mother by the arm.

Johnny slipped on his best fan-friendly smile.

"We're, like, your number one fans." The boy was practically bursting at the seams. "Right, Mom?"

The boy's mother stepped forward, taking Johnny's breath away.

He'd had several reasons to come to San Francisco. Eleven million obvious ones, and several others that he'd done his best to articulate to the fans. There was only one reason he should have stayed away.

"Alice." Just saying her name sent a line drive straight to his heart. Even fourteen years later.

"Congratulations on your new contract. I know you're going to have a great year." She sounded like any other fan, wishing him well. She just marched right up to his table to ask for an autograph. A freaking autograph? Like he meant nothing to her.

A slight breeze blew her hair around her face. She tried to smile as she tucked a loose strand behind her ear. Blond, straight, silky—and if he remembered correctly—oh-so-soft. She wore modestly cut jeans and a soft blue sweater that on anyone else would have looked plain and proper. He didn't need to glance at her left hand to know she was off limits. Yet, she still moved him like no other woman ever could. Made him long for what he'd had. What he'd lost. What he'd tried for years to forget.

"Wait." The boy gaped at her. "You guys know each other? For real?"

"Yes. Johnny was…" She held Johnny's gaze just long enough for him to catch a flicker of regret. She turned to her son, who was about an inch or two taller than her. "He was your dad's college roommate."

"You knew my dad?" The boy seemed more impressed by that than the fact that people waited in line for his autograph.

"Yes. I knew him." Johnny swallowed the lump in his throat. "Before he married your mom."

"Cool." The kid smiled and nodded his head, like it was no big deal. "I mean, I know you played for the Wolf Pack when they went to Nevada, but I had no idea you guys were, like, friends."

Sure. Friends.

"Zach." She placed her hand on his shoulder, ready to steer him away. "I'm sure Mr. Scottsdale is a busy man. Let's leave him alone."

They'd once been as close as two people could be. But now he was Mr. Scottsdale.

The boy shrugged, dismissing her and looking up to Johnny with admiration. "It's totally awesome to meet you."

Johnny nodded, giving his most sincere smile, even though seeing Alice, and her kid, hit him like a 97-mile-an-hour fastball.

They started to walk away.

"Give my best to Mel." As if he hadn't already done that.

Alice turned around.

"Mel died. Eight years ago." A pained expression flashed across her face.

"I'm sorry. For your loss." Johnny said the words. He wanted more than anything to mean them, but he'd carried that resentment around for so long, it had become as much a part of him as his right arm.

"Thank you." Alice gave him a sad little smile. It was forced. Polite. The kind of smile she'd give a stranger. "It was good seeing you. Really good."

"Yeah. Sure." He could say the same, but he'd be lying. Seeing her again only reminded him of everything he'd sacrificed.

* * * *

The minute she'd seen Johnny on the stage, Alice's heart had swelled big enough to fill the stadium. There he'd been, larger than life. Damn. The man looked good. Better than on TV. Better than she remembered. He'd gained some muscle. A lot of muscle. Even without the jersey, there'd be no doubt he was an athlete. He moved with the kind of confidence and grace that came with being totally in tune with his body. Like he'd once been totally in tune with hers. She ached at the memory, but shook it off, uncomfortable having such thoughts with her son sitting next to her. Like Johnny had clearly been uncomfortable onstage, addressing the media and the crowds. He never did like to talk about his game. He'd simply let his talent speak for itself.

Just as she'd predicted, women lined up at his booth. They all wanted his autograph. Some of them wanted a little more. She hadn't been able to handle it back then. And now? What he did was his business. Especially since she'd been the one to walk out on him.

"Mom. Are you okay?" Zach was protective of her. And a little too observant.

"I'm fine, Zach." She shook her head to clear the fog of memories that rolled over her. With only the briefest look into his eyes, she couldn't forget the three years they'd spent together, nearly inseparable. Studying. Hanging out. Making love. "I'm surprised to see him, that's all."

"But you knew he'd be here." Zach had that tone, the unspoken *duh*. They'd been coming to Fan Fest every year since Mel's death. She'd known Johnny would be here. She just wasn't prepared for the impact of seeing him again. She'd thought she'd put those feelings behind her. Packed them away with her college sweatshirts and student ID card. "You were so excited when you heard it on the radio. Your favorite player finally becoming a Goliath. Why didn't you tell me you guys were, like, friends?"

"I didn't want you to think it's a big deal." She tried to place her hand on his shoulder, but he squirmed to avoid the contact. That was new. Not unexpected, given his age, but she missed her little boy. The first time they'd come to Fan Fest, he'd held her hand. Until they'd gotten to the miniature version of the ballpark. He'd joined the t-ball game like he was born to play.

"It is a big deal." Zach looked at her like she was hopelessly out of touch. Something he did a lot these days. "Mom, you actually know Johnny Scottsdale."

There it was. The star-struck admiration bordering on worship.

"I *knew* him, Zach." Alice tried to keep her tone neutral. She couldn't betray her emotions. A wave of regret washed over her. The question of what might have been. "But that was a long time ago."

"Wouldn't it be cool if he came to the foundation's minicamp?" Zach couldn't know why it would be such a bad idea.

She'd hoped to avoid him. Avoid digging up the past. And the question that had plagued her more and more as Zach grew. "I already have a pitcher lined up. Nathan Cooper. He's done it for years."

Alice had worked for the Mel Harrison Jr. Foundation since its inception, a little more than a year after her husband's death. The initial donations were privately funded, set up to provide grants to community schools and youth organizations. As the foundation had grown, they were able to provide services for greater numbers of children, but the more successful they'd become, the less contact she had with the kids.

Until a few years ago, when the team had approached her about setting up a minicamp for youth players. It evolved from a Saturday demonstration and meet-and-greet to a weeklong afterschool program where the ballplayers worked directly with the kids, helping them learn fundamentals of the game while boosting their confidence with the attention and mentorship of the pro athletes.

"Cooper's alright." Zach sounded disappointed, bordering on whiny. "But he's not Johnny Scottsdale."

"Zach, we made a commitment to Nathan Cooper."

"And Harrisons always keep their commitments." Zach parroted the family motto. She could tell by the tone of his voice he had to restrain himself from rolling his eyes.

"Yes, Zach, Harrisons keep their commitments." No matter what. She'd made a commitment to Mel, to the Harrison family. She'd hoped her feelings for Johnny would eventually fade. She'd made her choice. A desperate one at the time, but once she'd committed to Mel, she wouldn't look back. She still couldn't. "Cooper's a good player. A good guy. We can't just tell him we don't want him anymore."

"Well, maybe they could both do the pitching clinic," Zach suggested. "Since Cooper's a lefty, maybe it would be better to have a right-handed pitcher too."

"Johnny's a busy man. He doesn't need us bugging him." And she didn't need to be reminded of what she'd given up.

"Yeah, but he probably doesn't know very many people here yet." Zach sounded hopeful. Like they'd be doing Johnny a favor. "It would be good for him to get involved in the community."

"Zach. He doesn't need us." She'd made sure of it.

"But…" Zach couldn't let it go.

"I think it's time for some lunch." Lately, food seemed to be the best distraction.

"I could eat." Zach shrugged. "You want to split some garlic fries?"

"You know I do." The ballpark's signature fries had become a tradition. But if she ate a full order herself, she'd be sorry later.

"Can I get two hot dogs, then? Or maybe some nachos?"

"You're that hungry?" Wasn't it only yesterday that she begged him to eat? Playing airplane with the spoon or bribing him with a toy to take three more bites.

"Yeah. I guess meeting Johnny Scottsdale increased my appetite." He grinned at her. For a second there, he reminded her of someone she used to know.

"Oh, Zach…" She sighed, her emotions getting the better of her. Seeing Johnny for even a few minutes had her all mixed up.

It had been easier when Johnny was on the other side of the country. When he'd been nothing more than a box score. An image on TV. She'd followed his entire career. From his earliest days in the minor leagues, to his first start in Kansas City, to when he was traded to Tampa Bay. She'd watched him. Cheered for him. Wished him nothing but success.

"Oh please, Mom. Don't go there." She was embarrassing him. As she often did whenever she talked about how quickly he was growing up. Becoming a man. Neither of them was quite ready for it, but that didn't matter.

She put her arm around him but felt him struggling with the idea of pulling away. Reluctantly, she let him go, knowing it was only a matter of time before he wouldn't need her at all.

"Order whatever you want. Just don't complain about a stomach ache later."

"I won't." He ordered a hot dog, nachos and a root beer.

She stepped up behind him and ordered her hot dog, the garlic fries and a Diet Coke. She struck up a conversation with the lady behind the counter while they waited for their order.

"Geez, Mom. Why do you have to talk so much?" He'd waited until they were at the condiment station before complaining.

"I was only being friendly. There's nothing wrong with that." She unwrapped her hot dog and placed it under the mustard spout.

"Yeah, then why weren't you very friendly with Johnny Scottsdale?" He kept his head down, concentrating on his food. She'd learned to pay attention more when he seemed least interested in making conversation. "You actually knew him in college and you barely said a word to him."

She hit the pump on the mustard a little too hard and it splattered all over her sweater. She quickly grabbed a napkin to wipe up the stain.

"Is it… Is it because he reminds you of Dad? Does seeing him make you sad?"

"Oh, honey." She put her arm around him, pressing him against her. How could she possibly explain why seeing Johnny again was so painful?

"It seems kind of weird that they didn't keep in touch after college." Zach had no idea how weird it would have been if they had. The three of them had been the best of friends. How many times had they let Mel tag along on their dates? Or how many times had she made herself at home at their place? But Johnny had been at the heart of their little group. And when he'd moved on, she and Mel turned to each other.

"Johnny was trying to make it to the big leagues." She used the same story she'd told herself over the years. "He had to work very hard to get to where he is today. Mel had a job here in the city, and I was busy raising you. We just drifted apart, that's all."

"But, maybe you and Johnny can be friends again." He had a tiny hesitation in his voice. Telling her there was more to the story than he was willing to share.

She waited. Pushing him would never get him to open up.

"Maybe…" Zach took a long slurp of his soda. "Maybe he could tell me more about my dad."

* * * *

Well, that was a mistake. By bringing up his dad, he'd upset his mom. Zach could tell because she got really quiet. They sat in the stands to eat their lunch and watch the next round of interviews. She nibbled on her hot dog and absently picked at the garlic fries. He ended up eating most of them, which was fine. He loved garlic fries. But it was weird with her not talking. Normally she would chatter on and on about the upcoming season and especially all the new players. He'd expected her to be really excited about Johnny Scottsdale. She was probably an even bigger fan than he was.

She'd actually cried when he pitched his perfect game. Cried and hugged Zach like they'd been there. But she barely said a word to him when they met today. And they didn't even get an autograph.

Now, she was all quiet, and he wouldn't be surprised if she said she wanted to leave soon. He'd seen what he wanted to see. Johnny Scottsdale's first interview as one of the Goliaths, and then he'd gotten to meet him. Sort of.

Kip Michaels stepped onstage to introduce the next set of players. He was one of the best. He never had anything bad to say about an opponent, but he was a Goliath to the core. He also managed to throw out a few tips for young players during every game. He'd point out simple things, like keeping balanced in the batter's box or following through on a pitch. Plus, he'd been there. Way before Zach's time, but he'd pitched in the majors for ten years. So he knew what he was talking about.

"Thank you, San Francisco!" Nathan Cooper stepped up to the mic for his turn in the spotlight. "It's going to be a great season. I guarantee it."

Yeah, he was alright. Kind of a showoff, though. Like it was more about him than the team. Cooper played to the crowd, making them laugh and cheer and get pumped up for the season. Even if he was kind of obnoxious, he was a pretty good pitcher. Most of the time.

Zach glanced over at his mother. She was trying to rub the mustard stain out of her sweater. He wondered if that would be her excuse for leaving early. He wouldn't mind. Not really. He just wished he could have talked to Johnny Scottsdale more. He had a lot of questions. Mostly about baseball. Like what it was like to pitch a perfect game.

He had questions about his dad.

He barely even remembered him. Only a few fuzzy memories—mostly good—of a guy in a suit taking off his tie and getting down on the floor to play with the Thomas the Train set. He remembered watching movies and going to the park, but he didn't think he'd ever played catch with his dad.

He'd played catch with a few different major leaguers. As part of the minicamp. He never really felt like he was part of the program though. It was more like he tagged along, just because he could. Because his mom ran the show and his grandparents had started the whole charity thing after his dad died.

Some of the other kids had it real tough, though. Single parents who worked two jobs just to pay their rent. So they didn't have time to play catch with their kids. There were foster kids who never lived in one place long enough to be part of a team. Some of the kids had dads in the military, serving overseas in Afghanistan or places like that.

Zach felt kind of bad, taking up a spot for a kid who needed it more. At least he didn't have to worry about money. Or his mom didn't have to worry, anyways.

"Hey Mom?" He had an idea.

"Don't tell me you're still hungry." She smiled at him, but she was kind of distracted.

"No." Not really. But he would be after dinner. They'd probably have a big salad or vegetable stir-fry—something healthy to make up for all the junk food. "I was just thinking. Maybe I'm getting too old to be in the minicamp."

"You're not too old." She folded up her napkin and wrapped up the last of her unfinished hot dog. "There will be plenty of other kids your age."

"I guess." He wasn't as excited about it as he'd been the last few years.

"You don't have to do the minicamp." She tried to sound like it didn't matter to her, but he knew she'd be disappointed if he wasn't there. "I hope you're not quitting because I haven't asked Johnny Scottsdale to join us."

"That's not it." He grabbed the last garlic fry. Except maybe that was part of it. "I just don't know how much more I can learn from the same guys."

That kind of made him sound like a jerk. Like he thought he was some great baseball player already. That's not what he meant. He just didn't know how to say it without sounding like he was spoiled or something.

How many kids got to work with real Major League baseball players every year? Not many. For most of them it was a once-in-a-lifetime kind of thing.

"If you don't want to come, that's okay. You won't hurt my feelings." She said that, but she didn't like when he didn't want to do stuff with her. It was hard for him to tell her he'd rather be with his friends. She always worked so hard at finding fun things to do together. Maybe it was because he didn't have his dad around anymore and she felt like she had to make it up to him. Or maybe it was because she didn't have his dad around and she was lonely.

"I'll come," Zach said. But he didn't really want to.

* * * *

Johnny plopped down in front of his locker to change out of his jersey and into his street clothes. He was wiped out, but not in a good way like after a game. His muscles were sore from tension, not exertion. He was still reeling after his encounter with Alice. For years he'd pretended they were both dead to him. Come to find out, Mel had died. And even though they hadn't spoken in years, it still came as a big blow. The man had once been Johnny's best friend. Almost a brother. And now he was gone. Was it an accident? A long and painful battle with disease? Whatever the cause, Alice was left to raise their son alone.

Alice was a mother. Not a big surprise. She'd always loved kids. She was going to be a teacher. Until she'd married Mel and didn't have to work. Mel was rich. Came from money and probably couldn't help but make even more money once he graduated and went to work for his father, helping make other rich people richer.

It bothered him more than he wanted to admit. Her having a kid. Not that Johnny had ever really wanted to be a father. But maybe a part of him would have wanted to be the one to give her that gift.

He was wrestling with that thought when his manager, Juan Javier, approached him.

"Just the man I need to see." Javier had been a catcher during his playing days. A pretty good one too, until his knees gave out. But he was still in good shape. Still had a commanding presence.

"Sure, what do you need?" Johnny didn't know the man well enough to determine whether he should address him by his first name, last name or just call him "Skip." His reputation around the league was that of a player's manager. Well respected and well liked, with a thorough knowledge of the game and an uncanny ability to get the most out of his players. Johnny looked forward to working with him.

"I need a hero." Javier parked himself next to Johnny. "Got word this morning that Nathan Cooper didn't pass a drug test. He's out fifty games, unless he appeals."

Did that mean Johnny would be moved to the bullpen? Cooper was a relief pitcher, a left-handed specialist. Johnny was a right-handed starter. At least he had been his entire career.

"Don't worry, you're still a starter." Javier clapped him on the back. "This is a PR nightmare. At least it didn't leak out this morning. That would have put a dark cloud on the Fan Fest."

"So what can I do?"

"Your reputation is spotless. It's one of the reasons the team was so interested in signing you." They didn't call him The Monk for nothing. His composure on the mound was only part of the story. "We had a few years where...well, you catch the news. The fans are sick of this stuff. Sick of the cheaters. We need someone like you. Someone the kids can look up to."

"I try to be one of the good guys." Johnny shrugged. It's all he'd ever wanted to be. He wanted his name to be associated with honor, integrity and respect.

"Russ Crawford, from the front office, had Cooper lined up for this charity event." His manager placed a sturdy hand on Johnny's shoulder. "We don't want a guy suspended for drugs representing us to the community."

"No. We don't." Johnny never understood what would drive a guy to take such a risk. Or why there were still guys who felt they could get away with it. He balled his fists, thinking about how much harder the rest of them had to work at proving they were clean.

"We need someone to take his place. I thought you'd be perfect." He gave Johnny a friendly pat on the back.

"I was perfect once in my life." Twenty-seven batters had faced him. Every one of them had walked back to the dugout shaking their heads. None of them had reached first base. No hits, no walks, no errors.

"You and only about twenty-three other guys." Javier gave him a smile of admiration. Of respect. Not only for Johnny, but for all the players who'd come before him. "But you're not just perfect on the field."

That was his reputation. No wild parties, drugs or women. When he went out with his teammates, he stuck with one beer. Just to be one of the guys. Then he would return quietly to his room. Alone. He politely refused advances and room keys from his female fans.

"What kind of charity thing are we looking at?" *Let's get to the point.* What really mattered. As long as it wasn't a speaking engagement. He could pitch in front of a sold-out stadium. Or an empty one where the few fans in attendance tried to make up for the lack of numbers with an abundance of noise. But talking to a room full of people? No thanks. He'd much rather run the bleachers, drag the field, or even cut the grass by hand, one blade at a time.

"It's a minicamp for youth players," Javier explained. "They come to the ballpark after school and we take them through a few drills, demo mechanics and basically share your knowledge of the game."

"That sounds like something I could do." Johnny was just beginning to think about what he might do after his career was over. Coaching was something to consider; it would keep him in the game. But he wasn't sure if he'd be any good at it. He didn't know if he could explain things in a way others would understand. He could show them, though. He could demonstrate what worked for him.

"So you'll do the pitching clinic." It wasn't a question. The new guy on the team had to prove himself, no matter his reputation, and picking up a teammate was a good way to do just that.

Johnny nodded. Why not? Anything to keep his mind off Alice and Mel. And their kid.

"Tell me about the kids." Johnny didn't have a lot of experience with kids. Like, none. Even when he'd been a kid, he didn't really know how to relate to them. He was the quiet boy in school and in the dugout. "How old are they?"

"I think anywhere from about nine to twelve or thirteen."

"Old enough to tie their own shoes, then." In other words, about Zach's age.

"Yet still young enough that they don't think they know everything," Javier added with a slight smile. "About baseball, at least."

"So these kids should be coachable." When he'd been that age, he'd soaked up every tip and tidbit of information about the game. He'd been eager to learn and apply the knowledge to his rapidly growing skills.

Could he be the kind of mentor he'd had back then? Could he pass down his knowledge of the game to the next generation? He hoped so.

"They're good kids. Some of them may have caught a bad break. Single parent homes, families fallen on hard times. Some of these boys might be homeless or in foster care." Javier was starting to make Johnny a little nervous. He'd been one of those kids. He'd known hard times.

Lived with a single mother who'd worked too much. Without a father or a man to look up to.

Until his coach had stepped up.

"I guess you've got your man." Johnny hoped he could be the kind of man these kids needed. "Just give me the time and place."

"I knew I could count on you. The camp starts Monday. Here's your contact at the Harrison Foundation." The manager handed him a slick business card. Johnny's heart seized as he read the name.

Alice Harrison, Director

"She's a great gal. Professional. Knowledgeable." Javier seemed not to notice all the air had been sucked out of the room. "You'll love her."

Oh yeah. Johnny had loved her. He'd once loved her even more than he loved the game.